I0561357

Life in the Park

Life in the Park

a novel

by Marion T. Smith

The Lichtenbergian Press
2017

Published by the Lichtenbergian Press.
Copyright © 2017 by Marion T. Smith
All rights reserved.

CATALOGING IN PUBLICATION
Smith, Marion T. 1962–
Life in the Park / Marion T. Smith
1. Georgia—Fiction. 2. Mobile home parks—Fiction I. Title
PN35XX
FIC

Book design by Dale Lyles
Fonts used: text, Minion Pro

For my daughter Raina, who reminded me that everyone has a story

Contents

I. A French Solution

"Aha!" Carl said as he put the seven of spades down on the table, but his excitement at claiming his sixth trick turned to frustration when Sophie's turn came. She put down seven spades in a row and took the round, something she frequently did. Carl, high on his fifth beer, hit the table with his fist, upsetting Rachel's glass and dousing her cigarettes with wine.

"Dammit Carl, my cigarettes!" sputtered Rachel.

"Take it easy Carl," Adam said, his voice slurred. "It's just a game."

"Yeah, you're right," said Carl, but not like he meant it. Sophie was a natural card player, which meant she beat him nearly all the time, but every time she did it, it hurt his pride. "Damn woman's got too much luck."

"It ain't luck and you know it," Rachel said as she wiped up the mess. "Sophie's just better than us at playing cards."

Carl grunted. Sophie didn't look up and said nothing.

"What happened?" said Benny Ben, a large, stocky boy of six, rubbing his eyes as he stepped out of the hallway of the trailer.

"Nothing, Benjamin," said Rachel. "Go on back to bed."

"I'll take him," Sophie said, and walked the child back to his bedroom.

"She's a good woman," Rachel told Carl in a loud drunken whisper as she searched through the pack of cigarettes to see if any one of them was still dry enough to smoke. "Better than you deserve. You need to treat her well. Now, hon, get me another pack out of the cabinet. These are all wet."

"Yes, ma'am," Adam said, with exaggerated meekness as he rose to do his wife's bidding. His subservience was made even more comical by the vast difference in their sizes. He was almost six-and-a-half feet tall and weighed just under three hundred pounds, which dwarfed his five-foot-nothing, one-hundred-and-five-pounds-soaking-wet wife. "Right away, ma'am. Will these do, ma'am?"

"Yes, Adam, these will do," said Rachel imperiously. "You may sit back down now."

Carl Thornborough knew they were teasing him. They had put on this little act just about every time he had seen them after he made the mistake of telling them how he felt about how a woman ought to treat a man, especially since he had married Sophie, a gawky little mouse with brassy brown hair and a stubborn streak. He just believed that it was a man's place to rule the household and a woman's place to mind him. That's how he was raised, and that's what he was taught on Sunday at Hall's Corner First Baptist Church. His mama certainly never said so much as a contrary word to his daddy, who was a deacon, because all he had to do was raise his hand. Women wanting to be the equal of men was the work of the Devil, his daddy told him many times, and the Great Deceiver constantly tempted them to give up their souls just so they could lord over men. It was unnatural, and it wasn't right, like it wasn't right for a wife to show up her husband, even if it was just a game of cards. It showed that Sophie still had a too much wickedness and willfulness of spirit in her, just like his father had said, and just as she proved on their first date. So, he decided right then and there he was going to make her "straighten up and fly right" once and for all. He just smiled at Adam and Rachel, though, because they were raised different and wouldn't understand.

Their game, as usual, was a half-case of beer, two bottles of wine, and three packs of cigarettes long, and in the early morning light Carl was only able to walk the short distance to their trailer next door with Sophie's help. That didn't keep him from berating her on the way.

"You showed me up. Again," he hissed.

"I'm sorry," she said softly. "I didn't mean to. Cards just always come easy to me."

"No, no," said Carl, his words slurred. "You did it on purpose, and I'm gonna put an end to it. You're never goin' to 'spute me or show me up ever again."

"I didn't mean to," she said, but she grew frightened when she felt his hand dig into her shoulder. "You're hurting me. Please, Carl."

"Shut up," he said and pushed her through the trailer door.

"Give me my goddamn cigarettes, woman!" a voice shouted from down the street.

"Get them you own damn self!"

He dragged her into the bedroom, where he exercised his prerogative as a husband without preamble, and Sophie bore the pain of it because it she believed it was the way of the world.

The next day, Sophie renewed her efforts to be a better wife to Carl. but her efforts weren't entirely successful. She was not a good cook, being only seventeen and raised by a mother who "cooked out of a can" as they say. And Carl insisted that she know all his likes and dislikes. She had tried to learn them in the four months they had been married, but it was hard because he was so contrary.

xxxxxxxxxxxxxxxxxxxxxxxxx

At first, when he was courting her, he had been so kind and sweet, bringing her presents and saying nice things about her mama and daddy. Things quickly got so that she felt her heart well up in her throat every time he smiled at her. She thought he was so handsome, with his thick black hair and angular chin, even though most would not agree, and when he looked at her with his sad coal black eyes it was like her head was enveloped in a honeysuckle fog.

In those sad eyes she saw a man afflicted with the cares of the world and she knew she could heal him with love. It made her feel so good inside to think that she could salve his pain. So, on their first date, when he tried to touch her there, and there, her innocence and church learning led her to resist at first, but not for long. How could she not let him when she wanted him to so much? She prayed silently. while his fingers wrote the name of the Devil in her flesh. that God would understand, especially since he too was a man.

That night in the bedroom of his trailer, was not a pleasant one for her. When he finally convinced her to take off all her clothes, he was so aroused that he entered her without further ceremony or any protection. She, with her passion just beginning to rise as she stood naked for the first time in front of a man, was unprepared, and cried out in pain as her hymen tore. It was all over quickly, which put the frustration of her burgeoning feelings of desire at war with the lessening of pain when he withdrew, and instinctively, she reached out for him to heal the breech.

"Damn, girl," he said, embarrassed at his quick ejaculation. "No woman's ever got me off so fast. Are you some kind of nympho?"

"Carl, I . . . ." she whispered, but he pushed her arms away and turned his back to her. Her tears came then, a stream trickling down her cheeks as silently as she could make it, and Carl, though he heard, let her cry it out. After a while, she got up and walked to the kitchen to search the refrigerator for something to drink. As she poured herself a glass of apple juice, she heard Carl padding down the hall in his bare feet. She didn't look at him. She couldn't. He stepped behind her and put one hand on her breast and the other between her legs, pressing his belly and his hardening penis against her back.

"Damn, you are a nympho or something," he said as he felt her body twitch beneath his fingers.

She didn't protest, but allowed him to have his way with her again. And this time it wasn't as painful as the first and he didn't turn away from her after, so she reasoned that things would surely get better over time with him. Besides, her pain was just God punishing her for her sin of the flesh. To want pleasure was to add the sin of pride, she thought, when his pleasure is what she should focus on if she wanted him to love her.

Over the next few weeks, she had tried to please Carl every way she could think of. She only knew how to make a few dishes well, chicken salad with grapes, chocolate chip cookies with M&Ms, and mustard potato salad with Vidalia onions, so she made those as often as possible. She also fixed her hair for him, wore perfume for him, and bought new dresses and underwear just to wear for him. And at night in the bedroom in his trailer, she let him do things to her because he wanted to, and she tried to enjoy it, not for herself, she insisted, but for his manly pride.

Yet for all her efforts, Carl was seldom pleased. He was still very nice to her parents and to her, in public, but when they were alone he grew more and more critical. He ridiculed her cooking because she could only cook three things well. Who ever heard of putting grapes in chicken salad, anyway, and besides, his mama's potato salad was a lot better, he said. He complained about her spending money on new clothes. He didn't like her hair up, but didn't like it when she took it down. He said her perfume smothered him. And he even resented her climaxes, which, after the first night, became more frequent and pronounced, and began to call her a slut in bed. Then, on one particular day, seven weeks since their first date, he said that one of her new dresses made her look fat. In this case, he was right. She had missed her period.

She had already taken a pregnancy test and it had confirmed her fears. She had been trying to work up the courage to tell Carl because she was by now a little afraid of him, but when she told him, he surprised her and said they had to get married right away. It was the Christian thing to do, he said, and he held her to him like a child while he stroked her hair. He started being nice to her again, most of the time, and Sophie was ecstatic. This proved that he loved her, and she knew that when they had a little baby to love and cherish, their lives would be complete. On their wedding night, he took her very tenderly and she responded with a surge of lustful passion that made her whole body glow pink with desire and shame.

Her dream was shattered three weeks later when she began bleeding and they rushed her to the hospital. She had a miscarriage. Sophie was disconsolate, and Carl at first was comforting. But after they came home, slowly Sophie saw that things were changing back to their old ways. Carl again became more demanding, and even more particular, and he quit touching her except in bed. Even there, her memory of the tender bliss of their wedding night struggled to stay alive against his increasingly insensitive, mechanical assaults.

xxxxxxxxxxxxxxxxxxxxxxxxx

After the card game, Carl treated her worse and worse, and when she complained, he told himself it only affirmed that she needed harder discipline. He insisted that the house be spotless, although he always found some fault regardless of how hard she worked, and his ridicule of her cooking escalated into occasional fits of rage, one in which he threw his plate against the wall, shattering it. He forbid her to wear pants anymore, but if she wore a dress, he complained that she looked like a slob if she wore anything old and that she looked like a whore if she wore anything nice. Sophie grew frantic when he started coming home drunk. If he wasn't too high, he forced her to have sex with him and called her names while he did it. When he was gone to work or out drinking, Sophie tried to keep away the tears, but there were times, in the middle of vacuuming the living room or making up the bed, when she doubled over in the floor with her arms wrapped around her waist and could not stem the torrent. Then, when things could not possibly get any worse for her, Sophie thought, they did.

xxxxxxxxxxxxxxxxxxxxxxxx

Hall's Corner wasn't much of a town, little more than a wide place in the road as the old folks say. It was originally a trading post in the Cherokee Nation, and before that a small village that rose up near a large spring, but was incorporated in 1855, nearly two decades after the removal. The town was backed up against Little Texas Ridge in the upper corner of Amama Valley between it and Sulagade Mountain to the west. Its buildings formed an "L," upside down and backwards, tucked up in the southeast quadrant of the intersection of Livingston Road, a north-south route, and the Brownsboro Road, which came to an end at a caution light. Across from it, Switchback Road continued on to the west up the mountain.

Hall's Corner had flowered and faded with cotton farming and the passenger and freight trains until now the fields were pastures and the tracks were gone, leaving only a long green berm like a giant mole tunnel running alongside Livingston Road. While it was in bloom, it was a quite prosperous hamlet, with several commercial businesses, including a hotel, five churches, three banks, two general stores, two groceries, two newspapers, a women's clothing store, a dance school, a drug store, a farm supply company, and four livery stables. The commercial enterprises were all arranged in the L-shape, the long stem facing west toward the tracks and the old Pinkus Hotel and a cotton warehouse. The shorter, north stem ran east along the Brownsboro Road. It ended at First Street, which ran parallel to Livingston Road behind the town between the Brownsboro Road and Talking Spring Road just south of downtown, and was dotted with a few old, stately houses, one of the largest and most elaborate of which was the Chamblee House, once an academy for young women that now housed the J. P. Pennick Funeral Home. On either side of First Street was an old pecan orchard that continued on past Talking Spring Road for a hundred acres.

Hall's Corner Drugs originally belonged to a man named Sam Wilson, one of the fastest human beings ever to live on the planet. He drove an old Ford pickup truck and would pull up in front of the drug store, cut off the switch, and be through the front door before the engine fully died.

The two general stores belonged to Abe and Albert Norris, two brothers who had a falling out years ago over a girl, and were in direct competition with each other. They tried to outdo each other at every turn, so their stores were piled high and deep with every thing imaginable, from overalls and boots and .22 shells to perfume and corsets. And their customers tended to be loyal, or at least very discrete, since the brothers tended to take it personally if one of their customers shopped with the other. The women's clothing store, Miss Clarie's Hi Fashion, belonged to Clarie Carver, who quietly drank gin all day just to pass the time. In the fifty-odd years she was in business, she never put anything on sale, even when she decided to retire in the early 1970s. The hoop skirts and crinolines still had their original price tags, so they only looked like they were half off.

Hall's Corner was only a little different now. All the buildings facing the old railroad track but one were still standing, although both the general stores were closed. The missing included the old hotel and the cotton warehouse, both of which were damaged by a tornado in 1951. The old feed store was also missing, having burned in 1955. The lot where it stood, at the south end of the long block, was cleared of debris long ago and grass grew in the sharp-edged shadows of the walls on each side of it. The back wall was missing, so the blue sky peeking through the pecan orchard behind it made it look like a missing tooth.

The town's few signs of an economic pulse were an antique store, which was a hobby of Julius Pinkus III, the present mayor, so it was open only three days a week; the old drugstore, now owned by Sam Wilson's grandson Gene, who expected a chain store to drive him out of business any day; a real estate office, a law office, a NAPA automotive parts store; the Curl Up and Dye Beauty Shop; and Linelle Dubose's Cozy Café, the local hotspot that took up the prime business location at the crux of the "L," hence its motto: "On the corner in the Corner." There was also a new Dollar General, Norris's Feed and Seed, and J's Grocery and Convenience Store around the corner facing the Brownsboro Road, and a half-mile farther east, on the north side, was the EZ Mobile Home Park.

Linelle Dubose was a rare woman. She was tall, independent, and a third-generation immigrant from France, but that was the least of it. Although she was a native of Hall's Corner, Linelle was more like the mountain women sometimes written about in Georgia histories, even though her bright red shock of hair made her look more like a giant troll doll than Granny Clampett. She had a natural fearlessness and fierceness in her demeanor that made some men love her at first sight, and some women fear her, at least until they got to know her. But little children and animals flocked to her like yellow jackets on a slice of melon lying in the sun, and their instincts about her were correct. So, when she went out walking, it was not uncommon to see two or three of them following her around like her constant companion, the fat blind pot-bellied pig Maurice.

The people of Hall's Corner were not unusually enlightened for North Georgia, which is to say they rarely wondered if there was more to life than what was right in front of them, but they accepted Linelle. It was not because children liked her, since there is no accounting for the likes and dislikes of children, but they accepted her for much more practical reasons: she was a native and so entitled to her eccentricities, and, more importantly, she was the best cook in twenty-five miles. And people drove farther than that for her chicken and dumplings on Thursdays, her pork barbecue and stew on Friday and Saturday, and her made-from-scratch biscuits and pies every day as long as they lasted. So, the people of Hall's

Corner had nothing bad to say about Linelle, at least out loud. It would have been biting the local hand that fed them.

Still, despite the out-of-town customers and a steady group of local regulars, Linelle made barely enough at the Cozy Café to support even her modest life-style, and so she had a few schemes for making money on the side. She raised her own vegetables out back of the café in an open patch of ground where a pecan tree had died, some of which she sold in the café, and she was widely sought out for her canned and pickled goods, especially her hot pepper pear jelly. And, occasionally, she read Tarot cards, although card reading was too close to card playing not to be looked down on by the local Baptists and Methodists and Pentecostals and Church of Godders as a snare set by the Devil. Some thought it was witchcraft, but the one or two who might have wished to run her out of town kept silent because even they couldn't stay away from the Cozy Café.

One a Friday evening in early August, after she closed the café at 3 p.m. as she always did every day because nearly everybody ate supper at home in Hall's Corner, she stepped into the narrow alley adjacent to the building to begin the ascent to her apartment upstairs with Maurice on her heels and was brought up short. At the bottom of the stairs was a woman, folded up in obvious pain, and she hurried to her side.

"Child," she said, because she could tell right away she was young. "Child, what hurts you so?"

"Oh," the young woman moaned as Linelle pushed back her auburn curls. Her pale white skin was flushed until it was near red, her hazel eyes were set back in her head by the swelling, and the last of her most recent tears still clung to her cheeks.

"Now, now, child. You're name is Sophie, isn't it. You just married Carl Thornborough a few months back."

Sophie moaned louder and threw up on the ground.

"Come, child," Linelle said as she helped her get to her feet. "Let's get you a cup of tea. It'll make you feel better. Tsk tsk, come along Maurice."

A short while later, Sophie did feel better, but only a little. She had stopped crying, and as she drank Linelle's tea, she looked around the apartment. She was surprised that it was so uncluttered. She had half expected Linelle's place to be a chaotic mix of exotic knickknacks and whatnots, like feathers and strange statues and glass cases holding small jars and vases and odd looking old books. Instead, the decor was simple, if an eclectic mix of styles and periods. The light through the pastel yellow gauze curtains on the windows at the front and back of the apartment cast a soft, creamy glow on everything as they rustled in a light summer breeze that left behind the sweet aroma of kudzu and wisteria blossoms as it undulated from one opening to the other.

Everything is balanced, Sophie thought, and she realized it reminded her of some photos in the interior design magazines she had pored over only a few months ago, back in her previous life.

"I am not a gypsy," said Linelle, drawing her back after a while. She swept her hand as if to take in the whole apartment.

"How. . . .?" Sophie asked.

"It is in your face. I am pleased you like my apartment," she said as she took the girl's chin in her hand again. "You have talent in your eyes."

Sophie felt like Linelle could see straight through her, soul and all. She started crying again and soon her head was lying on Linelle's shoulder as the older woman patted her back and spoke softly to her. "Now, now," she said. "Now, now."

"I want you to tell my future," Sophie finally said between sobs.

"But you already know it child," Linelle said.

"I don't. No, I don't. I want to know because . . . ." she paused to let her chest stop heaving, "I don't think my husband loves me anymore."

"It's an unusual man who knows what he feels," Linelle said. "Why do you think he doesn't love you?"

"Because," she suddenly wailed, "because he is sleeping with my neighbor, Rachel Willingham."

"Sssss. Sssss. And how do you know this?"

"Edna Wilson told me . . . at the drug store. She said . . . she didn't . . . want to upset me or anything, but . . . Hilda Broughton told her that Jessica Maples . . . from the beauty shop, was in Brownsboro this afternoon and saw Rachel and Carl at a motel restaurant, and Nellie Ann Biddle said she saw Rachel get into his car behind the Dollar General well before noon and drive out of town going that way."

The words came out of Sophie with increasing speed, as if she feared that they would stick in her throat and choke her if she stopped.

"Hildegarde and Nellie Ann," Linelle said with disgust. "Most towns only have one gossiping old biddy to worry about, but little Hall's Corner has two. And they compete to see who can spread any and every little rumor the fastest. If gossip was a horse race, they would be Secretariat and Seabiscuit."

"But they were right," sobbed Sophie. "After I talked to Edna, I walked down the back alley to the Dollar General and saw her car. So I hid and waited, and not more than a half-hour ago they pulled up. He walked her around to her car and he kissed her. On the mouth."

"Oh, child, oh, child," said Linelle. "Here, finish your tea."

Maurice, lying at her feet, snorted as if in sympathy.

"I love him. I do. And I try to please him, but I'm not good enough. What if he leaves me for her? Where will I go? What will I do? Daddy and mama said they wouldn't take me back after I got pregnant and married Carl."

"Child, listen to me. I'm going to tell you something about yourself that you do not know. It is not you who should be afraid; it's him."

"But . . . ."

Linelle interrupted her by wiping her tears away with a cloth that smelled of lemon, and shushed her as she quickly washed her face. Sophie could feel her skin tightening. Then Linelle opened the drawer on a lamp table by her chair and took out a makeup case. It was not like any Sophie had ever seen, mahogany gilded with ivory, with a lid held by a silver hasp. As Linelle opened it, Sophie craned her head around the lid and sucked in her breath when she saw all the small containers of rouge and lipstick and eyeliner lined up in tight little rows like an army of rainbows.

Linelle put the case beneath the lamp and paused a moment, studying Sophie's face, before she picked out a light almond rouge. The older woman worked quickly, adding blue eyeliner and light rose lipstick before she combed out Sophie's hair and spun it up in a tight whorl on top of her head. Linelle studied Sophie's face and nodded with satisfaction. She went over to an old chest against a wall in the middle room, and took out a bundle wrapped in paper and tied with twine. She unwrapped it carefully, then held up a shimmering blue strapless gown that was the prettiest dress Sophie had ever seen.

"Put it on," said Linelle as she left the room.

Sophie held the dress gingerly, as if she feared it would break, but excitement soon overcame her and she quickly exchanged the worn summer dress she was wearing for the luxurious old gown. She immediately looked for a mirror, but to her surprise, there wasn't one in the room. A moment later Linelle returned with a full-length antique one on rollers that she was careful to keep turned away from Sophie.

"Close your eyes and stand up straight," Linelle said.

Sophie complied with girlish enthusiasm, and stood tall, with her shoulders back and her chin up like she was royalty posing for a portrait.

"Now, open them."

Sophie couldn't believe it. She didn't recognize the stunning girl in the mirror, with the face like delicate porcelain, the elegant hairdo, and the gorgeous gown. She turned first one way, then the other, disbelieving her own eyes.

"You are blind to your own beauty, both in and out," Linelle whispered. "Look in your heart for it and you will find it. Can you see it now?"

"Oh, god," Sophie groaned at last. "Oh, god."

"Now, let us talk, cheri," Linelle said as she circled Sophie's shoulders with her arm. "You have much to learn about love and life. And cooking. But I believe you will see there is a solution to your problem, if you look at it with your new eyes."

xxxxxxxxxxxxxxxxxxxxxxxx

When Carl got home and found Sophie missing, he was both scared and enraged that she might have run off with someone else. He called the sheriff's department and the hospital in Brownsboro, but neither knew anything. He talked to several people in the park, including crazy Jake whose front deck was bigger than his house, the fidgety high school kid Bean, and Ekee the park manager, among others, and, finally, with trepidation, Adam and Rachel. He knew Rachel wasn't likely to know where she was, since she had been with him most of the afternoon, but Adam had been home all day because he was recovering from a foot injury at the machine shop where he worked and he might have seen her. He fought back his shame and guilt, and walked next door.

"Oh, hi, Carl," Rachel said with forced cheerfulness when she opened the storm screen. "Adam, Carl's here."

"Come on in, buddy," Adam said from the kitchen. "You look kind of pale. Have a beer."

"Ah, no," Carl said. "I . . . I was wondering if . . . either one of you has seen Sophie today."

"Why, is she missing or something," Rachel said.

"Yes. I got home about an hour ago and she wasn't there. I've called the sheriff's department and the hospital, and I've asked around the park, but no one has seen her."

"I saw her about two," Adam said. "She left the trailer heading toward town. I offered to give her a ride, but she said she wanted to walk. She said she was going down to the drug store."

"Oh," Rachel said with a little gasp, and Carl flinched at what it implied.

"I'll call Edna Wilson," Rachel said. The phone was in the living room, so she left Adam and Carl alone in the kitchen. When she came back, she looked bewildered.

"What did she say?" Carl asked.

"Ah, she saw her, about two-thirty, but she said she left the drug store and she hasn't seen her since."

"Is there something wrong, honey?"

"No, Adam. Edna was just acting odd, that's all. She hung up on me."

"Maybe she had something on her mind," Adam said as Rachel glanced at Carl knowingly. "I wouldn't worry about it. Get the phone book. We'll call everybody in it if we have to."

No one they called had seen her, except Julius Pinkus III, who thought he might have seen her running by his antiques store just before he closed. His eyes were as bad as his windows were dirty, so he couldn't be sure. Meanwhile, Sophie stayed missing right on through Saturday night and Sunday. Carl, who was produce manager at Aub's Famous Foods at Keown's Junction, a small burg nine miles south of Hall's Corner, went into work on Monday with no more than an hour or two of fitful sleep since Sophie went missing. He looked a wreck. Aubrey, the owner, commented on it, but Carl didn't enlighten him. Tuesday came, and Carl reported her missing, but Wednesday and Thursday and Friday passed and there was still no word. The *Brownsboro Beacon and Carter County News* ran her photo in its Thursday edition, along with a story that was necessarily short on information and unnecessarily long on speculation. The sheriff said they had questioned Carl, who was a person of interest in her disappearance, but so far there were no leads. The reporter, Brad Randall, who was also the editor and publisher, interviewed her mother Agnes, who pleaded for anyone who might know anything about her precious child to notify the authorities. The family put up a $1,000 reward for information leading to her whereabouts.

xxxxxxxxxxxxxxxxxxxxxxxxxx

Two weeks later, on Friday morning, Carl got a strange phone call, from Linelle Dubose. She invited him to a party that evening under the pecan trees behind her café. She said she had heard of his troubles and wanted him to be her special guest. Carl, who by this time was numbed with grief to the point of resignation, did not want to go except it would give him a chance to see if any one had seen anything that might explain Sophie's disappearance. Plus, it was hard to turn down free food, especially if it was Linelle's.

Just before three, Carl stepped outside his trailer only to find Adam and Rachel getting in their car. They told him they were invited to Linelle's party, too, and Adam, with a thin smile, asked him if he wanted to ride with them. In the car on the way, he tried to catch Rachel's eye, but she wouldn't look at him. She looked pale and angry, as did Adam, like they had just had a fight. It was only when they drove through the parking lot of the Dollar General to get to the back alley that Carl saw her glance at him in her makeup mirror. She looked drained, but she stared at him a second time with a mixture of wonderment and foreboding when she saw all the vehicles parked behind Linelle's. There was a crowd of fifty or more people milling around under the trees, inhaling the marvelous aroma of a feast only rivaled by the annual homecoming at Hall's Corner Baptist Church, spread out on six folding tables and covered with white cloths. Many of the people were from the trailer park, along with the Wilsons, Mr. Pinkus, and Sophie's parents, Agnes and James Truett. Most curiously, Brad Randall from the *Beacon* was among the crowd, too. Carl was about to say something about that to Rachel and Adam, but he was interrupted by the staccato pinging of a little dinner bell.

Linelle Dubose, dressed like a Southern Belle in a hoop-skirted gown she had bought when Miss Clarie's closed in 1972, commanded everyone's attention from the back porch of the café.

"Ladies and gentlemen, now that the guest of honor, Carl Thornborough, has arrived, please sit and eat before the food gets cold."

The crowd needed no encouragement. The cloths flew off the tables, and even the most voracious among them paused if only for a moment to take in the sight of platters of pork, sliced, chopped, and barbecued, Brunswick stew and chicken mull, fried sausage and fried pies, slaw, green beans, turnip greens, pinto beans, dirty rice, sweet potato soufflé with little marshmallows, Mississippi mud cake, coconut cake with cherry slices, sweet potato pie, lemon meringue pie, and blackberry cobbler with a homemade lattice crust. No one made special note that among the dishes was also a chicken salad made with grapes, a plate piled with chocolate chip cookies with M&Ms, and a large mustard potato salad with Vidalia onions.

Just over a half-hour later, when the first wave of unbridled gluttony had passed, and the early casualties were leaning back in their chairs or against the trees or lying on blankets on the ground groaning lowly like soldiers on a battlefield after the conflagration has passed on, Linelle rang the bell again to forestall the countercharge.

"Now, ladies and gentlemen, I trust you are all enjoying this wonderful feast."

The assemblage moaned their assent.

"Then let us pause a moment while our food settles a little, for I would like to introduce you to the woman who prepared all this."

Murmurs of confusion rippled through the crowd. Everyone had assumed, of course, that Linelle was the cook. Linelle gave them no explanation, but smiled as she turned to open the back door to the café. While she held the screen door aside, out stepped Sophie, her brassy brown hair gleaming in a tumbling waterfall framing her glowing face and spilling onto her sparkling blue gown. Some in the crowd gasped. Some didn't recognize her. Others whispered uncertainties among themselves. She stepped out to the edge of the back porch and a passing breeze jostled her curls gently while making small waves in her gossamer blue dress, silencing the crowd.

"Sophie?" Carl squeaked as he stepped toward her.

"Yes, Carl," she said softly.

"Where in the hell have you been?" His voice began to rise. "Did Linelle kidnap you or something? I've been worried sick. I ought to slap you into next week, you stupid bitch . . ."

Gasps peppered the crowd, but Sophie silenced them with a wave of her hand as Carl's cruel words died in his throat.

"Carl," she said, "I love you. I have loved you from the first time I saw you in the produce department at Aub's Famous Foods. I dreamed you were my prince charming, a white knight who would take me away to a fairy land where we would make babies and live happily ever after. But you taught me that chivalry is dead, Carl, and that only little girls live in fairy lands. I gave you my heart and you tried to crush it. I gave you my soul, and you tried to destroy it. I worked so hard to please you, but you were never satisfied with anything I did. I tried to heal you, but only succeeded in making myself sick. And when I found out you were having an affair with Rachel, I wanted to swim out into Lake Coosawattee until I knew I was too far out to swim back."

Carl blanched before the cold murmuring of the crowd, except for Rachel, who could only cry, "Oh my god. Oh my god" with her head in her tiny hands.

"Now Sophie," Carl started to whine.

"It's OK, Carl," she said. "The reason I was so disappointed was because I had false expectations, about you, about me. Well, I have seen through those illusions. That's why I had sex with Adam."

"What!?!" Carl shouted. Everyone looked at Adam. The red-headed giant wrinkled his mouth and shrugged. Rachel looked up at him and wailed, but he folded his arms across his chest and would not look at her. Meanwhile, Carl's rage was trying to decide on a direction when Sophie spoke again.

"I also made love to your widowed father, Rachel," she said, "and Carl, I made love to your father, as well as your cousin, Grace."

Carl spun around and scanned the crowd for their faces and, upon finding each one, each one just shrugged, except for Grace, a petite tomboyish woman. She was not a lesbian, she was always quick to say, but only a woman who liked to make love to other women sometimes, and she was irrepressibly grinning from ear to ear like she had won a bet. Carl was overwhelmed with a cacophony of conflicting emotions of anger, rage, shame, and guilt, and just as they threatened to tear his sanity to shreds, he looked back at Sophie. A beam of sunlight pierced the pecan canopy and set her face aglow, and she smiled at him without a trace of either triumph or condemnation.

"Oh, God," he said, the words gurgling up from deep within him. "My sins have been visited upon me ten-fold."

He dropped to her feet and kissed her hand while tears flooded his cheeks.

"I am so sorry. I am so sorry."

"I know, Carl," she said, with a tiny quiver in her voice as she pulled her hand from his and stepped past him down into the little human sea.

/|\

II. Who Wants Pie?

Adam and Rachel Willingham sat in silence at a cloth-covered table beneath a pecan tree in the yard behind the Cozy Café, pointedly not speaking to each other. After all, their friend and next door neighbor Sophie had probably just blown their marriage all to hell by publicly exposing Rachel's affair with her husband Carl to half the town of Hall's Corners, or so it felt. Then she announced that she had taken her revenge by making love to Adam, not to mention Rachel's father, Carl's father, and his cousin, Grace. Sophie was thorough if she was anything.

Every one of the fifty or so people among those that café owner Linelle Dubose had invited over just for the occasion who had any sense of history knew that they were experiencing a definitive moment in the town's history. It was one that would rank with the five-alarm cotton feed store fire of 1955 that threatened to burn down the town, and with the scandalous events surrounding that hot October day back in 1892 when Mac Peterson, the head of the lodge, shot and killed Cade Norris, owner of the town's largest store, in broad daylight on Main Street over the affections of Priscilla Howard, daughter of the county judge and widow of one of its most respected lawyers. Peterson was found not guilty by reason of "anticipatory self-defense" since Norris had threatened to kill him, but the scandal forced the widow Howard, by all accounts innocent of any wrongdoing, to go live with relatives in Marietta for good, and Norris's wife Ellen never recovered from her loss. The story made daily papers as far as New York and St. Louis.

But times had changed, and scandal was no longer what it once was. Besides, none of the main players in the present drama were of great social prominence or among what remained of Hall's Corner aristocracy. Rachel, a well-rounded brunette of a little over five feet with a face society had deemed passably pretty because of her two large blue eyes, was the daughter of Elwood Brady, a cook. But Elwood had not worked since the Great War because his Army service as an artilleryman in North Africa and the Italian campaign left him partially deaf and so skittish he was pretty much useless for anything that paid money. Rachel had grown up about as poor as poor can be since they were on disability and welfare, living on oatmeal eaten without butter or sugar, beans, cornbread, and whatever they might grow, gather, or get extra through the kindness of others.

Of all the parts of Sophie's revenge, her making love to Elwood was one to wonder about. Most people didn't think that at 72 and increasingly infirm, he was still capable of performing. And people wondered how Sophie, 17 and now clearly so beautiful, could sleep with a man so old and bristly and wrinkled, and who had no natural teeth. There was something so . . . diabolical . . . about the whole idea.

Adam was a giant at six-six and over three hundred pounds, up twenty-five pounds plus from his high school days when he played right tackle for the Carter County Wildcats. His step-daddy was Ollie Willingham, who was now retired after working at Ostow Mills until the New York Jews who owned it closed it and moved everything to Mexico. He had provided what is called a "decent living" for Adam, his two brothers Zach and Pete, and his mother Yvonne after his real daddy, Franklin Pinson, an automobile mechanic, ran off with a pretty young blonde in a red Corvette when Adam was five. She had left Franklin in Texas after a month when his money ran out, but Franklin had too much pride to come crawling back to Yvonne, and just kept on going. The last anyone heard of him, he was in Alaska, but that had been years.

So Adam and Rachel lacked pedigree or a social standing of any significance. He was in the trades, a machinist, and she was a housewife. Plus, they were both high school dropouts (although he was taking night classes at the off campus center of the University of Georgia in Brownsboro), and they lived in the EZ Mobile Home Park because it was all they could afford, as did a sizable number of the people now leaving the pecan grove behind the Cozy Café. Altogether, this made their plight less one of awe and more a source of either sympathy or amusement, both of which could be expressed by saying,

"Bless your heart."

"Go to hell, Grace," said Rachel, and she dropped her head so she did not have to make eye contact. Grace, with the slender hips and square shoulders of a tomboy even at 30, giggled as she sat down by Adam.

"Oh, man, can you believe Sophie?" she said, as if to herself since Adam and Rachel weren't responding. "Whew, nobody saw that one coming, especially Carl. He looked like a whipped dog, not that he didn't deserve it. No offense, Rache. But that Sophie, wow! Anybody see where she went? Linelle! Linelle! Where's Sophie?"

"On her way to New Orleans to live with her aunt," Linelle yelled through the back screen door. "Says she's getting her GED and enrolling at Tulane."

"New Orleans. Wow, people will be talking about this one for a while, and look at us. Hell, we're supporting actors in the whole damn melodrama. We ought to take this thing off-Broadway."

"Dammit, Grace, we're humiliated. All of us, including you," Rachel said. "How can you be so damn chipper."

"Yeah," said Adam with dull resignation. "When she took down Carl, she took down a lot of people."

"My god, they *are* alive. Don't you see that that's what makes it so funny? I mean, who would a thunk it. Sweet little church mouse Sophie finds out Carl is messing around, no offense again Rachel, and ups and drops a damn nuclear bomb, not just on his ass, but on all our asses. She even did it with your daddy, and his daddy, too! Eeow. And me. Course I ain't complaining and they were grinning like Cheshire cats, both of them a good forty-fifty years older than her, although Carl senior had his grin wiped right off his face when he saw his wife's expression. Man, Mattie Belle tore out of here like a bat out of hell. Hey, that rhymes."

Adam and Rachel remained silent and downcast.

"Ah, come on guys. There are some times in life that are so painful that all you can do is laugh. Like that time when we were seniors and we got drunk and took off for the Everglades to go fishing, and when we got there they said the swamp had dried up and there weren't any fish. We were so drunk we didn't care, but the AC went out on the truck and we about died from mosquito bites in the swamp and heat exhaustion all the damn way home. Remember that?"

Adam coughed.

"Yeah, and what about the time when we were going to turn the sprinklers on at Brownsboro High before the Shrine Game, just to slow down that jackrabbit running back they had," said Brad Randall, editor and publisher of the *Brownsboro Beacon and Carter County News*, as he sat down at the table beside Grace. "And we got arrested for trespassing and you and I almost missed the game. Boy, coach was really pissed when he came to bail us out."

"Yeah, Rache, Remember? We were driving the getaway car."

"And that's just what you two did, get away as fast as possible. Then, to top it all, they beat us 27-3 and that running back had nearly two hundred yards."

Still Adam and Rachel said nothing, and in the momentary silence she could be heard sobbing.

"Oh, Rache," said Grace soothingly as she reached across the table and took her hand. "Adam. Come on guys. So you got a little strange and now everybody knows about it. So, you're even. You can't let this tear you apart."

"Hey, look, I've got some scotch that's older than Sophie over at my house," Brad said. "Why don't we go there, and have a few drinks. We can really blow it all out. You won't even have to drive home, cause there's plenty of beds."

"Yeah," said Grace. "and I've got something for 'dessert'."

"You've been to see George, Gracie?" Brad said, dropping into an imitation of George Burns. *"Gracie, did the nurse drop you when you were a child?"*

"No, we were too poor. My mother had to do it." said Grace. "Snark snark. Ah, c'mon, guys, it'll be like old times. Remember when we used to get so blitzed we couldn't see straight."

"Or at least Grace couldn't see straight, if you catch my drift," Brad said, imitating Groucho Marx.

"Your George Burns was always better than your Groucho, and that ain't saying nothing," Adam muttered.

"That's the spirit!" Brad cried.

"And don't think I'm not still mad at you, Adam Willingham, for screwing that little slut," Rachel said with the barest trace of a smile as she wiped her eyes with the back of her hand. Adam started, but before he could come back with a retort, Gracie jumped in and said:

"There you go, girl. Now, let's go get high."

Brad Russell's house was fifteen miles out of town just off the Old Brownsboro Road in a patch of old oak and walnut trees at the end of a quarter-mile dirt driveway. It was a dark green "plantation plain" with black trim, and had a two-story porch on the front. In the back was a dining room and kitchen to the left side of the dog trot hallway, with its own porch and an old cistern at the end. Brad inherited it from an aunt and when he began to restore it, discovered it was built around an old log cabin. The house dated back at least to the 1850s, only a little while after the Cherokee removal. He had been researching for years trying to find out who built the original cabin, with no success since it apparently dated to before the Cherokee Land Lottery.

"Brad, this looks so good," Rachel said as she entered the dog trot. Brad had renovated the outside of the house, but had left the old log cabin's walls exposed inside, which included the two front rooms on the first floor plus the hallway.

"Very nice," Adam said.

"That's right. This is the first time you guys have been here since I renovated the place. Man, that's been nearly six years."

"Since right after Benny Ben was born," Rachel said.

"Where is the boy?" Brad asked.

"He's at mama's. Boy what a scamp," said Adam proudly.

"OK. OK. Enough of old home week," Grace said. "Brad, you go break out the hard stuff and meet us up on the top porch. Let's get things rolling here."

"Yes, drill sergeant, sir!" said Brad as he saluted her and turned on his heels toward the kitchen.

"I'll help," said Rachel and followed him without looking back at Adam, whose eyes followed her.

"C'mon, big guy," Grace said as she took Adam's hand and entered the narrow stairwell on the left side of the hallway. She looked down at the soft cast on his foot. "What happened to your ankle?"

"I hurt it at work, but it's about healed."

"Can you make it up the stairs?"

"No problem."

"Then let's go breathe some fresh air."

In front of the house, to the right of the driveway, was a very old spring house that Brad still used to chill liquor, and Adam and Grace settled into an antique metal glider on the second floor porch in time to see Brad and Rachel run across the yard to it and go inside. Beside the spring house was a large pool of ice cold, clear water fed by the spring which was shoulder-deep in the center, and, as the breeze was moving in just the right direction, they could smell its coolness in the air. The breeze also carried a small whoop, then a woman's laugh, clear and clean as the spring water, like a short soprano solo, fading quickly into the bass line of tree frogs, the melody of whippoorwills, and the occasional percussion of a flying beetle buzzing repeatedly against the front porch light below them. Grace thought she saw Adam flinch.

"You know, I had the hots for you in high school," she said as she handed him a lit joint.

"Oh, I can't," Adam said. "If I get injured on the job and they find pot in my system, I can lose my workman's comp."

"No problem. I'll show you how to make some of my special tea and if you drink it before you take a piss test, they won't be able to tell a thing."

"You sure?"

"I know it for a fact. And besides, have I ever lied to you?"

"OK, Grace, but I might have to drink a lot of it, since I'm such a big guy."

"That's what I've always liked about you."

"Now Grace, you know and I know that your fence doesn't swing that way."

"I never said I didn't like guys," she said with a mock pout. "I just like girls better sometimes. But sometimes I like guys. Some guys."

Their conversation ceased as the pot began to take effect. Adam, a little uncomfortable and confused at the line their conversation had taken, tried to keep his mind focused on the spring house, to see when Brad and Rachel came back. But things kept intruding on his consciousness, like the moon rising and the rough moan of a cat far away on a ridge, or a barred owl that flew to the top of a broken top pine tree in the thicket at the far edge of the field, his eyes flashing in the moonlight.

"This is good stuff, Grace," he murmured, but she didn't reply. When he turned to look at her, she was lying back in the swing, her green eyes closed, and his breath caught at how beautiful she was, in her boyish way. He felt the ache of desire rise in him and even though he tried to reason with himself that it was only because he was high, he saw a sudden flash, like from a camera, and he was mesmerized by her soft chin, her flat breasts with their small nipples barely making an impression in her shirt, her short collar-length dirty blonde hair, her narrow hips encased in cargo shorts from which two thin freckled legs poked out like sticks, her small feet dangling leather sandals, all so suddenly, strangely, and painfully beautiful he swallowed hard and gasped for air to keep from touching her.

"So, I see you guys started without us," Brad said, his voice slightly slurred, as he entered the porch with three bottles of liquor in hand. "Well, we did too."

Rachel giggled as she stepped onto the porch behind him with glasses and a pitcher of ice.

"I brought some Chivas for me and you, some Southern Comfort for our Janis wannabe, and, of course, some Jack Daniels to serve the queen. Are you ready, your highness?"

"Yes, my lord," Rachel said as she spread the glasses out on the table. "You may pour at will."

Soon the porch was silent once again except for the tinkling of ice in glasses, the pouring of liquor, and the inhalation and exhalation of pot smoke against a muted chorus of frogs, whippoorwills, and beetles.

"I pink mah tumb is dumb," said Brad, shattering the silence. Adam, with his mouth full of scotch, lost it, and sprayed a mist into the night air, which led Grace to whoop, Rachel to cackle, and all four of them to laugh uncontrollably.

"This is some really good shit, Grace," said Adam.

"Shhh, shhh. Just live the moment, Adam," she said. "Feel your body. Feel the rhythm of your breathing, the pulse of your heart. Listen."

The other three thought her words were hilarious and the renewed uproar shattered the stillness until they were all teary-eyed and gasping for breath.

"Hey," said Brad, suddenly and without preamble, "did you girls really get it on that night in the Cohuttas when you were sharing a tent?"

"Brad!" Rachel squeaked.

"You devil!" shouted Grace, who tried to kick him but her leg wasn't long enough. The women looked at each seriously, but a smile began to erupt on both their faces and they burst into laughter again, Grace so hard that she doubled over in the glider.

"Damn, you could always do that, Brad," Adam said with wonder. "When we were in school, you could say the damndest things in front of girls and get away with it. But if I said 'em, I got my face slapped."

"That's because Brad is so handsome, in a boyish sort of way," said Grace in a slow Southern drawl.

"And he is, shall we say, well endowed," Rachel said, then turned bright red.

"And how the hell would you know?" Adam exploded. "Don't tell me that you . . . and he . . . It was that time you two walked out to that old barn while we were skinny dipping in the river, wasn't it?"

Brad just looked at Adam, his face blank, but Rachel dropped her eyes.

"So, we're not even after all. Quick, who on this porch has screwed everybody else on this porch? Can I see a show of hands? How about you Rache? Have you done the nasty with everyone here?"

"Bastard!" she spat, and began to cry.

"Whore."

"Guys, guys," said Grace. "Calm down."

"Go to hell, Grace," Adam and Rachel said as one.

"My dog got hung up once," Brad said, obviously wasted. Adam lunged at him, but Rachel jumped in between them.

"Leave him alone! C'mon Brad, let's take a walk," she said haughtily as she pulled him up from his chair. "I know, let's walk out to the barn. You want to walk out to the barn, Brad? I know I do. Meanwhile, you stay here with Marine Corps Barbie."

"Hey!" said Grace, "I was in the Air Force."

Adam slumped back down in the glider. He heard Rachel and Brad laughing and giggling as they navigated the stairs, with their voices fading away once the back screen door slammed. Adam's anger had dissipated almost as soon as it erupted, because he always saw too many sides of things to be self-righteous and there were many sides to this. He sighed and stared out on the patchwork of fields and hedges dotted with small copses of trees that now swam before his eyes between the house and the road. Then he felt Grace's presence, and when he looked around, she was leaning backward and staring at him through half-closed eyes, her mouth slightly open. He hesitated, but when she tucked her lower lip beneath her teeth, he groaned and reached for her and she rolled over to straddle him.

xxxxxxxxxxxxxxxxxxxxxxxx

In the middle of the night, with the moon risen high and bathing the fields of sagebrush in a soft yellow glow, Brad stumbled onto the front porch naked, with a glass of scotch in his hands and said, "Hey, where did everybody go . . . oh, hell."

Grace lay on top of Adam in the glider, with her knees clasped against his sides and her arms draped around his neck like she was climbing his body. They were both naked and appeared to be asleep.

"What's that you say, lover?" Rachel said as she stumbled onto the porch behind him, also without clothes. "Oh."

Rachel strove hard to be nonchalant upon seeing her husband locked in a carnal embrace with her best friend. After all, she had just been in a similar embrace with Brad, and there was something in the combination of nudity, sex, pot, liquor, and the balmy night that made everything seem charged with electricity.

Grace awoke. She turned her face to look at Rachel through squinted eyes, and said, "You are beautiful."

"No, Grace," Rachel said, responding to something implied in Grace's tone, but Grace, with the stealth of a cat, got up from where she lay on Adam and stepped softly across to Rachel. Without hesitation, she pressed her nude body against Rachel's and kissed her deeply. Rachel's moan of protest evolved into a groan of desire as Grace pushed her back into Brad's bedroom.

"Oh, hell," said Brad as he stood in the doorway. "Adam, wake up!"

Later, in the quiet stillness that comes just before the sky first begins to lighten with the dawn, Adam lay wide awake nestled between Rachel and Grace, with their backs against his sides, and Grace spooning Brad, in Brad's king size bed. The ceiling was pressed tin in a teal color. Adam wondered if the color was true to history. He wondered if Brad had installed it himself. He wondered that life had been so kind to Brad, and that it wasn't just the money he had inherited, although it helped since it got him this house and made it possible for him to buy the newspaper. But Brad was one of the chosen ones, he thought, handsome, charming, the high school quarterback, president of the Key Club, naturally blessed with success, just as Grace was blessed, but with a bliss born of good humor and indifference to opinion, or at least the ability to fake it. Suddenly aware of her body next to his, he shivered. She shifted slightly against his side.

And he thought of Rachel and the first time he saw her, a gawky freshman transfer from Greenville, South Carolina, and obviously poor as dirt. His throat tightened now as it had tightened then with an unexplainable urge to hold her and tell her everything is going to be all right. But pitiful, helpless freshman transfer Rachel was an illusion. She was knowing, in ways that life on the bottom rung of the social and economic ladder taught children early on, and hungry as only someone who has gone to bed with an empty belly night after night could be. So, his urge to rescue her was really only an urge to ward off the close horizon of Hall's Corner and Carter County that pressed in on him more and more each day as adulthood drew nearer. He knew what he felt was what his father felt, and it was why he just kept on going when he ran out of money in Texas. He couldn't figure out how to hate that in his father without hating it in himself. But whatever it was in him in which was contained that hate, and whatever it was in her in which was contained her hunger, drew them together like opposite poles of a magnet and they called it love. And now, lying in bed, in this moment, Adam could see the future and sense the end of their marriage, not today, not soon, but someday, like the inevitability of awakening from a dream.

xxxxxxxxxxxxxxxxxxxxxxx

Later that day at about a quarter to three, when the Cozy Café was empty and Linelle was cleaning up and preparing to close, the quartet trudged in, clean but disheveled, and obviously tired and sated. Linelle, appraising them at a glance, brought glasses of iced sweet tea to the table and, when they started to speak, put her finger to her lips mysteriously, then turned and walked back to the kitchen. They each wondered at her behavior, but in their condition that was all the energy they could muster. They did not look at each other, either, but sat in silence like monks in meditation, staring blankly at anything and nothing. After a while, in which time in the kitchen moved faster than time at the table, Linelle returned to softly disturb their muted silence with a simple tomato and cucumber salad lightly sprinkled with balsamic vinaigrette and feta cheese. Each of them was soon absorbed in the flavors and textures. Then, after a further while, Linelle appeared with heaping plates of vermicelli covered in a lightly herbed butter sauce, and a bowl of toasted slices of homemade French sourdough bread. Adam and Rachel and Grace and Brad stayed lost in their own worlds as they savored Linelle's creation. And when they were sated beyond satedness, Linelle appeared at their table with four cups of strong, dark coffee.

"Who wants pie?" she said.

Rachel began to twitter, then Brad groaned and Adam laughed softly as if it hurt to do more, before Grace, gasping, with tears filling her eyes, said "I think we've had enough."

Anyone passing by the long block of buildings that made up Hall's Corner proper that one Saturday afternoon, the day after what came to be known as "Sophie's Revenge," might have wondered at the four adult citizens of the town who were sitting quietly and still on the steps of the old depot, out of the sun but still in the heat. They could have been part of a performance art project. They were in an interminable present caught between a past that had now changed forever the future in unknown but inevitable ways, and so they lingered at precisely the point between. Past them moved lives both dead and still alive in memory as ghosts walking the street, passing between them and the past and the future and the sun beneath which they sat so still, floating in the liquid syntax of time.

III. Sea of China

Chenglei, wearing a dark blue suit with a bright red tie, knocked rapidly on the door of the old, rusted trailer on lot 80E in the EZ Mobile Home Park. Behind him he could hear the auxiliary fan on his Altima siphoning off the heat of its now quiet engine.

"Ru!" he said, "Ru!" in that type of hoarse whisper people use when they want to be heard by someone in particular but not by others in general. No one answered. He tried the door and it was unlocked.

"Ru?" he said as he entered the living room. He stopped for a moment, or something stopped him, long enough to take a deep breath of the sparse simplicity of the room. The only furnishings were a wicker love seat and chair, a handmade coffee table, a small stand by the door that held a vase of orange ditch lilies in the process of decomposing, a small rug pockmarked with the faint vestiges of stains and wear left over from a previous life, and two posters, one in the Japanese style, of a small hut on a distant mountain side near a waterfall, all surrounded by a mist made of emptiness, and the other a bright Georgia O'Keeffe print of a pitcher plant (No. VI).

"Ru!" he cried.

Again, no one answered. He checked the front bedroom just off the living room—it was empty—but as he turned back into the living room, he noticed the coffee table. It was made out of some old rough-hewn lumber. It was about two feet by three feet, and the wood was gray with age. The top was planed and sanded, but the sides and legs were rough. Chenglei noticed was there was no gap in the seams. Each piece was cut and fitted meticulously, such that the top was smooth and level. And despite the fact that the legs were full two-by-sixes, the table did not wobble. Instead, the table was so structurally sound, and square and true, it seemed grounded in the very earth itself.

"Ru," he said, with a note of despair. He raced out of the room and down the hall, but as he suspected, no one was in the bathroom or the back bedroom. The bedroom closet was empty, except for a few hangers, and Ru's sleeping mat was gone.

"Open up!"

Chenglei froze. Someone pounded on the door.

"Open up! Federal agents."

He heard heavy footfalls come around the trailer to the back deck and heard someone shout, "We're in position!"

Chenglei's shoulders slumped first, then his whole body slid to the floor. He slowly inhaled and exhaled resignation to his fate, but as his mind became clear, Chenglei saw something that marred the empty serenity of the room. It was a matchbook, on the floor, as if cast there carelessly, but in the seconds before the front door and the bedroom door came crashing in, he grabbed it. Embossed on the cover was "Sea of China," the name of a Chinese restaurant in Atlanta and a phone number, 725-4316, and written over it was the Chinese character for "duckling." He pushed it through a heat vent in the floor. When the feds broke the doors down, Chenglei was sitting on the carpet, but far, far away.

He was with Ru. They were living in a Zen story. Chenglei was a young monk mocking his master Ru's mannerism of wagging one finger to emphasize a point. But once, when he did, holding up his own finger to imitate Ru, the master caught him, quickly seized his finger, then just as quickly cut it off cleanly with a sharp knife. And when, in shock and pain, he howled and looked up at Ru through tearing eyes, Ru wagged one finger. Then, Chenglei understood.

When the federal agents grabbed him and pulled him to his feet, he offered no resistance, but bowed to them as they cuffed his hands behind his back.

xxxxxxxxxxxxxxxxxxxxxxxx

Jake watched as the old pickup pulled up beside his trailer. It looked so rusted and dented that it already had one wheel in the junkyard. But the old man who emerged from it was dressed neatly in faded jeans and a yellow cotton short-sleeve shirt, and was wearing a worn but still serviceable pair of brown cowboy boots.

"Hello," the old man said.

"Hello," said Jake, from his lawn chair under the shade of a large willow oak that grew beside his trailer.

"My name is Yao Ru, and I recently moved into the trailer at 80E." The man extended his hand. He spoke with just the trace of an Eastern accent if anyone noticed because otherwise he looked like any other average joe to Jake, except when he got up close and you could see his eyes were slightly slanted.

"80E. eh? That's about the worst piece of crap in the whole park. The county ought to condemn it."

"It suits my purposes," Ru said, smiling. "I am . . . good with my hands and think I can make it habitable."

"Well, good luck with that," Jake said. "So what can I do for you?"

"Do?"

"Yeah, you know, help you with. I assume you didn't just come over to hear yourself talk."

"Hear myself? Oh, that is humorous," the old man laughed, deeply and genuinely, and Jake found himself laughing too, although he didn't consider what he said to be funny.

"I come to ask if you know of any places of work," Ru said, finally, still grinning. " I am new to Georgia and need to find employment."

"OK, sure," Jake said. "You're good with your hands. What kind of work did you do in . . . wherever it was you came from?"

"China," Ru said. "I was a horticulturalist. I grew plants."

"Hmmm," Jake said. "Well, there is only one big plant nursery in the county, and that's Pilgrim's down at Keown's Junction. . ."

He stopped when Ru looked confused.

"It's over on the Brownsboro-Keown's Junction Road, halfway to Oak Log.'"

Ru looked even more confused.

"Sorry. I'll draw you a map. But I wouldn't put any eggs in that basket . . . have any hope of getting a job there . . . because old Millard Pilgrim is about as ornery as a cornered rattlesnake. Hell, the only reason his wife and daughter put up with him is because they're related, and I guess maybe don't know any better."

"Pilgrim's Nursery? For babies?"

"Oh, no, no, Mr., ah . . ."

"Yao."

"Yao. It is a plant nursery. They sell flowers and shrubbery, turf grass, concrete yard art, stuff like that."

"Very good," said Ru. "If you will direct me to Mr. Pilgrim, I would greatly appreciate it."

"Stay right here. I'll be right back," Jake said. He went into his trailer, and in a moment came back with a carpenter's pencil and a piece of paper, on which he drew a simple map for Ru to follow.

"Gracias," Ru said, which was so unexpected that Jake couldn't help but grin.

"De nada," he said. "And next time, don't be a stranger."

"Oh, I will not," said Ru, quickly grasping Jake's meaning. "I will not."

Jake watched as the old man got back into the pickup and turned west out of the park toward the junction at the Livingston Road. Curious old man, Jake thought. I kind of like him. I wouldn't bet on his chances with old man Pilgrim though.

xxxxxxxxxxxxxxxxxxxxxxxxx

Ru ran up the steps from the truck parked by the curb in that busy, ambling style of older men, and knocked insistently on the door of the 50s-ish style house with a big front porch supported by wooden pillars, painted gray with white trim, on a residential street lined with huge oaks and maples in an old neighborhood in East Point, just south of Atlanta. He heard noises coming from inside, sounds like that of people running about, then he heard a door slam just before the front door opened. An Asian woman of indeterminate age because of her heavy makeup opened the door and peeped through the small space allowed by the safety chain.

"Madame Hong?"

"Yes."

"I am Mr. Yao. I am here to see Ling."

"Yes, of course," the woman said. She opened the door wide and stood aside to allow Ru to come in, but glanced up and down the street quickly before closing it behind them. "She is through there, the last room."

Ru hurried through the door and down a short hall. He encountered only one other person, a young Chinese girl, barely a woman, wearing a silk gown that clung to her body like a mountain waterfall. She was standing in the doorway to a bedroom, and her face was a fluid mix of emotions: expectation, resignation, fear, hope. Ru found her presence overwhelming and averted his eyes as he passed her. She said nothing. At the door at the end of the hall, he paused to collect himself, then knocked. "Come in," a soft voice said. He entered.

Sitting on a plain single bed without a headboard or footboard in a drab Spartan room was Ling, wearing a brightly colored robe whose gaiety of hues only made its contrast with her sunken, pale features more noticeable. Without looking up, or removing the long, white cigarette from her lips, she said, "You are in the wrong room. I am ill and Madame is not sending any men to me today."

"Ling?"

She looked up and slowly recognition changed her blank expression into a smile.

"Ru!" she said, rising to embrace him before quickly backing away and bowing. "Oh, I will make you ill. I am sorry you have to see me when I look so unpresentable."

She wobbled and he grabbed her arm to help her sit back down on the bed. He pulled a cheap plastic chair from the corner and sat beside her.

"Ling. What is wrong? Have you seen a doctor?"

"Yes, I have. He says it is only the flu, the Asian flu," she said with a small laugh, as she urged Ru to sit closer beside her. He did, and it immediately reminded him of their time on the ship coming to America, when they sat and talked often. "Madame Hong was worried that I might infect the household, so I have been confined to my room. The worst has passed and I should be able to resume my . . . duties tomorrow."

A long silence followed, one that inevitably must come to an end, but they lingered in it for as long as possible because they both knew they stood in a doorway through which time was passing, and in this moment futures existed that would no longer exist once this moment was passed.

"So this house, it is . . ." Ru said.

"Yes. Do not say it."

"It is as I feared that night as the boat carried us away. I saw you running along the deck and heard the harsh shouts of the snakeheads. But now it is over. I will take you from here. You will be free."

She dropped her head into her hands and began to cry softly.

"I will never be free again," she whispered.

"But your contract. You have fulfilled your obligations." He could not say it, or even look at her, knowing that fulfilling her obligation meant intercourse with many, many men. "I can take you away from here, where no one knows who you are."

She groaned.

"But you will know," she said. He started to speak, but she held up her hand. "I am staying here. Madame Hong can be harsh, because she must or the snakeheads will punish her. But she is not cruel. She is training me, so one day I will take her place."

"But the snakeheads? These men are dangerous."

"Only if we defy them," she said. "And maybe I can help some of the women through their . . . ordeal."

Ru sat quietly, his hands folded at his waist, breathing softly. She watched him intently, burning this moment into her memory, of Ru, sitting peacefully like a monk, in an orange plastic chair like he was sitting in Buddha's palm. Finally, she reached out and took his hand.

"You must leave," she said softly, "and never come back. Once I complete my training I will be moved to a new location, and I will only know where it is after I arrive."

"Yes," he said.

"And Ru. Do not tell Chenglei."

"Yes." A simple word, not only of affirmation but of comprehension, of knowing that doors close in time and doors open. "I will not forget you, duckling."

"Nor I you, Ru," she said and kissed him on the cheek. Without another word he rose and left the room.

xxxxxxxxxxxxxxxxxxxxxxxx

"I don't mean to show my ignorance or anything, but are you some kind of guru or something?" Jake asked Ru one evening in September as they drank tea in the living room of the Chinese man's trailer. Ru laughed uproariously, grabbing his stomach and bending over in his chair.

"No, no, Jake. No, Gurus are Hindu holy men. I'm Chinese. Back home in Fujian, I was just a gardener."

"But this place. I mean, I came in here once, when I first moved into the park, and thought about renting it because it was so cheap, and, god, it was awful. But now . . . hell, you actually made it livable. But not just that. There's something about this room . . . and this table. Why did you go to so much trouble to make this table?"

The table, which served as a coffee table of sorts and held their tea glasses, was about two feet by three feet, and the wood was gray with age. Ru had made it out of some old rough-hewn lumber he found beneath the trailer. He had planed and sanded the top, but he left the sides and legs rough. The first moment Jake looked at it, he almost dismissed it as a crude bit of practical furniture making, but he looked again, and then again. The first thing he noticed was there was no gap in the seams. Ru had cut and fitted each piece meticulously, such that the top was smooth and level. And despite the fact that the legs were full two-by-sixes, the table did not wobble. Jake couldn't quite believe it.

"Why did you go to so much trouble to make this table?" he asked again.

""We must draw on the strength of the inner attitude to compensate for what is lacking in externals. Then even with slender means, the sentiment of the heart can be expressed."

"Even with slender means, the spirit of the heart can be expressed. You are! You are some kind of guru!"

Ru laughed again, and when he stopped, he said, "No. What I said was from the *I Ching*, an ancient Chinese book of wisdom. It is like a saying you might take from the Bible, such as, consider the lilies of the field. They reap not, neither do they sow, yet God provides for them."

"But what you said still sounds different. Even with the simplest means . . . You know, I took taikwondo. Even earned an orange belt, but my knee started giving me too much trouble."

"Taikwondo is a Korean martial art, Jake."

"Oh, sorry. I didn't mean any offense. There aren't many Asians around here, although I hear there are a bunch of Laotians or Vietnamese or something living near Carter. They've got their own subdivision, complete with rice paddies in the back yard."

"I understand. All human beings see the world sometimes in terms of stereotypes. I even think it is a natural first step in trying to understand, like a secretary's shorthand. I am guilty of it, too. When I first came to America, I did not think there was any difference between Los Angeles, Atlanta, and New York, but now I see that your cultural differences are almost as great as ours. In China, our dialects can be so distinct that people from different parts of the country have trouble communicating with each other."

"Well, I might have trouble communicating with someone from the Bronx, or East LA. People are so different. I worked with this Yankee woman once, from New York City, and she was a trip. She always seemed to be in a hurry, and she had a mouth on her. If you weren't careful, you'd get your feelings hurt, but she didn't really mean anything by it. It was just the way she was."

"Hmmm. She sounds like a Confucian. In my country, the young people follow Confucius, some literally and some only in spirit. But life for them is a big, complex game with a set of fixed rules. You work hard. You follow the rules. You succeed."

Jake laughed, and at the questioning look in Ru's face, said: "That's the way it was in America when my daddy was a working man. He worked for the GM plant in Atlanta for twenty-five years, a good union job, and retired with a pension. Life was supposed to unfold like it was according to some plan, and for a lot of people I think it did. But Daddy, he was one mean crazy SOB. He was what the doctors call a Type A personality. Two weeks after he retired, he had a massive heart attack and died. He was just 51."

"I am sorry for your loss," Ru said.

"Don't be," Jake said without emotion. "He was one of those people who are running so hard they never look up to see where they are, or who they are with, even their children. That's why I think you've got to stop and eat the roses every once in a while."

"Eat the roses?" Ru asked, then he saw Jake smile. "Ah, very funny. My father was a local government official, a bureaucrat. I only saw him early in the morning before he left for work and I for school, but I was usually in bed before he came home. He worked very hard. In China, no one stops to eat the roses until they retire."

"Then what do they do?"

"They become Daoists."

"Daoists?"

"Yes. It is an ancient way of life. Daoists believe that life is like standing in a doorway through which time is passing. Moment by moment the future becomes the past, but always in the present. The present is all we have."

"Is that like Buddhism? I read a little of Alan Watts when I was in San Francisco once."

"Yes and no," said Ru. "Most Buddhists sit on the bank and contemplate the river. Daoists swim in it."

"Ha, ha. I think I get it. In the South, we say you either fish or cut bait."

"Oh, Jake, it is not like that at all, but it is just like that," laughed Ru.

xxxxxxxxxxxxxxxxxxxxxxxx

"Goddamn it," Millard Pilgrim shouted. "Where in the hell are those peat pots, Doris? Dammit, I said I wanted them out here on the work table."

"A customer just came in, daddy," Doris said meekly. She was a pale, harried, skinny woman, almost all of one color, drab.

Ru could see Millard through the half-open sliding glass doors off the retail showroom. He was standing by a large wooden table under the shade of a big yellow maple tree. He was a thin, wiry man of average height whose features seemed drawn as tight as his personality. It was hard to imagine that he had ever been cute, even as a child. Doris skittered about like a drop of water on a hot grill, flinching at his every word.

"Yes, I am a customer, but I would like to speak to you, Mr. Pilgrim."

Millard was about to say something that could easily have been taken as rude, about being too busy to talk to anyone, when he noticed that the customer was Asian.

"I see that your azaleas appear to be struggling. I think it is because your soil is too alkaline. And your begonia cuttings need more potassium. Not much, just a little. And you are over-watering the roses."

"Well, I'll be damned," Millard said. "Dammit, Doris, did you pot the azaleas in regular potting soil?"

"Ah," said Ru, looking at the natural topiary of a pine thicket just beyond the last row of shrubbery. "I see you are growing kudzu."

Millard Pilgrim was stunned for a moment, but then he started laughing like he had not laughed in his adult life. There was something about this man standing before him that suddenly made everything so funny. For one thing, he didn't look Asian until you saw him up close, and for another he didn't talk Asian. Yet there was something about him that marked him.

"You don't grow kudzu," he finally said. "It grows itself. You just try to keep from getting lost in it because you might not find your way out."

This time, Ru laughed.

"So, you looking for work?" Millard asked.

"Yes," Ru answered.

"It's spring and I need some help for a few weeks, but I can't pay much."

"I do not need much. I just need it in cash."

"Cash?"

"I don't like the government taking what is mine."

"Then, I guess you're hired."

"When do I go to work?"

"Any time you want?"

"Then how about now?"

"Fine."

And just like that, Ru went to work for Millard Pilgrim.

xxxxxxxxxxxxxxxxxxxxxxxxxx

The smell of urine and vomit and feces made the stale air difficult to breath. It had been better earlier when they were at sea and the snakeheads had opened the hatches to let in fresh air and light, but now they were in port and they had to wait for nightfall before they would see the sky again.

"Ru, what do you think it is really like in America?" Chenglei asked uncertainly.

Ru smiled in the darkness because throughout their long miserable voyage, Chenglei had kept up a sustained monologue on the wonders of America, and of his plans and dreams for great success there.

"Don't worry, you will be fine," Ru said, answering a question Chenglei had not asked. "Americans are people like we are. They just have different rules and different behaviors. Just pay attention and proceed cautiously, and you should be fine."

"But I want to be very successful," Chenglei said with fervor. "I want a big condo, a big luxury car, a country club membership. And I want a blonde Swedish wife."

"Ah," said Ru, chuckling. "The American dream."

"And what is wrong with a Chinese woman?" Ling interjected playfully. "Are we not beautiful? Do we not have grace? Are we not obedient? What does a Swedish blonde have that we do not have?"

"They're not Chinese," Chenglei said.

"Duckling, it is getting dark soon and we will be separated," Ru said. "When you find out where you will serve out your contract, you must contact me and I will come to see you."

"Me, too," Chenglei said.

"Ru, do not call me duckling. You make fun of my name."

"No, it is a pun in English. The last day when we went up on deck and you were about to hit your head on the door frame, I told you to duck. In English, a duckling is a little duck. It is a term of affection."

"Oh," she said, "you are being nice."

"And me?" Chenglei asked, with a large, exaggerated smile on his face.

Ling could not help but laugh.

Suddenly, the hatch door flew open with a loud clang and one of the snakeheads yelled down the hatch, "Hurry! Hurry!" The trio scrambled to grab their meager belongings and scurry up the ladder onto the dark deck along with the other immigrants. The brisk offshore wind smelled of brine, but to the immigrants it might as well have been chrysanthemums. Chenglei, Ru, and a few other men were separated from the rest and put on a small launch. As they pulled away from the freighter, toward the lights of

Savannah, Ru could see Ling running along the deck with members of the other group, and he could hear the shouts of the snakeheads ordering them to hurry. A feeling of foreboding came over him.

"Welcome to America!" Chenglei said as he grabbed Ru's arm. "Welcome to America!"

xxxxxxxxxxxxxxxxxxxxxxxxx

The old man strode nonchalantly along the sidewalk, stepping lightly across the broken sections, his slightly slanted eyes scanning ahead as if he was looking for something. But no one passing by could see his eyes, shaded beneath a narrow brimmed hat. He wore faded jeans, a yellow short-sleeved shirt, and a pair of worn boots. From his shoulder hung a small bag not unlike that worn by several graduate students common in this area so close to the university. Little distinguished him at all. At the end of the block, he saw the restaurant on the other corner. After crossing the street, he turned down the street beside it and stepped into the alley behind. Within few steps, he stood before the restaurant's service entrance and knocked. A young Chinese man opened it.

"The plum trees should bloom so beautifully this year," he said, bowing.

"But only if we get good spring rains," the young man answered as he bowed and opened the door.

IV. Life in the park

"Enough already, Sandy," Jake said as he pressed the receiver against one ear and covered the other with his hand so he could hear her over the noise of a feed truck on the highway. "Look, I've had some trouble, OK? . . . I know. I know. Walt's been late a lot, but he swears Plum Thompson's going to pay him this week, so I'll have the money tomorrow. . . . Hey, wait a minute. I know I'm already a month behind, but I love that kid as much as you do. You know that. . . . No. I told you I stopped drinking. Christ. It's just that Walt says he keeps having cash-flow problems . . . Oh, don't give me that crap, woman. You know you could never manage money."

Click.

"Hey . . . Hey!" Jake slammed the receiver down in the cradle of the pay phone in front of J's Grocery and Convenience Store. Beside him he could see the neon sign behind the plate glass that flashed in bright orange letters, "cold . . . beer, cold . . . beer, cold . . . beer." It beckoned like a siren's song.

"Ah, shut up," he said. Beer's the reason I'm in this mess, he thought, this mess being divorced, poor, and living alone in a trailer park just a half-mile from downtown East Jesus, otherwise known as Hall's Corner, Georgia. It wasn't supposed to be this way, but, at 30, he had had enough time to figure out that 'sposed to and a dollar might buy you a cup of coffee. But I'm not bitter because things with Sandy and me didn't work out, Jake thought. For a while there, it was pretty special. There was that afternoon at the lake when we drank a six-pack of beer apiece, played chess, and then had sex in the water, floating inside a big truck inner tube, right in front of everybody and nobody knowing. Or when I held her at the hospital while she pinched the bejesus out of my arm when Punkin forced her way into this world like an ugly little red train roaring out of a tunnel. And that day at the state park when we walked that path along the mountain creek and stopped to picnic. I can still see the crawdads scooting around, like little soldiers defending their territory, in water so clear and clean that looking at it made my eyes cold.

That was before I knew about big moments and little moments, he thought. I only learned about them later, after everything had gone to hell, when I talked to the old Chinaman, Ru, who disappeared. He talked about each moment being a gateway between the past and the future, like we're standing in a doorway and time is flowing through it.

Jake had never thought about life that way, but he had not found out quick enough to stop himself from tearing his marriage all apart, to prove to himself that Sandy couldn't really love him, like women had never really loved him, even his mama, who was the one who made the template. And when neglect and indifference weren't enough, beer and belligerence did the trick.

I'm not bitter, he thought. So why don't I feel not bitter? Because I had a sense of déjà vu when we broke up? Déjà vu, hell, déjà vu. Because I woke up too late to do a damn thing about what I had done? Bitter because I lost one more possible future?

Sandy had already remarried, to Luther Johnson, an English teacher and girls soccer coach at Carter County High, and he admitted begrudgingly, a decent fellow by all accounts. Since her marriage, the only time she talked to him anymore was to bitch at him about his late child support payments. He knew it was no more than what he deserved, considering what he had put her through the last few months they were together, but he struggled to fully admit that to himself. And her quick remarriage had hurt his heart despite his best efforts to deny it.

There is no use going there, he thought; it's all water under the dam. But it was a life lesson he couldn't just put away on a mental shelf with a little label on it that said "Don't be this stupid next time," not living in a trailer park, with work scarce, and both his truck and his little girl needing new shoes. He laughed to himself. He couldn't help it. It sounded too much like a country song.

He tugged at the waistband of his pants, a habit from childhood, then turned to walk across the store parking lot beneath an oil-painted evening sky of bright blue fading to gray and fluffs of white clouds steadily oranging in the west. J's sat across and just west down the Brownsboro Road from the EZ Mobile Home Park. It was a big park, with close to 90 spaces, but there would have been a lot more of them if Ekee's uncle, Zebediah Schultz, had not made the lots two or three times the usual size. He left a lot of trees, too, so as mobile home parks went, the EZ wasn't so bad.

"Hi, Mr. Peterson."

Jake snapped out of his thoughts to see a very tall and very thin boy with dark frizzy hair pull his bicycle up beside him. He nodded.

"Bean."

"Mr. Peterson, I'm getting my car this weekend, if I can get the money."

"Yeah?" Jake said, with a hint of sarcasm, the emotional residue of getting hung up on. This was not the first time they had had this conversation. Bean had been talking for weeks about buying a twenty-five year old Toyota Tercel with a bad transmission that he had seen rusting in the weeds on the school bus route. But Jake regretted his tone almost immediately.

"No, really. I'm going to get it. Milton Pinkus at the antique store is going to give me $100 for my stereo, and I'm going to buy it."

"Bean, you've been going to get that car every weekend for the last two months," he said, turning to the boy with a thin smile. "And, as I remember it, your grandmother's old hi-fi doesn't even work."

"No, no. I got it working. I did."

Jake watched Bean's Adam's apple bob up and down, which it did when he was excited or nervous.

"And how did you do that?"

"How, what? Mr. P-P-Peterson," Bean stuttered, suddenly very self-conscious.

"How did you fix the stereo? You don't know anything about electronics."

"Well, I didn't actually fix it, I . . . I just turned it on and it's working now, I don't know how."

"Then you better get it over to Milton in a hurry," Jake said, and burst out laughing. Bean hesitated, licking his lips nervously, then smiled when Jake slapped him on the shoulder.

xxxxxxxxxxxxxxxxxxxxxxxx

The next morning, Friday, right at 6:30, Walt Carter pulled up beside Jake's trailer in his pickup. Since the truck had a lifter kit and oversized tires, Jake had to pull himself up into it by grabbing the door frame and the seat. He grunted with the effort.

"Putting on a little weight, ain't you, Jake?" laughed Walt, a fat and balding man of 45, whose face and head always seemed to shine like he had just scrubbed it with a washcloth. His words were often accompanied by spittle.

"You're one to talk," Jake said as he tried to find a place to put his feet on the floorboard of the new Ford quad cab, which nonetheless was already packed with junk mail, receipts, small plastic bags, soft drink cans, and fast food wrappers, while at the same time not knocking any similar pieces of the effluvia of Walt's life off the dash.

"Just big-boned for my height. What time are we going to get our pay?"

"Won't be 'til tomorrow. Thompson says he's going to catch me up for the last month."

"I sure as hell hope so. My ex-wife is giving me trouble about child support."

"So what else is new?"

That day, their work went well, as usual, and they finished putting the exterior trim on a home in a subdivision being built by Thompson Development a few miles east on Highway 253 called Hall's Creek Village. Walt was the site manager, as well as their crew chief, which meant he had to oversee all aspects of the development. The crew, which did the interior trim, and all the exterior finish, was efficient and productive as construction crews go, and Walt liked them. He would even work with them sometimes, especially if they were behind, but most of the time he only saw them once or twice a day if then, since it was a big development and was months away from completion. Walt had to spend a lot of time with his other subcontractors, and they ran the gamut from grading to landscaping. And he frequently had to go to Brownsboro on business, too, although it was widely known among the workers that that "business" was often his girlfriend Gail.

Sometimes, when he came back, there was liquor on his breath, and sometimes he didn't come back at all. And several times he had shorted their pay or missed paying them altogether, always blaming Plum Thompson, although he had always made it up in a week or two. Still, the men had an easy camaraderie, in part because they also shared an awareness of their likable boss's shortcomings, and complaining about them made the long summer days pass quicker. But this was truly a long day, made to feel longer by Walt's report that evening that their pay was going to be another day late, and Jake was beat by the time he returned home late that night at 9:30. The tires of Walt's truck crackled to a stop in front of the old brown single-wide on 51C.

"What the hell?" Jake said.

"Looks like a load of lumber to me, Jake, and treated at that. You building a deck?"

"Hell, I can't even afford to re-floor the bathroom," said Jake as he stepped down out of the truck. "One of these days me and the throne are going to wind up on the ground. Somebody screwed up."

Walt just laughed.

"You'll have the money Saturday, right?"

"No, I pick it up too late Saturday to cash his check at the bank. I'll have it Monday morning after the bank opens."

"I guess that'll have to do."

Jake stood by the stack of lumber and began to scratch his head as Walt pulled away. There was enough lumber, precut, to build a large deck, including step risers, metal braces, boxes of treated nails and deck screws, and a complete set of plans in a plastic sleeve. This is hundreds of dollars worth of stuff, Jake thought. No way I am going to pay for this. He searched through the paperwork until he found a copy of the bill of lading. Bean had signed for it.

"I'm going to kill that kid," he muttered.

The lumber was shipped from the Lumber Barn which, like every other major national retailer was over twenty-five miles from Hall's Corners in any direction, in this case in Brownsboro, the county seat. Jake was very familiar with the company since it was the only wholesale building supply outlet in the county, and he was a frequent customer. He knew it was late, but he walked back down to the pay telephone across the road anyway.

"Hello, this is Jake Peterson in Hall's Corner. I want to talk to someone about a load of lumber that was delivered to my house today. . . . What? An answering service? OK, OK, I'll call tomorrow I guess."

He walked back to the trailer and frowned when he saw Ekee pull up in his white Ford Galaxy, a luxury car now showing signs of its age like an old woman in a prom dress. The park manager leaned toward the passenger window, which stopped with a loud squeak halfway down.

"Building a deck, Jake?"

"No, Ekee. Somebody delivered it by mistake."

"Well, you know the park rules about junk in the yard. No. 7: No resident shall . . ."

"Yeah, I know. Like I said, it's a mistake. I'll get somebody out here tomorrow to get it. By the way, Ekee, when are you going to get a plumber over to fix that leak in the water line?" He pointed to a large damp spot on the ground behind his trailer.

"Tomorrow. The guy's supposed to be here tomorrow. Well, I got to run."

The park manager pulled away.

"That's what you said yesterday," Jake said out loud, but Ekee didn't hear him over the noise of his car. Jake went into the trailer, which was like a sauna since October was unseasonably warm, and turned the air conditioner on high. He unfastened his utility belt, dropped it on the floor, and slumped on the couch. Within five minutes was sound asleep.

Jake slept late the next day, and it was after lunch, which was really breakfast–a bowl of Cheerios in milk that was just beginning to turn–before he called the Lumber Barn. They told him he would have to bring the bill of lading in. With the worn out brakes on his truck squealing with every stop, he drove over to Brownsboro.

"I need to talk to someone about a load of lumber," he said to the young man behind the counter in customer service. The "associate" was dressed in a sport coat and tie, but he was so thin and lanky with youth that it hung on him as loosely as his sense of responsibility. On his name tag were the words "Ed Ward."

"Our computers went down about ten minutes ago," he said with natural indifference. "We can't access any of the records."

"Well, when will the computers be back up?"

"Don't know," he said.

"Then, who does?" Jake asked, growing impatient and his voice rising.

"I don't know," Ed said, sitting up a little straighter. His lack of real concern for the problem of the man on the other side of the counter was unchanged, but he could see the department manager walking toward them. "Perhaps you can come back Monday."

"Monday!" For a moment he forgot that the founder of the Lumber Barn was a devout Christian and none of their stores were open on Sunday.

"May I help you, sir," said the manager, a tall and handsome young black man whose ebony skin shimmered in the fluorescent light.

Jake explained the problem to him and got the same answer, although with more detail and a little more certainty. The system was down. The IT people were saying it would be hours before they could have it back up. He didn't tell Jake, but the problem was with new automated inventory software the corporation had installed a week ago. The system had gone down three other times since, although this was the worst of the four by far.

"I am sure the system will be back up by late tonight," the manager said, "but you might want to wait until Monday just to be sure."

Grimly, Jake gathered up the paperwork. He wanted to say something to the manager, to cuss him out, but he knew there was nothing the manager could do about either Jake's problem or his own. And he wanted to cuss out Ed, mostly because he was such a little punk, but he figured he couldn't help it either.

The incident had Jake talking to himself as he drove back to Hall's Corner, but when he pulled into the park, he was rendered speechless. Beside the large bundle of lumber in front of his trailer was another bundle almost as large. He examined it long enough to determine that it was to be used for an elevated extension of the deck to be built with the previous bundle. He could only grin sardonically as he sat down on the steps of the small, dilapidated little porch at his front door.

"That's gonna be some deck," said Bean as he braked his bike to a stop.

Jake just stared at the new bill of lading in his hand. "No, Bean. It's all a big mistake. It will be out of here Monday, or . . . maybe Tuesday. And tell your grandmother not to sign for anything for me, OK? And don't you sign anything else, either."

"Uh, Ok. Uh, Mr. Peterson, I'm going to . . . I'm going to get my car this week, for sure."

"Yeah?" Jake said, absently.

"Yeah. See ya."

Bean rode through Jake's yard to his trailer just behind Jake's on D Street as Ekee's car pulled up.

"I thought you said all this stuff was going to be out of here today, Jake, not add to it."

"I can't explain it, Ekee," Jake said. "Some computer mixup at the Lumber Barn. It'll all get straightened out . . uh, early next week at the latest."

"I hope so, Jake," he said. "I wouldn't want to serve you notice or anything. Can't have people junking up the lots."

"Oh, go to hell, Ekee. I got enough trouble already. I didn't order this stuff."

"You . . . you . . ." Ekee sputtered, but when Jake stood up, he put the car in gear and let slinging gravel complete his retort.

That was a dumb thing to do, Jake thought. Ekee could give him thirty days notice. Could, but wouldn't. They had known each other a long time, since that day in fifth grade when Jake had pulled a bully off him and bloodied the kid's nose. Ekee owed him, but more than that, coward that he was, he feared him. Still, there was no use venting his frustrations on Ekee, however tempting it was, especially when his backyard was slowly becoming a mud hole from the water leak,

Jake took the new plans inside and sat down on the couch to examine them. The first set was for a large deck, complete with built-in seats, plant boxes, and wide rails, but with supports and bracing heavier and stronger than usual. The second set of plans explained why. They were for a stairway leading to a deck terraced off the first, eight feet off the ground. Jake marveled, as he sometimes did, at the possibility of a life in which spending thousands of dollars just for something like a deck was no big deal. And he looked at the simple line drawings and tried to visualize what the decks would look like, but sleep soon overtook him.

xxxxxxxxxxxxxxxxxxxxxxxxx

On Monday, he waited and waited, but Walt didn't showed up. He was considering walking over to the pay phone when finally, just before eight, another member of the crew, a wizened old carpenter named Louis, pulled up in his beat up old Chevy truck. Jake knew something was up when Louis struggled to look him in the eye.

"You seen Walt?"

Louis's face screwed into a deep frown.

"The son of a bitch skipped out on us, Jake."

"Hell and damnation," said Jake. "What about our pay?"

"He took it. His girlfriend Gail says she ain't seen him since Saturday night. Said he was going over to Thompson's to pick up the payroll and never came back. I waited for y'all this morning for forty-five minutes at the new site, and when y'all didn't show up, I figured his truck must a broke down. That's when I went by his house."

"That . . . that . . . What am I going to tell my ex?"

"I know, Jack. I got three mouths to feed at home myself. He left us high and dry. But I figure, heck, Thompson still needs work done. Maybe we can make our own crew. You could run it."

"I don't know, Louis. I gotta think about this a little."

"Yeah, I reckon. Well, I'm going to see if I can work a few days for Bude Meadows."

"You know you can't trust him either," Jake said.

"I know," Louis said, "but I gotta do something right away. They're gonna cut my power off Friday if I don't pay the co-op something. You want me to let you know if Bude's hiring?"

"Yeah, I guess so. Thanks Louis."

"See ya, Jake."

Jake walked across the road to the pay phone and took some coins out of his pocket. Heads it's Sandy, tails it's the Lumber Barn, he thought and flipped a quarter into the air. When it landed in his palm face up, he dialed Sandy's number.

"Sandy, listen. I got bad news. Walt skipped out on us with the payroll and . . . no, I haven't been drinking. I don't drink anymore; I told you that. Listen . . . Listen! Don't get all upset. Yeah, yeah, I know you are entitled to your anger, but . . . Child Support Recovery? You did what?"

Click.

After kicking the steel post that held the phone, an act to which the post was wholly indifferent but his foot wasn't, Jake called the Lumber Barn.

"What do you mean the numbers don't match your records? Yeah, I got them right here in my hands. They've got your name on them. I don't care what the computer system says about your inventory. I just want to know what I am supposed to do with all this friggin' lumber. The park manager is giving me hell about it. Call your Atlanta office! Hell . . . OK. OK. Give me that number."

Jake dialed the 800 number and waited through three recordings of "Everything is beautiful (in its own way)" before he finally got a human. But even the human couldn't help him. The numbers on the invoices did not match any on record, and the human insisted that their inventory records were all copacetic now that the new system was in place.

"Are you sure the invoices say Lumber Barn?"

This time Jake hung up the phone. He cursed to himself all the way back to the trailer, but when he came around the street corner, he was stunned. Two Lumber Barn delivery men were getting in their truck after unloading a third bundle of decking.

"Hey, hey! Wait a minute, you guys. I didn't order this stuff."

"You Jake Peterson?" asked the driver as he looked at the LCD on his new personal digital assistant.

"Yeah."

"Says here you did. Man, you are building a hell of a deck."

"I'm not building a deck," Jake said through gritted teeth. "Dammit, I didn't order this stuff."

"Hey, mister," said the guy in the passenger seat. "Give us a break. We're just doing our job. Call Customer Service in Brownsboro if you got a complaint."

"I did and they said they didn't have any records of the deliveries. You guys got to take all this stuff back."

"Pardon my French, buddy, but you're full of it," said the driver, waving the personal digital assistant. "According to the this, you did order all this stuff. Besides, we can't do anything unless the warehouse tells us to. Now, we got to go. We've got three more deliveries to make. Our 800 number is in the phone book. Just call them and they'll get it all straightened out."

"I did already," Jake sputtered, but the truck was already pulling way.

Jake kicked the new bundle of lumber before he remembered that he had already bruised his toe on the metal pole holding up the pay phone. While he was dancing around in pain, Ekee's car stopped in front of the trailer. He held a sheet of paper out the window and fanned it up and down.

"What's this, Ekee?"

"Notice, Jake," Ekee said with a squeak. "You got 30 days to get this stuff off the lot or you'll have to move."

"Ekee, don't be an asshole," he said as he stepped toward the passenger window.

Ekee flung the paper at him and sped off. I knew I shouldn't have pissed him off, Jake thought. It was pouring stupid gasoline on a bad luck fire. He tried to get his mind around what had happened, but he couldn't. Too much bad luck to get a grip on, especially in the hot midday sun. Maybe a glass of tea in front of the air conditioner would help. Jake picked up the third set of plans and was about to go inside the trailer when a county deputy drove up.

"You Jake Peterson?" he asked.

"What now?" Jake said.

"I got a warrant for your arrest for failure to pay back child support."

Jake's shoulders slumped. "Could you tell me when the complaint was filed," he asked.

"Sure," the man said as he looked over the papers. "July 26."

Almost two months ago. Jake would have laughed, but it hurt too much. He thought about men in prison for twenty years for crimes they didn't commit. Children kidnaped and killed. Whole families that died in war. Bad luck is bad luck, but it can be good luck. Like the old Chinaman had said, "Sometimes it's hard to tell which is which." My health is good, except for my toe, he told himself. My little girl is healthy. But I don't have a job, don't have any money to speak of, I'm getting kicked out of my home, and now I'm being arrested. Any way you slice it, this bad luck ain't good luck. Others might have their bad luck, but this was his own particular piece of that pie.

The deputy took Jake down to the county jail and booked him. His bond was set at a thousand dollars initially, but the judge the next morning was sympathetic because he knew old man Thompson, who was a long-time friend, and he verified Jake's story about the stolen money. He let Jake go home on his own recognizance, and set a hearing for a month later.

Jake had the deputy who took him home drop him off at J's, where he bought a six-pack because he was feeling so ornery and sad. He opened one of the beers as soon as he stepped outside the store, and threw the can into the trash can beside Ekee's office as he walked to the trailer. Once inside, he slouched down on the sofa and took a big drink out of another can, then leaned forward to look at the third set of plans, which were lying on the coffee table. They were for a second extension, off the first one, and a full fourteen feet high. He leaned his head back on the sofa and closed his eyes.

For the first time he could see it, all three parts. His mind began to wander, from the image of the majestic decks to the long front porches on the house he lived in as a boy where a spring practically in the front yard formed a pool of water so clean watercress grew in it. And from there his mind slid to the little pool in the cold creek at the state park where the crawdads marched about backwards, then on to the little house he and Sandy had planned with the big sunroom. Then he fell rapidly down a long, undulating tunnel, on and on, until he flew out of it into a deep purple sky flecked with images of distant thermonuclear explosions. His mother's face floated before him. "Is this a big moment or a little moment?" she asked.

His own anguished cry roused him from the dream, and he gasped for breath like a drowning man. When he opened his eyes, the beer in his hand might as well have been a poisonous snake. He threw it in the trash, along with the other four cans after they had been drained into the sink, then stepped outside into the muggy heat. He shook his head to clear it, then realized he had all three sets of plans in his hand. He walked about in the front yard, looking down at the plans and up at the empty space above his narrow lawn. Finally, he turned to the three bundles of wood.

He remembered the old Chinaman who had lived in 80E. When he had walked into his trailer at Ru's invitation, an old trailer that Zeb should have got rid of years ago, he had been amazed. Ru had cleaned and polished everything down to the nub, and patched and painted until the place actually looked like something fit to live in, at least on the inside. But the most amazing thing to Jake was a table.

Ru had made it out of some old rough-hewn one-by-sixes he found beneath the trailer. It was about two feet by three feet, and the wood was gray with age. Ru had planed and sanded the top, but he left the sides and legs rough. The first moment Jake looked at it, he almost dismissed it as a crude bit of practicality, but he looked again, and then again. The first thing he noticed was there was no gap in the seams. Ru had cut and fitted each piece meticulously, such that the top was smooth and level. And despite the fact that the legs were full one-by-sixes, the table did not wobble. In fact, the table was so structurally sound, and square and true, it seemed grounded in the very earth itself. Jake couldn't quite make sense of it.

"Why did you go to so much trouble to make this table?" he finally asked Ru.

"The *I Ching* says one must draw on the strength of the inner attitude to compensate for what is lacking in externals. Then even with slender means, the sentiment of the heart can be expressed."

Jake eyes focused on the bundles of lumber. Then he began to roar with laughter. "So, what's the problem?" he gasped.

It took him the rest of that day, all night, and over half of Tuesday to assemble the deck. As he worked, he thought, each piece is an expression of all of them, so he carefully fit them together, trimming and planing and sanding where necessary to make each fit flush. And when he tired, or was tempted to take shortcuts, he remembered what Ru had said. "This is a deed that will go out a thousand miles," he said over and over to himself as he worked. When he finished, the first level fit snugly against the front of the trailer and ran over half its length. The second slid off it like the wing of a bird cleaning itself and stretched up into the branches of a 40 foot oak tree growing near the door. The third deck hung over the trailer like the hand of a supplicant, open beneath the sky.

He marveled at it and, although he was weary and craved sleep, he took a lawn chair, a pitcher of iced tea and a cigar up onto the top deck. From there a short while later he saw Ekee's car coming toward him.

"What the hell is this, Jake?" Ekee yelled out the window.

"Decks, Ekee," Jake yelled back. He took a puff on the cigar.

"I know that! But I told you to get this stuff out of here, not build a Taj Mahal."

"Number 46, Ekee."

"What?"

"Park regulation No. 46. A tenant may build porches, decks and room additions so long as they do not present any hazards or detract from the overall appearance of the park."

"Yeah! Well, I say this detracts from the appearance of the park. It's all out of proportion."

"I don't think so, Ekee."

"Why?"

"Because this place sure looks a heck of a lot better from up here."

Ekee jammed the car into drive and pulled away.

"Boy, Ekee's mad," said Bean as he rode up on his bicycle. "Man, this is some deck, Mr. Peterson. This is the best one I ever saw."

"Thanks, Bean."

"Mind if I come up there sometime. I bet you can see for miles."

"Sure Bean. Come by at sunset. It should really be something."

"I will," said Bean. "Oh, and Mr. Peterson. I'm getting my car this weekend for sure."

"That so? Drive it over. I'd like to see it."

V. The Poker Game

Just out from the tiny community of Talking Springs, Georgia, in Carter County, there is still standing today a small collection of weathered buildings by a clear, cold little body of water known as Cannon Pond. It is so-called because local legend has it that a wealthy early settler bought a small cannon for home defense during the Civil War, and that he was either forced to push it into the pond to keep a fingerling of the Union Army from taking possession of it on Sherman's March to the Sea, or it fell into the pond when it was fired at them. There are no historical records that anyone has actually ever seen the cannon at the bottom of Cannon's Pond, even though the spring-fed water is remarkably clear and there is little silt, but the legend persists.

The first of the group of buildings, the Talking Spring AME Church, was the first black church in Carter County. The congregation met regularly there from after its founding in 1871 to sometime during the Great Depression, when they disbanded and joined the congregation at a much larger and more accessible church by the road in Hall's Corner four miles north. The church building quickly fell into disrepair, but because it was made of very wide and thick rough-hewn oak timbers on a tall rock base, the weeds and the weather could not destroy it in decades of trying, only collapse its roof and part of its chimney.

In 1940, the land upon which the church and the pond sit was bought by Travis "T" Lumpkin, the local sheriff, and it is he who restored the church to usable shape and assembled the other buildings. It was his hobby, although one not without purpose. He repaired the chimney and replaced the roof and the four windows allowed by the thick timbers, and even put in an new pine floor. He painted the church white and had a bronze plaque affixed to the wall by the front door that said, "Talking Spring AME Church, Est. 1871."

The other buildings he gathered from around the county. There was a corn crib he got from a man up on Switchback Road on Sulagade Mountain a few miles to the northwest, the small old Six Mile General Store he got free from the state just for moving it when they rerouted the road between

Brownsboro and Hall's Corner, and the old train station at Hillsborough, a community a couple of miles to the east, which he bought from the railroad when the trains quit stopping there. He added several old sheds, including a spring house which he moved atop a small spring by the pond, and he built a very long, screened house with a barbecue pit right next to the church.

The buildings became collectively known as Lumpkin Town, and the sheriff made them available to churches (including the black church at Brownsboro) for homecomings, to civic clubs and, later, youth baseball and football teams, for picnics, and to families for reunions and weddings. They were political capital that T used to help win his first election in 1948, and every subsequent election until 1972, when he retired.

His first year in office, T began to hold regular Wednesday night poker games in Lumpkin Town, and it quickly became a mark of social and political status in Carter County to be counted among the men invited to attend. T purposely kept the number fairly low, usually no more than sixteen or twenty, but he did allow the regulars to bring guests if they asked. And he made sure the regulars included the majority of white men of any real social or political clout, which meant that the state representative, several county commissioners, some members of the mayor and council of Brownsboro, the mayor of Hall's Corner, the superintendent of schools and a member or two of the county school board, one or two bank presidents, and several wealthy landowners usually had a seat at the tables.

Each Wednesday night, known only to a few, the real business of Carter County was conducted over plates of barbecue and stew on folding tables set up in the pit house and quarter-limit games of five-card stud and seven-card draw. Candidates for office were discussed and chosen for support, and, in general, the future course of the county was plotted. And T made sure that that course included his continued service as sheriff.

Just as very few of the citizens of Carter County even knew of the Wednesday night gatherings, and only a select few of those who attended knew of the sheriff's other poker game, played for matchsticks, once a month on Thursday night, the winner taking home some prize the sheriff put up. This smaller group, usually no more than four to eight, consisted of like-minded men who were friends. Counted among them one April night in 1958 were "Uncle" Dave Wallace, the state representative for Carter County who came into office when T did and served for decades, Luke Palmer, Sr., and Phil Thompson, the county's two wealthiest men, and Willard Baker, the former state representative and former mayor of Brownsboro.

"I got a special prize for the winner tonight," T said with a big grin as he dealt the first hand.

"What are you up to this time, T?" asked Luke. "Not another country ham."

"Oh, no, it's better than any ham," T laughed. "It's better than even a whole hog."

"Well, tell us what it is," groused Phil, his thin face set in its customary scowl.

"Oh, you'll see. It will be here in a little bit. Now let's play cards."

"T, this better be good," said Uncle Dave, but T only winked at him.

Of the five players, Luke was the best. He was lucky at cards just like he was lucky in life. He was born handsome and charming, and even though from a poor farm family, had acquired a million dollar loan from the government to build quonset huts during World War II. After the war, the government forgave the loan, instantly making him rich. He was naturally a shrewd businessman and by now was the richest man in Carter County, second only to Phil. He did exceed him in girth, however.

T was the next best player, although many times he purposely lost, and the rest knew it. He was not anything like the fat, comical Southern sheriff portrayed in the movies. He was very tall, six-feet four, and had broad shoulders and a narrow waist. It helped that he could look down on almost everyone he dealt with, especially since his cratered face was not even passably good looking.

Phil and Willard and Uncle Dave were about equal in their lack of poker-playing ability. Phil, who had inherited all of his father's massive land-holdings but not any of his intelligence, was the county's richest man only because he did have the good sense to know he wasn't very bright and let his wife advise him. He also knew to keep his mouth shut when opening it would likely embarrass him, so he said little even among his friends.

Willard had been a good card player in his day, but now at almost eighty, he usually fell asleep halfway through the evening, and the others just dealt him out and continued the game.

Uncle Dave was much more intelligent than Phil; in fact, he was the smartest of the group, but he was terrible at bluffing and was usually easy prey for Luke or the sheriff. They often took pity on the him, though, because he took the game too seriously, and let him win a few hands early just to keep him happy. He was, after all, the county's link to the governor.

But it was hard to dislike Uncle Dave anyway. He was a jovial, if sometimes volatile, little bantam rooster of a man with a powerful bass voice that belied his small stature. That voice, and an ability to think quickly on his feet, kept his majority above sixty percent during his entire time in office, although it helped that he was very adept at convincing the governors he served under to keep allotting money from their emergency fund for various local projects.

After the first few hands, Uncle Dave had almost enough matchsticks piled up in front of him to build a tiny two-room cabin, but he knew not to trust his luck. And sure enough, over the next few hands the stack began to dwindle. By the time the four men who were awake saw the headlights of a car coming down the long gravel drive, Luke and the sheriff were well ahead, with Uncle Dave trailing badly and Phil needing a miracle to survive.

"Who's that?" Luke asked.

"That's the prize," T chuckled as a county sheriff's deputy's car pulled up beside the screen house in the edge of the shadows. The men could just make out the deputy as he got out of the car, then opened the back door. A figure emerged, hidden in the dark, and the deputy led it around to the door. When he entered, all but the sheriff gasped.

The figure was a slender young woman of above average height and no more than eighteen, her hands cuffed behind her back and her legs in shackles. She had chocolate almond skin and was dressed in a strapless red polyester mini-dress that clung to every curve it didn't reveal. Her curly black hair shimmered down on either side of big bright eyes, high cheek bones, a small flat nose, and a wide mouth set in a small, oval face until it touched her shoulders. As she entered with the deputy, she shook herself free of his arm and stood facing them, her full breasts out-thrust. After T dismissed the deputy and he drove away, he addressed the group.

"Gentlemen, this is Polly Ann Johnson, the daughter of Card Johnson from over in Carter," said the sheriff as he got up and walked over to the woman. He put his arm around her shoulder and she tried to twist out of his grip, but gave up when it proved to be too difficult. "Now, some of you may know Card. He's a good nigger farmer with a big family that never caused anyone any trouble. But, as you can see, his gal here is no farm girl. Despite her good raising, she has gone down another path. We caught her whoring for money two nights ago in the projects over in Brownsboro.

"Now, after two nights in the county jail, she's not looking her best, but I think you will all agree that even so, she's still something special. I never saw a nigger gal as pretty as her in my life and I grant none of any of you have either."

"She's the prize?" Phil sputtered, his mouth open. "I can't . . . Evalene would kill me if she ever found out."

"Well, there's not much chance of you winning, now is there Phil?" the sheriff laughed. "Polly Ann here is facing a charge of prostitution, which you all know Judge Chamblee frowns upon, and assaulting a deputy and resisting arrest. He's liable to make an example of her and put her away for some hard time. And then, after the state gets through with her, Card is liable to beat her within an inch of her life and she knows it. So, Polly Ann and I came to this little agreement, didn't we darling."

He squeezed her shoulders tightly, but she never looked at him, although her lips began to tremble.

"If I drop the charges, Polly Ann agrees to make herself available to the winner for one night for whatever they might like to do to her, short of leaving a mark. And tomorrow, she's going to high tail it out of Carter County. Isn't that right, Polly Ann?"

Polly Ann didn't answer, but seemed to right herself and stared openly at the men.

"Isn't that right?" T said with a shake of her shoulders.

"Yes," she said.

"So, you see, this cute little nigger gal goes to the winner of her own free will. Now sit right over here so we can look at you while we finish the game."

He led Polly Ann to a chair a few feet from the card table, behind Phil. The chain on her leg irons scraped the floor as she hobbled beside the sheriff, and when she sat down, she had to sit on the edge of the seat because of her handcuffs. She pressed her thighs tightly together.

"Phil, you're going to have to move to the side so we can all see her," Luke said.

"I guess," Phil said as he reluctantly moved his chair to a corner of the table, which still forced Uncle Dave to crane his neck slightly to look around him.

"T, are you sure about this?" Uncle Dave said. "If the NAACP got wind of it, they would raise hell. Y'all know that trouble's coming since the Supreme Court ruled that segregation is illegal. It's already happened in Little Rock There's not more than a couple hundred or so black kids in the whole county and they've got a pretty good school, but no matter."

"Nah. They'll never integrate the schools in Georgia in my life time," T said. "And as far as the NAACP, whose going to tell? You Phil? Evalene would strip your hide. You Luke? Luke's tongue is hanging out already just thinking about tonight. And I sure as hell ain't going to tell, nor is Polly Ann, since she knows what's good for her. So, that leaves you, Uncle Dave. You gonna tell? I bet the Atlanta papers would have a field day with it."

"That's blackmail!" Uncle Dave said, his voice booming, as he stood up, knocking over his chair.

"No it ain't," T said as he stood up in front of him. He towered over Uncle Dave and craned his head down to stare in his face, but Uncle Dave bowed his shoulders and glared at him. After several long seconds, T stepped back. "It ain't blackmail because none of us can afford for any of this to get out, see? It's perfect. One of us gets a cute piece of nigger pussy and the rest don't have any choice but to keep their mouth shut about it, including Polly Ann. I already told her she might wake up dead if she ever let out a peep. I didn't threaten her, mind ya. I was just speculating."

Uncle Dave gritted his teeth, obviously not ready to quit the argument, but instead sat down and said, "Let's play."

The sheriff grinned broadly as he sat down too and dealt the cards. As the hand progressed, both T and Luke kept leering at Polly Ann as their piles of matchsticks began to grow. She looked past them like they were invisible. Phil started to fold on every hand and was soon out of the game altogether. After sitting through another hand, pointedly not looking at Polly Ann, he mumbled something about "not having any interest in any of this" and left. Since he was Willard Baker's ride, the old man went with him, although not without gawking at Polly Ann all the way out the door as if he could not determine if he was awake or still dreaming.

Uncle Dave played with his mouth set in a hard line, only occasionally looking at the red-dressed prize a few feet from him. The warm night air was sexually charged and he was not immune to it, but the whole situation felt like a surreal anachronism to him. He had been to the old slave market in New Orleans and he couldn't shake the feeling that he was in some kind of time warp. He could imagine that there had been other times like this where white men gambled with a black woman as the stakes. He could even imagine that his great-grandfather might have done it, since he owned a plantation in South Carolina before the war with over fifty slaves. As he glanced at the girl, so defiant and yet so vulnerable, he grew bitter. He didn't like this being forced into this. He didn't like it at all.

Three hands later, it really began to look like T and Luke would be left to fight it out for the prize. As he dealt the hand, Uncle Dave knew that if his luck didn't change soon, he would lose and be left with a huge moral dilemma. But when he picked up his cards, his eyebrows twitched. T saw it, too, and raised the ante ten matchsticks. Luke took a look at Polly Ann, and then at his hand and matched it, then raised it twenty more. Uncle Dave fingered his cards as he looked back and forth from his rapidly dwindling pile of matchsticks, then matched the bid. T's face was solemn, but inside he was grinning. He raised the bet thirty matchsticks. Luke looked over his cards at Polly Ann and smiled. He matched the bet. Uncle Dave didn't see it. He was watching Polly Ann, who now had her chin down on her chest.

"It's down to you, Uncle Dave," T said. "You still got thirty matchsticks in that pile?"

Uncle Dave counted them.

"Thirty-five," he said and pushed them all on the table. "I call."

T waited for Luke to show his cards. When he saw the pair of fives, queen high, he grinned and put down three nines, king high. Both of them turned to Uncle Dave.

"So, what have you got?"

"Oh," he said, and laid down three kings.

"Well, I'll be damned," Luke said in wonder as Uncle Dave claimed the pile. The three stacks of matchsticks were now about the same size.

"He wasn't bluffing," T marveled to himself.

"Well, it's getting late," Luke said. "We're all about even. What say we cut the cards?"

"Nah, let's play it out a few more hands," said T, but not before Uncle Dave said, "I'm in."

"I hate cutting cards," T said. "What about if we play one hand of five-card draw, nothing wild? Winner takes all."

The other two men agreed, and all the matchsticks were put in one big pile in the center of the table. T began the deal. Luke got the four of clubs, Uncle Dave the seven of diamonds, and T the jack of hearts.

"Jack's lead," he said and dealt the second card.

Luke got another four, of hearts, Uncle Dave got a six of diamonds, and T got the deuce of spades.

"Fours lead," said T as he dealt the third card. Luke got a queen of diamonds, Uncle Dave the seven of spades, and T the ace of spades.

"Sevens lead," he said grimly.

Luke's fourth card was the king of diamonds.

"No help," T said.

Uncle Dave's was the three of clubs.

"No help there either."

T got the nine of spades.

"No help, either. Sevens still lead. OK, boys, it's a pair of fours against a pair of sevens."

He dealt the last card face down and got the jack of hearts.

"Hot damn," he cried as he threw the card down. "A pair of jacks!"

"Well, shit!" Luke said as he threw down the eight of clubs.

"So, what it is?" T said to Uncle Dave, who wasn't paying attention. He was staring at Polly Ann and her slumped shoulders.

"Uncle Dave?"

Without taking his eyes off her, Uncle Dave dropped the six of clubs on the table.

"Well, fuck," T shouted. "You lucky bastard."

Uncle Dave turned around to see the other two men staring at him like they had just woken up right where they were. While they watched, he scooped up the pile of matchsticks and put them back in the plastic tub used to store them. Then he gathered up all the cards and shuffled them, then put them on top of the matchsticks. He sat back then and looked at them. The silence of the heavy spring air was broken only by the buzzing of beetles and the fluttering of moths against the screens, and the deep roar of bullfrogs around the pond.

Finally, with a long look at Polly Ann, Luke said somberly, "I guess it's time I went home," and got up to leave.

"Me, too," T said with resignation as he stood up. "Y'all can stay here as long as you want, Uncle Dave. Here's the keys to her handcuffs and shackles. Just turn out the lights when you go."

Uncle Dave didn't speak, not until long after their tail lights had disappeared around the wild privet that lined the drive near the road. When he turned to Polly Ann, she was staring at him. He got up and went over too her. Her eyes widened, and she trembled. He knelt down in front of her to unshackle her ankles, and reached behind her to free her hands, then got up and went back to his seat.

"You can go now," he said. "Just make sure you are out of Carter County by tomorrow morning."

She smiled broadly in relief as she rubbed her ankles.

"Thank you! Oh, thank you!"

She ran to the screen door, but as she opened it, she stopped and looked back at him. He was sitting in profile, staring out through the screen at the pond. He had his feet stretched out, his ankles crossed, and his thumbs were looped in his pants. She closed the door and stepped back in the room.

"I'm not a whore. I just needed some money real bad and I borrowed it from this guy named Sweet Sammie. He lives in the projects. When I couldn't pay it right back, he said I had to work it off. He threatened to cut my face if I didn't do what he said."

When Uncle Dave made no response, she continued.

"I was going to run away. I just needed enough money for a bus ticket to Atlanta, that's all. Sweet Sammie takes nearly every dollar from his girls. I knew right away he wasn't going to let me make enough to pay him off for a long time."

He turned his face to her then.

"I just kept thinking of the old slave market in New Orleans," he said softly.

"Oh, Jesus," Polly Ann gasped as she bent forward, grabbed her stomach, and began to sob. He went to her and helped her back to Phil's seat at the table.

"Here," he said, handing her his handkerchief. "Would you like some water or coffee? I think there's still some left in the pot."

"Coffee," she whispered.

He brought back two cups and poured a shot of bourbon in each of them. She sipped the hot bitter liquid with her eyes down. He could see tears streaking her cheeks. He listened as her sobs faded into the night sounds.

"I always liked to hear bullfrogs at night," he said finally. "I was never afraid of the dark, even as a little kid."

She raised her eyes and sniffled. His voice was deep and resonant, and seemed to spread out in the room like a low fog.

"I remember one time when I was just a boy, my brother and some of the older kids took me snipe hunting. They took me down to the creek on my daddy's farm, where a cow path ran between a big blackberry patch and an old overgrown privet hedge before it crossed, and left me there. I knew they were up to something. My brother was always picking on me since he was five years older. It was a moonless night and it was so dark that I could barely see my hand in front of my face. But as I stood there, I could hear the creek a few feet father on, and bullfrogs and crickets, and I realized that they were still the same as they were in the daytime; I just couldn't see them. I stood there for I don't know how long just breathing and listening, then I went back to the house. But you know what?"

"What?" she asked.

"I was gone so long, mama made all of them go search for me. When they got back, looking pretty scraggly after fighting their way through briars and thickets for an hour and scared to death that something had happened to me, I was sitting at the kitchen table drinking buttermilk. I laughed and laughed."

Polly Ann smiled. Her big sparkling eyes, high cheek bones, small flat nose, and wide mouth, individually would have been out of proportion on any other face, but on the small oval of hers they melded into a rare, even startling beauty when she smiled. Uncle Dave could only stare at the transformation.

Polly Ann felt like she was standing on a rope bridge high over a gorge, gently swaying back and forth. Who is he? she thought. He is white. He's nearly middle age. There are tiny streaks of gray in his hair, and little wrinkles around his eyes. He's so small, he would look like a boy if it weren't for that. But his voice drew her into his hard blue eyes until she felt like she was drowning.

She got up and walked over to the screen, and knew without hearing or seeing that he followed her. They peered out into the new light of a sixth-night moon that rendered one wall of the old church in a yellow glow before it cleared the tops of the far trees to shimmer like a crocus in the pond.

"It is so beautiful," she said softly.

Uncle Dave watched the buildings and the landscape take shape and form in the pale light. They are just as they were in the dark, he thought. Just as they were.

"It will be dawn in a little while," he said.

"Yes."

She swallowed, and turned to him. He was smiling at her.

"I'll take you to the bus stop in Hall's Corner," he said quietly. "Don't worry about the fare. I'll give you the name of a man I know in Atlanta. He's a good man and you can trust him. He'll rent you an apartment, and help you get set up and find a job. I'll see you in a couple of weeks."

"I won't be kept," she said.

"Nor will you be. I wouldn't want you if you were."

He kissed her then and the bridge gave way. She tumbled over and over into the depth of the dark shadows.

Sylvester "Sammie" Smith was arrested the next day by county sheriff's investigators and charged with six counts of running a house of ill repute, three counts of contributing to the delinquency of a minor, three counts of enticing a minor for illicit purposes, three counts of statutory rape, one count of assault on a law officer, and one count of obstructing an officer in the performance of his duties. At the next term of the Carter County Superior Court, he was tried and convicted on all counts. His sentence was 20 years to life in the Arrendale State Prison.

VI. The Highly Probable Thing

When he was seventeen, Ezekiel "Ekee" Schultz and his friend Danny Wade were both stock boys at Aub's Famous Foods in Keown's Junction and one suffocatingly hot day in August of 1965 were fishing half-gallon cartons of ice cream from an outdoor freezer that stood beside the store at the time, a weekly task all the stock boys relished in the summer. They would stick their heads and shoulders as far as they could into the hard air and breath deeply until its bitter cold seared their throats. This particular day, during the height of the racial troubles that gripped Georgia, Danny was bragging to Ekee about his girlfriend Ramona.

"I tell you, she's an easy piece," Danny boasted as their upper bodies hung suspended over cartons of vanilla, chocolate, and strawberry. "You could get you some on the first date. I did."

Ekee laughed excitedly, but then stopped and turned to Danny, their breath fogging the air inside the freezer.

"But she's your girl."

Danny tried to be nonchalant, but couldn't quite do it.

"Ah, I'm tired of her, ya know, and I want to break it off. She's talking about getting married and shit. If you went down there Saturday night and asked her out, she'd go. She ain't hardly got a mind of her own when it comes to men. It would really help me out. I could accuse her of screwing around and quit her clean, and you'd get some pussy in the bargain."

The plan was very alluring to Ekee; so far, six years past puberty, he had never gotten past second base.

"I'll borrow Floyd's car," he said, the words churning the misty air.

"Yeah, that's it," Danny exclaimed as they each pulled an armful of half-gallon cartons of Neapolitan out of the box and put them in a shopping carts. Ekee heard footsteps and turned to see a young black woman about his age walking across the side parking lot behind them, heading for the front of the store. She was wearing a simple dress made of store-bought cotton print, bright yellow with small red and blue and green flowers, and her butt swayed like a tree in a spring breeze as she walked.

"Ummm, ummm," Ekee moaned for Danny's benefit. "Take a look at that."

"You like dark meat?" laughed Danny, bumping his hip against Ekee's for emphasis.

"Huh?" Ekee said distractedly.

"You'd fuck a black pussy."

"Hell, no!" Ekee shouted loud enough to suppress a forbidden desire.

They didn't hear the heavy footsteps behind them until they stopped. Both boys turned around and saw a large black man staring at them from thirty feet away, his eyes smoldering.

"Oh, shit," Ekee whispered. "Let's get the hell out of here."

They slammed the door on the freezer and pushed the shopping carts around back of the store as fast and noisy as a drumstick on a cymbal, anxiously looking over their shoulders as they turned the corner to see if the man pursued them. They hid in the stockroom for a half hour, until they were sure the man and woman had left the store, and caught hell from Aub for letting the ice cream get soft.

On Saturday night, Ekee drove his friend Floyd's '54 Chevy down Brownsboro Road to Six Mile, never getting over 30 miles per hour to keep the throaty roar from its busted muffler to a minimum. Following Danny's directions, he slowed down even further as he reached the pass over the ridge so he did not miss the pig trail dirt road to the left that would lead him to the Promised Land. He turned on to it and drove even slower when the car threatened to bottom out in the deep ruts. The road soon crossed the railroad track that had led to the construction of the new Brownsboro Road and relegated the old one to an often neglected tar and gravel two-lane. The dirt road connected the old and the new roads and was unmarked, but was widely known as Pumpkin Jones Road for a former county commissioner long dead and largely forgotten but for his namesake. A half-mile past the railroad track, Ekee saw the lights of an old farm house on a small knoll on his right, and turned up the driveway. He was glad the weather had been dry, because he figured that in wet weather he would never have made it up to the house.

Ekee pulled up in front of a rusted Ford pickup and cut the engine. He tried to calm his growing excitement by taking a deep breath, but it had little effect on his mental state or the turgidness that had settled in his groin. He got out and walked up the high wooden steps and across the porch, only the creaking of the wood and the distant roar of bullfrogs from Lake Coosawattee another mile down the road breaking the silence. The porch was partially illuminated by light streaming out of the screen door. He knocked.

The room beyond the door was a living room, with a sofa and chair and a worn oval rug before the fireplace pocked with black circles where it had been burned by sparks from previous fires. He could see no one and knocked again. Muted voices skittered into the living room from the back of the house and soon a girl, who looked a year or two younger than he, followed them. She was a plain girl, with limp brown hair draped over her shoulder in a long ponytail that ended near her waist. As she stepped up to the screen, he could see she had a long, oval face with flickering gray eyes, their beauty offset by her thick nose and tiny chin. She wore no makeup. She wore a long dress, printed with tiny flowers, made of flour sacks, ending at her ankles; and her body was pear-shaped, her shoulders narrow, her breasts small, and her hips wide.

"Hello," she said in a small voice.

"Hi," Ekee replied with as much nonchalance as he could muster. "I'm a friend of Danny's."

"Oh," she said. She looked back over her shoulder briefly, and then stepped out onto the porch. "We can sit in the swing."

She led him into the deep shadows at one end of the porch and sat on large wooden swing hanging on chains from the open porch rafters.

"Where is Danny?" she asked as he settled in close beside her. She scooted over a little until her the arm of the swing pressed against her side. She wouldn't look at him.

"He couldn't come, so he sent me," Ekee said.

"I like Danny," she said as her fingers fidgeted with her dress, smoothing out the wrinkles and pushing the skirt down until the hem touched her shoes.

"Do you go to Brownsboro High?" he asked, casually. He wanted to just grab her and kiss her, but he figured from Danny's description of her that she would just slump in his arms and let him, so there was no rush. He could toy with her as a cat toys with a mouse.

"No," she said, glancing at him and quickly returning to her dress.

"You graduated."

"I dropped out."

Ekee could wait no longer and put his hand on her shoulder.

"You're really pretty, Ramona."

She shrugged her shoulder beneath his hand, but when the gesture didn't shake it off, she leaned back against the seat.

"I don't . . ." she started, but Ekee slid up against her, trapping her at the end of the swing, and kissed her. Her mouth was soft and slack, and her tongue lay still against the bottom of her mouth as his darted across it. When he broke the kiss, she gasped as if she had been holding her breath.

"I like Danny," she said quietly.

Ekee kissed her again and ran his hand up her chest to cup a breast. She shivered, which he took as assent, and rubbed his palm across her nipple.

"Hehehe."

Ramona stiffened at the high-pitched giggle coming from behind the screen. Ekee turned to it, but only caught a glimpse of someone standing there before he heard the soft patter of fading footsteps. He turned back to Ramona and kissed her again as he took her nipple between his thumb and forefinger. She grunted.

"Why don't we go for a ride," he whispered in her ear.

"I don't want to," she said, so Ekee kissed her again.

She still did not respond, but Ekee didn't care. He had only French-kissed one other girl in his life, a girl at school when they were both thirteen and curious, and he was determined to hold this beachhead. He unbuttoned two buttons on the top of her dress and slipped his hand inside. He could feel the warmth beneath the cup of her white cotton bra.

"Oh, come on, it'll be fun," he said softly as he kissed her neck. Ramona squirmed like a butterfly on a pin.

"I like Danny," she said, her breath coming in soft pants.

"Don't you like me, too?" he whispered in her ear. "I'll make you feel good."

"I . . ."

"Hehehe."

Ekee yanked his hand out of her dress and she straightened up, smoothing her dress again. Ekee saw a old woman behind the screen this time. She was very short and time had settled on her in that way which made guessing her age impossible, but she held her palm to her mouth.

"Hehehe," she giggled, then fled when she saw Ekee looking at her.

Ekee was getting frustrated at her interruptions. He turned back to Ramona and unbuttoned three buttons on her dress this time despite her feeble attempts to stop him, and this time slid his hand into her bra. He smiled as he felt the warm flesh of her breast and took its nipple between his fingers. Ramona shrank back against the seat as he squeezed his fingers together and kissed her again.

"C'mon, go out with me," he said, breathing into her mouth. Something about her reluctance and the strange giggles of the old woman made him desperate. He withdrew his hand from her bra and pushed it into her crotch, making a scoop with his fingers.

"Uh uh," Ramona grunted and shifted her hips in an effort to escape his probing hand.

"C'mon," Ekee hissed. "C'mon."

He pulled up her dress and Ramona pressed her thighs together tightly, crossing her knees. Ekee poked his fingers deeper into her crotch and put his arm around her shoulder. He pulled her mouth to his hard, bruising her lips and forcing her mouth to open wide. His tongue flickered along the edges of hers, which suddenly came to life and darted around his. Her thighs opened slightly, allowing his hand to flatten against her vagina, and she sighed.

"Stop," she said, but made no effort to make him stop. "Not here."

"You'll go then!" Ekee exclaimed as quietly as he could.

"Yes," she whispered.

"Hot damn."

"Hehehehehehe."

He turned to see the old woman staring at him, giggling beneath her hand. She was shifting her weight back and forth on her feet like she had to pee, and flatted her nose against the screen, her eyes squinted as she peered into the dark shadow of the porch. When she saw Ekee looking back at her, she squealed and ran back into the house.

Ekee stood up quickly and took Ramona's hand. He tried to pull her up beside him, but she was like dead weight. He tugged again, but then heard heavy footsteps from inside the house that grew quickly louder. A dark shadow fell on the screen and Ekee could see a tall, wiry man dressed in overalls standing on the other side with the old woman beside him.

"Git back in the house," he said as he pushed the old woman back. "Damn you boys, coming up here and kissing on my daughter. I'm pretty goddamn tired of it! I think I'll go get my shotgun!"

Ekee's heart stuck in his throat. The old man disappeared back into the house and Ekee looked at Ramona for one last time. She had pushed her dress back down, and was huddled up at the end of the swing, her chin against her chest and her arms wrapped around her, shivering. All thoughts of paradise fled his mind, and he leaped down the long stairs, stumbling half-way to fall on his face in the yard. He felt something wet and squishy soak through his shirt and onto his stomach, but he scrambled quickly to his feet and bolted to the car. He was shaking so much he could barely get the key in the ignition, and when he tried to crank it, he flooded the carburetor.

"Oh, shit!" he yelled as he stamped the pedal to the floor, never taking his eyes off the screen door. The engine turned over and over five times before it began to sputter to life. He kept the pedal down and it revved up until he heard the hard knocking sounds of the crankshaft grating against the main bearings. Black smoke poured out of the tail pipe. Ekee put the car in reverse and it lunged backwards down the driveway, bouncing like an old wagon over the deep ruts. As he turned the car out into the road in a cloud of dust and gravel, he slammed on the brakes and slid up to the edge of the ditch on the other side. He quickly jammed the shifter into first, and took one last look at the house. The old woman was standing at the screen door again. He couldn't see the porch swing.

With a groan, he popped the clutch and floored it. The car fish-tailed down the road with a large plume of dust rising behind it. Although he was now out of any danger, Ekee never slowed down. At any moment he feared he would hear a shotgun blast. He flew over the railroad crossing, the wheels coming up off the ground. When the car crashed back into the dirt, the muffler fell off, and from the house Ramona could hear the engine's roar until it was practically in Hall's Corner. She tightened her arms around her chest and, peeked out from underneath her eyebrows at the screen door, but it didn't open. She saw the man's shadow appear in the skewered rectangle of light on the porch, and thought she saw him turn toward her. She pushed the swing to one side, hiding deeper in the shadows. With a grunt, the man turned and walked back into the house. Ramona breathed then and began to cry. She stayed out on the porch long after the light went out.

xxxxxxxxxxxxxxxxxxxxxxx

"You bastard," Ekee cried as he hit Danny on his upper arm. They had snuck back into the stockroom the next Monday, and Ekee cornered him against a stack of boxes of paper hand towels.

"Whatcha hitting me for?" Danny groaned. "Didn't ya get any?"

"Hell, no. It took me a half hour just to get her to go out with me, and just when I had talked her into it, her old man came out and threatened to shoot me with a shotgun."

Danny let out a yawp that could be heard all the way to the front of the store, and doubled over laughing.

"It ain't funny, dammit," Ekee said, trying to hush him. "You made a dang fool out of me."

Danny was laughing so hard he couldn't say anything.

"I said, it ain't funny, you shithead," Ekee hissed, hitting Danny in the upper arm again.

"It's the funniest thing I ever heard," Danny gasped. "I set you up with a sure thing and you almost get an ass full of buckshot."

"Why didn't you warn me about the old woman," Ekee said angrily.

"Her mother?" Danny said, sobering. "She's like a little kid. I never had any problem with her or her old man. He's never said a word to me. I just show up and Ramona and I leave right away and inside fifteen minutes we are doing the wild thang. She can't keep her hands off me, like she's some kind of nympho."

"She ain't no nympho. I barely got to third base. She just kept saying, 'I like Danny.'"

"No shit?"

"No shit."

"Well, fuck," Danny said. "I guess I am going to have to bust us up the hard way. I'll go down there tonight and just tell her straight out it's all over but the crying. He really said he was gonna go get his gun?"

"I 'bout tore up Floyd's car getting out of there. He says I almost blew the motor, and I tore the muffler off. He was really pissed."

"You are something, Ekee, you know that? Really something."

When Danny went to see Ramona that night, just as he was about to tell her it was over for good, she whispered seven little words to him that choked his own back down his throat.

"I love you," she said as she pressed her face against his bare chest in the backseat of his car. "I missed my period."

Two weeks later they were married, and seven and a-half months later had the first of five children. They moved in with her parents and Danny quit Aub's to go to work in the new Ostow Mills textile plant near Hall's Corner. He barely made enough there to afford a trailer at the Lazy Acres Mobile Home Park outside of Brownsboro after he and Ramona's step-father almost came to blows within a week over the old woman's meddling.

Ekee quit Aub's soon after the incident to return to school for his senior year, turning down a part-time job at the store to work for his uncle Zebediah as a handyman at the EZ Mobile Home Park in Hall's Corner. Their friendship quickly faded. Ekee never really forgave him for almost getting him shot, and Danny couldn't see him without thinking of his hand in his wife's crotch.

VII. Benny Ben and the Gorilla

Ezekiel "Ekee" Schultz was of that particular category of men of whom others, upon hearing that some calamity has befallen them, short of death or dismemberment, if of the more callous and indifferent type themselves, would laugh outright. Some among them might even laugh at the loss of a limb. The sage would only shake their heads in amusement at the peculiarity of the human species, while the religious would piously see such an event as evidence of God's divine justice. And a few, those not often confused by appearances and given to deeper speculation on the vagaries of the human condition, might simply wonder at the peculiar workings of fate in a man's life.

Ekee was not a man without redeeming qualities, but they were not easy to discern. He was a short, florid, fat man whose girth was in inverse proportion to his intelligence, although not his cunning. It was common wisdom in the EZ Mobile Home Park in Hall's Corner, Georgia, that if you assumed that anything the park manager said was a lie, you would be right more times than you would be wrong. For years, he had let the naive and those not versed in local history think that the "E" in the park's name referred to him, as if he were an owner. The letter actually stood for Elizabeth, his late aunt who had died of pancreatic failure. The "Z" stood for Zebediah, his uncle, and the real owner of the park. But it wasn't just a lack of intelligence or honesty that made Ekee annoying to everyone but the small children who sometimes instinctively burst into tears or ran from him like he was an ogre. He was a major source of frustration to anyone whose trailer needed repairs.

To many, Ekee seemed willfully stupid. His view of the world was composed of an eclectic mix of childhood certainties and cultural mythologies, all taken whole cloth and all held to be beyond dispute. As with many such people, it hid deep fears of being wrong, and, in Ekee's particular case, being made a fool. Like the roots of a tree sprouting in rocky soil, Ekee grew up a crooked mirror reflecting the family violence born of the ignorance, religion, and racism endemic in the South. He never held his head straight when he talked, but cocked to one side and turned, his chin slightly tucked, so he was always looking at the world out of the corner of his eye. Of course, that which we seek to avoid often seems to seek us, like water moccasins will swim head up out of the darkness of a swamp toward the light of a boat out frog-gigging. Without knowing it, Ekee's rigid fear of being made a fool was what most made him one, a recursive vortex of imagination that plagued all his hopes.

Ekee assumed the position of manager of the EZ in the summer of 1985, and like a former lieutenant puffed up by shiny new captain's bars, he used every opportunity to assert his new authority. But he ran into a roadblock immediately. His first act was to serve an eviction notice on Polly Ann Jones, the old black woman in 78D at the back of the park. Polly Ann was a nettlesome mystery to him, an irritating force of nature like the oppressive mugginess of a Georgia summer, and he had long sought to avenge her rejection of him when he secretly sought sexual favors from her one hot muggy night in 1983. But now, years later, with his newfound authority, he felt supremely confident in throwing her out. In the last six months, Zeb seemed to have lost interest in the park all together, anyway.

Ekee chose the wrong hill to die on. His complaints to his uncle Zeb about her, fabrications of her whorishness he felt sure his uncle would believe because she was black, surprisingly fell on deaf ears.

"She stays and that's that," Zeb told him dismissively.

"But Uncle Zeb, she's got strange men coming and going in the middle of the night," he said.

"I said she stays," Zeb said with finality, staring hard at his nephew. Ekee's frustration only grew when Zeb insisted that Polly Ann and Mama Wallace, an old woman whose brother-in-law was once state representative, alone among the tenants, would keep paying their monthly lot rent directly to him. Mama Wallace he could understand, since she was the matriarch of one of the most prominent families in Hall's Corner who had simply fallen on hard times in her old age, but is the old man getting some from Polly Ann, he wondered. He couldn't imagine it. Polly Ann almost never left her trailer, and he never saw Zeb's Cadillac parked in her space or anywhere near it.

"But, Uncle Zeb . . . "

"Listen to me, boy," Zeb snarled, his face hard, and his brown eyes tightening into small black circles as he pulled Ekee to him by his shirt. His breath smelled of peppermint. "Leave that woman alone, or I'll kick your ass so hard your teeth will rattle. I told you once, and I won't tell you again, leave her to me."

He released Ekee then, pushing him back with his fist, and Ekee knew better than to say anything more. He was convinced now that Zeb must be getting a little on the side from her, although he couldn't for the life of him figure out how. He got in his car and fumed the short distance back to the park office from Zeb's house. As he pulled into the park, his mouth fell open when he saw a huge deck rising above the trailers two streets over. He was seething and spun gravel as he turned down the park's front access road to the entrance of C Street. As he suspected, it was Jake Peterson's deck. Somehow, Jake, despite being out of work, had obtained three loads of decking materials in just the last few days. He insisted that it was all a mistake, a computer glitch he said, but now he had built this incredible monstrosity with it overnight. The deck was huge, with three levels that corkscrewed up clockwise. The first was half as long as the trailer, the second tucked up against the roof line and into the middle-aged oak tree at the back of it, and the third was suspended over the roof on two big beams.

"What the hell is this, Jake?" Ekee yelled out the window.

"Decks, Ekee," Jake yelled back. He took a puff on the cigar.

"I know that! But I told you to get this stuff out of here, not build a Taj Mahal."

"Number 46, Ekee."

"What?"

"Park regulation No. 46. A tenant may build porches, decks and room additions so long as they do not present any hazards or detract from the overall appearance of the park."

"Yeah! Well, I say this detracts from the appearance of the park. It's all out of proportion."

"I don't think so, Ekee."

"Why?"

"Because this place sure looks a heck of a lot better from up here."

Ekee jammed the car into drive and pulled away. with no target for his rage until he saw Benny Ben, a boy of six, playing in a sewer pipe behind the trailer that served as the park office, part of an extension of the county sewerage system under construction. Benny Ben was big for his age, well on his way to being a very large man like his father Adam, who lived in 33A with his wife Rachel, but Ekee gave no thought to how his father might react when he skidded the car in the gravel and without bothering to close the car door, descended on the boy.

Benny Ben was playing Luke Skywalker, the vertical concrete access tile a gun pod on the Millennium Falcon, shooting at Imperial Troops with an old bent five-iron.

"Git out of there, you little shit," Ekee roared as he descended on the boy, and Benny Ben, this eyes wide, scrambled out of the tile and ran all the way home. "And don't you let me catch you playing in it any more, you hear me!" he shouted. The startled look on the boy's face gave him a feeling of satisfaction, and his chest swelled as he got back in his car and returned to the office.

Later, his bravado evaporated as images of a very angry Adam rose in his mind, and he periodically pushed the curtain on the office window aside a little to look up A Street toward their trailer. He wondered if he could out-run him, since Adam was still on crutches from hurting his foot at work. When night fell and he could no longer see much because the security light was out, he cursed himself for not calling the co-op days ago to report it, and kept the TV low, alert for any sound outside his door. Finally, when it grew late, he went to bed, but could not fall to sleep until well into the middle of the night.

For several days, Benny Ben played elsewhere, mostly in the pine thicket across the road from the park, harassing a flock of feral dominiques that roosted in the trees, but the lure of the gun pod was strong, and finally he snuck back to it, careful to give the office a wide berth. He knew instinctively that the county would complete the extension of the sewer system soon and close off the access tile forever. Only a broken water main that flooded the site in late October, caused by a backhoe digging the sewer trench, had kept them from finishing it already.

That day, and the next, he was once again killing Imperial Troops, this time with a Blastech A295 blaster rifle, as if blissfully unaware that Ekee would eventually discover him in the tile. It occurred on the third day and Ekee, his confidence growing, chased him away once more with belligerent righteousness.

"I said, git out of here boy!" he yelled at the boy's back, and when that night Adam never appeared at his door, his sense of rightness was complete. But on the night of his Halloween party, the conflict arose anew.

Ekee loved Halloween. It was his favorite holiday of the year, and as a child he went trick-or-treating until even he was too embarrassed to be seen competing with all the little kids for candy. So, some years after he went to work for his uncle Zeb, he began to hold elaborate costume parties in his trailer next to the park office, and invited all the residents to attend. Only about a dozen people usually did, drawn more by the abundance of food than by any true regard for the park manager. After the first one, when only Adam and Rachel, showed up, Ekee had his parties catered by Linelle Dubose, who owned the Cozy Café in Hall's Corner and was the best cook in nearly thirty` miles. He easily convinced himself that their hunger passed for friendship. For their part, the party-goers felt at ease with masks to hide their true feelings.

While most of those in attendance wore simple plastic masks held on their faces by thin rubber bands, a few bothering to enhance their costumes with a sheet or old clothes they dug out of the corner of the closet, Ekee went all-out. He had several full costumes, including a demon mask that covered his entire head, complete with a long flowing black robe bedecked with red runes and one grotesque hand with gnarled fingers and long, black curling nails. But his favorite was a gorilla suit. He saved for it for months, and when he got finally got it on mail order, he tore open the package and immediately put it on, sweating profusely since the air conditioner was broken and it was July. Reluctantly, gasping for breath as sweat dripped down his round face from his matted black hair, he took it off and put it away, but every day he thought of how impressed everyone would be at his next party when he greeted them at the door.

Jake was the first to show up, and laughed when the door opened.

"Some costume, Ekee," he said.

Ekee knew right away it was Jake. His costume consisted entirely of a Richard Nixon mask, the same one he wore every year, and Ekee only grunted, "Come in."

But soon others showed up, most of them taking no more pains with their costumes than Jake had, although they all said something about what a great costume he wore. But Ekee felt the party was made when he saw Bean at the door. Bean Wallace was a strange kid, always full of pipe dreams, but Ekee tolerated him more than most because he looked so odd. The rumor in the park was that the kid was part black, something no one dared to speak openly of since his grandmother, Mama Wallace, with whom he lived with on C Street, was white, from a prominent local family, and mean besides, and Bean could pass. But nothing in his appearance completely dispelled that notion. Bean, at 16, was six feet tall and skinny as a rail, with skin that was a light shade of almond and a mass of reddish curly hair that untended formed a riotous helmet over his head. Ekee was especially delighted when he saw Bean at his door, wearing an old green leisure suit with green makeup and green hair.

"What the hell are you supposed to be, Bean?" Jake shouted from his post at the end of the couch.

"I'm an asparagus," Bean said in all seriousness. Jake hooted, and ripples of laughter spread through the room. Bean flushed, but it only made his face look greener.

As the gorilla welcomed the vegetable inside, Ekee was ecstatic that finally someone had put a little effort into their costume, although not so much that it trumped his own. Free to be a magnanimous host then, Ekee was everywhere at once, serving his guests the beer or wine they had brought with them, except for Bean, of course, and joking with them, by all appearances, the perfect primate host. Ekee grew a little tipsy, and, feeling expansive, he even took the liberty of goosing Mandy Bush, his part-time bookkeeper, the only woman present and by all lights one of the prettiest girls in the county, not counting her older sister Debbie, who had been a finalist in both Miss Teen Georgia and Miss Georgia.

Mandy was a slightly plump dishwater blonde with a gregarious personality who lived in a new subdivision off the Brownsboro Road four miles east of Hall's Corner with her husband, Bud Jenkins, produce manager at Aub's Famous Foods in Keown's Junction. She wasn't too much of a flirt, but men sensed sexual possibilities in the way she held herself and the way she moved. It reminded them of the natural sensuality of a cat. At twenty-two, she was the object of more than one male fantasy in the park, most especially those of Ekee and Bean. She wore no mask, but her costume consisted of small tree branches tied to her torso, heavy rouge on her face, and bright red hair. Several male hearts skipped a beat when she announced herself as the "burning bush," especially since her husband Bud wasn't with her. And as the night wore on, the bush burned ever more brightly as she got drunk on wine coolers.

Mandy shrieked at a gorilla's hand squeezing her butt, then turned to smile saucily at Ekee. He laughed hilariously and danced away to crank the music up louder than he usually permitted the residents to, until everyone had to shout to be heard. With casual conversation effectively prevented, Ekee stepped into the middle of the floor and began to do a gorilla dance. He flailed his arms and beat his chest and hopped back and forth on his feet as everyone laughed, and for a moment Ekee believed they truly were laughing with him.

"Hey, Ekee!" Jake shouted, but the park manager didn't hear him. "Ekee!"

The park manager was lost in a fantasy involving a primate and a flaming shrub.

"Ekee!" Jake shouted again, waving his arm.

Ekee stopped then and leaned toward Jake.

"What," he yelled in frustration.

"There's a kid in the sewer hole!"

Bean turned down the stereo.

"What?" Ekee shouted, his frustration now evident to everyone as his voice boomed in the suddenly quiet room.

"I said, there's a kid playing in the sewer hole," Jake said. "It looks like Adam's boy."

Ekee stumbled over to the window behind the couch and pulled the curtain aside. On the edge of the large illuminated circle formed by the security light, he could barely see Benny Ben, jumping up out of the hole armed with his five iron to fire off a few rounds, then duck back inside.

"I told that kid to stay of that hole," Ekee said angrily to no one in particular. "I've told him and told him."

"Ah, he ain't doing no harm, Ekee," Jake said. "Let him play. Besides, they'll probably cover that pipe as soon as everything dries out."

"But as park manager, Jake, it is my duty to prevent any accidents. Hell, Adam could sue us for a million dollars and bankrupt my uncle if the boy got hurt."

"You ain't liable, Ekee. It's the county's pipe and it's on their right-of-way."

"No, you're wrong, Jake. That boy gets hurt and lickety-spit I'm out of a job."

"Ekee, I'm telling you . . ."

But Ekee refused to hear, and interrupted him.

"Y'all watch. I'm going to give that boy a fright that'll keep him out of that pipe forever," he said, and ran out the door.

As the party-goers pulled back the curtain to watch, they saw Ekee stealthily walk in the deep shadows around the bright circle of light until he was barely visible on the far side behind the tile. He crept up to the edge of the shadows and waited for Benny Ben to jump up out of the hole.

"Use the force, Luke," the boy shouted as he popped up in the opening, club in hand, laying down laser fire at waves of Imperial fighters, the blasts from their guns bouncing harmlessly off his energy shield.

"Agggggh!" Ekee shouted as he jumped up and raced toward the boy.

Benny Ben quickly turned and was, quite naturally, horrified. A gorilla was bearing down on him, and all sorts of terrible thoughts raced through his brain. He never considered that it might be a man wearing a costume, even though it was Halloween. It was realistic enough, and there was no time for questions. That thing was going to kill him, and maybe eat him, and adrenalin surged through his body like a wildfire in sagebrush.

Ekee roared again in triumph. The boy was trapped. He figured he would grab him and toss him out of the tile, after a final roar right in the child's face, and beat his chest as he watched the boy fly down the street. He'll probably pee his pants, Ekee thought.

The park manager soon loomed over the tile, and the trembling boy backed up against the far side of it, but just as he lunged to grab the boy in his big paws, a blinding flash of pain erupted in his temple and he saw stars. Without even a moment to think about what had happened, he slumped over the side of the tile and fell to the ground unconscious.

Only the collective roar of the party-goers from inside the trailer broke the silence of the night after Benny Ben's footsteps faded down A Street. Ekee never saw the boy transform his laser cannon back into a five iron. The party-goers, many of whom had misgivings about scaring a child that way, were ecstatic at the poetic justice of it all. It was several minutes before they could catch their breath enough to wonder if the boy might have killed him.

Jake and Bean ran down to him then, and were relieved that he was still breathing. They dragged him back to the trailer and sat him down on the couch. Bean pulled his feet up on one end and Jake tugged off his mask. A large red bump had risen on Ekee's temple, but everyone soon ignored it. They were momentarily amazed that, unconscious, Ekee's face was as innocent as a sleeping child.

"Get a cold washcloth," Jake shouted, and an asparagus and a burning bush rushed to the sink, colliding in front of the faucet.

"Sorry," Bean said, suddenly feeling very sheepish as he felt her hip against his.

"No problem," Mandy replied, her voice slurred, her hip not moving away, a pink blush lining her rouge.

Bean dawdled beneath an azure sky full of exotic portents, or so he would write later.

"What the hell is taking y'all so long," Jake shouted, and they scurried to find a cloth and wet it under the faucet.

"Here," said Mandy, breathless, as she found one in a drawer and handed it unsteadily to Bean. His eyes never left hers as he fished for the faucet knob, then thrust the cloth aimlessly into the cold water. He squeezed it out quickly, then handed it back to her. His hands were cold, and hers were warm.

"Goddammit, bring me the washcloth," Jake bellowed, not looking at them, and, the spell broken, the asparagus ran to take the cloth to Jake with the burning bush trailing along behind.

Jake took the cloth and immediately put it on Ekee's forehead. The park manager grunted.

"Ekee, wake up," Jake shouted, then as an aside to the rest said, "I bet he's got a concussion."

Jake tried to stifle a laugh, but his lips began to quiver as he remembered how the boy cold-cocked Ekee in a smooth, upward stroke worthy of Arnold Palmer. Bean tittered, Mandy giggled, and then no one could hold back any longer and laughed out loud. Jake couldn't stop himself then and joined the raucous chorus.

"Ohhhh," Ekee groaned, quieting the room.

"Ekee!" Jake said, mirth slow to die in his throat as he slapped the park manager's cheeks. "Wake up, Ekee!"

Ekee's head lolled to one side, then turned back upward as his eyes opened.

"Ow," he said as he tentatively felt the bump on his head with his gorilla paw.

"Next time, Ekee, pick on someone your own size," Jake sputtered, and the room erupted again. Ekee looked confused as he scanned their faces, but in his addled state could only smile back.

"Great party, huh?" he said as he slipped back into unconsciousness again.

It was only on Monday, after an overnight stay at Carter County Memorial Hospital and a groggy Sunday, that Ekee found out what had happened to him, and then piecemeal.

"That bump looks awful," Mandy said when he entered the office. "Who knew a boy that young could be so strong."

Ekee was too embarrassed to inquire further, but later at J's Grocery and Convenience Store across from the park, he overheard Teg Barton, the owner and local tee-ball coach, say to Marvin Wade, who was setting up a Budweiser display in the front of the store, "That kid was a holy terror last spring in T-ball. He hit it over the fence nearly every time, even when he fouled off my pitches and had to hit off the T."

"Those fences are ninety feet," Marvin said in wonder.

And when he had to go to the Lumber Barn in Brownsboro to pick up a quick coupling to fix a leak behind Jake's trailer, feeling somewhat obligated toward him now for getting him to the hospital, he was humiliated when the clerk, whom he had never seen before in his life, said, "Whatcha needin'? We've added a sporting good department. We got a special on golf clubs today."

Ekee grimaced as he searched the man's face for any sign he knew anything, and even though his face revealed nothing, he realized that within a couple of days more surely everyone in Carter County would have heard the tale of how this mobile home park manager dressed in a gorilla suit got knocked out by a little kid on Halloween night. He could just hear them saying, as Jake had, "Next time, he oughta pick on someone his own size" and laughing uproariously.

But the story was quickly quashed by even more startling news. Plum Thompson, a local developer and the county's richest man, killed his wife and himself on the Sunday after Halloween. Ekee didn't know him, but his uncle Zeb did. Zeb was their adopted son.

"I never wish ill on anyone," Ekee thought, "but thanks, Plum."

VIII. An Azure Sky, Full of Exotic Portents

Mandy Burns took a sip of gin and tonic as she ran the vacuum cleaner over the living room rug of her new house. She and her husband Bud had saved every penny they could for four long years to get up the down payment, and finally purchased a fairly modest two-bedroom, one-bath cottage-style home with a garage in Hall's Creek Village on Brownsboro Road just a few miles east of Hall's Corner. The house was so new that the yard was unfinished, and it was impossible to keep the red clay out, even walking on the wide boards that connected the front porch to the driveway. It wouldn't be such a problem, but Bud kept the garage locked to protect his model trains. He had a huge miniature layout of Hall's Corner and the northwest corner of Carter County that he had been working on for years, and he spent the first week in their new home just putting it all together for the first time. It filled the entire garage.

"Sweetie, wipe your feet," Mandy said every time he came in the front door.

"Sorry," he would say, stomping his feet on the green welcome mat on the small concrete front porch, but he never got all the dirt off his shoes.

Their new beige carpet had a wide red streak running from the front door to the bathroom hall and Mandy knew they were going to have to shampoo it. *She* was going to have to shampoo it. Bud spent every available minute in the garage.

"Shit," Mandy said. She turned off the vacuum cleaner and fixed another drink, then flopped down on the Early American couch they had moved from their trailer in EZ Mobile Home Park. There it had looked fairly nice against the dark wood paneling of the living room. It was a little faded, but it had no tears in its floral print fabric anywhere. But in the new home, with sandalwood walls and bigger windows, it looked old and worn. Mandy decided she hated the thing, and the maple-stained coffee table that went with it. She put her feet up on the table and sighed as she looked at her legs.

"I'm getting fat," she said, then kicked off her shoes. "Now I'm barefoot, too. All I need now is to get pregnant."

"What, honey?" Bud shouted from the garage.

"Nothing." she shouted back.

She was still a little resentful that Bud had made such a big deal about her getting snookered at her boss Ekee Shultz's Halloween party. He was the park manager at the EZ, and she worked for him part-time as a secretary/ bookkeeper. It was true that she was so drunk that Jake Peterson, one of the park's residents, had to drive her home, but nothing had happened. She didn't dare tell Bud that she was the only woman at the party, and that by the end of the evening something might have happened, but Jake was too much the gentleman. Besides, to her way of thinking she deserved a little fun. It was the first time in years she had gotten to cut loose, so long that she had forgotten how much fun she used to have at parties her senior year at Carter County High after her parents decided she was old enough to go out on dates without a chaperone. Because her parents had been fairly strict, even over-protective, going out on her own was like breathing the fresh air after a storm. Within a month of her release, she had gotten drunk, smoked pot, and had sex, all for the first time, and decided she liked them all a lot. She soon had a reputation as a "party girl," but it was a label she wore with defiant pride. Then she met Bud.

xxxxxxxxxxxxxxxxxxxxxxxxx

He caught her eye at a private party just for seniors at a cabin on Lake Coosawattee on Pumpkin Jones Road, a dirt crossroad that connected Old Brownsboro Road with the new Brownsboro Road. The land belonged to the Palmers, whose oldest son, Luke Jr., was the star running back for the Carter County Wildcats. Luke, who had a scholarship to Furman, invited everyone out to his family's cabin without bothering to tell his parents. He knew his mother might get upset if she found out, but it wouldn't matter because his father would just reply, "Boys will be boys," as he always did when his sons got into trouble.

Some members of the football team brought a couple of kegs and someone else brought a boombox, which they cranked up full blast since there was only one house on Pumpkin Jones Road and it was nearly a mile away and had been vacant for years and was about to fall in. With no adults to restrain them, the party grew wilder and wilder as the night progressed. While some students danced and danced in the cabin, one group went skinny-dipping in the lake and others sought out glens in the old hardwood forest to smoke pot and sing and grope each other in the shadows. More than one boy, drunk for the first time, lost his lunch, and more than one girl lost her virginity that night.

Mandy was not among the latter. Luke Palmer had already secretly asked her out, secretly since he was going steady with the captain of the cheerleading squad, Alicia Kensington, gotten her drunk, and taken her "precious pearl" as Mandy derisively called it. She knew Luke was just taking advantage of her, but she didn't blame him. Besides, even drunk, she could sense that he wasn't all that great in the sack, and she knew that he knew it. She didn't even get upset when he didn't ask her out again, or when he told his friends and they began to pester her for dates because they thought she was easy. She actually liked her newfound popularity, but she wouldn't go out with just anyone who asked. She might be easy, she decided, but she wasn't free.

Bud Burns had graduated from Brownsboro High five years earlier, and came with Lisa Cunningham, a member of the senior class and a friend of Mandy's, as her date. Bud had a reputation as a "stoner" and brought a quarter-ounce of weed with him to the party. He was high when he arrived and the chaos proved to be too much for him, especially since he knew almost no one, and within a short while he was sitting in a small circle of students in a clearing over a hundred yards away from the cabin. Mandy was dancing in the cabin, her blouse off after drinking three glasses of beer, when Lisa came in to use the restroom and took her aside.

"Want to get high?" she whispered.

"Yeah," Mandy said.

"Bud brought some pot. Just keep it quiet. We're out in the woods. Follow me, OK?"

"OK."

Once they were in the woods, the girls could barely see the trail and stumbled several times, which only made them giggle until Mandy stumbled into a briar patch.

"Ow!," she cried.

"What?" Lisa said. She could barely make out her friend's face in the dark.

"I got a thorn in my finger."

"Shit."

"It's OK. I pulled it out."

Lisa started laughing.

"Prick your finger?"

"Oh, shut up," Mandy said, laughing with her despite the pain. She rubbed the wound and flinched. "I can't tell if I got it all."

"C'mon. We'll do something about it later."

In their inebriated states, it seemed to be taking forever to reach the clearing, so by the time they got there, they were almost sober.

"Hi," Lisa said as they entered the small opening in the trees.

"I guess I am," Bud laughed, which caused everyone else to laugh.

"This is my friend Mandy," Lisa said as they sat on either side of him in the circle. "She has never gotten high."

"A virgin, huh?" Bud laughed again as he handed her a fat joint. "Well, this'll take your cherry."

"He's cute," Mandy thought as she took her first toke. "Real cute. Tall, dark, and handsome cute."

She was sitting so close to him that their arms were touching, and as Mandy's senses entered a new world, she became increasingly aware of how warm his arm felt against hers.

"Would you look at that?" Bud said as he took her hand and held their forearms up, pressed together. His tan skin was in sharp contrast to her white skin. A tension settled in her groin as she looked at his black eyes and chiseled features, but Bud seemed blissfully unaware of it. He just smiled at her and she felt as if something was melting to liquid inside her. Lisa sensed it, however, and pulled his other arm up against hers.

"My skin is just as white as hers," she said.

"Nooo," said Amber Slade, a classmate, from across the circle. "If a boy and a girl have forearms the same length from wrissst . . . elbows to wrists, it means they are compatible. Bud's and Mandy's were . . ."

"That's just a silly superstition," Lisa swore. Her forearm was clearly a half-inch shorter than his.

"Yup," Bud said amiably and dropped Mandy's hand while putting Lisa's to his lips. "I just love your skin. I love it here, and here, and here."

Lisa exploded into a fit of giggles that were soon muffled by his mouth. Mandy could only watch in stoned silence as Bud pressed her body back against the ground and was lost to her.

xxxxxxxxxxxxxxxxxxxxxxxx

A week later, Bud dumped Lisa. Two weeks later he asked Mandy out. Six weeks after that they got married. Now, four years later, Mandy struggled to remember how it all happened, it was such a blur. She tried not to regret the loss of Lisa's friendship, just as she tried not to regret the way Bud's personality changed so radically after they married. The way he morphed from seductive party boy to dutiful husband was breathtaking. He was like an actor changing roles. She knew she should be grateful anyway that he was so hard working and focused on securing their future, but she felt like what she got didn't match the picture in the catalogue. Unconsciously, she rubbed the small bump of scar tissue on her finger and felt a faint jolt of pain, like a static discharge deep in the muscle. Ignoring it, she got up to fix another drink.

Soon Mandy was storming around her house, stomping and cursing and drunk, flailing her arms like she was a bug ensnared in a spider's web and slowly being enveloped in a motley cocoon.

"Four years!" she cursed. "Four fucking years."

xxxxxxxxxxxxxxxxxxxxxxxx

"You're drinking too much," Bud had yelled at her Friday morning when she got up and immediately fixed herself a bloody Mary. "It's embarrassing."

"You're embarrassing," she had snarled at him. It was the only retort her throbbing temples could come up with.

"Me? You're the one who made a damn fool of yourself at Ekee's party. What the hell were you thinking wearing that stupid costume?"

"I thought it was hot," she had said, cocking her hips.

"It was slutty! I don't know what's come over you lately. The house is always a mess. You stay drunk all the time. It's like I don't know you any more."

"You haven't *known me* in weeks.".

"What's that mean? You're the one who passes out every night."

"We never have any fun anymore. I want to have some fun."

"Fun? You call it fun to get so drunk at a party full of strange men that you can't even drive home!"

"It's better than playing with toy trains."

"I thought we had a plan. We worked hard for this," he said, ignoring the bait and opening his arms wide. "I thought this was what you wanted."

"It wasn't fun."

"No, we didn't have the money to do anything, but I thought you understood that."

"We had money for trains."

"Dammit!" he had said as he grabbed her by the shoulders and shook her. "It's just a hobby! And lately it's the only thing that is even remotely enjoyable about this house."

She began to cry, and Bud immediately felt ashamed of himself.

"I'm sorry, baby. I'm so sorry," he had said softly as he took her in his arms. "I've got a few minutes. Let's sit down."

But when he attempted to get her to sit on the sofa, she groaned and threw up on the cushions.

"Shit. You're drunk."

He sat her down in his large vinyl recliner and she closed her eyes. After cleaning up the mess with a wet towel, then spraying the cushions with an air deodorizer, he turned to her. She was snoring softly.

"God, I can't believe this," he had said in disgust, grabbing his travel bag and storming out the door.

When Mandy awoke after noon, she knew he was gone before she realized what time it was. The foul taste in her mouth drove her to the bathroom. As she churned mouthwash around her cheeks and gums, she looked at the stranger in the mirror. She was obviously still young, but her youth was hidden beneath a mask of pallid cheeks and swollen, red eyes.

"It's like I don't know you any more," she said silently, mouthing the words.

She fled from her reflection into the kitchen where she fixed another drink, and realized that since she was free of Bud for the next three days while he attended a modeling convention, she could be free of a lot more. The phone rang. It was her younger sister, Debbie.

"Hey, sis, what's up?"

"You just wake up? You sound like shit."

"Headache."

"Well, maybe this will cure your ills. I'm in town, over at mom's, and you'll never guess who came in the bar a couple of weeks ago."

Mandy didn't reply.

"Ted! Ted Jacuzzi! Your old flame from high school."

"Ted."

"Damn, you do sound wasted, sis. Yes, Ted. The guy you dumped for Bud."

"You stole him, you mean."

"Ha! He graduated from Tech at the end of the summer and said he is working at Aub's supermarket with your husband until he starts graduate school in January. You know, they're cousins. I never knew that. Anyway, he's an assistant manager or something, and he's still as handsome as ever, although he is a lousy tipper. He's rented a trailer in Hall's Corner and I thought we could go over and see him tonight, with Bud out of town."

Mandy wondered why Bud had not told her Ted was working with him. She knew he had talked about the assistant manager's position Aub had been considering. It really must have chaffed him that Ted got the position, even if it was temporary, especially since he was his cousin and a former flame. She threw back the last of the vodka and said, "I really liked him, you know? He was a lot of fun."

"So, you want to go out 'cattin'?"

"Yeah."

Ted Jacuzzi was a tall, skinny kid when his family moved to Hall's Corner when he was a junior, but almost overnight he filled out into a lanky dark-haired hunk. His real name wasn't Jacuzzi; it was Jaworski, but he got the nickname his first day in class and it stuck. Ted was the brainy type. His degree was in mechanical engineering. But like so many men who are analytically inclined, he could be something of a doofus when it came to girls. Mandy thought it was cute the way he blushed and hemmed and hawed when she spoke to him for the first time in the fall of her senior year. And, frankly, from the way he kept sneaking peeks at her breasts, she knew he was an easy mark. So she hooked him, and when he proved to be as meticulous in his love-making as he was in everything else in his life, she decided not to throw him back.

Mandy put down her drink and rushed to the shower. She stood in the cold spray until at least some of the puffiness around her eyes washed away, then began her preparations. She would wear her little black cocktail dress, she decided, the one with the spaghetti straps and low neckline that had been hanging in a dry cleaner bag in the back of her closet for over three years. She would wear her black pumps, with the three-inch heels, and put her hair up in a twist. She would use the violet blue eye-shadow in her makeup drawer, if it had not caked and crumbled, and her "Red Hot" lipstick if it had not suffered the same fate. She fixed herself a cup of strong black coffee.

By the time Debbie arrived at 7:30, Mandy had shoe-horned her way into her little black dress, which seemed to have shrunk a size. Her eye-shadow and lipstick had proven to be still usable, if barely so, but it took almost a half-hour for her body to remember how to walk in three-inch heels, and even longer to get her hair to give up its unruly ways. In all, the image she saw in the full-length mirror on the back of her bedroom closet door gave her a feeling of triumph, because it had not come without a struggle. She licked her palm and patted down one curl that had escaped its bobby pin, and smiled.

When she opened the door, Debbie whistled, and said, "Looking good, sis," but Mandy's mouth fell open. Debbie had bleached her hair almost platinum, and she was dressed in a strapless red mini-dress of a kind rarely seen in Carter County except on television. She looked like a snake shedding part of her skin, and had almost got it below her hips but not quite past her nipples. Over the past decade, there had been only one similar sighting, when two strippers from Atlanta turned off the interstate and got lost. They walked into Linelle's Cozy Café in Hall's Corner right at lunchtime when the place was packed. Everyone turned to look at them, and more than one man swore later that they just smiled and struck a pose. Reports of the sighting spread faster than the time an alligator was spotted on Pumpkin Jones Creek, reaching all the way to Brownsboro before nightfall.

"You, too," Mandy said, begrudgingly, and Debbie smiled. "Are you wearing any underwear at all?"

After a quick look around, Debbie slid the dress up a couple of inches to reveal a matching red triangle of cloth, then shimmed it back down.

"I got them at the mall in Atlanta. There's nothing but a string in the back. It's a thong. Aren't they cute?"

"I guess," Mandy said, suddenly very aware of the black bikinis she had on, with the little hole right below the waistband on her right hip.

As they drove to Ted's trailer, Mandy listened as Debbie chatted on and on about how exciting her life was now. She was making scads of money, she said, and with a sweep of her hand took in her car, a late-model Camry. She had a two-bedroom apartment downtown, in one of the better complexes. It even had a hot tub. And she had a rich boyfriend. In fact, he was the owner of the club where she worked. Mandy heard her, but wasn't listening until, without preamble, Debbie said, "Oh, and I had an abortion."

"You what?" Mandy said.

"I had an abortion. It was nothing really. I just forgot to put in my IUD. Well, actually, I didn't have time. You know how that goes. Tim, that's my boyfriend, sometimes gets a little overeager. There's no way I wanted a baby. Yuk! How would I ever take care of it? I work practically every night until two or three in the morning. So when I told Tim I had missed my period, he found me a doctor and that was that. Tim paid for everything. Do you like my new car?"

Mandy watched her face for any sign that might contradict her sister's off-hand, dismissive attitude, but she saw none and looked out the passenger window.

"It's nice."

"Tim got it for me," Debbie said. "I think he really loves me. Want a wine cooler? They're in a cooler in the back floorboard. Get me one, too."

As they drank the wine, Mandy couldn't shake her disbelief that her sister could be really be so cavalier about such a momentous thing as having an abortion. She knew she couldn't. She didn't want a baby yet, either, and not just because she and Bud had decided to wait until they were in better financial shape, so she took her pills religiously. She shuddered and wondered if living in Atlanta had made her sister into someone strange and alien to her. It, and the wine, put her in a pensive mood she could not completely shake when Ted opened his door.

"Surprise!" Debbie shouted and was delighted at the stunned look in Ted's face.

"Debbie? Mandy?" he stuttered, his eyes briefly focused on her breasts before he blushed self-consciously and quickly raised them.

"Same old Ted," Debbie said with a big grin, and barged past him into the room.

"Hi, Ted," Mandy said, just above a whisper, as she followed her sister, leaving Ted, his mouth open, to close the door.

"Got anything to drink in this dump?" Debbie said with a laugh as she walked into the middle of the room, her back to them. "Just teasing. I've got some wine in the car if you don't."

"I . . . I have some beer," Ted said. "I didn't know you were in town."

"Just in for the weekend, to see my sis," Debbie said as she turned to them. "Her old man's on some trip, so we are just out having a good time. When the cat's away and all that. Is it in the fridge?"

"Huh? Yeah. Help yourself."

"Want one, sis? How about you, Ted?"

She didn't wait for a reply and got one for each of them.

"Where's your stereo?" she asked as she handed them each a bottle. "Oh, I see it."

Debbie soon found a rock station playing "There's Going to be a Heartache Tonight" and turned the volume up. She leaned back against the stereo, her eyes closed, and began to sway in time with the beat while she took a drink. Ted watched as the skirt of her dress threatened to disprove Zeno's Paradox.

Debbie stopped, her hip cocked to one side, and looked at them, but not like she was actually seeing them.

"Got any pot, Teddie Bear?" she asked, her voice slightly slurred. How many wine coolers has she had, Mandy wondered? She had only seen her drink two.

"Ah, no, I haven't smoked in long time."

"Well, I can fix that," Debbie said with a giggle and fished a joint out of her purse. "Let's get high."

"I don't think . . ." Ted started, but Debbie advanced on him like a cat until she was directly under him and said smoothly, "Me neither." She lit the joint and took a deep drag, then handed it to him. When he didn't accept it right away, she exhaled into his face, and put it between his lips.

"Like my dress?" she said, wiggling her hips.

"Yes," he said as he inhaled. His eyes suddenly locked on Debbie's nipples and remained there seconds later when Mandy took the joint out of his hand and took a deep toke. In an instant, she felt a rush unlike any she had ever felt from any pot before.

"What is this stuff?" she asked Debbie.

"Oh, just something special I got for tonight," Debbie said coyly. "It's laced with coke. Oh, don't worry. It's not enough to get you hooked. It just gives it a little kick, that's all."

Ted took the joint from Mandy's hand and took a deep toke. When she saw him sneak another peek at her breasts, she giggled as she took the joint from him and led him to the couch.

"Don't bogart it," she said as she pulled him down beside her so close their hips touched. Mandy was suddenly jealous. Even though she told herself that she had gotten over Ted long ago and was happily married, or married at least, the sight of her sister snuggling up to her old boyfriend made her angry. She sat down beside him, with her hip pressed against him, too, and looked at her sister defiantly. Debbie paid her no attention.

"So, Ted, what's up?" she cooed as she placed her hand on his knee. Ted blushed and looked very uncomfortable.

"Yes, tell us?" Mandy said as she mimicked her sister.

"N . . . not much," he stammered.

"I'm sure there's something," Debbie purred as she pressed a breast to his arm. Even though she realized her sister was up to something, a game that was exciting to play but whose outcome was uncertain, Mandy followed suit.

"We want to know," she whispered.

With a lurch, Ted stood up, throwing both of them aside.

"I just graduated with a B.S. in engineering and I'm working at Aub's until I can find a better job or maybe go to graduate school. Bud's one of my department managers," he said in a rush as he turned to face the women, then gasped. Debbie's skirt now clearly disproved Zeno's theory. Debbie slowly stood up and stepped up to Ted, rubbing her body against his. She pressed her crotch against his and winked at her sister, then threw her arms around his neck and kissed him.

Mandy wondered if Debbie was bluffing, or if she really meant to do what it looked like she was about to do. Mandy hesitated to call. The mention of her husband's name had taken the edge off her mood. As she watched her sister do a little bump and grind against her old boyfriend, she caught Ted's eye. He looked dismayed. It was almost a plea for help.

"Debbie," Mandy said, raising her voice, but her sister ignored her.

Debbie broke the kiss and with a wanton smile, said, "Want to do us both, Ted?"

"Debbie!" Mandy got up. She pulled her sister away from him. "What the hell are you doing?"

"I just thought Ted might like a little fun," Debbie pouted, then looked over her shoulder. "So what do you say, Teddy Bear? Want a threesome?"

"You might have asked me first," Mandy said hotly, yanking her back around to face her. She blushed when she saw Ted staring at her with a blend of expectation and total confusion. In an alternate universe, Mandy knew she might have gone along with it. And certainly, in another universe, where she was alone with Ted now, her marriage vows would have been toast, especially because little sparks of electricity seemed to be crawling across her skin. But this wasn't either of those universes. This wasn't even reality. It was just a game.

"I just figured that since you hadn't had any in so long . . ."

Mandy slapped her hard across the cheek. A dark whirlwind of betrayal, jealousy, anger, and frustration twisted in her gut.

"Get off me!" Debbie cried, clutching her cheek, as she pushed her away. "What's the matter? You gone frigid or something?"

Mandy raised her hand, but Ted caught her wrist.

"Both of you cool it," he commanded, surprising both of them. He took Debbie's wrist in his other hand and led them to the door. "I don't know what kind of game you two are playing, but you better work this out somewhere else."

And just like that he pushed them out and closed the door behind them.

"Damn! You had to go and screw everything up," Debbie snarled.

"Screw what up, sis? Didn't you see the way he was looking at you?"

"Yeah. He couldn't keep his eyes off me."

"No, Debbie. You were just making a fool of yourself. What made you think that we could just waltz in and Ted would forget the way we both dumped him and just hop in the sack?"

"It's what every man wants, Mandy," she said, her eyes tearing up. "Don't you know that? It's what they all want. It's like some super fantasy, two women at one time."

"C'mon, let's go," Mandy said. She put her arm around Debbie's shoulders and led her down the hall.

Mandy awoke the next day in a fog. The combination of wine and beer and pot and coke she had consumed the night before made her sleep like she was in a coma. She only vaguely remembered taking Debbie home to their mother's and sitting in the car with her until the middle of the night while she cried.

It turned out that the week Debbie found out she was pregnant, she went to the club eager to tell Tim the news. She waited until after work, just so they could make love first and she could tell him cuddled in his arms. But after the bar was closed and cleaned up, when she went into the office to let him know she was leaving, he was sitting on the couch with a stunning brunette Debbie had seen him briefly talking to earlier in the bar. She didn't know who she was, but her tube top and short vinyl skirt told her everything she needed to know.

"She was a hooker!" Debbie sobbed in Mandy's arms. "And he made me do it with her! I never even told the bastard I was pregnant. I just found a clinic myself. I left him, sis, even though I still love him. I do. He can be so sweet."

"I know," Mandy said, stroking her hair, even though she really had no idea what kind of man Tim really was. He probably was a real jerk, like her sister said, but Debbie was known to remember things the way it suited her best.

She called her mother's house, but Debbie was already gone.

"She left before I got up," her mother said. "Is she having some kind of problem? She was all fidgety when she got here yesterday. She couldn't sit still and she wouldn't stop talking."

"Well, you know how Debbie is, mom," she said and hung up.

As she lay back down in bed still dressed in her nightgown, an image of Ted, poor, confused Ted, rose in her mind and she frowned. She had not known Ted was in town, and she wondered, if she had, would she have gone to see him alone? From the look on his face last night, the one after the one that looked like a stern father throwing a couple of squabbling children outside to settle their differences, the one with a touch of sadness he gave her as he closed the door, she thought it might have been different if she had been alone. She could still feel the way he gripped her arm so swiftly, and held it so tightly she had no hope of breaking free. No, it would definitely have been different. But now Debbie had come in like a tornado in a trailer park and left any future possibilities just debris scattered over a wide area.

The phone rang.

"Mrs. Burns, this is Attorney Layton Elrod with Thompson Development. I'm glad I caught you. We've been trying to reach you for days, but I just learned we had the wrong number. Is your husband home?"

"No, he's out," she replied.

"Well, Mrs. Burns, tell him it's going to be a little while before we can get around to fixing your yard. We've had . . . a problem. You've heard about Mr. and Mrs. Thompson, I presume."

"No."

"Oh. Well, they died. And now, as you might expect, their estate is yet to be settled."

Mandy, staring at the red streak in her carpet, said, "How long?"

"Ma'am?"

"How long before you can fix it?"

"Oh, don't you worry about that ma'am. Just have your husband call me."

"But . . ." Mandy stopped. He had hung up. "Goddamn it."

Mandy thought about calling him right back and cussing him out. She stormed around the house until she found her purse, but when she looked inside it for his card, she realized that it wasn't hers, it was Debbie's. "Crap," she thought, then felt the plastic baggie. She too it out and saw another joint inside, one just like the one they had smoked the night before. She shivered, and took it with her to fix a drink. She poured a shot of whiskey in a glass, tossed it back, and poured another one. She rolled the joint between her fingers.

"It's Debbie's," she thought as she stopped in the doorway to the living room. "She'll be back for her purse. She's crazy. Last night she was a total slut. Poor Ted. He looked so uncomfortable. What the hell were we thinking? That he would just welcome us in like old times after the way we treated him. I remember the way he looked at us when he opened the door. Same old Ted, but who could blame him for looking. Hell, our boobs were practically hanging out. But when he shooed us out the door, he wasn't same old Ted, was he? The look in his eyes made me shiver. I never wanted him like I did in that moment, even when we were dating. Maybe it was the pot. Was Debbie serious? Did she really want us both to do him? Would I have gone along with it if she had just told me first? Maybe. Maybe I would have. What time is it? 1:15. Is anybody coming by here today? Shit no, now that we're going to have to wait for the landscaping. Bud won't be back until tomorrow. I wonder if I saved it if he would get high with me? If he were here right now, would he do it? Would we get so high he couldn't keep his hands off me, like he used to? No. He would worry about having to take a piss test if he got hurt at work. 'I could lose my job, Mandy.' Is that Debbie? No, just an old car turning around in the cul-de-sac. God, Bud, what happened to us? Damn, I'm so horny. You love those goddamn trains more than you love me. Is it because I'm fat? Is my ass too big now? I know my legs look like tree stumps. Shit! Shit! Shit! How did I get here?"

Tammy quickly took the joint out of the baggy and lit it. She took a deep drag, then another.

"Jesus, this is some shit," she said, then burst into laughter. She stepped into the living room, her hands holding her sides, and sat down on the couch. She watched in anticipation as everything around her seemed to get brighter and more colorful. Funny, she thought, giggling. Funny old house, Funny old walls. Funny old sofa. Funnnnny. Ooooo, my body . . . . I'm tingling. Better put this out.

She used the remote to turn on the stereo and sighed when she heard REM. She lay back on the sofa and closed her eyes, her head gently swaying in time with the music. She didn't know how long she lay there. She only knew that the music sounded so wonderful she never wanted it to stop.

The doorbell rang.

"Fuck," she said. "Who could that be? Debbie?"

She tried to act normal, and took a deep breath as she opened the door.

"Yes," she said.

"M . . . M . . . Mandy, I brought you these."

Bean, a tall skinny boy of sixteen she had had fun teasing at Ekee's party, held out a bouquet of wildflowers. His hands were trembling and his mouth was gaped open. Mandy blushed when she realized that she was still in her gown and he could see practically everything.

"Wait, Bean," she squeaked and closed the door in his face, returning moments later wrapped in her robe. "I'm sorry. What were you saying?"

"I . . . I brought you these flowers."

"Oh, Bean, how sweet," she said. She took them and buried her nose in them.

Bean was mesmerized. After their hands had touched by the sink on Halloween night, sending shivers up and down his spine, he just knew they were in love and had come to declare it. After the way she had rubbed her body against his, he thought she would fall into his arms and kiss him. They would run away together and live in New Mexico, or Montana. But when she opened the door and he could see the outline of her naked body beneath the gown, backlit by a lamp, he felt like a silly boy who had gotten caught up in some fairy tale, a fairy tale that evaporated without a trace and left him feeling as naked as she was. He blushed.

"Want to come in?"

Bean couldn't speak. He just followed her into the house like a puppy.

"Sit down here on the sofa," she said, patting the cushion next to her. "I was just listening to some music."

She sat back against the cushions and closed her eyes. Her head was bent back, and she almost looked like she was asleep. Her pink lips curled slightly in a smile. Her breasts steadily rose and fell. The robe ended just above her knees, and her feet were bare. She wiggled her toes.

"I love you," he blurted.

"What did you say?" she said softly, opening her eyes.

Bean blushed.

"I . . . I love you."

He was leaning toward her so far their arms were almost touching. Without speaking, she took his hand and held his forearm up next to hers. They were the same length from elbow to wrist. Mandy gasped. She could see herself then as if she were floating above them. She saw the disheveled woman, looking a little care worn, and she could tell she was a little drunk and very, very high. She was holding the boy's arm up, staring at him. The boy was squirming. She could see the bulge form in his pants, the bulge he tried to hide by crossing his legs. It was like some scene out of a trashy Southern novel: The Young Virgin and the Faded Belle. But the self looking down on them could not stop the self on the couch for pushing his knees apart as her face descended on his crotch.

Bean didn't know what to do, so he did nothing. Only in his wildest fantasies, late at night before he went to sleep, was there anything to compare to this reality. Nothing in his dreams could have felt like this. He never knew a woman's mouth could feel so warm. With a quick jerk of his hips, he spent, too quickly but not soon enough, and groaned. Mandy rose up to look at him, her eyes narrow. Bean stared back at her in awe. She licked her lips and smiled.

"Mandy! You home? The door was open, so I . . ."

Debbie stopped in the doorway. Mandy scrambled up, pulling her robe tightly about her, leaving Bean to fend for himself. He jumped up, yanking on his zipper, and ran out the door past her.

"I just came back to get my pur . . . Damn, he's just a kid."

"Oh, shit," Mandy groaned, her head in her hands.

Debbie watched her sister tremble in shame.

"What in God's name is going on, sis?" she said. "Were you doing the kid? Look at me!"

"Go to hell, Debbie," Mandy said without looking up. Her face was flushed.

"No, you go to hell, sis. If anybody found out what you just did, they would throw your ass in jail. Here's your purse. I'm outta here."

Debbie threw Mandy's purse on the couch and picked up her own, then left. With a start, Mandy ran after her.

"Debbie!" she cried, but her sister was already in her car and backing out of the driveway. She only looked at her once, as she hit the gas. Mandy's cry was drowned out by the squeal of the Camry's tires. "Bean?"

Mandy was embarrassed and angry at the same time. She slammed the door shut and locked it. They wouldn't really throw her in jail, she thought. Bean is sixteen. But she worried anyway. What if it got out? Would Bean tell? Of course he would, he's a boy. What if Bud found out? He will be home soon. She beat her fists against her thighs in frustration.

"Shit," she said and picked up the joint.

IX. The Poet's Curse

Bean Wallace trembled as he stood before all the older students in his senior English class. He was not only just sixteen and the lone junior since he skipped freshman composition, but he was naturally shy. He wouldn't be standing there at all except Mr. Dooley insisted he read his poem for everyone. Bean's self-consciousness forced the words out like quail rousted to flight by a shotgun.

"My poem is entitled 'Swedish Girls in Tahiti,'" he gulped.

Then, his voice surprisingly deep and resonant, he said:

"Swedish girls
with hair like margarine
and teeth like new snow
smiling at the supermarket
on posters for suntan oil –
their eyes fifty miles of open sky
above a crystal beach
are almond angels advertising
just one other idea of heaven."

"Right on!" a boy in the back shouted and several others hooted. Some of the girls giggled and Marsha Collins, who was a natural blonde with a tan and the reigning homecoming queen, blushed. Only P. J. Frazier, a budding feminist, looked at Bean curiously, as if she had just noticed he existed.

"Excellent," Mr. Dooley said. "Class, how do you interpret Bean's poem?"

"It's about hotties!" laughed Josh Palmer, starting quarterback and Marsha's boyfriend. He, like Marsha, immediately assumed it was about her since she was the closest thing to an Hawaiian Tropic model that Carter County presently had to offer. He could laugh because Bean was obviously no threat.

"Anyone else?"

"Yeah. I think it is about wanting the impossible," said Tom Irwin, STAR student and president of the Honor Society.

"How so?"

"Well, these girls are not real. They're just images. They airbrush out any imperfections."

"No they don't," Josh said in disbelief. "You ever see those Hawaiian Tropic girls? Remember *Dumb and Dumber*. Man, those girls weren't fake. They were hot!."

Marsha, sitting in front of him, turned around and, with a look of disgust, blew an errant tendril of hair out of her face.

"What'd I say?" Josh said as a ripple of laughter spread through the class.

"Everybody has dreams," Tom continued, ignoring the interruption, "but some of them are impossible. They're illusions. Isn't that what you meant with 'just one other idea of heaven.'?"

Before Bean could reply, Elsie Pilgrim spoke.

"Don't you believe in God, Tom?" she asked. Elsie was a member of the Hall's Corner Church of God. She never wore makeup, had only had her hair cut once in her life, and wore long dresses every day.

Tom blushed slightly.

"I have doubts," he finally replied.

"Haven't you accepted Christ as your personal savior?" Elsie said, staring at him intently.

"OK, OK, we've gotten off the subject," Mr. Dooley said. Tom looked at him with gratitude. "Any other comments, on the poem?"

"Yeah, I think it's a commentary on how materialism has corrupted American culture," P. J. said. The class seemed to collectively groan, and the whispered words "feminist" and "Communist" could be heard. P. J.'s face reddened.

"Interesting," Mr. Dooley said, his stare quieting the class. "Care to explain?"

"Well, these women aren't real, like Tom said. They're just used to sell a product," she said hotly. "They're just using sex to sell suntan oil. But they create an idea of beauty that almost no women can match. Guys look at them and then they look at real women, and they think they're flawed and imperfect when they are not. It's degrading."

"Speak for yourself," Marsha said, tossing her hair back. P. J. looked like she could kill.

"What do you say, Bean?" Mr. Dooley said to break the tension. "What does the poem mean to you?"

Bean had gotten caught up in the discussion and forgotten he was still standing in front of the class. Everyone suddenly turned to him and it felt like he was standing in a spotlight.

"I . . . I . . . just saw the poster and decided to write a poem about it," he sputtered.

"Spoken like a true poet," Mr. Dooley laughed as the bell rang. "Don't forget your essays on 'The Red Wheel Barrow' are due Friday."

As the class streamed out the door, Mr. Dooley called Bean back.

"Yes, sir?"

"Bean, you're a natural poet. I liked your poem, but you know what I say about criticism?"

"Yes, sir. It's worse than worthless if it's not honest."

"Right. So I want you to dig deeper, Bean. Poetry comes from the soul."

"OK, sir, I'll try."

"But don't worry. You're young. Sometimes great poems come from life experiences you haven't had yet."

"Like what, sir?"

"Like death, or heartbreak. It's only through the loss of life or love that the truth of them are known," Mr. Dooley said, suddenly pensive. When he saw the confusion in Bean's face, he laughed. "So go out there and get your heart broke, kid."

"Yes, sir," he said with a crooked smile, but his teacher's words were already burrowing into his mind. When Bean wrote poetry, it did come from his soul, but it only felt like a malformed lump in his stomach. He had a deep longing for something he never had but still felt like he had lost it somehow.

xxxxxxxxxxxxxxxxxxxxxxxx

"Crap," Bean exclaimed as he sat up in bed and tore yet another sheet out of his notebook. "It's crap."

Ever since Ekee Schultz's Halloween party he had been trying to write a poem about how he felt in that one small moment by the sink when his hip bumped up against Mandy Burns'. Ekee was the park manager at the EZ Mobile Home Park where he lived, and Mandy was his part-time secretary. It wasn't just that she had dyed her blonde hair red, rouged her round face and hands, and had on bright red lipstick, a costume she called "the burning bush" that had men circling her all night like a pack of hounds on the scent. Not just that. And not the way she smiled at him, slightly off kilter, when their hands touched, which caused him to stop breathing. No, it was everything. It was the vision of her shrouded in the smoky haze of the room, the very air unable to avoid caressing her, and the way he felt drawn into a vortex of lust and love and deep abiding longing for . . . something, something that made sense of everything, like . . . like

"Like the whorl in her hair made sense of its flames."

"Shit, shit, shit," he groaned and ripped the sheet out.

"Are you OK, honey?" Mama Wallace, his adopted mother, asked as she looked in his door. Bean suddenly realized where his other hand was and slammed the notebook down on his lap. He grimaced.

"Yeah, Mama Wallace. I was just doing my homework and I got a little frustrated. Sorry."

"Well, just keep working at it and I'm sure you'll figure it out," she said kindly. "I'm going to go down to Polly Ann's for a minute, but I'll be right back. I'm going to take her a pint of the strawberry jam I made this morning."

Without waiting for a reply, she left. Had she seen him? Bean couldn't tell, but he cringed and blushed anyway in unbidden and uncontrollable shame.

"Oh, fuck," he whispered angrily, and lay back on his bed. As his hand settled once again in his crotch, the image of Mandy re-materialized, but this time only her bright red lips, the soft undulations of her breasts rising and falling beneath the red maple leaves on her chest, and the unsteady swaying of her drunken hip as it bumped against his like an incoming tide. It was an impossible image of possibility in the eye of a vortex of realities impossible to describe. Yet he knew then that he had to seek her out. He had to know.

xxxxxxxxxxxxxxxxxxxxxxxx

Bean spit and shook his head as a cloud of caked red mud and grease fell from the transmission mount on a faded red Tercel parked in his yard. He was taking out the torque converter, which he hoped was the only thing wrong with the car. He had watched the car for months, sitting in a patch of weeds at a house at Six Mile crossroads. His school bus passed it every day as it turned onto Brownsboro Road toward Hall's Corner. One day, he stopped at the house and the old man who answered the door told him that the car had belonged to his son, who drove it while he was in high school.

But it had torn up about the time he had gone into the army, and he didn't come back from Desert Storm. He said he had not thought about selling it.

Bean saved every penny he could, but it still took help from his aunt for him to come up with what he thought was enough money to entice the old man. She had given him an old stereo which turned out to be an antique, and told him he could sell it if he wanted. It didn't work until Bean opened the back, looked inside, and closed it back up. When he turned it on then, music blared out of the speakers. He quickly sold it to Milton Pinkus, who ran an antiques store in Hall's Corner.

"Ah, sir, I want to talk to you about the car," Bean stammered as he stood at the old man's door a second time. The air was crisp. The first cool night of fall was coming in on the heels of a cold front.

"I told you last time I'm of no mind to sell it," the old man said. Bean could not read his face, and nothing in the tone of his voice was of any help, either. He was a shrunken old man, with the bony features, large ears, and big knuckles of advanced age. His skin glistened like parchment through the rusted screen door.

"I . . . I know sir, but I'm willing to pay. I've got some money."

"Belonged to my son. He got killed in Bush's war."

"Yessir. You told me. I'll fix it up and everything. It's a shame to let it rust away in the weeds."

"I told him not to join the damn army."

"Yessir."

"What the hell were we doing over there in the first place?" the old man said, his voice rising. "Oughta just guard the coast, I say."

"Yessir. About the car . . . "

"Broke his mama's heart, my boy did when he got hisself killed. He wasn't even in the fighting, they said. He died in an car accident. Mamie ain't been the same since."

Bean gulped. Through the door he could see down the unlit dogtrot until the walls disappeared in the dark shadows. He felt as if he was standing on the edge of a cliff and if he made just one small step, he would fall.

"Well, it can't be helped now," the old man said. "Can't be helped."

He looked even smaller now, as if Bean were looking at him from far away, but even then his dark eyes seemed to go right through Bean's skin. His face wrinkled up even more and softened.

"Just take the car, son. I don't want nothing for it. Just get it out of the yard," the old man said, and turned away.

Bean watched as the blue door closed. The paint was peeling, exposing patches of dark mahogany stain that looked gummy and soft. Bean struggled to grasp what had just happened. The car he had longed for so long was his for nothing, but it came with a ghost.

As he shook the red dust out of his eyes later, he said, "It's gonna be all right now, Ghost. It's gonna be all right."

xxxxxxxxxxxxxxxxxxxxxxxxxx

Mandy was dressed all in white and floated toward him. There was a bright white fog behind her, and she was smiling. Her hazel eyes were sparkling.

"Bean," she whispered. "Bean."

The ground began to turn to boiling foam that kept swelling and swelling until it covered him to the waist. He felt anxious, as if he might drown in it, but it was so warm, and turned into a swirling mist that parted as Mandy moved through it. Bean could see the curved shadow of her body beneath the gown. Light streamed out from the triangle at the top of her thighs.

"I love you, Bean," she said as she extended her arms toward him.

He reached for her. Her body flowed into his and her pink lips opened. The foam roiled about them, warmer and warmer.

Bean sat up in bed and turned on the lamp. He took a notebook and pen from the night stand and wrote, "Like a lighthouse guiding ships to safe harbor." Frowning, he ripped the page out and threw it in the trash. As he lay back down, he rubbed the sheet over his groin and shifted over to one side of the bed.

xxxxxxxxxxxxxxxxxxxxxxxxx

Is this a dream, too? Bean asked himself as Mandy opened the door. He knew her husband was out of town for the weekend. This might be his only chance to be alone with her. He had not seen her in the week since the party, and his memory of her that night had changed in her absence. Small parts had fallen away, and other parts had been added. In his mind, she had morphed into a white sorcerer queen who, with a wave of her wand, would transport them off beyond the sea, or at least that's what he had written in his notebook. This Mandy, the one standing before him, was no less a sorcerer. Her almost transparent gown was like a spell of chaos.

Mandy squeaked when she realized she was wearing only her gown, and slammed the door in his face, then opened it up again. Bean knew none of it. He was as stunned as a moth in a spider's web, waiting to be entombed in a gossamer casket.

"Bean?"

"I brought you these flowers," he said.

"Oh, Bean, how sweet." She buried her nose in the petals. "Want to come in?"

Bean couldn't speak. He just followed her into the house like a puppy.

"Sit down here on the sofa," she said, patting the cushion next to her. "I was just listening to some music."

She sat back against the sofa and closed her eyes. Her head was bent back, and she almost looked like she was asleep. Her pink lips curled slightly in a smile. Her breasts steadily rose and fell. The robe ended just above her knees, and her feet were bare. She wiggled her toes.

"I love you," he blurted.

"What did you say?" she said softly, opening her eyes.

Bean blushed.

"I . . . I love you."

He was leaning toward her so far their arms were almost touching. Without speaking, she took his hand and held his forearm up next to hers. They were the same length from elbow to wrist. Mandy gasped, and as Bean watched in disbelief, she spread his knees apart and put her face in his crotch.

Bean didn't know what to do, so he did nothing, at least voluntarily. Nothing in his dreams could have felt like this. He never knew a woman's mouth could feel so warm. With a quick jerk of his hips, he spent, too quickly but not soon enough, and groaned. Mandy rose up to look at him, her eyes narrow. Bean stared back at her in awe. She licked her lips and smiled.

"Mandy! You home? The door was open, so I . . ."

Bean looked up to see a woman in the doorway. Mandy scrambled up, pulling her robe tightly about her, leaving Bean to fend for himself. He jumped up, and ran out the door past her yanking on his zipper.

"Damn, he's just a kid," he heard her say.

xxxxxxxxxxxxxxxxxxxxxxxxx

Bean knew Mandy loved him, and even though their night together had ended in disaster, he ran from the bus stop to the park office after school just knowing she would run into his arms. But when he arrived, Mandy was gone. Ekee sat at her desk, cursing.

"Where's Mandy?" he asked, dreading the possible answers.

"She's gone. The little bitch never came in today, and when I called her house, no one answered. When I called her husband at work, he just said he didn't know where she was. He sounded pissed. He just said she was gone and hung up."

Bean was in a panic. What could have happened to her?

He tasted iron on his tongue. He tried to swallow, but couldn't. He turned and ran out the office door before Ekee could see his face and the guilt written there. For the next two days, Bean walked down the halls at school like he was part of the dull green paint on the walls, and he came home each day and ran to his room like a rabbit seeking its warren. He slept only fitfully, and by the third day he had the sunken eyes and pallid cheeks of a boy down with a fever.

"I think you ought to stay home, today," Mama Wallace said when she went in to see why he had not come to breakfast. "You might be getting sick. You just try to rest and I'll fix you some chicken soup."

Bean sighed as she closed the door. He never wanted to leave the dark comfort of his room again. In a while, Mama Wallace returned with the soup in a heavy mug and put it on the night stand, then sat down on the bed beside him. The bed springs creaked in protest.

"You don't seem to have a fever, at least," she said as she felt his forehead and smiled at him. "That's nearly always a good sign, although my daughter Dena once had a temperature of 96. We didn't think anything of it until this lump came up on her chest. We took her to the hospital and they said she had pneumonia. She stayed in an oxygen tent three days, but she was the sweetest child. She just played and played with the toys we brought her and never complained. That's my Dena, though."

Bean looked up at her without expression, but because he was at least paying attention to her, she continued.

"Did you hear about Alonzo Allen's pig? You know, that little potbellied thing that they kept in the pen out back of the house, when it wasn't following Raynelle around like it was tied to her ankles. They even let the thing run around in the house, like it was a dog or a cat. But anyway, Lizzie Lou, that's the pig's name, remember, Lizzie Lou got out over the weekend and got into that new subdivision down on the Brownsboro Road. Well, when this Yankee woman saw that thing in her yard, she grabbed up her children and ran into the house to call 911. She said there was a wild boar on the loose. Imagine that, mistaking that fat little thing for a wild boar? My Elton would have set her straight right off. He used to hunt boar, you know, up in Tennessee. Best pork you ever tasted."

Bean nodded his head.

"Well, to make a long story short, this deputy shows up and shoots the thing. Raynelle said she cried and cried. She said all that deputy had to do was hold out a cookie in his hand and Lizzie Lou would have followed him anywhere he wanted to go. I wonder if he was one of those city boys from Brownsboro."

Bean began to take sips of the soup.

"Be careful, honey. It's hot. Oh, and did you hear about that girl who works for Ekee? Mandy. Mandy Burns."

Bean choked.

"I told you it was hot, baby. Well, it seems her husband threw her out of the house. Something about some shenanigans she was up to while he was out of town. Polly Ann didn't tell me what she had done. She said she didn't know, but you know Polly Ann ain't one to gossip. She must have been up to no good, though I don't have much to say for her husband. Bud Burns is tighter than a tick when it comes to money, and that poor girl never wore a new dress that I remember. But I ain't one to judge."

"What happened to her?" Bean whispered.

"Well, she went over to her mama's, but she's not there now. That Ann Cochran is a hard woman to live with, fretting about things all the time like she does. No wonder those girls went wild the minute they got out from under her thumb. Polly Ann said she thinks she's gone to Atlanta, at least according to Ann. I do so hate to see a young couple have trouble. These days, if their marriage hits the least little bump in the road, they call it quits. Not like me and my Elton, God rest his soul. We had plenty of troubles but we stayed together until he died. Not that I didn't want to wring his neck plenty of times. He could be such a grouch."

Mama Wallace chuckled. Bean sat up in bed and drank the soup down in a gulp, scalding his throat.

"Mama Wallace, I really didn't feel too well when I woke up, but I'm much better now," he said hoarsely. "The bus has already run, so can I just go work on my car a while? I only need to put the starter back on and reconnect the battery."

"Well, I don't know. You still look pale as a sheet, although I do see a little color coming back. I guess it's OK, but if you get to feeling worse, you get right back in the house."

"Yes, ma'am," Bean said.

"And don't forget you've got to get a tag and insurance on that car before you can take it out of the driveway."

"Yes, ma'am. I've got the money. I'll get someone to take me to town."

Within an hour, Bean sat behind the wheel of the Tercel and put the key in. He waited, and waited some more, an unknown being better than a bad known, but finally he inhaled deeply and turned the switch. He patted the gas pedal and the old car sputtered briefly before all he could hear was the grind of the starter.

"You probably got it flooded," Jake Peterson said as he walked up. "Put the pedal on the floor and hold it."

Bean did and after he counted eight turns of the engine, it began to sputter again.

"Keep turning it," Jake yelled from underneath the hood. "I think the choke's stuck."

Soon the little engine roared to life then with various clangs and clatters, and white smoke billowed out the tail pipe.

"Easy, Bean. Let off the gas until it won't stall out. There's no telling when the last time this motor was cranked, and it needs some time to get its bearings, or get oil to its bearings. For a minute there, I thought you were going to blow it all apart."

"Th . . . thanks, Mr. Peterson."

"Just let it warm up good and we'll see if it will idle," he said as he looked the car over. "Well, you said you were going to get it, and you did. And all things considered, it ain't bad. Of course, you've got some body rust, but I haven't see an old Japanese car that didn't. Metal's too thin to hold up long. But I don't think it's ever been wrecked. And you've got some dry rot in the tires, but the tread is good on all four wheels. Take your foot off the gas."

The car settled into a high idle. Jake stuck his head back under the hood and slowly the rpms decreased until the engine smoothed out, with only an occasional misfire.

"She needs a tuneup. Did you change the oil? Well, you better do that right away. In fact, go ahead and cut it off. There could be water in it."

The engine raced just slightly, and died with a shudder.

"Yeah, with a little more work, this little car might do you fine. How much did you wind up paying for it?"

"N . . . nothing. I got it for free."

Jake laughed. "Well, you probably paid too much."

"Mr. Peterson, could you take me to Brownsboro and get the stuff I need? I also got to get a tag and insurance."

"Sure, kid. I ain't got nothing to do but twiddle my thumbs, anyway. We can stop at that new barbecue place for lunch. The Red Pig, I think they call it. A couple of the guys on my old crew ate there and they said it was the best barbecue this side of the Cozy Café. When we get back, I'll help you put it together."

"Thanks, Mr. Peterson."

"No problem."

By late afternoon, the Tercel was road-worthy, although it was going to need new tires soon and perhaps new front brake pads even sooner. Mrs. Wallace insisted that Jake ride with Bean the first time he took it out on the highway, and he came back with a stamp of approval for both the boy and the car. Bean didn't smile much, and he didn't even turn on the radio. That's not the way I acted with my first car, Jake thought.

"He seems responsible enough," Jake told Mama Wallace. "I told him not to get it over 50 until he can replace those tires, but for the time being, I think you can trust him, and the car."

"Can I go now, please Mama Wallace? I need to go see somebody."

"Well, I guess it's OK. I'll have supper in a couple of hours, so don't be late."

"I won't." Bean said as he put the car in gear and it lurched forward down D Street. Jake and Mrs. Wallace watched it turn into the highway and head east on the Brownsboro Road.

"Must be going to see some girl," Jake said, smiling.

"I guess," Mama Wallace replied with a shake of her head.

Bean gripped the steering wheel tightly as the little car raced along Brownsboro Road at 65 miles per hour. He flinched every time he met a car, and his arms trembled when he met a logging truck, but he kept his foot on the gas. Still, the few miles seemed an eternity before he reached the entrance to Hall's Creek Village. The tires squealed as he slammed on his brakes to make the turn, and the little car bounced as two wheels slid off the pavement and skidded in the gravel beside Cat's Den Drive. The driver behind him blew his horn, his tires squealing as well, and Bean could hear him curse as he looked out the driver's window into the deep, red clay ditch just below him. Bean gulped and the car lurched forward when the left front wheel escaped the gravel and hit pavement

"Steady, Ghost," he muttered.

Bean slowed the car to a crawl as his hands suddenly began to shake so much he could barely steer. Small starter homes lined the street like pastel monuments of azure blue, coral green, crocus yellow, sandalwood brown and sea foam white. Each one, whether the Bay Shore, the Retreat, the Hilton Head, the Cambridge, or the Huntington, sat in the middle of bright green postage stamps marked by small Bradford pears and red maples, and short paths of red-streaked concrete. One had a boat under a faded blue tarp beside it. One had an old Chevy pickup, primer gray and tottering on large black knobby tires, protruding from the carport. Two had abandoned Big Wheels, red and blue, one on a driveway, one on the sidewalk, and four had small bicycles, three pink with white baskets and pink and white plastic streamers on their handlebars, one black with no fenders and muddy tires, all seemingly scattered at random on the grass.

Five houses in, Bean looked down two side streets lined with the same monuments, each ending in a cul-de-sac backed up against a sagebrush field. But after another block, there were no lawns, only muddy sloughs of clay sliced by long, thick boards that left a red patina on their driveways and along their foundations. One bicycle stuck up out of the mud as if it were trying to escape, and two small cars sat on the curb as if they were afraid to venture onto the driveway for fear of falling off into the muck.

Bean stopped in front of a blue Huntington deluxe model with a one-car garage and turned off the engine. Through the windshield he could see the line of homes broken by vacant lots bearded with golden sage, the occasional scrub pines and sassafras bushes and coralberry plants sticking up like unruly hairs. The house, like all the rest, sat mute in the diffuse amber glow of the afternoon sun. The garage door was covered with all-weather plywood.

He knew she was not here, and he didn't know why he came except to convince himself he was not in a dream. He cranked the car, pulled into its driveway, then turned around and back toward Brownsboro Road with the engine whining in protest. He turned east on the road and drove to the Oak Log-Six Mile Road three miles ahead, and turned south onto it. Five miles later, he turned west on to Macedonia Church Road, a narrow blacktop, drove past the church a half-mile farther, and pulled into the driveway of a large white farmhouse surrounded by pastures. To the right, a short line of black cattle was following a well-worn path that snaked across the pasture from Cochran's Creek to a weather-worn red barn. A man of old age, wearing overalls and a straw hat, was walking down to the barn when he stopped at the sound of the car and turned around.

"Mr. Cochran," Bean shouted as he got out and walked toward him. He was breathless by the time he reached the man. "Mr. Cochran, I'm a friend of Mandy's."

The man's dark eyes raked over him and then his face softened, if only a little as he turned and continued toward the barn.

"Mr. Cochran, where is she?" Bean asked as he trailed along behind. "I'm worried about her."

He grunted.

"Someone told me she just up and left town."

Mr. Cochran stopped and turned to him.

"How is it you know her, boy?" he said, his face as stolid as a mask.

"I . . . I . . . live in the EZ and I do odd jobs for Ekee Shultz," Bean said. "I talked to her in the office a lot. Is she OK? We were friends."

The man grunted again. Bean, not knowing what else to say, said nothing.

"She's gone to Atlanta," he said.

Bean waited, his body rigid, trying to control his breathing.

"She's living near Emory University. That's all I know. She said she got a job at Chinese restaurant there. Now my cattle are waiting."

Mr. Cochran walked on to the barn without turning around. Bean looked over him at the wide arch of the sky. He turned and looked back over the rise, his red car barely visible, and saw the late afternoon sun still well above the horizon. He felt his wallet in his back pocket, then ran to the car. As he slammed the door and turned the key, his eyes narrowed and his mouth stretched from cheek to cheek in a thin line.

"OK, Ghost, don't fail me now," he said grimly as the engine sprang to life.

An hour and a-half later, Bean was shivering uncontrollably as he turned off the interstate and navigated the maze of streets, frequently stopping to look at his map. It seemed like an eternity before he got to Emory, and another before he finally saw the red and black lacquered walls of the Sea of China sitting on the corner of a back street. He pulled in behind the restaurant as an old man was taking out the trash. Bean rolled down his window.

"Excuse me, sir, but do you know Mandy Burns?" he asked.

"Yes," the old man said. His open smile unnerved Bean for a moment. Does he know me, he thought. There was something vaguely familiar about him.

"Is she here?"

"No. This is her off day."

"Do you know where she lives?"

"Yes."

"Can you tell me where it is?"

"No."

Bean groaned. For the first time since he left Carter County, he could feel the ache in his arms and hands. An abiding weariness settled in him and he slumped back against the seat. The old man walked across in front of him to put the trash bag into the dumpster, then walked to the back door. He stopped then and turned to face Bean. He took a small pad and pencil from his pocket and scribbled something down. He walked over to Bean and handed him the slip of paper.

"You did not get this from me," he said.

Bean's heart raced as he read the address, but when he turned to thank the old man, he was gone.

Fifteen minutes later, he knocked on the door of a rented room in an old house near Piedmont Park. His hands felt cold and damp, and sweat popped out on his brow.

"You!" Mandy exploded when she opened the door. "You ruined my life, you little shit."

She was wearing the same faded robe she had worn that night and Bean gulped.

"No! No!" he shouted as he put his hand on the door to keep her from slamming it in his face.

"I know. You just had to brag, didn't you," she hissed as she tried to force the door closed.

"No, Mandy. Oh, god. I didn't tell anyone."

Mandy glared at him. His face was trembling and tears were welling in his eyes. She looked confused.

"Well, if you didn't . . . Oh, shit," she said as she released the door and walked back into the room. Bean followed, watching her shoulders clinch. "That little bitch! That stinking little bitch! I should have known."

"I'm . . . I'm so . . . so . . . sorry, Mandy."

She turned to him, and her red scowl softened.

"Oh." she said. "Bean. How did you find me? How did you get here?"

"I . . . I drove my car."

"But how did you find this place?"

"I ca . . . ca . . . can't say. I promised."

She smiled wryly. She thought she knew.

"I love you," Bean whispered.

Mandy's brows lowered and her mouth curved in a half-smile.

"Oh, Bean, you can't," she said.

"B . . . B . . . But I do."

"But Bean . . ." He interrupted the sentence by taking her into his arms and kissing her. Mandy struggled against his eager tongue at first, but with a sigh kissed him back.

"You love me, too," Bean gasped.

"Oh, poor Bean," she laughed, pushing his arms off her waist. "You're too young to even know what love is. I'm not sure myself, for that matter. Besides, you really want some cute little teenager who will coo and sigh when she looks at you all mooney-eyed, not an old woman like me. Besides, I'm ruined."

"No!" Bean cried as he tried to take her in his arms again. "I want you."

Mandy pushed him away and walked over to the small table beside her bed. She took a sip from a short glass on the table, and picked up a joint. She turned to him as she lit it and took a drag, then extended her hand toward him.

"Want a hit? It's just cheap local stuff, but it'll give you a buzz."

Bean could not speak.

"When you get that girl, you really ought to make love high. It's the best," she said as she took another hit.

"I . . . I . . ."

"Shit, I'm late! I gotta go meet Johnny. He's this really cool guy I met. You know, he went to Carter County High? Class of '84. It's a small world. It really is. He plays guitar in a jazz band now. You'd dig them. They're playing tonight at a club just down the street. He's got some really good pot," she said, giggling. "Want to come?"

Mandy suddenly seemed so far away, like she stood at the intersection of lines receding into the distance. Bean's heartbeat slowed until he thought it would stop and he struggled to breath.

"Seriously. You're underage, but I can get Johnny to make them let you in."

Bean haltingly found his voice again.

"I can't," he said. "I've got to go home. Mama Wallace will be worried."

"Suit yourself." she said as she took his arm and led him to the door. "You really are a sweet boy, you know that."

She kissed him on the cheek.

"Uh huh," he said.

"Oh, Bean, don't look so sad. Next time you are in town, stop by and we'll hang out, OK."

"OK," Bean said, trying to smile but not very successfully.

As the door closed behind him, his stomach clinched and he doubled over in agony.

xxxxxxxxxxxxxxxxxxxxxxxx

AN AZURE SKY, FULL OF EXOTIC PORTENTS
I drove a dead man's car to seek a sorceress,
Red rusted casket rolling on cracking wheels.
His corpse rode shotgun and would smile at me
As if he thought he knew just how it feels
To be a an errant knight out on a foolish quest
For something that he knew did not exist.
They way was long, the burden hard to bear.
In a concrete canyon's cloistered room
I found the sorceress at last. Worn weary
From my task I faced her ruins but could
Not sing my fable's song. She laughed,
Her spell cast shards of broken glass.
I took her in my bloodied arms but gasped
She had no flesh and no eyes peered
Back at me from her bleached white skull.
I held her fast until her bones were dust
That wafted on the long lines of my soul,
Then clapped my hands to shake the red clay
Off of them. The Ghost clapped, too.
I don't know why.

"Well, Bean, this is definitely an improvement in some ways," Mr. Dooley said as he looked up at the boy from behind his desk. "I like the imagery in places, and inner rhymes. You've developed the theme well, although you give the journey short shrift. Where is it? Oh, 'The way was long. The burden hard to bear.' There's a lot left unsaid here. But you know

I don't like to critique anyone's poetry too much, because who can sit in judgement on a poem, 'eh? It's just my opinion, to be taken with a big grain of salt, but there's a little too much teenage angst in it. And it's a little too sentimental for my taste. But, you are a teenager after all, and you'll grow as a poet. I'm sure of it. I expect to read your work someday in anthologies. I'm serious. Just keep writing and don't ever stop."

"Thank you, sir," Bean said with a weak smile as he took the sheet of paper from him and left.

Mr. Dooley shook his head and smiled.

"Wait up, Bean. Bean!" P. J. Frazer shouted as she ran by his door.

X. Hall's Corner, Midday

I was in an old house and I was waiting for the women to arrive. When they did, they went into the kitchen. They were happy and chatting amiably when they went by me (there were a lot of windows. It was like the helm of a ship). There were three of them and they asked me if I wanted any coffee. They were fixing instant. I drank real brewed and joked with them. No, I said, but if you would like some real stuff, I have it in my car. They laughed and this one, dark-haired and thin, said, everybody knows you only drink brewed coffee. She said it sarcastically. I was leaving the room and turned back. I said I will have a cup of instant . . .because I wanted to be with them. They didn't hear me.

"Ah ah ah," Dave Stone gasped when he jolted awake. It was the same dream again. Always the same dream. Not in any of its particulars, but in how it felt. It always felt the same.

It was 4:12 a.m. Youthful Folly leading to Disjunction. He knew he couldn't go back to sleep, so he got up and turned on his computer.

"Hall's Corner, Midday."

The words sat atop an unwritten page, the same unwritten page they topped yesterday, and the day before.

"His staccato heartbeat echoed in his ears when he heard the distant howl. He didn't know how, but they had found him," he wrote, then with a groan, he backspaced until the words were gone.

"Shit!" he said. He went to the kitchen. He fixed a cup of coffee and sat down in his brown leather recliner. The coffee was very hot, so hot it burned his lips.

He turned to see Papa sitting on the sofa in front of the fireplace in the old farm house near Winchester. The winter wind was moaning around the house corners. He was talking to his cousin, Edie, his uncle's oldest girl.

"Papa, the water for your coffee is boiling," she said.

"Let it boil a few more minutes and make me a cup," he said.

Papa liked his coffee hot, even if it was instant.

He laughed.

"Hmmm," he said softly as the trailer room reappeared. He shook his head vigorously. He must have nodded off again, but it didn't feel like he had slept. He took another sip of coffee. It was cold. It must have been all that cinnamon in Doris Pilgrim's apple pie, he thought. Cinnamon always made him restless.

He looked at the clock. It was 5:31: Waiting leads to Influence. He wanted a cream cheese Danish. J's Grocery wouldn't be open for another half-hour.

"Can't eat it anyway," he thought. "We're diabetic, remember? That stuff's poison. Besides, it's artificially flavored and tastes like shit."

"*Never stopped you before.*"

"Oh, shut up. Maybe we ought to take Doris out. She is kind of nice, and she's going through a divorce, too."

"*Might even get some nookie.*"

"She looks too much like my mother."

xxxxxxxxxxxxxxxxxxxxxxx

"My ex was a real bastard," Doris said. She took a big bite of her hamburger. Faint yellow light blinked on and off the white laminated table at the front of the Cozy Café from the caution light at the junction of the Livingston and Brownsboro Roads.

"She really doesn't look like mother at all," he thought.

"*Too pretty?*"

"No, smart ass. Too plain."

"He just up and left me with Elsie. Cleaned out the bank account and took the car. I don't know where he is, and DFACs can't find him. All we had was a little money I had hidden away that he didn't know about. I was lucky Ekee let me make the deposit in payments, or we would be out on the street."

"Elaine said she just couldn't live like this anymore, but she never said what 'this' was. She just told me I had to change. I tried. I started helping her more around the house, at least as much as I could with my job. I took her places. We took a trip to Niagara Falls, and we went to New York City. But she said it wasn't enough."

"He wasn't much to look at, you know. And he never held a job for more'n a month or two at a time. I allus just told myself he hadn't found his place in the world, you know. I prayed and prayed that he would take Jesus Christ as his personal savior."

"I don't think I could have done anything to keep her. I think she might have been cheating on me, anyway. Within a month after we separated last year, she had taken up with some guy from over in Stockbridge."

"My Johnny ran around on me all the time. I knew it. Oh, he was sly about it, but I just knew. Woman's intuition."

He watched her take another big bite of the burger. She had ketchup on her lips.

"Did you like my pie?"

"Yes," he said. "It was real rich."

"No. It was awful."

"Y'all set," asked Linelle, proprietor of the Cozy Café. She was grinning.

"Linelle, you sound like a Yankee," he laughed.

Doris looked confused.

"We're fine. That's what waitresses say up North," he said as Linelle walked back to the "house table."

"Oh," Doris said as she licked the ketchup from her lips.

"Nice lips."

"What! White people have always eat black folks' cookin'. Hell, some of them even sucked at a black teat!"

The words exploded from the back of the dining room where Linelle sat with a large black woman.

"That's Polly Ann Jones," Doris whispered, spitting bits of hamburger out into the air before she took the time to swallow. "She's that old nigger woman who lives in the black section, 87D. You want to stay away from her. I hear she is a witch. Let's get out of here."

Doris gobbled down the last bite of hamburger and grabbed her coat off the wooden rack as she went out the door.

"Hey Yankee," someone said as he paid for the meal at the register. He groaned in mock frustration and turned to see Jake Peterson, whose trailer was at the end of C Street, two trailers from his on D Street.

"Hey, redneck," he said with a grin.

As they talked for a moment about trivialities such as getting his water line insulated now that the nights were sometimes below freezing and traveling the country in a trailer, Dave thought he's an amiable, helpful sort. He had found a few others like him in other places. They made up for the rest, like the two young men at the counter, who took his Boston accent as proof he was alien and strange, and wouldn't look at him.

"Check out the pixie."

Jake's small tomboyish companion was smiling openly at him, her green eyes sparkling.

"She's all bone. Nothing to get a hand hold on."

Later, when they sat in the dark at the Cherokee Cineplex, Doris leaned against him, and when he dropped her off at her trailer in the EZ Mobile Home Park, he kissed her. She tasted of onions.

xxxxxxxxxxxxxxxxxxxxxxx

I am going up through a house. The house is old and the walls are burnished, as if in amber . . . they have a sheen. I float up and on the first level I see a man and a woman in a bedroom naked and making love. The man turns into a big pink pig. On the second level I see an old man talking to a large pig who stood erect like a man. He is much taller than the old man, and his bearing is one of dignity. His arms are folded across his chest. The two are facing each other and I know they are talking about me, but I cannot hear anything they say. They never look at me. I go on up until I reached a landing with a narrow spiral staircase leading up to the top.

"Not too many people rent these rooms because it is so difficult to get to them. But it has a great view," says a voice.

I stand at the doorway to the top room, then walk in. The walls are all glass and I can see the Boston skyline far below. The room trembles and shudders as the wind rakes the window panes. I wonder if a gale might twist it right off the top of the building. I know it would be very difficult to get groceries up this far. The floor begins to shake.

"Damn!" Dave gasped as he sat up in bed. He gritted his teeth and lay back down. "OK, let me have it. I'm tired of running."

The fear rose up again. The building appeared briefly, then faded away. Suddenly, he was flying down a winding road, careening around curves at a high rate of speed. To the left was a white fence, and beyond it a cliff. He couldn't see to the bottom. He sped up until the fence was a white streak. Ahead he saw a tunnel. When he entered it, it became an undulating tube. On and on he went until, with a gasp, he emerged into a dark night sky. There were no stars.

He remembered his mother whipping him with a switch, one she had made him cut. He cut her a sturdy one. As she lashed his legs, he felt no pain, only a dead pressure against the legs of his jeans. He and his sister Annie had only snuck off to see their friends next door. They did it all the time and she had just scolded them before. But then daddy had caught them and raised hell and red welts with his belt. He didn't know which hurt worse, dangling in his iron grip like a fish on a line, thinking he would die from the pain, or watching Annie scream.

"You're just like him," he had thought. He could taste blood.

"Cry, damn you, cry!" she yelled, but he wouldn't. He could see a flicker of fear cross her face. She stopped whipping him. She threw the switch down.

"Damn!" he said.

xxxxxxxxxxxxxxxxxxxxxxxx

"Uh uh uh," Doris moaned.

Her face was flushed with sweat; her body quivering. He thought she was close, and he longed for release.

"Uh ... oh ... wait.... I'm ... too dry."

He didn't stop. He could feel the tightening in his groin.

"Ayah, ayah, ayeh, hu hu hu," she groaned. "Stop. Stop!"

He stopped. He still pulsed inside her. With a groan, he rolled over. He lay back against the pillow, his chest heaving.

"Are you all right?" she asked.

"Yes," he said. He could just make out the profile of her shining face in the dark.

"*No!*"

"She doesn't look like my mother at all," he thought.

"I'm sorry. I thought I had some KY Jelly in the bathroom, but I'm out."

"Don't worry about it."

"Are you sure?"

"Yes."

"It's all my fault. Oh, God, I have sinned. God punishes the wicked," she moaned as she began to cry.

"Doris, it's all right," he said, but she was no longer hearing him.

"The Lord is my shepherd. I shall not want," she cried. "He maketh me lie down in green pastures. He leads me beside the still waters. He restoreth my soul. He leads me in the path of righteousness for His name's sake. Yea though I walk through the valley of the shadow of death, I will fear no evil, for Thou art with me, Thy rod and Thy staff, they comfort me. Surely goodness and mercy shall follow me all the days of my life; and I shall dwell in the house of the Lord forever. Amen."

When she finished, he listened for her breathing until she began to snore softly. He got up and walked into the living room. Out the picture window he could see a circle of D Street illuminated by a security light. He looked at the clock on the microwave. It was 4:56: The Folly of Youth leads to The Wanderer. He rubbed his stomach, then lifted the small roll of fat in both hands and squeezed. He sighed, then picked up the flask of Scotch and went out on the porch.

It was a clear, cool night. The air was dry. He took a drink. He shivered a moment, goose bumps popping up on his arms and legs, until the warm liquor settled in his stomach. In each direction, single-wide mobile homes like a rag tag fleet of ships that had all run aground lined D Street for almost a hundred yards until it ended in crossing streets that had no name. A portion of some stuck out into the circles of yellow light that dotted the street, while others, like missing teeth, left dark holes in the line. The homes were dark as well except for small rectangles of light coming out of the bathroom, and then only the few that he could see. Near the back end, there was the blue flicker of a television behind thin curtains. A dog barked over on A Street, then another farther away. He walked over to the edge of the porch and peed in the yard. He wished he had a cigarette.

He heard a noise inside and opened the door. Doris sat naked on the sofa with her legs pressed tightly together and her elbows on her knees. Her breasts spilled out between her arms and her nipples were pebbled. She looked up at him.

"I woke up and you weren't in bed. Close the door. It's cold."

He felt like he stood there for a long time, half his body in the warm and half in the cool, but it was only a second. He saw himself close the door before he closed it. He wanted to say something, but the words were still only a formless stone in his gut. He wanted to stand in front of her and press her face to his groin. It was the only explanation.

"Close the door. I'm freezing."

He closed the door and took her hand.

"Let's go to bed," he said.

"I think you ought to go now."

"OK, Doris."

xxxxxxxxxxxxxxxxxxxxxxxxx

I am going down a road in a truck and encounter a pile of dirt, the type used to block impassable or closed roads. I am wearing glasses and holding a cup in my hand. There is a wooden barrier that has been pushed to one side. I stick my hand out the window and put my glasses and cup on top of the barrier. I go over the mound in the truck. Although I cannot see it, I feel that what lies ahead is impassable because of water, as in a flood. The pile looks like a mountain range, with sharp ridges, and I am surprised that the truck will cross it.

I see a dragon, very large and dark, dark green, off to my right. I know this dragon. I cross the mound of dirt and I am surprised to find that I am back at the same place. My uncle Eddie is driving and there are two old people and a small boy with us. I look down the slope in front of us – it looks like the sides of two converging ridges, and I say, "I don't think we were intended to go this way."

I am sitting facing my mother. We have our legs spread apart and she is shelling peas. I am stringing beads. As I am working, I realize that I am getting an erection. With my elevated arms and hands, there is no way to conceal it and I realize that my mother, if she looks, will see it. I am surprised when I feel the tips of her fingers gently slide along my thighs. I look at her and she smiles. It is a warm and accepting smile. I am emotionally paralyzed.

"God!" he shouted, bolting up in bed. His body was shaking. He was gasping. Grimly, he lay back down and closed his eyes.

He thought about Susan. It was late summer. August. His parents had gone to Connecticut on vacation. His little brother was with them. His sister was already married and gone. It was Saturday. He and Susan were lying on the covers of his bed naked. It was hot. The old house had no air-conditioning. A halting breeze caressed the window curtains. They were sweating. They had just made love. He marveled at the pinkness of her skin. She said she was thirsty and he got up to go to the kitchen. As he walked through the living room, he felt so free that he could pee on the floor. He got two Cokes out of the refrigerator. In the humid air they began to sweat, too, by the time he got back to the bedroom. She had her eyes closed. He held the cans over her naked body and the beads of cold water fell one by one onto her belly. She squealed. He lay down on her, propped up on his elbows, still holding the cans, and could feel the cold droplets warm between their skins. He kissed her. He breathed her air.

"You're not supposed to be doing this!" his mother shouted later. She was standing in the hallway in front of the bathroom. It was Sunday. They came back early. They stayed one night and drove straight back. Without stopping, he knew. That's the way his father was. He never stops. My mother is holding a condom by the rolled-up end. It did not flush. He couldn't speak. He couldn't feel. He could only stare at her and turn away. He didn't tell Susan. She wouldn't understand.

xxxxxxxxxxxxxxxxxxxxxxx

Doris sat in a lounge chair under the canopy of his trailer. It was misting rain and she was huddled in her coat. He was standing by the grill cooking steaks in a long-sleeve shirt. The weather was warm, for November.

"I heard that Johnny is in Atlanta somewhere," she said."His sister told me he is living with some tramp. He is a musician, you know. Plays jazz guitar. I want to find him and just go up to him and ask him why. I just want to know why."

"That's the million dollar question, isn't it. A month after Elaine and I divorced, I heard she was living with this guy in a cabin on a creek outside Stockbridge. This old friend of mine said he saw her with him. They were bathing in the river naked, in plain sight of the bridge. I am not a violent man by nature, but when I heard that, I wished I had a deer rifle and I was standing on that bridge. That's when I hit the road."

"It's so hard. He never said anything to me. Not a word. He just left. One night we were in bed; in the morning he was gone. Why would someone do that? We had been married fifteen years."

"How do you want your steak?"

"Done."

"Medium well or really well?"

"Done as in done. I want to go back in the house."

"Goddamn it, get me a beer!" yelled a loud, drunken voice from a street over.

"Get it yourself, you bastard!" a female voice yelled back. Dave chuckled.

"Such is life in the park," he mused to himself, then turned to Doris. "But it's such a wonderful day. It's November, but it's cool, not cold. There's a light mist but no wind. We've got two steaks on the grill and two drunks over on E Street for entertainment. I tell you, Doris, it doesn't get much better than this."

"For you, maybe. I'm freezing."

"Where's your sense of adventure? Have a drink of this. It will warm your insides."

"Yuk. I hate that stuff. Do you have any wine coolers?"

"Nope. Fresh out."

"I'm going inside to get some coffee."

"Coming back out?"

"No! I will set the table."

The door slammed. He pushed his steak aside, but left hers over the red coals. He watched the steady drip of raindrops falling from the edges of the canopy. As the sky began to darken as evening came on, the gray air settled down on the homes on D Street like a shroud until one by one they disappeared. The security lights came on early, but only the closest trailers were visible. Beyond them was only a string of receding suns. He breathed in the mist and exhaled the mist. The clean air scraped his throat. It really was a very fine day. For November.

By the time he checked it again, her steak was almost black.

"Doris, why don't we go to Chattanooga," he said later as they ate.

"Whatever for?" she said as she chewed the meat.

"We could eat at that restaurant, the Choo-Choo."

"I can't afford it."

"I'll buy."

"No. I told you we're strictly Dutch."

"*Except when I'm buying.*"

"We could go to Rock City. Have you ever been there?'

"Once, when I was a kid."

"Did you see Ruby Falls?"

"No. There was no way I was going in a cave. Uh uh. It's too spooky."

"It's amazing. I never saw so many colors."

"Johnny tried to get me to go up there once, but I told him I didn't want to. I never was much for traveling. It's just the way I am."

"You would have a good time."

"When I was a girl, I used to like to sit in front of the fireplace on days like this and drink hot cocoa. Mama would wrap us both in a big downy coverlet and we would snuggle while we watched the fire. I got Johnny to do it once. It was wonderful. That's what I like."

"I bet you did a different kind of snuggling."

She blushed.

xxxxxxxxxxxxxxxxxxxxxxxxxx

I am riding a bicycle on the same road with Eddie. There is a house on the other side of a railroad track up ahead. I am wobbling on the bike because I am carrying a big winter coat. I am frustrated and throw Eddie the coat. He holds it for a few seconds, then throws it down. I don't care and ride on.

We stop at a street corner. There is a street lamp between me and Eddie.

"Are you going to go get the truck?" I ask him.

"Yes," he says.

"Are you going to get someone to do it or are you going to do it yourself?" I ask.

He replies, "I am going to get someone to do it for me."

I feel as sense of resignation, as if to an impending loss.

Dave awoke breathing heavily and immersed in a dull sense of doom. When he lay back down, the details of the dream quickly faded away. He remembered Susan again.

He was working at a service station. He and Susan had been dating for seven months. It was Christmas Eve and the station was open late to serve last-minute shoppers coming out of the mall. They were few. It was a cool, crisp night and he was standing in an open bay looking out over the scattered cars in the parking lot across the street. He saw a white sedan cross the street and come toward him. As it stopped in front of the bay, Susan got out and ran toward him. She threw her arms around him despite his dirty clothes and kissed him. "I love you," she said, and ran back to the car. He saw her parents wave. He waved back. Eleven months later she was in college and they were history. He didn't know that then. It would not have made any difference if he did. He wouldn't have believed it.

xxxxxxxxxxxxxxxxxxxxxxx

"*You're a liar.*"

"No, I'm not."

"*Yes you are. And you don't just lie with words. You lie with your whole life.*"

"No, I don't."

"*What about Susan?*"

"That wasn't a lie. She was the most wonderful girl I ever knew."

"*After a year and a-half, she dumped you like a rotten fish.*"

"It was her parents. They didn't want her getting too involved with anyone before she went to Cornell."

"It was her. She's the one who said she wanted to date other people."

"I wanted to marry her."

"And the first time she goes out with this other guy, she screws him, and then tells you all about it. Some wonderful."

"I . . . I . . ."

"You couldn't take it. Hell, you married Elaine because she looked like her."

"No. I loved Elaine."

"Bullshit."

"I did. It just didn't work out, that's all."

"Because she wasn't Susan, was she?"

"No! We broke up because I . . . because she . . . we just drifted apart. It happens. We weren't compatible."

"Compatible shmatible."

"We just fell out of love."

"Love? You don't even know what love is ."

"I do. It's . . ."

"I'm waiting."

xxxxxxxxxxxxxxxxxxxxxxxx

I am standing in the dirt road. It has rained. A stream has swollen and has made the road impassable. "I have to go back and get my glasses and my cup," I say and Eddie nods, with a touch of resignation, too. "How do I get there?" I ask. He is slightly impatient. He attempts to explain, then rethinks it. "See this road?" he says, indicating a side road just in front of the creek. I nod. "Go down it, beyond the county line. It will take you to them."

I race down the road. My bike has no fenders and a rooster-tail of mud arcs out behind me. I can feel the cold liquid clay soak my back. The road is pitted with mud holes. I hit every one on purpose.

Dave woke up. He stared at the white ceiling of the travel trailer. He sighed. He went back to sleep.

xxxxxxxxxxxxxxxxxxxxxxx

"Doris, have you ever smoked pot?" he asked. They were lying in bed, naked under the covers. Her head was resting on his arm. The clock by her bedside read 8:43: Unity leads to Revolution.

"Once, when Johnny was in college, he took me to visit his English professor. He took us down to the basement and tried to get us high. I took a couple of puffs, but I didn't feel anything."

"Sometimes that happens. Did you ever try again?"

"No."

"Why not?"

"I just didn't want to. It's illegal. I was always scared of getting caught."

"You don't know what you've been missing, Doris. I don't smoke it regularly. I've gone for years without it. But there are times when there is nothing like it, like now. Want to try again?"

"You've got pot!"

"Yes. A joint. It's pretty good stuff."

"Oh, Jesus, throw it out! Flush it down the commode!"

"But, Doris. . . ."

She threw back the covers and scrambled out of bed like he was a snake. She stood over him. Her body was shaking.

"Johnny smoked it all the time. It's addictive. I begged him to stop, but he wouldn't. He said he could quit it anytime, too. Then he got busted. I couldn't take it any more. When he got out of jail, I told him it was either me or the pot. He left."

"It's never that simple, Doris."

"Get out! Get out, now! Oh, God, what have I done? For the sins of the wicked will be visited upon them ten-fold."

"But Doris . . ."

"I said, get out!" she cried as she fell to her knees and began to pray. Her body was hunched over in agony and her shoulders jerked like she was flailing herself with a lash. If he had his camera, he would have taken a picture, but he was sure he would not forget the moment anyway.

It was a cool night and it was raining. A stiff wind was blowing so hard the rain was falling aslant. In no time his pants and long-sleeve shirt were soaked. He leaned into the wind as he walked over to D Street to his trailer. The droplets stung his cheeks. He opened his mouth wide and drank.

"Nice weather we're having, isn't it?"

"Yes. Very nice. For November."

"I wonder what time it is."

ϟ

XI. The Dominecker War

Marvin Lewis knew he shouldn't be doing what he was doing. Not only because it might get him beat up if not worse, but also because it hurt so damn bad. But he had liked the white girl from the first time he saw her through the window at the soda fountain at Sam Wilson's drug store in Hall's Corner three years before. Her name was Jennifer Ann Butler. She was a graduated senior at the Chamblee School for Women who had stayed on as an aide, and she had the longest, sweetest legs Marvin had ever seen. Last year, at the Miss Hall's Corner Festival, when he and his daddy and mama and sister sat in the balcony at the old Hall High auditorium along with a few other black families to watch the pageant, Marvin's throat got so tight when he saw Jennifer Ann in a bathing suit that he thought he would choke.

"You're staring at that white girl again," his sister Chanelle had scolded him in a whisper. Her eyes were flaring like black embers above her charcoal cheeks. When Marvin's daddy and mama turned to see what the children were talking about, Marvin dropped his head and said nothing.

It wasn't the first time Chanelle had gotten her back up about it.

"Why don't you go out with Angel? She's cute, and besides, I think she likes you," Chanelle had said to him only yesterday.

"She is too silly," Marvin said.

"Then what about Polly Ann Jones?"

Marvin blanched. Polly Ann was the prettiest black girl in the county, if not the prettiest girl, period, but there was something so imposing about her that Marvin never even considered the possibility that she might like him. Besides, she was two years older than he was.

"She is pretty," he said.

"But you still got a thing for that white girl, don't you? Marvin, I don't understand it. She ain't that pretty you know. Besides, you got to think of the time we're living in. Black people are finally going to get their rights. The Supreme Court said so. The change hasn't gotten here yet, but it's coming. It's happening in Little Rock right now, so it's going to happen in

Carter County. Now's not the time for a proud black man like you to be chasing after some white girl."

"Thank you, Rev. King," he had said, and he thought she was so mad she was going to slap him. But he really loved his sister, and he knew she was right. Jennifer Ann wasn't that pretty. He nose was too long and her chin too prominent. But she was just so tall and thin, with long, soft black curls on one end and long slender legs on the other. Besides, there was no accounting for feelings.

So, here he was, hiding in the dark in the bushes on the lawn of Chamblee School spying on her and Phil Thompson, whom they called "Plum." He was the richest young man in Carter County since his daddy owned a big part of it. He was a veteran of the Korean Conflict and had just graduated from the University of Georgia. And if all that was not enough, he was called Plum because he was "plum handsome." Marvin knew that even if he was white, he wouldn't stand a chance against that kind of competition, but from the first he had resolved to love Jennifer Ann from afar, like a knight at court in love with the queen.

"Plum, stop!" Jennifer Ann giggled as she sat next to him on a bench partially hidden in the shadows of some crepe myrtle. She was holding his hand away from her breast.

"Well, I might just call up your sister," he teased. "I bet Genie would be more accommodating."

"Plum Thompson, she's just a junior. You leave her alone!"

"OK, OK, I didn't mean anything by it. I just want a little loving, that's all," he said as he nuzzled her neck. "Let's go over to my house."

"Oh, Plum," Jennifer Ann moaned. She released his hand.

Marvin watched in chivalric agony as Plum's hands began to travel here and there on her body until they rested on her bare knee, then began to slide upward.

"Plum! We can't. Not here," she said hoarsely.

"Like I said, let's go to my house."

The implied promise of her words made Marvin feel something heavy and dull form in his gut, dispelling his momentary illusion that she might be in distress and need rescuing.

"Jennifer Ann!" a girl's voice shouted. "Jennifer Ann!"

"Oh, shit," Plum said as Jennifer Ann straightened her dress.

"Over here, Genie."

"There you are!" the sixteen-year-old said as she ran up to them, breathless. Genie Butler was almost as tall as her sister, and a little prettier, although she had about the same nose and chin. At sixteen she was still as skittish as a colt.

"Hey, kid, to what do we owe this interruption?" Plum said, arching his eyebrows. He hugged Jennifer Ann to him.

Genie stopped in her tracks and her whole body seemed to blush.

"Hi, Plum," she said, biting her lower lip.

"Hi, kid," Plum said as he stretched his legs out from the bench, crossing his ankles. "Like I said, to what do we owe this interruption?"

Genie stood stock still. Marvin thought she looked like a hen that was charmed by a puff adder.

"Genie?" Jennifer Ann said impatiently.

"Oh, huh? Oh, Dr. Pinkus wanted me to ask you if you would play piano for the reception he is having tomorrow for State Representative Wallace and his wife. Effie has come down with the chicken pox."

"Oh, Lord, I don't have anything prepared except the old stuff," said Jennifer Ann as she rose to her feet. She swatted Plum's hand away when he tried to touch her butt, then turned and whispered to him, "Stop! She'll see."

"That old stuff seems pretty good to me," Plum said as he looked up and down her body.

Genie giggled.

"Come along, Imogene," Jennifer Ann said curtly. She took her sister's hand and led her back toward the school.

Genie looked back over her shoulder and Plum winked at her.

"Yes, sister dear," she said with a wiggle of her butt.

Marvin, from his station in the bushes nearby, clinched his fists tightly.

xxxxxxxxxxxxxxxxxxxxxxxx

After she had graduated, with honors, Jennifer Ann had stayed on at the Chamblee School as a teacher's aide because of her sister, and just before school started in the fall, Plum rented a small old house just a little ways east across Brownsboro Road from where First Street intersected it. Late on the afternoon of the first day of class, she was walking in the flower garden behind the small ridge on which the school sat with a basket of late peaches under her arm, picked from the school's orchard, and thinking of how she might sneak over to his house after dark. It thrilled her to think they might actually have a place where they could be alone and free. When she reached the end of the garden and saw the old dirt field road that ran along the back side of the small ridge and came out right across from his house, she thought, "Perfect."

She heard clucking sounds and turned to see a flock of black and white speckled chickens scratching the ground around the plants.

"Shooo!" she hollered, "Shooo!"

The chickens ran a short distance in the garden, then resumed their scratching. Jennifer Ann tapped her feet in frustration.

"They're eating bugs," a voice said, and she turned to see a young black man, roughly her age, stacking corn stalks in the vegetable garden nearby.

"What?" she said as she looked around. There was no one else in sight.

"They're eating bugs. It's good for the plants," Marvin said. His words were hoarse, like he had something in his throat. He tried to smile.

"How do you know?"

"I just know, that's all. Chickens always eat bugs, if they can catch them. Domineckers like them a lot."

"Domineckers?"

"That's what they're called," he said. In her long blue dress, he thought she looked like a giant cornflower. "It's really dominiques, but that's the way folks say it. They come from England."

"Hmmm. What is your name?"

"Marvin. Marvin Lewis. I'm the groundskeeper and gardener."

"You're new."

"Yes, ma'am."

"I'm not a ma'am."

"Sorry ma'am, I mean, sorry."

"What happened to the old man who used to do this?"

"His name is Dub. He retired. His back hurts too bad for him to work any more."

"Dub," she said as if the word were a lemon drop she was worrying with her tongue. She turned to the chickens.

Marvin watched her lips move with fascination. He knew they would feel so soft and warm.

"Then, what they're doing is good for the garden."

"Yes, Jennifer Ann. It's very good," he said. Saying her name made his heart pound in his chest.

Startled, she turned to him. Her face was flushed.

"How do you know my name?"

"Everyone in Hall's Corner knows who you are, Jennifer Ann."

He said her name again. She stared at him. He was a stocky boy, with broad shoulders and thick arms. He had a broad, flat nose and large lips, and his eyes were dark and deep. His black, curly hair was combed out in a tight Afro, and the sun on his brown sweaty skin transformed his arms and face into carved mahogany.

"I have to go," she said and quickly walked back up the hill to the school. His eyes followed her until she went up the back steps and into the building. Without looking back, she knew they did, and he knew that she knew.

That night, she was anxious as she snuck over to Plum's house on the dirt path, but not because she was afraid of the dark. She chaffed at having to sneak around at all. Why couldn't they just live openly as lovers? The moon had yet to rise, and the small ridge blocked the lights from Hall's Corner, so staying on the path proved to be more difficult than she had imagined. She had only the light of the top floors of the houses along First Street to guide her, and where the privet grew too high, she had nothing at all. She thought of the young black man with skin like carved wood. Marvin, he said his name was. Marvin Lewis. He had unsettled her when he called her by name. She wondered if she could even see him in the dark.

She stumbled into a fence post by the side of the path and cursed. Something out of the shadows answered her with low murmurs. She yelped and tried to run, but her dress was caught. She ripped it loose and ran until she could see the lights of Plum's house. As she ran across the Brownsboro Road, a small dog somewhere in the dark started barking, and then another. Once inside, she slumped back against the door, gasping.

"You seem a little distracted," Plum said to her that night over dinner. He struggled to wrap the soft spaghetti noodles on his fork.

"It's nothing. Just a little hay fever. Do you know anything about chickens?"

"Chickens? Yeah. Daddy's got about ten houses just north of Six Mile. Half of them are layers and half broilers."

"Do they eat bugs?"

"Nah, just feed."

"Are they domineckers, I mean, dominiques?"

"Hell, no. They're white leghorns. You city girls don't know a thing about farming, do you?"

He was teasing, but that didn't smooth the wrinkles in her brow.

"Domineckers are an old breed," he said. "They're pretty good layers, and they're pretty good meat, but they can't beat a white leghorn. You overcooked the spaghetti."

"Sorry," she said. She was not looking at him.

"Why the sudden interest in chickens?"

"I was just curious. Someone told me they ate bugs."

"Well, they do, if they're yard chickens. Yard chickens will eat about anything."

"Yard chickens?" she said.

"Yeah. Granddaddy had all kinds, domineckers, Rhode Island Reds, banties, game chickens, even Guinea fowl and those weird little cochin chickens with the feathers growing over their feet. He let them run loose because he built a big coop for them, and as the saying goes, chickens always come home to roost."

He laughed. She didn't.

"Did you bake a pie?"

"Yes," she said, suddenly smiling at him. "It's peach. I took some from the orchard behind the school."

"Why Jennifer Ann, you're a thief and an outlaw," he laughed.

She cut him a slice of the pie, and watched anxiously for his reaction as he took a bite.

"Crime never pays," he said, choking. He forced down another two bites, washed it down with milk, then threw down the fork. "You know, the old man gave me hell all day today because the framing crew screwed up a wall on the courthouse annex. Hell, those boys won't listen to me and he knows it. I told him, 'If you want me to be a supervisor, then make me a damn supervisor.' But he won't because he's just too goddamn hard-headed about me working my way up from the bottom. I just want to go to bed."

"Are you through? I've got to go help Genie practice for her recital."

"Well, I guess I better take a shower."

Jennifer Ann scowled as he went into the bathroom. She stood in the middle of the living room of the small, three-room house with anger and frustration smoldering inside her. For the first time, they were alone in their own house, like man and wife, and she had ruined dinner.

"You wanted this," she thought. "And you got it. You're engaged to the most handsome man in Carter County, and one day he'll be rich. Hell, half the girls in the county would kiss the ground he walks on. So, why are you so mad?"

The question hung silently in the air like a magic rune cast by a wizard that glowed briefly then disappeared.

"Because we don't really suit each other? He wants a Sweet Rosemary who can cook, and I can barely boil water without burning it. Because he doesn't make love to me any more like I'm a goddess? Oh, how eager and hungry he once was to please me. But I knew that wouldn't last. I don't know how, but I knew. Or is it because he was so tired he only wanted to go to bed until I reminded him of Genie's practice? I've seen the way he looks at her every time we get together. He can't take his eyes off her, and she's no better. If she wasn't my sister, I would think she was being a whore."

The future stretched before her like lines into infinity that never crossed.

She felt no better after an hour of watching him flirt with Genie and Genie flirt back as she mangled the Bach piece she was perform in a month. When she frowned at him for sitting on the bench next to her and bumping her with his hip, which made her giggle, he got up and took her aside.

"Relax," he said. "We're just having fun. Surely, you are not jealous of her. She's just a girl."

"I know it, and you know it, but I don't think Genie knows it," she said hotly.

He smiled crookedly and shook his head, then sat back down on the bench. When Genie looked at Jennifer Ann with trepidation and at him with curiosity, he shrugged his shoulders and mugged, causing her to laugh. Jennifer Ann sat silently and let him take over the instruction. "It's the blind leading the blind," she fumed, as the piano gave up the minuet as if were being tortured into it.

When the hour was over at nine o'clock and Genie had to go to bed, her sister quickly kissed her. She stepped back and hesitated, then hugged Plum hard and kissed him on the cheek with a loud smack.

"Thanks," she said, giggling and blushing, before she turned to run up the stairs to her room.

"Now, let's sneak over to my house," Plum said. He hugged Jennifer Ann. His breath was warm on her neck. Her body stiffened.

"I've got to go to bed. Classes begin at eight and I've got to finish my preparations."

"Aw, c'mon, Jenny. Don't be mad. It'll be fun," he said, kissing her neck again.

"I said I've got to go to bed."

"Well, have it your way," he said, his voice rising. He turned and went out the door, slamming it behind him so hard she thought the glass would break. She locked the door, turned out the foyer lights, and sat down on a small, armless antique chair by the door, daring herself to cry.

The next afternoon, she explored the path behind the school in the light and saw the source of her fright. It was a chicken pen. A small piece of her dress was a little blue flag flying from a twist of wire. The gate was open and none of the chickens were anywhere to be seen. Across the back of the pen was a coop made of wide boards like the kind she had seen on old sheds and barns. It had a half-roof, sloping toward her, with an eave that extended a couple of feet beyond the wall. The front wall itself was wood halfway up with chicken wire covering the rest, except for a half-wood, half-wire door at one end. It was well made, she concluded, a perfect merger of function and form.

"Like it?" Marvin said.

She turned to see him walking up the path toward her. She shivered even though it was a warm afternoon.

"Did you build this?" she asked.

"Yes, I did, Jennifer Ann," he said as he stopped five feet away.

She glared at him.

"Why do you keep saying my name like that? It's impertinent."

"Why?"

"I don't know. Just because it is, that's all."

"Because I'm a nigger and you're a white girl?" he said. He didn't know why he was suddenly so angry, but he was.

All the blood fled from her face.

"No! It's only . . ." she said as she stared into his hard eyes.

"Am I being too uppity?"

"Stop it!" she cried.

"Then what is it, Jennifer Ann?" he said, his voice soft and sinister, as he stepped up to her. She saw his nostrils flaring with each breath and could smell the sweet muskiness of his sweat. Her heart was beating so fast she felt that any minute it would burst right out of her chest. She stepped back, but she never took her eyes off his.

"I'm not prejudiced, you know," she said, straightening her shoulders.

"Lot of white folks don't think they are, but they are," he said.

"Well, I'm not one of them. I'm just not used to . . ."

"Talking to a black man your own age."

"Being around any black people at all."

"You know, at one time I would get lynched for doing this," he said. "Some crackers would come get me out of bed tonight and string me up with a rope from that old oak tree there and set me on fire."

"Please!"

"Hell, they might call their whole families to come and watch, little kids and all."

"Don't! I can't stand it!" she said in anguish as she dropped her head and began to cry.

She looks like a woman, but she cries like a girl, he thought. Marvin felt like scales had fallen off his eyes. He reached out to her. She felt the shock of his hand on her arm. The rough calQlouses scraped against her skin.

"I'm sorry," he said, "I won't say your name if it makes you uncomfortable."

She looked up at him. The call of cicadas rippled through the trees and a crow flew overhead, cawing four times. A gentle breeze rose to ruffle the browning leaves of the old oak just down the road, and a thrasher rustled its leaves on the ground. She sniffled and held her head up.

"No, it's OK," she said.

He dropped his hand and smiled at her. His white teeth and pink gums glared from between his dark lips. He turned toward the chicken coop.

"I built it out of some lumber I got from an old shed that used to sit back of the orchard," he said.

"It's looks well made," she said. Her eyes lingered on his mouth before she turned, too.

"Oh, I got something for you," he said. He reached in the pocket of his overalls and took out a folded sheaf of papers.

"What is it?"

He handed it to her. She unfolded it and saw written across the top of the first page in a steady hand, "The Dominique Chicken. By Marvin L. Lewis."

"It's a report I had to give in school." His face was beaming.

"Thanks . . . Marvin," she said.

The muted roar of a pickup truck caused them to turn toward Brownsboro Road. A new, black Ford was approaching them, careening wildly around the ruts in the old road. It skidded to a stop beside them.

"Well, lookee here!" a fairly handsome, clean-cut looking boy said, leaning out the passenger window. "You trying to teach that nigger to read? He'll sweat himself to death!"

He and the driver, another boy about his age, hooted.

Marvin said nothing. but Jennifer Ann could see his jaw tremble. She put her hands on her hips.

"Y'all just get on. This is none of your concern."

"My, my, don't she speak like a proper lady," the boy said, leering at her. A sliver of fear ran up Jennifer Ann's back when she realized he was drunk.

"I said, get on!"

"Yes, ma'am," he said with a tip of his baseball cap. "Drive on, Gabriel!"

The truck lurched forward and slung a rooster tail of dust and gravel into the air. When it settled, she looked at Marvin and laughed. It confused him until she held up his arm next to hers. They both were coated with a light patina of reddish-brown dust.

"Thanks for the paper . . . Marvin," she said.

Marvin nodded blankly, his mind addled by the touch of her hand on his. He wanted to kiss her brown lips.

In the distance, they heard the squeal of the truck's tires as it hit the pavement of Talking Spring Road a quarter-mile away. But the sound gave way to the loud roar of the engine and the flinging of gravel. They looked down the road to see the truck coming back toward them very fast.

"Damn," she said. "Marvin . . ."

Marvin was gone. She ran down the road the short distance to the school's garden, then up through the rows toward it before stopping and turning around. The truck skidded to a stop down below her.

"Where's that nigger boy?" the driver yelled at her. "Me and Taz want to talk to him."

"You leave him alone!" she shouted.

"Why, Gabe, I think she's sweet on that nigger," said Taz.

"Is that right? Are you a nigger lover?" Gabe said, his voice sweetly foreboding. Jennifer Ann scowled at them and walked away.

"Oh, come back, honey," Taz yelled. "I got something right here between my legs that will make you forget all about that nigger boy."

She never looked back, but their raucous laughter burned in her ears long after she heard the roar of the engine fade.

Jennifer Ann was more angry than she was afraid. She had never been so angry in her life, so in an act of defiance, she walked the old field road in the dark that night to Plum's house just like she had done the evening before. As she walked, she tasted bitter gall. She was angry at the boys for being so obnoxiously stupid. She was angry at them for spoiling her encounter with Marvin. She was angry at them for presuming that they were lovers. The whole idea was so . . . alien.

Lost as she was in emotion, she failed to see the hound until she was upon it. The huge dog barked at her menacingly from Plum's porch.

"Plum!" she yelled.

"Down, Judd!" he yelled as he came out the door. The dog quieted and lay down by the door. Plum took her arm and led her into the house. "He ain't dangerous."

"I thought you were keeping your dogs at your daddy's house," she said once she was safely inside.

"Well, I was, but Judd got into a little trouble. You remember that flock of wild guineas that live in the woods behind the house? Judd got ahold of one of them and killed it. Daddy said he's a suck-egg dog now, and he was going to put him down until I pitched a fit. He's a Walker hound. They're too pretty to kill. Were you really that scared? You're shivering."

"It's been a long day," she said, sighing deeply. "I brought us some sandwiches for supper since we've got to go to the reception in less than an hour."

"I hope you didn't burn them?" he said, grinning, but Jennifer Ann didn't smile. "What? I can't even tease you anymore?"

"Sorry," she said as her face relaxed into a small smile. "I'll set the table."

The reception for Representative Wallace in the old Hall's Corner High School gymnasium was the event of the season for the school, and for Hall's Corner as well. "Uncle Dave" as he was called, one of Hall's Corner's most famous residents, had been representing the county in the Georgia Legislature for nine years and was very popular, winning each election with over sixty percent of the vote. Upon first glance, he was not an imposing figure. He was very short and had a bony face that few would consider remotely handsome. When he shook Jennifer Ann's hand, she towered over him and thought he looked like a little rooster. But when he smiled, his whole face lit up, and she could not help but smile back.

"Hi, Jennifer Ann," he said, shaking her hand vigorously "You've grown into a fine young woman."

His voice rumbled like a bassoon. When he saw her look of confusion, he continued.

"I saw you when you were no more than ten, at a campaign rally in Brownsboro. You were with your aunt and uncle, Merlene and Joe Bunch," he said. "I was so sorry to hear of their passing."

"Yes," was all she could say.

"I look forward to hearing you play tonight. And you must be Imogene," Uncle Dave said as he shook her sister's hand. "I hear you're doing well here at the school. Well, hello, Plum. How's your mother?"

As the long line quickly moved on, Jennifer Ann felt like someone had turned on a lamp in the dark, then turned it off.

Uncle Dave was the county's primary conduit to the largess of the state treasury, and had, through friendship with the governors he served, been very effective in securing state funds for various county projects, so the audience included practically every person of any prominence in the county, their husbands or wives, and many of their children. Jennifer Ann had never performed before such a large group, but had given up early on playing any of the new pieces she was working on, so her rendition of an old favorite by Chopin was competent if not spectacular.

Afterwards, the school's headmaster, Dr. Julius Pinkus, Jr., gave a long introduction to Uncle Dave. His high-pitched monotone contrasted so sharply with the representative's basso profundo that Jennifer Ann couldn't help but smile. But despite Uncle Dave's powerful delivery, the events of the day kept leading her mind astray. The two boys in the pickup truck were simply being intolerable. She didn't think they were really more than talk, but she understood why Marvin didn't want to stay around to see. As her eyes wandered over the crowd, she suddenly gasped.

"Who are those two boys down on the end of the front row?" she whispered to Plum.

"Them? That's Uncle Dave's nephew Gabe on the right, and Taz Lumpkin, the sheriff's oldest boy. Why?"

"No reason," she said. "I was just curious."

"Neither one of them is worth a damn," Plum said, "and together they are always up to some kind of meanness. You stay away from them, Genie."

Genie, sitting on the opposite side of Plum from Jennifer Ann, smiled at him adoringly.

After Uncle Dave's speech ended, Jennifer Ann and Plum got separated when they each recognized friends in the crowd. It was more than a half-hour later, when people began to file out of the old gym, that she began to look for him and Genie. She asked a couple of girls from the school if they had seen her, and they said they had, but it was a while ago, so she walked around the gym until she concluded they were not present. Thinking that they must have gone outside, she left and began to walk toward the school, with the intention of sneaking over to Plum's house later, when she ran across Dr. Pinkus.

"Sir, did you see Marvin late this afternoon?" she asked.

"Yes, I believe he rode down to Keown's Junction. Why do you ask?" he replied.

"Oh, it's nothing really. I just wondered if we might use some of the corn stalks from the garden for decorations for the Halloween dance."

"That's a good idea, Jennifer Ann," he said. "I'm sure he'll put some by if you ask him."

"Have you seen Genie?"

"She and Plum came out ahead of me. I think I saw them go up toward the school."

"Thanks," she said.

xxxxxxxxxxxxxxxxxxxxxxxxx

She didn't see them outside the old house, nor were they in the foyer. She heard voices coming from the library, a small room off to the right, and went to ask whoever was inside if they had seen her sister and Plum. She didn't have to ask them. When she walked in the door, she saw Plum press Genie back against a table in the back and kiss her. Genie had her arms around his neck and her eyes closed.

"You bastard!" she shouted and stomped out of the room.

"Oh, God, Jenny!" Genie cried as she pushed Plum away.

"Shit! Jenny!" Plum shouted as he ran after her, but she had already gone upstairs. "Oh, fuck!"

He started up the stairs, but Genie grabbed his arm.

"You can't go up there," she said. She was crying. "I'll go."

Genie found the door to Jennifer Ann's small bedroom locked.

"Jenny," she cried. "I'm so sorry, Jenny. Oh, god, I'm so sorry."

"Go away, whore!" Jennifer Ann shouted through the door.

"Oh, no, Jenny! Please!" Genie cried, but there was no further reply. She slumped down beside the door and hugged her knees as she rocked back and forth in misery.

Jennifer Ann immediately regretted calling her sister a whore, even if her kissing Plum deserved such an epithet. When she saw them kiss, it did make her angry, but it was a hollow anger that she struggled unsuccessfully to turn into righteous indignation. She knew, then, that she had always known it was inevitable that she and Plum would part. It was even somehow fitting that he would turn to Genie. She was even sure, she had to admit, that they would probably be happy together.

"Damn," she said as she sat down in a chair and turned on the lamp on the table beside it. Marvin's report was right where she had left it, and she picked it up.

xxxxxxxxxxxxxxxxxxxxxxxxx

"The Dominique Chicken"
By Marvin L. Lewis

Dominiques are medium sized-chickens with heavy black and white feathers that form a tight, irregular pattern called "hawk coloring" or "barring." They have a distinctive comb called a "rose" comb because it looks something like the open petals of a flower. The wattles on their head and face are bright red. They are the oldest known breed in America, and were brought over to this country by the colonists. Early names for the Dominique were American Dominique, the blue-spotted hen, the hawk-colored hen, and, in New England, the Pilgrim Fowl and the Plymouth Rock. Sometimes they are also called "Dominikers" or "Domineckers." By the 1850s, they were the most popular breed of chicken in the United States and are called, "The Chicken of America."

The origin of the breed is a matter of dispute. They are known to have existed in Southern England in the 1700s, but some authorities believe they originated in France. In the early days of the American Colonies, there were not many of them since few farmers raised chickens due to the abundance of native game. But as cities in the East grew in population, they quickly became very popular because of their hardy ways.

Dominiques are very adaptable, and thrive both in pens and in the wild with little care. They are excellent foragers and can survive in very cold weather due to their thick feathers. They are called dual purpose chickens because they are steady layers and produce medium brown eggs with a rich flavor, and they also yield a quality meat good for frying, baking, and stews. Dominique cocks can weigh seven pounds, cockerels six, hens five, and pullets four. Their feathers were also used in pillows and featherbeds. Dominique hens tend to be calm, personable birds, which makes them desirable both as laying hens and family pets. They are also good mothers, and produce chicks that feather early and mature quickly. They survive in the wild very well due to their heavy feathers and protective coloring.

The popularity of the breed declined in the late 1800s due to the introduction of fancy Asian breeds and the rise in popularity of the Plymouth Rock as a separate line. Plymouth Rocks are larger than Dominiques, and they do not have a rose-like comb. Their coloring is also different. The feathers of Plymouth Rocks form distinct regular patterns of black and white, while the feathers of Dominiques form irregular patterns and have less contrast. This makes them appear not quite black but not quite white. In 1849, the breed was officially recognized in order to distinguish it from the Plymouth Rock

Today, Dominique chickens are thought by many to be nearing extinction, or already extinct, but I know of at least one flock that exists in Carter County. I hope the breed survives because dominiques are pretty birds, and they have many attractive qualities.

At the bottom of the last page was written, "B. Good effort, but needs sources."

xxxxxxxxxxxxxxxxxxxxxxxxxxxx

The next morning, Sunday, Jennifer Ann was expected to attend Sunday services in the chapel along with the students, but she was too worried about Marvin and snuck out of the building by the back stairs. As she walked the lawn down to the garden, she searched for him even though she knew it was his day off.

When she reached the chicken pen, she cried out in dismay. The front fence was torn from its boards and lying on the ground, and the chicken wire across the front of the coop was ripped open. A dead chicken was lying in the coop, and black and white feathers were everywhere. She immediately thought of the two boys in the pickup, but then she saw the tracks of a large dog. They were all over the little yard, and outside it in the road. She searched until she saw them go north up the road toward Plum's house.

"Judd," she growled.

Her first impulse was to go and confront him about the dog, but her feelings were too raw. Instead, she decided to ask Dr. Pinkus if he knew where Marvin lived.

She waited outside the chapel door behind some bushes to avoid seeing Genie, but her sister came out with Dr. Pinkus, so she had no choice but to reveal herself.

"Oh, Jenny, Jenny," Genie cried as she ran to hug her. "I'm so sorry. He lured me into the library, I swear."

When Jennifer Ann did not hug her back, but stood stiffly, looking off toward First Street, Genie began to sob and ran back into the school building. Dr. Pinkus looked after her with concern, but was not one to interfere in private matters.

"You were not at the service, Jennifer Ann," he scolded her.

"There was an emergency," she lied. "Do you know where Marvin lives?"

"Oh, poor child, there has been a terrible accident. If you had attended the service, you would know, because I made an announcement. Marvin was badly hurt in an automobile accident late last night on Livingston Road. He was on his way back from Keown's Junction when his car ran off the road and hit a tree. The state patrol said that from the skid marks it looked like someone ran him off the road."

"Where is he?" Jennifer Ann said frantically.

"Now there's no reason for you to get upset, Jennifer Ann."

"Where is he?"

"They probably took him to the Gradys in Atlanta," he said as Jennifer Ann turned and ran down the hill to her car. He shouted after her, "They don't expect him to live, Jennifer Ann. Where are you going?"

A little over an hour later, Jennifer Ann, trembling in fear and guilt, pulled into the parking lot at Grady Municipal Hospital in downtown Atlanta. When she asked about Marvin Lewis at the receptionists desk, the old woman behind the counter said she had no record of anyone in the hospital by that name.

"He's a Negro male, about twenty," Jennifer Ann said. "He was in a terrible car wreck."

"Then I am sure I would not know," the old woman said officiously. "He would be in the black section."

"How do I get there?" Jennifer Ann said in great agitation.

"Miss, I said he would be in the black section."

Jennifer Ann grabbed the arm of a passing doctor and asked him directions, then ran off down a hall toward the back of the hospital. An elderly black nurse in the section looked at her curiously, and asked her when he would have come in, then told her to wait. She walked over to a white nurse nearby.

"Miss Childers, do you know of any young black males admitted overnight?"

"No, baby, you know the rooms are all full," the nurse said dismissively.

"No one was admitted last night, Miss," she told Jennifer Ann. "We've got a waiting list. But he might have gone to Harris Memorial. It's on Hunter Street. It's a black hospital. I can give you directions."

"Thank you," Jennifer Ann said after the nurse had written down the directions on a sheet of paper and handed them to her. She turned to leave, but stopped and turned back.

"What's your name?"

"Lizbeth, miss," the nurse said, smiling.

"Thank you, Lizbeth."

Jennifer Ann followed the directions into Southwest Atlanta and was struck by how the city progressively changed, from the new to the old, from a preponderance of white faces to almost none. Black men and women and children, more than Jennifer Ann had seen in her life, even growing up in Macon, lined streets dotted with a cacophony of buildings and houses of various ages and states of repair. She saw an old black woman leaning in the doorframe of a weathered house that looked like even her slight frame might tip it over. She saw a young black man wearing a shiny three-piece suit emerge from a church, his hair slick with grease, and confidently walk down the street. She saw four black girls giggling and laughing as they jumped rope on the sidewalk, the skirts of their dresses flaring.

At an intersection, she stopped for the light and found herself surrounded by a dark sea of what seemed like hundreds of black men and women in either direction. The sounds of laughter and singing and shouting melded with the smells of barbecue and greens and burnt hair. She gripped the steering wheel tightly. A quartet of young black boys who were singing in sweet harmony suddenly stopped and looked at her. Then she noticed others stop and stare. Her heart raced, and when the light changed, the tires on her car barked as she went through the intersection. A few moments later, Jennifer Ann sat in the parking lot of Harris Memorial trembling and began scolding herself for it. But her heartbeat refused to entirely return to normal, and with a quick, deep breath, she got out of the car.

When a young black nurse inside the hospital told her that Marvin had been admitted last night, Jennifer Ann fidgeted with her car keys and could barely look the woman in the eye as she asked her for his room number and directions. By the time she stood before the door to his room, she was out of breath.

"God, don't let him be dead, don't let him be dead," she whispered, then opened the door.

Marvin was lying in a bed in a tiny room with his head heavily bandaged, and casts on his left arm and leg. Sitting by his bedside was a very dark young woman nearly her age, and standing nearby was an old couple.

"What are you doing here?" the young woman asked with open hostility. Jennifer Ann blanched.

"Quiet, Chanelle," the old man said sternly, then, his voice softer, said, "You're from the school, aren't you?"

"Is he going to be all right?" Jennifer Ann asked nervously.

"He's in a coma," the old man said. "He's been hurt pretty badly. In addition to breaking his arm and leg, he got a bad concussion and his brain's swelled. It took so long to get him here, the doctor said he may have suffered brain damage."

"Oh, God," Jennifer Ann said. Tears began to roll down her cheeks.

"Why would anyone want to hurt my boy like that?" the old woman wailed. The old man hugged her.

"Now, now, momma, you're going to upset the other patients. Let's take a walk outside for some air. Chanelle will come get us if there is any change. Now mind your manners, girl."

After the old couple left, the young woman glared at her but said nothing. Jennifer Ann walked to the side of the bed opposite her and stared down at the almost lifeless form. Marvin was laboring with each breath. She touched his hand.

"He let me read his paper on chickens," she said. When she looked at Chanelle with her eyes full of tears, the young woman's scowl softened, but only a little.

"I told him not to be messin' with no white girl," she said.

xxxxxxxxxxxxxxxxxxxxxxxx

For the next few weeks, Jennifer Ann numbly went about her duties at the school with concern for Marvin never far from her mind. She slept poorly and had little energy. When Genie worked up the courage to apologize again, she forgave her sister, but Genie wasn't sure she was sincere. And when Plum tried to explain himself, she simply told him coldly that it was over and walked away.

One wet, overcast Saturday morning, the last weekend of the month, she thought of the chickens for the first time and quickly walked down to the pen, her shoes sticking in the muck of the garden. It was as she had last seen it, and the chickens were missing. She cried then, deep, rasping sobs that drove her to her knees in the muddy path. But as her grief subsided, she heard a quiet clucking sound, then others. She jumped up and her eyes searched the brush and trees along the path. She found the flock roosting in a privet thicket across the road, not fifty feet from the pen. There were more big dog tracks in the mud of the path and into the edge of the thicket, but her heart leaped when she saw how many of the Domineckers there were scratching the ground underneath the bushes.

She walked back to the pen with a lighter heart. They really are a hardy breed, she thought, but she worried about how they would fare in the coming winter. She walked into the pen and pushed the fallen fence back up, but the nails of the top board had been pulled out of the post and it sagged back down to the ground. She tried again, and got a splinter in her finger.

"Ow!" she cried. She yanked it out, then stalked back through the garden to the equipment shed. The door was locked. She was thinking of putting on her work clothes and going across Livingston Road to the feed store to buy a hammer and some nails when she saw an old pickup truck come up the dirt path and stop in front of the pen. The old man from the hospital got out. He was carrying a carpenter's box. She ran down to him, losing a shoe twice in the garden mud.

"He came out of his coma a few days ago," he said as he put the box down.

"Is he going to be OK?" she said.

"Don't know yet. His mind seems to be working fine, but he don't remember a lot of things anymore. The doctor said it might be permanent."

"But he remembered the chickens, didn't he?"

The old man watched emotions flicker across her face.

"No," he said flatly. "He told me about them before. I just ain't had the time to come and check on them till now. Looks like some dog's been after them."

The old man took a hammer and a handful of nails from the box and stepped into the pen. He nailed the top board back up, and then tacked the chicken wire screen on the front of the coop back into place.

"It's going to have to be stronger. It's a big dog," she said.

The old man turned to her.

"A town ain't no place to raise chickens," he said stoically.

"There are some more old boards up by the equipment shed."

His mouth twisted into a wry smile.

"Then I guess we'll go get 'em," he said.

When they were finished, Jennifer Ann's dress was streaked with wet red mud and the color of her shoes and socks was no longer discernable. The labor left her tired, but it was a different tired from that which she had been feeling for weeks. It was a righteous tired, and as they stood admiring their improvements, she felt a sense of satisfaction. The pen was much sturdier, with both the chicken wire of the pen and the coop heavily reinforced with the old boards.

"How will you get them back in the pen?" she asked.

"Oh, they'll come if we give them a little feed. But I don't think even this will keep that dog out for long if he is as big as I think he is."

"It won't?"

"No. Like I said, a town ain't no place to raise chickens."

"Then maybe something's got to change," she said, her mouth set in a firm line. The old man just looked at her curiously.

xxxxxxxxxxxxxxxxxxxxxxxxx

```
MINUTES OF THE REGULAR MEETING
OF THE MAYOR AND COUNCIL OF HALL'S CORNER
October 7, 1957
```

<u>Present:</u> Mayor Julius Pinkus Jr., Aldermen Clayburn Jackson, J. P. Pennick, Sr., Abraham Norris, and Albert Norris, Police Chief Harold Dunning, Fire Chief Darby Elliot, and City Judge Victor Simms.

<u>Absent:</u> City Attorney James Elrod.

<u>Location:</u> Hall's Corner City Hall.

<u>Welcome:</u> Mayor Pinkus.

<u>Invocation:</u> The Rev. Billy Thomas of the First Baptist Church of Hall's Corner.

<u>Pledge of Allegiance:</u> The Royal Ambassadors of the First Baptist Church of Hall's Corner.

Mayor Pinkus made a motion that the minutes of the September 2 regular meeting be approved, seconded by Aldermen Norris and Norris. Motion was unanimously carried.

<u>Old business:</u> There was no old business to discuss.

<u>New business:</u>

City Judge Victor Simms requested $800 for improvements to his office and the courtroom, including new chairs and drapes. Mayor Pinkus made a motion to approve the expenditure, seconded by Aldermen Norris and Norris. Motion was unanimously carried.

Darby Elliot, Chief of the Hall's Corner Volunteer Fire Department, requested that the mayor and council purchase a used pumper tank from the Brownsboro Fire Department at a cost of $2,000. Mayor Pinkus made a motion to approve the purchase, seconded

by Councilman Pennick. Discussion followed.
The motion was tabled until an accurate
assessment of the condition of the tank
and pump could be determined. Mayor Pinkus
commended the Volunteer Fire Department.

Mayor Pinkus made a motion that the Mayor and
Council hire a city manager, seconded by
Councilman Jackson. Discussion followed.
Motion was tabled until the next meeting when
City Attorney Elrod could provide information
on how city ordinances would have to be
changed.

Jennifer Ann Butler, a teacher's aide at the
Chamblee School for Women, requested to speak
to the Mayor and Council about the problem
of dogs running loose in the city. Miss
Butler said that a large hound belonging to
Phillip Thompson, Jr., had recently killed
several chickens belonging to the school.
Mr. Thompson, who was in attendance, said
that there was no proof the chickens were
killed by his dog. He also said that his dog
was no longer being kept at his residence.
Mayor Pinkus reported that he had received
a number of similar complaints in recent
weeks. Councilman Jackson made a motion that
the City Attorney be requested to draw up a
proposed ordinance banning uncontrolled dogs
in the city limits for consideration at the
next meeting, seconded by Councilman Pennick.
Motion carried 3-1 with Councilmen Jackson,
Pennick, and Albert Norris voting yea, and
Councilman Abraham Norris voting nay. Mayor
Pinkus abstained.

There being no further business, the council
adjourned.

(s) Julius Pinkus, Jr., Mayor

(s) Hazel Smith, City Clerk

xxxxxxxxxxxxxxxxxxxxxxx

Jennifer Ann's car skidded and slipped in the gravel of Switchback Road even though she drove very slowly. The high ridges on one side of the road and the deep declines on the other unnerved her, so she was relieved when she pulled the car off the road into the dirt yard of the old shack.

Even though it was a cool day, there was little wind and the door to the shack stood open. Chanelle stood in the doorway surrounded by the warm smells of collards cooking.

"I came to see Marvin," Jennifer Ann said, defiantly meeting Chanelle's cold stare. The woman did not immediately answer.

"He's in the back," Chanelle said finally with a shrug of her shoulders, and led her through the small living room and kitchen into a small back porch converted into a bedroom. The old woman was standing by the stove stirring a large aluminum pot, and as they passed, said, "He don't remember much."

Jennifer Ann was in awe of the rooms. The swept floors and clean table tops and warm smells of wood burning and collards cooking contrasted sharply with the cardboard stapled to the walls.

The small porch room was chilly. She could see daylight through gaps in the boards. Marvin was sunk deep in a featherbed mattress suspended on the ropes of a wooden bed frame, all but his head covered with by a large thick quilt. There was a long, red scar from the crown of his head to his right ear. He was sleeping.

"Marvin, wake up. There is someone here to see you," Chanelle said, jostling his shoulder.

Marvin opened his eyes.

"Hi," he said to Jennifer Ann, breaking out in a broad smile. Two of his teeth were missing. "Who are you?"

Jennifer Ann's heart fell into her gut.

"I'm Jennifer Ann," she said softly. "I talked to you about the Domineckers behind the school."

"My name is Marvin," he said.

She looked at Chanelle, who stood in the doorway as if on guard, but the woman only shook her head and frowned.

"Will his memory come back?"

"Some, maybe, the doctor said, but he can't remember anything at all of the last six months."

"I talked to you about domineckers?" Marvin said, his brow furrowed. "They are a hardy breed."

With a gasp of dismay, Jennifer Ann put her hand over her mouth and fled the room. She stopped in the kitchen and shivered.

"Honey, you got to play the hand the Lord gave you. Don't waste your time wishing for another hand," the old woman said while stirring the pot. With a cry, Jennifer Ann ran out of the house.

As the sound of her car's tires spinning in the gravel reached the porch room, Marvin looked confused. Chanelle searched his face for any sign of recognition.

"You really don't remember her, do you?" she asked.

He closed his eyes and said nothing. When Chanelle had left the room, he shivered and pulled the quilt tighter around his neck.

XII. The Misadventures of Ted Jacuzzi

"Excuse me." The voice was raspy and low. Assistant Manager Ted Jaworski was standing in the Express Lane being teased by Sydney Cromer, the newest employee at Aub's Famous Foods, and didn't hear it. She had just asked him if he liked the new nametags and pulled hers out a little by lifting it with two fingers, her palm on her ample breast.

"Excuse me!" The voice was a harsh shout, but still barely loud enough to rise above the ambient noise of people pushing squeaky grocery carts, women dragging whining children, and the beep of the bar code scanners. Something bumped against Ted's leg and he yelped as he involuntarily jumped onto the conveyor. In spinning around, his foot brushed an old woman in a motorized chair on the shoulder.

"You don't hear very well, do you," the old woman said harshly as she pushed a lever on the chair arm and sped to the front crossing aisle of the store, then turned ninety degrees and disappeared behind the candy rack. Ted was left with his feet dangling over the edge of the conveyor, his face red, and his mind imprinted with the scathing look the old woman gave him as she passed.

"You've done it now," laughed Marvin Lewis as he squeegeed the front windows.

"What have I done, Marvin?" Ted squeaked.

"Don't you know who that was?" Sydney giggled. "That's Aub's mama."

"The owner? Oh, crap. I better go apologize."

"Uh uh," Marvin said as he wiped the squeegee blade with a cloth. "That won't do at all. Best just keep your mouth shut and hope she never realizes who you are."

Sydney nodded her head.

"Fact is, I think someone is calling for you in the meat department."

"Oh . . . oh!" Ted said as he jumped off the counter and disappeared down aisle five.

"I swear that's the dumbest smart boy I've ever seen," Marvin laughed. "And you better quit teasing him like that, Sydney. You're going to get yourself in trouble."

Sydney just laughed. She thought he was pretty cute for a dumb smart boy.

On the way to the back, Ted passed Ronnie Chavez, one of the stock boys, a lanky kid of sixteen who usually wore an air of supreme disinterestedness.

"Ronnie, put a sign on that Halloween stuff up front that says twenty percent off, and be sure to tell Sydney and Juanita about it. And straighten up the display. Kids have been in it."

"But I was dusting the cans," Ronnie said. "That's my job."

"One of your jobs, Ronnie," Ted said. "You can do this when you've finished."

"Right, dickhead," Ronnie whispered as he watched the assistant manager's back disappear into the meat department.

"And to what do I owe this pleasure, cousin Jacuzzi?" Bud Burns, the meat department manager, said, his hands caked in hamburger meat.

"I'm just looking for a place to hide temporarily," Ted said as he looked through the one way mirror than took up most of a wall.

"Wo ho, that's a good one! Wait'll Aub hears that his assistant manager, temporary assistant manager, is hiding in the back of the store like the stock boys."

"I kinda ran into Mrs. Folsom."

"I gotta hear this."

"It's nothing," Ted said in a loud whisper as a young couple stopped at the pork cooler. "She just ran into my leg in the Express Lane and I kinda kicked her in the shoulder when I jumped up on the conveyor getting out of her way."

Bud threw back his head in laughter and dropped a handful of hamburger on the tile floor. He bent to pick it up, looked at Ted, who was facing the window, and weighed it in his hand. When Ted turned to him, he threw it in the garbage can.

"Not a month on the job, and you're already in the shit with Mrs. Folsom. You're a walking train wreck."

"I didn't know who she was."

"Well, you do now. Listen, stay here and I'll go scout the coast," Bud said, still chuckling. He wiped his hands and went out through the swinging doors.

Ted took a deep breath, trying to lift the shroud of unreasoned fear that he suddenly realized had settled on him.

"Dammit, stop," he whispered. "Why do you have to do this?"

xxxxxxxxxxxxxxxxxxxxxxxxx

Mrs. Folsom, leaning forward as if trying to extricate her girth from the clamps of the arms of her chair, jerked the lever on the arm, banging the chair against the steps to the office, which was elevated three feet above the floor. Aub stuck his head over the side, and quickly stepped down the short stairway and opened the door part way.

"Mama, you're going to have to pull your chair back."

She huffed, and the chair jerked back a couple of feet.

"Are the receipts ready?" she asked.

"No, mama," Aub said, a little breathless. His jowls and stomach quivered. "It's only the fourth. I'll have everything for you tomorrow."

"The fourth? Are you sure?" she asked.

"Yes, mama. It's the fourth of November."

"I thought it was the fifth."

"No, it's the fourth."

"I thought it was the fifth," Mrs. Folsom grunted and turned her chair around.

"Mama, wait. I've been thinking about putting in a full section for women's cosmetics. I think they will sell pretty good, since there's not a drug store in nearly twenty miles except for Hall's Corner Drugs, and Gene Wilson doesn't have the space."

"I tried it once. Didn't sell," she said as she sped away without looking back.

Aub's mouth gaped open as he turned to step back up into the office. I'll tell her about the new assistant manager later, he thought.

"Juanita, I think they're going to need you on the registers," he said.

A plain woman of thirty-five with long brown hair, wearing a loose dress that came to her ankles and only occasionally fell against the thin body beneath, pushed past him out of the office, but not before he patted her on the butt.

"Mr. Folsom!" she yipped lowly, hunching her shoulders and blushing.

As Mrs. Folsom zoomed down the front aisle, Bud stepped back into the dog and cat food section and watched as she passed. She slowed as she neared the Express Lane, but there was a line, so she swerved around it and zipped in front of a line of customers, past register two and out the automatic door, her chair hitting the glass door with a loud crack. Outside, a thin, frail-looking woman helped guide her chair onto a lift and into a large blue van, then closed the door. The woman paused to look at the storefront, as if she was looking for something, then got into the driver's seat and drove away.

"Did she break it?" Bud laughed as he stepped out into the aisle and caught Sydney's eye, then sobered and lowered his voice when he noticed the line of customers.

Sydney shook her head, smiling, then pointed her finger at him. "You've got hamburger on your apron," she mouthed.

He mouthed back, "I know. Did Jacuzzi really kick her?"

Sydney nodded her head, which caused the white streaks of hair around her face to close partly over her eyes. She tipped her head back quickly and blew it out of her face, then winked at Bud when she saw him watching.

"She didn't, but one of these days she's gonna," Marvin said to himself, his voice drowned out by the squeaking of his squeegee on the front window.

"Bud! Find Ted and tell him to come to my office," Aub shouted from his perch.

Bud and Sydney burst into laughter. Sydney's customer, a fat woman holding one child in her arm and another by its wrist, looked confused, so she meekly said, "Sorry," and put her purchases in the cart.

Bud ducked his head to avoid the curious stares of the others in line, and scurried to the back. A few moments later, Ted emerged from the frozen foods aisle across from the office and knocked on the door. Aub told him to come in.

Aub was sitting in a large office chair with his round stomach pressed against a wide desk piled high with stacks of paper. Other stacks, and merchandise books lined the wall to his left and to his right was a small metal typing table devoted to a coffee maker and shakers of sugar and creamer, with a plastic bag of white styrofoam cups underneath. Scattered sugar crystals glittered on its surface around dried coffee drops. Ted took the only seat he could, a backless stool just to the right of the stairwell.

"Want some coffee?" Aub said without turning around.

"No, thanks."

"I'll be with you in just a minute."

Ted wiped his eyes with the back of his hand and took a deep breath.

"Ted, we might have to wait on putting in the cosmetics," Aub said abruptly as he spun the chair. "Mama doesn't think they'll sell."

Ted's shoulders tightened as he watched Aub's chins weave to a stop.

"Did you show her the marketing data?"

"No. Mama wouldn't understand it anyway. Said she tried it once and it didn't sell, that's all."

"But it will work, Aub. After the initial costs for displays and stocking the aisle are recovered, the profit margin will be the highest in the store."

"I know, I know, but mama gets these ideas in her head and there's no getting them out. You know she's only been swimming once in her life. Her uncle threw her in the swimming hole down at the old trestle when she was little and told her to swim or drown. He was just kidding, of course, but she went under like a rock. She was a skinny one in those days. Anyway, she's not been in the water since. She's just that way."

"But Aub . . ."

"I'm not sure if we can handle the up front costs right now anyway," Aub said as he turned back to his desk. "Maybe after the fall when things settle down."

Ted sat on the chair, his back against the wall, rubbing the back of one hand with the other. When he noticed, he slapped his hand softly and stood up.

"I understand. Just keep it in mind. I think it will draw new customers."

"Uh huh," Aub said as he heard Ted's footballs on the steps. When the office door closed, he slumped back in his chair and sighed.

xxxxxxxxxxxxxxxxxxxxxxx

By the middle of October, Ted had earned enough to move out of his parents' house into a two-bedroom trailer in the EZ Mobile Home Park in Hall's Corner. Although his rent was not very high, Ted really wanted to save the money. He knew he would need it in the spring, but after four years of college, he felt like a square peg in a round hole at home. To his mother and father, it was as if he had never left, while he lived in a universe that was so much larger and totally incomprehensible to them. He took occasional trips to Atlanta, just to reaffirm its existence, and he didn't look up any of his old high school friends because he was afraid that if he did he would somehow be sucked back in to his old life. It was only through his cousin Bud that he found the job at Aub's, and he took it because he knew that few of the customers would be from Hall's Corner since a national chain had opened up a supermarket just west of Brownsboro last year. When he did see people who knew him, he avoided them if possible, but when he couldn't, he always found some excuse to keep the conversation short. Still, he felt like his old life kept trying to ensnare him like the tentacles of an octopus.

"Ronnie!" he shouted, waking the stock boy in his makeshift bed atop boxes of paper towels in the back corner of the stock room. "I told you mark down the Halloween displays."

"Shit," Ronnie said as he scrambled to his feet and tried to get by Ted, who grabbed his arm. Ronnie cocked is fist as if to hit him and Ted turned him loose.

"You're fired. Get your stuff and leave," Ted said hotly. The stock boy smirked at him.

"No I ain't. You can't fire me," Ronnie said. He pushed Ted aside and went out of the stock room.

"What's all the commotion?" said Carl Thornborough, the produce manager, as first Ronnie and then Ted passed through his section.

"I caught Ronnie sleeping in the stock room again and I fired him," Ted said.

"Oh," Carl said and grinned. The produce manager was short and wiry, and in the time Ted had worked at Aub's his skin seemed to have tightened on his face like cowhide on a drum. When he grinned like he was now, Ted almost expected to hear his cheeks go thump thump.

Ted turned to leave, but Bud suddenly appeared from the back of the store.

"What? Somebody see Sophie?"

Carl scowled at him, drawing his skin even tighter.

"Man, I still can't believe that girl," he laughed, poking Carl in the ribs. "You know she caught him fooling around with Rachel Willingham, don't you? I woulda died if my old lady had screwed half of Hall's Corner just to get back at me, and then announced it publically like she did behind the Cozy Café. She even did it with Rachel's sister Grace Brady and her father Elwood. Nobody even knew that old man could still get it up. Hell, he can barely walk."

"She didn't do none of that," Carl groused. "She just said it to humiliate me. My daddy told me he didn't touch her."

"Not according to Rachel's husband Adam, and everybody knows Grace's gate swings both ways."

"They just had too much pride to admit it."

"So, is the divorce final yet?" Bud said.

"He fired Ronnie," Carl said.

"Shit, you didn't?" Bud said, looking to Ted as if he meant "Bless your heart."

"I caught him sleeping in the stock room again," Ted said, drawing his elbows to his sides.

"But don't you know . . ." Bud started, but Carl's stare hushed him.

"Don't know what?" Ted asked, his brows furrowing.

Ronnie came racing down the aisle and Ted yelled at him.

"Where are you going?"

"Back to work," he said without looking back. Carl and Bud began to laugh.

"What is it this time?" Ted said in dismay.

"He's Juanita's boy," Bud whispered as he gathered the three of them in a huddle.

"Bu . . . but he's a Chavez and her name's Jackson."

"She took her old name back after her husband Julio got killed," said Bud.

"He was a wetback," said Carl.

"I don't care if he was a Mexican, he was a hell of a mason," Bud said. "Her family hated him, though, and shunned her after they got married. When he died–he was killed when a wall fell on him while they were building the ICU at the Brownsboro hospital–Juanita had a baby and no place to go. But her family would only take her back if she changed her name back to Jackson."

"And some say the boy is Aub's."

"That don't make any sense, Carl. She was already pregnant when she came to work here," Bud said.

"Yeah, but do you ever wonder, Ted, why she spends so much time up in that office? They ain't going over the books, if you know what I mean. You've done it this time, Ted," Carl said, grinning from ear to ear. "You've really done it this time."

"But she's a Pentecostal!" Ted said hoarsely.

"Yeah, I bet she is a real holy roller," Carl smirked.

"Ted. Aub wants to see you in the office," Sydney said over the store PA.

"Shit, shit, shit," Ted groaned as he started up front, Carl's cackle burning his ears.

xxxxxxxxxxxxxxxxxxxxxxxx

Sydney Bates was just out of high school and had an unusual beauty. Any of her physical parts taken alone—her narrow eyes, thin nose, small mouth, pointy chin, long neck, or her plump breasts, narrow hips, and slender torso—were not of themselves very notable, but in combination the sum of them caught many men by surprise. Sydney knew it, too, and drank of their attention, even though most of Aub's customers were too old or too fat for it to be of much satisfaction.

"Hey, Sydney!" shouted Troy Latimer as he headed a column of five football players into Aub's on that Thursday after Halloween. "We've got an off week and coach asked me if I would come down and give these kids some tips before they get in the playoffs, so I thought I'd stop in. I heard you were working here."

Sydney's face glowed. She had dated Troy before he enrolled at a Division III school in Tennessee, where he had walked on as quarterback.

"How's it going?" Sydney said, as casually as possible.

"I made the team."

"That's great, Troy."

"Yeah. We run the same kind of wing-T coach runs, so he asked me if I would come down one day and show the boys a few things."

"Yeah, I guess we learned a little from the old man," grinned Josh Palmer, the current starting quarterback for the Wildcats. Troy grabbed him by the shoulders and shook him. "Hi . . . Hi, Sydney."

"Hi, Josh," Sydney said, smiling. "Hi, Floyd, Hi, Ben. Hi, Doug. Hi, Tracy."

"Hi, Sydney," the boys said as they gathered around her. Sydney beamed.

"Dori, can you watch my register?" Sydney asked, turning to a tall brunette on register three.

"Sure. Just let me lock up my cash drawer."

"Dori? Dori Cunningham?" Troy said with a chuckle. "You look like you swallowed a watermelon seed."

"It's Dori Ward, now," said Dori, smiling broadly as she patted her round stomach.

"You mean, you and Petey? Well, kiss my ass and call me Aunt Suzie."

"Troy, watch your language!" Sydney giggled as she led the boys outside onto the sidewalk. They circled around her, backing her up against the front window, and Sydney stood with one foot on the brick base. All the boys were grinning ear to ear and occasionally they would hoot with laughter.

"Is that Troy Latimer?" Ted asked Dori as he walked up to the register.

"The same. He's down here helping coach or something."

"Hmm," Ted said. He watched as Sydney wiggled her rear end between handmade posters festooned with turkeys and pumpkins and ghosts advertising specials on canola oil and bananas. The laughter grew louder and suddenly Troy grabbed her by the shoulders and she squealed, pushing him away. Sydney tried to escape the circle of boys, all laughing uproariously, but the boys locked arms and threw her back against the glass each time she tried.

"She's going to break that glass," Marvin said as he walked up, pushing a mop bucket.

"I guess you better go rescue her, Ted, before those hounds tear her apart," Dori smiled.

Ted stuck his head out the automatic door.

"Sydney, there's a line," he said, and the group's laughter died.

"Ted! Ted Jaworski," shouted Troy as he pushed his way out of the circle and shook Ted's hand. "Fellows, this is the guy who hit three three-pointers in a row in overtime to beat Athens Academy in the state semifinals."

"Wow," Doug Marshall said, and the rest murmured their assent.

Ted blushed at the attention, and was grateful that Troy didn't mention that the three buckets exceeded his season average by almost three points.

"We'd have won state if that forward from Sardis-Garrard-Alexander hadn't put up a prayer at the buzzer and had it answered," Troy said.

Ted was also glad that Troy didn't mention that it was he who was guarding that forward after his brother Paul fouled out, although there was really nothing he could do to stop the shot. The kid was going out of bounds and scooped it up over the backboard.

"Good to see you, Troy. How's your brother?"

"Oh, he ruptured his sternum against Appalachian, so he's done. Dallas was looking at him, too. They want him to come back next year as a graduate assistant, working with the quarterbacks."

"Sorry to hear it. Well, we've got to get back to work," Ted said, putting his hand on the back of Sydney's shoulder and guiding her through the automatic door.

"Bye, Sydney," the boys hollered and she waved at them over her shoulder.

Once inside, Sydney turned to him and winked. Her nipples made twin dents in her faded blue Aub's Famous Foods smock.

"Were you coming to rescue a damsel in distress?" she teased.

Ted glanced from her breasts to her face, and smiled weakly, blushed, and returned to the empty office; Aub was gone for the day. Ted stepped to the left side of the stairway to stare over the half-wall at Sydney. His groin tightened when she smiled back at him and dropped her customer's change. As she giggled an apology, punctuated with her hips, he readjusted the arrangement of elements in his crotch, leaning over slightly to do so. As her customer, a white-haired old man in a red acrylic jogging suit and black tennis shoes, walked away, she said something to Dori over her shoulder and Ted watched her skitter to the office door. His mouth was dry.

"Teddy Bear," she whispered as she reached the top of the steps. She pushed him back into the chair and stood over him. With a quick look around, she ducked down and straddled his waist. She pressed her body into his. He could feel each ridge and valley of her. Her blue eyes glittered. Her pink lips parted. She kissed him. He grunted. She giggled. "Thank you," she said softly. Then she was gone. Ted felt like he had just stuck a butter knife in a wall socket. He leaned back in the chair, groaned, and fell over into the floor.

For the rest of the day, the vivid visceral image of her lying on him kept rising up in his brain whenever he saw her, when he lay in bed that night trying to go to sleep, when he rubbed the bruise on his butt, or for no discernible reason at all. Sydney seemed to know it, too. When she saw him looking at her, she would toss her head and look away, but not before she cut her eyes at him and pursed her pink lips into a small smile.

"Go out with me," Ted blurted in a loud whisper when they were alone at the front of the store on Friday. She gasped in pretended shock, momentarily covering her mouth. Her eyes danced above her palm.

"You want to go out with *me*, Teddy Bear?" she said softly as her hand moved from her mouth to her heart.

"Yes," he said hoarsely. His palms were sweaty. His nostrils flared. His body clinched in rigid anticipation. A flash of guilt crossed her face. She frowned, her lower lip protruding and her eyebrows slanted downward as she cocked her head to one side.

"Oh, Teddy Bear, I wish I could, but I can't."

"But why?" He inwardly cringed at the touch of desperation in his voice.

"I just can't, Teddy Bear." She shrugged her shoulders and looked off. When her eyes came back to his face, they were sad. She touched his arm. "I want to. I just can't."

Ted felt as if he was trying to balance on a rope strung across a gorge of can't and want. His mind teetered and tottered as he looked down and gasped, his heart pounding in frustration. He nodded his head, and gave her a mechanical smile. He stared at her until she blushed self-consciously, then turned and walked away.

Ted kept his distance from her for the rest of the day. As he totaled up the receipts for October, he stopped to stretch, then lean on the half-wall like a sailor might lean on the rail when his ship was becalmed in a fog, with only the blinking of a distant lighthouse piercing the gloom. And when he could not avoid being close to her, Sydney looked at him with the innocent shyness of a child who had heard the words of forgiveness but doubted their sincerity. His heart hurt so he had to remember to breathe.

Such intense pain could not be long endured, and Ted admonished himself angrily for his suffering with scores of rationalizations. What he felt was mere infatuation. They weren't really compatible. She didn't really like him or she would have gone out with him anyway. While none of them rang true, collectively they reduced the pain until it throbbed like a bruise after the purple has begun to fade. "You are a fool when it comes to women," he told himself. "Grow a spine!"

And he did, although he felt it was a crooked, malformed thing the next night when Mandy, Bud's wife, and her sister Debbie, both of whom he had dated in high school and had dumped him back to back, came barging into his trailer in cocktail dresses and three sheets to the wind.

"Surprise!" Debbie shouted as she came in the door wearing a tight-fitting strapless red dress that went from almost to barely enough. Her long hair was bleached platinum. In her wake was Mandy, in a little black number that looked like it had shrunk in the wash. He couldn't help but stare.

"Same old Ted," Debbie said with a big grin.

"Hi, Ted," Mandy said as she brushed past him, leaving both the door and his mouth open. He shut them.

"Got anything to drink in this dump? Just teasing. I've got some wine in the car if you don't."

He could tell right away she was drunk, and maybe Mandy, too.

"I . . . I have some beer," Ted said. "I didn't know you were in town."

"Just in for the weekend, to see my sis. Her old man's on some trip, so we are just out having a good time. When the cat's away and all that. Is it in the fridge?"

"Huh? Yeah. Help yourself."

As he watched her hips sway saucily as she walked to the fridge, he felt like a mouse in a cage with two snakes.

"Want one, sis? How about you, Ted?"

He was struck dumb when she bent over to get three beers out of the refrigerator. He knew the snakes were hungry. His body quickly launched a major assault on his mind, scattering his thoughts in all directions. "Is this for real?" was fighting valiantly to hold the right flank, but "What the hell are these two bitches up to now?" was crumbling on the left. The middle of "What am I going to do if they try to do what I think they are going to try to do?" was faltering in the breach.

Debbie turned the music up on the stereo and leaned back against it. Her eyes closed, she began sway in time with the beat while she took a drink. The skirt of her dress threatened to disprove Zeno's Paradox.

"Got any pot, Teddie Bear?" she asked.

When he said, "No," she produced a joint.

"I don't think . . ." the right flank started, but Debbie advanced on it stealthily like a cat until she was directly under him and said smoothly, "Me neither" and stuck the joint in his mouth.

"Like my dress?" she said, wiggling her hips. It was a diversionary tactic designed to draw his eyes away from her face and down her body.

"Yes," he said as he inhaled. The right began to falter under a two-pronged attack. All seemed lost when she pulled him down beside her on the couch so close their hips touched. Mandy snuggled up beside him in a pincer movement, and Debbie pressed her breast against his arm. The middle was about to give way, but when he looked at Mandy, something in her eyes told him her morale was low. Suddenly the right rallied and began to drive the enemy back enough for him to withdraw and form a new line. He stood up.

"I just graduated with a B.S. in engineering and I'm working at Aub's until I can go to graduate school. Bud's one of my department managers," he said in a rush. Debbie brought in the heavy guns: her skirt now clearly disproved Zeno's theory. Having established that position, she advanced until her line met his in a full frontal assault. She pressed her crotch against his, then threw her arms around his neck and kissed him. But he could see Mandy's forces were wavering, and when Debbie asked him, "Want to do us both, Ted?" the tide suddenly turned.

"Debbie!" she cried as she got up. She pulled her sister away from him. "What the hell are you doing?"

"I just thought Ted might like a little fun," Debbie pouted, then looked over her shoulder. "So what do you say, Teddy Bear? Want a threesome?"

"You might have asked me first," Mandy said hotly, yanking her back around to face her.

Ted could only watch as his opponents turned on each other. The right and left flanks quickly closed to cover the wavering middle of the line.

"I just figured that since you hadn't had any in so long . . ."

Mandy slapped her hard across the cheek.

"Get off me!" Debbie cried, clutching her cheek, as she pushed her away. "What's the matter? You gone frigid or something?"

Mandy raised her hand. Ted's right flank flew into the breach and he caught her wrist.

"Both of you cool it," he commanded, surprising both of them and turning them to rout. He took Debbie's wrist in his other hand and led them to the door. "I don't know what kind of game you two are playing, but you better work this out somewhere else."

And just like that he pushed them out and closed the door behind them. But the battle wasn't over until he drank himself into oblivion.

He woke up the next morning groggy. Later that day, just before close, he was further shocked when from his office perch he saw Debbie come blowing into the store like a Siberian Express and go straight back to the meat department. Soon, Bud came out and stalked out of the store without a word. Debbie followed in his wake until she stopped to talk with Carl. Ted ducked behind the wall when they both turned in his direction. He thought he heard them laugh, but when he looked back over the wall, Debbie was gone and Carl was animatedly telling something to Dori and Juanita, both of whom were blushing.

Monday was his off day and he never left his trailer, dreading Tuesday morning. He just kept imagining that everyone, employees and customers, would burst out laughing the moment he entered the store when Bud began beating him senseless. But as with many such expectations of doom, reality proved to be different. When he tried to talk to Bud, his cousin just scowled and turned his back, When he walked back to the front of the store, he realized that everyone up front had watched. Sydney was giggling as was Dori, Juanita was blushing, and Aub grinning. Marvin said, "Uh uh" as he passed and shook his head while he cleaned up a spill.

"Ted, you got to be as dumb as a box of rocks," Carl said later when their paths crossed in the stockroom. "I know what I would have done."

Ronnie laughed at him derisively from his throne of toilet paper.

Ted was glad he had to spend most of the day in the office getting a final tally on the month's receipts. When he was done, he carefully lay back in the chair and closed his eyes, but could not rest. With a grunt, he walked out of the office to mark off the counts on a late delivery, and when he finished, he took the long way back to the office through the dairy section to avoid Carl.

"Did you hear Bud threw her out?" It was Sydney. She was just around the office corner, past the short health and beauty aides aisle, in the Express Lane.

"His wife?" Dori said.

"Yeah. His sister-in-law or something told him she walked in her house on Sunday and found her with some man, you know, in a compromising position."

Dori gasped. Ted slipped into the aisle and a new world.

"I heard they had a huge fight," Juanita said.

"Man, did they," Sydney said. "And she was so drunk that when she got in her car, she drove it right into the garage door."

"That's where he kept his model trains!" Dori gasped.

"No shit?" Sydney cried, then lowered her voice. "No shit?"

"Yeah. You know how Bud's always wanting us to come over and see his setup. Well, he told me it took up the whole garage."

Juanita and Sydney laughed, but concern creased Dori's face.

"Where'd she go? I knew her, you know. She used to be a friend of my sister Lori. She was Mandy Cochran. That was her sister Debbie who came in here Sunday right before Bud left."

"I remember her! She was a senior when I was a freshman," Sydney said. "I heard all kinds of stories about her that year. She was a real wild child."

"Mama said she stayed at her parents' house Sunday night," Juanita said. "But she left yesterday evening for Atlanta."

"I wonder what made her do it," Dori said. "They had just bought a new house."

"Well, enough of that," Sydney peeped. "Let me tell you the latest on me and you-know-who. My parents went to see my grandpa and grandma over the weekend. We had the whole house to ourselves. So, you know what we did?

"What?" said Juanita in a hushed voice.

"We did it in every room!"

"You didn't!"

"Yup, even the bathroom. But you know what's so funny? He slipped in the shower and his knee broke through the wall. You can see all the way into the kitchen. Man, what a time I had explaining that when my parents got home!"

Ted angrily stepped back to the office and let the slam of its door silence their laughter. He would be leaving soon, he thought. Less than two months, but when he thought of graduate school, it only tangled up his mind with emotions. He had yet to find a place in Atlanta and he knew he was procrastinating. He had yet to turn in his notice on his trailer in Hall's Corner, too, and had even let Aub continue to nurture the hope that he would become the permanent assistant manager. It was not that he was happy here; far from it. He was in an impossible situation. All the employees knew that if they didn't like what he told them, they could go to Aub and he would try to please them just like he tried to please Ted,. And now he felt more powerless than ever since one of his department managers, and his cousin to boot, wouldn't speak to him, and the other, Carl, would, he knew, from now on would never miss a chance to rib him about Mandy and Debbie. And now he knew that even when Sydney was kissing him that day in the office, she was screwing someone else. Despite his resolve, the tentacles of his old life had ensnared him.

Over the office wall, he heard the rhythmic squeak of the mop bucket stop. "Pity the fool," Marvin said, imitating Mr. T. "Pity the fool." The squeaking resumed, only to fade away like the call of geese merging with Southern sky.

By Thanksgiving, the tentacles were crushing him so tightly he could barely breathe. The lights of the store seemed dimmer each day, and the riot of colors along the aisles and on the handmade posters seemed dull and lackluster. Bud soon got over his mad, but Ted could only shrug when his cousin tentatively tried to be civil. Carl's constant jibes played out like songs on a radio turned down low in a back room. Ronnie walked past him in a dream. He tried to be convincingly friendly when Dori or Juanita or especially Aub greeted him, but he was not sure he carried it off. And when Sydney looked at him shyly in concern, he smiled broadly even though it galled him. A deep loneliness congealed in the pit of his stomach and he carried it through the day and then on his way home, until he could finally lock it behind his trailer door.

As the days grew shorter, the warm days of early November lingered. They would hold in abeyance the damp cold of the Georgia winter for another two weeks, until it settled over everything in thick, gray clouds from horizon to horizon.

"Everyone please come to the front," Aub said over the loudspeaker. "We have an important announcement."

It was late on the day before Thanksgiving and the store was to close in five minutes, at five o'clock, so everyone working could go home to their families. All day the store was packed with people buying up the last of the pecans, frozen pie shells, pumpkin pie mix, paper plates and cups and plastic sporks, but by 4:55 only a couple of customers remained.

Ted was meandering through the store like an inspector. He moved a can of pinto beans to line it up with its companions, and straightened up a section of barbecue potato chips. He found a candy bar in the aisle and put it back on the shelf. He was watching the clock, longing just to get outside. Two more weeks, he thought. Just two more weeks.

When he heard Aub's announcement, he slowly made his way to the front. He rounded the corner of the dog and cat food aisle, and saw the other employees gathered in a bunch like a herd dog had driven them there. Aub was standing in front of them, and Carl and Sydney were standing beside him, holding hands. Ted gulped.

"Everyone. Is everyone here. Ted? Oh, there you are. OK. Carl and Sydney have an important announcement."

The group's murmur of expectation echoed off the stone in Ted's stomach. On Carl's face, triumph was almost succeeding in disguising uncertainty, while Sydney squirmed like a child about to ride the Ferris wheel.

"Ah, we're a . . ." Carl said.

"We're engaged! We're getting married!"

Sydney held up a diamond ring, and Dori and Juanita descended on it. Carl stepped back, his brow furrowed in pique until he saw Ted and look-what-I-did bloomed on his face. He stepped up to his intended and took her waist firmly in one hand while shaking Bud's with the other. Aub patted Carl on the back.

"Pity the child," Marvin said softly as he walked past Ted to join the fray of celebration.

Ted saw the future run before him like cow paths disappearing into the wilderness. He was standing in a muddy slough at a point where they converged and diverged.

"So, Ted, have you given any more thought to staying on permanently?" Aub said, suddenly appearing before him in front of register two.

"What?" Ted said, still on the edge of the wilderness.

"Staying on," Aub laughed, then lowered his voice into a conspiracy. "Surprised me, too. That Carl is a slick one. While everyone was thinking that wife of his had ruined him for good, he was tapping a new keg. And look at her."

Ted did. She was a path that disappeared over a slick hill of rutted mud. The path waved at him with the tips of its fingers and smiled from between the privet and sweet gum and blackberry vines. He waved back. Carl saw them look at each other and stepped between them.

"Well, what do you say, now, Jacuzzi?" he crowed.

He shook Ted's hand like he was untangling a rope.

"You know, I had a cousin once who couldn't go to sleep at night for nothing," Marvin said as he walked up.

They three men turned to him in curiosity.

"The minute he crawled into bed, his leg felt like it was burning. He said it was like it was on fire. He tried creams, lotions, went to doctors and tried a bunch of pills, and two chiropractors. He even got acupuncture. None of it worked."

"So, how did he ever get to sleep?" Carl asked.

"He set fire to the other leg."

XIII. November 4, 1998

The puppy was yelping, like it was afraid, and she could never bear to see an animal suffer. She ran out the back door of the house into a cold, low fog and gathered her robe tightly around her. The path to the barn was wide and old, but dark and overgrown, and she felt the wet branches of unkempt privet lash her face and arms as she ran. The puppy began to howl, a mournful, guttural sound that ran up and down her spine.

When she reached the barn, she ran into the hall and stumbled into a round bale of hay, which almost knocked her over. She blindly sought support to keep from falling and felt the large tires of the tractor. She was gasping for breath. She steadied herself on the wheel. The puppy cried out from beyond the light of a three-quarter moon that filled the opening before her. She realized that when she entered the barn, there had been no moon, but she had no time to think of it. She plunged into the light and gasped in fear. She was standing near the edge of a large, ragged-edged erosion ditch that split an old cotton field in full bloom, covering it in brown stalks and white cotton balls bursting from their hulls. The plants tore at her clothes as she fought her way to the ravine and the puppy, whimpering now. The poor thing, with bony ribs and the wet eyes of disease, was clinging to the rim with tiny claws, only its head and chest visible. She could not see bottom of the ditch until farther on, and knew the puppy would die from the fall. It was so weak and pitiful she wondered if the merciful thing to do would be to let it go. It would be an easy thing to do. But she couldn't, and fought against the rough stems and branches and hulls of the cotton plants to reach it. She must save it. But the plants grew larger until they closed over her head, blocking out the moon, and she cried in anguish to free herself from them.

"Lois! Is breakfast ready yet?"

The hard, dry voice snatched her awake. She found herself pressed tightly against Aub's wide naked back, and eased away from him and out from under the covers. The old house was chill and she shivered as she searched for her robe.

"It's five a.m., Aldora," she said in a loud whisper.

"Lois! Is breakfast ready yet?"

Lois hurriedly walked out of the room and almost ran over Mrs. Folsom, whose electric wheel chair was parked in the middle of the hallway. The fat folds of the old woman's body were quivering as she scowled at her.

"You don't hear well, do you girl?" she said, her eyes squinting and her lips pursed tight.

"It's five a.m., Aldora. Aub doesn't have to get up for another hour," Lois said.

"I want bacon, but we don't have any."

"Yes, we do, Aldora. Aub brought some home yesterday. It's in the refrigerator. It's the thick sliced kind you like. He has Bud make it up special."

"I didn't see it in the refrigerator."

"It's there, Aldora."

"I didn't see it."

"You're going to have to move your chair. You're blocking the hallway."

"Well, all you had to do was ask," the old woman said, her voice suddenly shrill. She jerked the lever on the chair's arm back hard and the chair slammed against the wall, knocking a small hole in the wallpaper. Oblivious to the damage, the old woman turned the chair around abruptly and scooted down what remained of the house's original dogtrot, now narrowed by a closet in the middle and closed-off by a bathroom at the back, and into the kitchen.

"Turn off your chair," Lois said as she entered the room. "You've only got three red lights left."

"It was on charge all night. The battery must be bad. I told Aub he needed to get me a new one."

"The cord is unplugged."

"What?"

"The cord is unplugged where it goes into the chair."

"Why do these things keep happening to me?" Aldora cried. It was the low wail of a child and tears suddenly filled her eyes.

"It's all right, Aldora. Cut off your chair."

"Oh," she sniffled.

"Here, take your pills. What do you want to drink with them? We've got milk or orange juice."

"OK."

"Well, which is it?"

"Juice."

Lois took a carton from the refrigerator and filled a small glass.

"Pull your chair up to the table, Aldora."

The old woman stabbed at the buttons on the arm of her chair with her stubby finger until she found the right one, then ran the chair into the table, spilling the juice.

"Now turn your chair off," Lois said as she wiped up the mess.

She took the carafe from a coffee maker on the counter and filled it, then cleaned the filter and scooped fresh grounds into it. Before she put the filter back, she put it up to her nose and inhaled deeply.

"I don't want any coffee."

"I know, Aldora."

"My daddy tried to feed me coffee when I was a little girl. He would dip a biscuit in it and put it in my mouth. I would spit it out every time. He finally gave up."

Lois turned on the oven to preheat, and put eight slices of bacon in a baking pan lined with tin foil. She took out a covered bowl of flour from beneath the counter and scooped out a cup into a smaller, plastic bowl. When she went to the refrigerator to get the milk, she noticed Aldora had fallen asleep with her head leaning far over to one side. She had not taken her pills. Yawning, she rolled out four biscuits while the bacon sizzled in the oven. When it was done, she replaced it with a pan holding the biscuits all bunched up at one end, then sat down to drink her coffee. When they were done, she turned the oven down on "warm" and put the bacon back in.

She thought about going ahead and cooking the eggs, but it was only 5:35. They would be dry and tough by 6. That gave her fifteen minutes to sit at the table and drink her second cup of coffee. She closed her eyes and sniffed as she took a sip while she waited. The liquid was so hot it almost burned her lips. It was perfect, as the moment was perfect since no one was awake but her. Even the old house was asleep. She dropped her head and rested.

When Aub came into the kitchen twenty-five minutes later, he walked past the sleeping woman softly, kissed Lois on the cheek, and poured a cup of coffee before sitting down beside her, his rear end spilling over the sides of the yellow plastic kitchen chair.

"Good morning. How long have you been up?" he whispered.

"She got me up at five," she whispered back. "I think she's constipated. She was up and down four or five times during the night."

"Uh uh," he said as he shook his head. He took two eggs, four strips of bacon, and two biscuits from bowls in front of him and put them on his plate. She watched as he ate.

"How is the new assistant manager working out?"

"Ted Jaworski? He's fine. He's a sharp boy. I wish he would stay, but he's got his head set on going to graduate school in January."

"Have you told her about him yet?"

"Mama. Nah, she wouldn't understand."

"It's been two months."

"I know, but I figure that since I've waited this long, he'll probably be gone before she notices."

He said it with a grin and a shrug. Her eyes softened.

"Jacuzzi's, eh, Jaworski . . . now the guys have got me saying it . . . has got some good ideas. What do you think about half an aisle just for women's cosmetics and beauty aides?"

"Hmmm. You could relocate the automotive stuff and picnic supplies to the drinks aisle now that the distributor is taking up so much space with the displays up front."

"Right. Just what I was thinking. Ted did this market analysis–nothing fancy, it was just from the census and the Extension Service County Guide–and he said it looked like it could be a real profit maker. "

"It makes sense. Keown's Junction is growing, and the closest drug store is Gene Wilson's place in Hall's Corner. With that old soda fountain, he barely has room for a tube of lipstick in that place."

"But his daddy made a mean orange cream soda."

"Yes, he did," she smiled. "Seems like I remember sharing one with this handsome young boy just out of the army one time."

"Swept you off your feet, did he?"

"Ummm hmmm."

"Is breakfast ready yet?"

"Yes, Aldora," Lois said as she got up and patted her husband's shoulder. She stepped around the table to fix the woman a plate of one egg, three strips of bacon, and a half-grapefruit.

"This is not that store bought-bacon, is it?"

"No, Mama. I had Bud slice it thick just for you," Aub said.

"I don't like that store-bought bacon."

"I'll see you this evening," Aub said as he stood up from the table.

"We will come by to pick up the receipts."

"It's the fourth, mama," he said. He leaned over to kiss the old woman's cheek. "The receipts won't be ready until tomorrow."

"I thought it was the fifth."

Aub waved to Lois as he went out the back door, and she waved back before starting to clean the table. She scraped the scant leavings on Aub's plate into the garbage disposal even though it didn't need it. She slowly chewed the last strip of bacon, then looked at the remaining biscuit and egg a moment before she dumped it all into the disposal.

"You trying to lose weight?" Aldora said as she picked at her food.

"No. It's just all that fat and cholesterol."

"You're skinny as a rail now."

"Don't forget your pills, Aldora," Lois said. She sat down and ate the other half of the grapefruit.

As Aldora finished eating, Lois put the dishes and pans in the dishwasher, but didn't turn it on. She wiped down the stove and counter top, then went into the bedroom to make the bed. She was in the living room vacuuming the floor when Aldora entered.

"You forgot my doctor's appointment," the old woman snarled.

"No, Aldora. It's at eleven."

"They called yesterday and said it was at nine."

"It's at eleven. Are you ready?"

"I've got to go to the bathroom. My bowels haven't moved in a week. Where's the hemorrhoid cream?"

"On the sink. Try not to strain so much, Aldora."

Lois had just finished vacuuming the carpet when she heard Aldora scream.

"Lois! Bring me a diaper!"

When Lois entered the bathroom, the old woman was standing between her chair and the commode crying, holding her skirt up. Her diaper lay on the floor. The commode lid was smeared with her gray feces, as was the seat of her chair.

"I couldn't make it," she said hysterically.

"It's all right, Aldora. You just had an accident."

Lois wet a washcloth and handed it to her, then took another and wiped the seat of the chair.

"Now here's a fresh diaper. You'll have to sit down on the chair."

When Aldora sat down, Lois backed the chair up, then cleaned the toilet seat while the old woman struggled to get the diaper on over her heavy thighs. Her skin crawled when she looked into the basin. She quickly flushed the commode and rinsed out the washcloths, then washed her hands twice with hot water and soap.

"We'll ask the doctor today about your bowel movements," Lois said as she turned to leave the room.

"There's nothing wrong with my bowels," Aldora said.

"We'll be leaving in fifteen minutes."

As Lois drove the blue van from Keown's Junction to Hall's Corner, Aldora intently watched the green rolling pastures and hardwood forests pass.

"My Aunt Charlie lives out there," she said as they passed a two-lane blacktop on the right marked by a sign that said "Talking Spring 3 miles." "Her name is Charlotte, but when I was little, I couldn't say Charlotte. I said Charlie, and it stuck. She said if I stopped by, she would give me some of her pear preserves. She said she made a hundred pints this year."

Lois thought of the dining room cabinet and closet filled with jars of preserves, jellies, soup mix, green beans, and pickled cucumbers, green tomatoes, squash and peppers.

"We can stop on the way back."

"When we get home, we've got to cut the okra," Aldora said. "If we don't cut it, it will get too hard."

"The okra's gone, Aldora. It's November."

"It didn't grow this year like it did last year."

"You put up twenty quarts in the freezer, and made two dozen quarts of soup mix."

"You did. I just watched. If it had not been for you, I wouldn't have put up anything this year."

"You helped prepare everything."

"I had a garden when Daddy and I lived in Talking Spring before he died. I broke the ground with a hoe. It was the prettiest thing. It didn't have a weed in it. Daddy said, 'Mama, that's a good garden.' This gal from the newspaper came out and took my picture. When they ran it in the paper, it said, 'One old woman with a hoe.' I don't know why they said that. I'm not old."

They rode on in silence until they reached Hall's Corner and turned off onto a narrow asphalt lane named First Street, then into the driveway of an old house with a sign out front that read, "Albert J. Jenkins, M. D. General Practitioner."

After Lois signed her in, they sat in the waiting room.

"Get me a magazine," Aldora said.

"You might like this," Lois said as she handed her an old worn issue of Southern Living. While Aldora thumbed through the magazine, Lois watched the television hanging on the wall. The sound was down so low she couldn't hear, but she just watched the images pass of a police chase and a flood and cars stuck in an early blizzard interspersed with images of immaculately dressed men and women talking to her.

"Mrs. Folsom?" the nurse's aide called, standing in the doorway to the back of the office.

"Yes," Aldora said.

"You can come back now."

"It's about time."

The clock read 11:45.

"Let's get your weight."

Lois and the nurse, whose name tag said "Eloise," helped Aldora up on the scale.

"Three twenty-five," the nurse's aide said as she wrote it down on a clipboard.

"You've lost five pounds," said Lois.

Eloise led them to an examination room and Lois slowly backed Aldora's chair inside.

"I need to get your blood pressure," Eloise said as she wrapped an inflatable band around the old woman's arm. She had to tug it to get it far enough for the velcro to hold.

"One-fifty over ninety," she said as she wrote the number down on the clipboard, then put it on the counter. Lois watched her face for any sign of judgment, but there was none.

"I think it's up a little, Aldora," she said as Eloise left, closing the door behind her.

"I hope we don't have to wait long like we did last time," Aldora said, squirming a little in the seat. "My hemorrhoids are hurting."

The air of the white-walled examination room was warm and soon grew close. Lois felt herself begin to nod off, and shook her head. The steel blue plastic clock on the wall with a drug company logo behind its hands said ten minutes had passed.

"I wish I had a cup of coffee, or tea," she said out loud.

"I don't like coffee. My daddy tried to feed me coffee when I was a little girl. He would dip a biscuit in it and put it in my mouth. I would spit it out every time. He finally gave up."

"Maybe the doctor will be here soon."

But the clock seemed to be in no hurry and the minutes multiplied. Aldora squirmed in her chair.

"You forgot my hemorrhoid creme," Aldora said as she glared at Lois.

"You put some on before we left," she said drowsily.

The clock said 12:15.

Outside the door, she heard the muffled voices of Albert Jenkins and Eloise, then the clack of a door closing.

"Maybe the doctor will be here soon," she said.

"I went to school with his brother Edward," Aldora said. "He's got three brothers. All of them are doctors. He used to throw bugs at me and pull my hair. I wore it in pigtails."

"I wore mine that way when I was a girl, too," Lois said. "My hair was long, so they came down below my shoulders."

"He was a handsome rascal. I might have married him, but he went away to college. That's when I met Aubrey. We only dated a month, then we got married. We'll be married sixty-four years in April."

"Hi, Mrs. Folsom. How are you feeling today," Dr. Jenkins said as he entered the room.

"We've been waiting too long," Aldora groused.

"Her hemorrhoids are hurting her," said Lois.

"Have you been using the creme I recommended?" he said as he listened to her heartbeat through a stethoscope.

"Yes, but it ain't working," Aldora said.

"Then I'll write you a prescription before you leave. Now what did you want to see me about today?"

Aldora stared off into space with knitted brows.

"She's constipated a lot and she's been forgetting things more and more," said Lois.

"How's your diet going? I see you've lost a little weight," he said as he began filling out a pink preprinted sheet on the clipboard. "Your blood pressure is still high, though. We've got to get that down. Have you been taking your medications?"

"Yes," Aldora said.

He took Aldora's hand in his.

"How's your circulation? Your hands are cold."

"She says her feet get numb sometimes," Lois said.

He released her hand and turned back to the form.

"Well, just keep taking your medications. It's important. Get her a stool softener for her constipation. I want to see you again in a month. But if you have any problems in the meantime, just call and get an appointment."

He got up to leave, but then stopped.

"Oh, I've got to write you a couple of prescriptions," he said as he sat back down. He filled out one for a suppository.

"Now what was the other thing?" he said, his brow furrowed.

Aldora couldn't say.

"Her memory," said Lois.

"Oh, yeah," he laughed and wrote out a second prescription. "Take this once a day. When you come back in a month, I'll increase the dose. I like to start patients off slowly on this, but it is much more effective at a higher dose."

At the check-out desk, the medical assistant, whose name tag read, "Vicky," said, "He wants to see you in a month. That will be $10."

Aldora fished her credit card out of her purse and handed it to Vicky, who took it and processed the charge, then handed it back to Lois with a copy of the pink form and an appointment card.

"Put these in your purse."

Lois loaded Aldora and her chair in the van, then turned south out of the doctor's driveway onto First Street. But instead of following it back to Highway 94, she turned left down Talking Spring Road.

"Where are we going?" Aldora said.

"To see your Aunt Charlie."

"Her name is Charlotte, but when I was little, I couldn't say Charlotte. I said Charlie, and it stuck. She said if I stopped by, she would give me some of her pear preserves. She said she made a hundred pints this year."

"Turn off your chair, Aldora," Lois said as she watched the road. She remembered when she and Aub had snuck off after church and rode down to a spring that lay ahead. Some kids were already swimming in the big pool below it that fed the gurgling stream that fed Cannon Pond farther south, so she and Aub walked up to the spring head. The cold, clear water poured from a crack in a rock face and made a little waterfall. It was a hot day, but she still yelped when he pushed her head under the stream, then she forgot how cold the water was when he kissed her.

"Turn here," said Aldora.

Lois guided the van to the right around a curve in the road, past the short spur that connected to the Six Mile-Keown's Junction Road. A quarter-mile farther, she turned into a gravel drive that wound up around a small knoll and ended at the carport behind a simple white frame house. Empty flower pots lined the metal free-standing carport, and fruit trees ran down the side of the hill.

Aunt Charlie, a woman not quite as old or as large as Aldora but still hobbling on bad knees, greeted them at the door. Lois followed Aldora up the ramp into a den, then turned to go back out.

"You're not staying?" Aunt Charlie asked as she settled back down into a big plush Early American chair.

"I want to walk to the spring," Lois said.

"It's too cold," Aunt Charlie said as Lois closed the door. "She's not wearing a coat. She's liable to get pneumonia."

"She's trying to starve me to death, Aunt Charlie," Aldora cried, her face in a tearful grimace. "She would put me in a nursing home if she could, but I won't have it. I just won't have it and she knows it."

It was not a cold day, but the air was getting cooler as evening approached and Lois would have liked to have been sitting in her kitchen drinking a cup of warm tea. But Aunt Charlie's house was always so hot and humid and musty with odd smells of human decay that she could barely breathe.

"Where's your sense of adventure?" she said to herself as she reached the road, then laughed as she shivered in her shirt sleeves. "I'll tell you when I can feel my ass."

She walked up to the turn-off. She watched little wrens flitting about in the privet and cedars and dead weeds that lined the road, and smiled. She stopped where a culvert let the water from one of the small springs that were everywhere in the low grassy plain escape to join Talking Spring Creek, and searched for bream in the water. She found none, but father downstream she saw a beaver working diligently to repair a broken dam of sticks. She stood and watched it for a long time, and almost didn't notice the pickup come across the old railroad crossing and stop at Talking Springs Road, then turn north toward Hall's Corner. The driver, a young man, and a young woman beside him, waved to her and she waved back. She thought the woman looked familiar, but she couldn't place her. She turned back toward the beaver dam, but the beaver was gone. A single brown leaf came out of the culvert and moved with the stream until it breached the dam and then flowed on. She watched it until it was out of sight.

xxxxxxxxxxxxxxxxxxxxxxxxxxx

"Thanks for the preserves, Aunt Charlie. We really need them," Aldora said as Lois struggled to get a cardboard box of pint jars into the van. When she turned, Aunt Charlie shrugged at Lois and Lois nodded her head.

"Her name is Charlotte," Aldora said as the van backed out of the drive, "but when I was little, I couldn't say Charlotte. I said Charlie, and it stuck."

"Turn off your chair, Aldora."

"I know what you are trying to do, Lois," the old woman suddenly hissed, her voice rising. "I know you want to put me in a nursing home. But I won't have it! I'll tell Aub!"

"Calm down, Aldora. Remember your blood pressure."

"I'll tell him! I will! When we stop at the supermarket to pick up the receipts, I'm going to tell him."

"But it's only the fourth, Aldora."

"Lies! Lies! You didn't like me from the day you got married. I know. I see how you look at me."

"Please, Aldora," Lois said, her eyes liquid.

They passed a sign reading, "Keown's Junction, pop. 881." A half-mile farther on, the road ended in Livingston Road, and Lois turned the van south into a small group of buildings consisting of a convenience store, a tire company, a small brick post office, a weathered little wooden building used as a polling place on the left and on the right a small shopping center that included a beauty shop, an insurance agency, a take-out pizza with a closed sign on the door, a video rental store, and Aub's Famous Foods. A three-way stop with a caution light just beyond the store signaled both the entry of Highway 146 from Brownsboro to the east and the end of all commercial activity on Livingston Road for the next ten miles.

"Stop! Stop!" cried Aldora, scowling at Lois as they pulled up to the caution light. "You forgot I've got to pick up the receipts!"

Without comment, Lois turned the van in a small loop and into the parking lot. She parked it in a handicapped space in front of the grocery store, and let Aldora out. With the last two red lights on her chair blinking on and off, the old woman drove up a short concrete ramp and into the automatic door. The footrest hit the glass with a loud crack before the door opened and she went in.

"It's getting cool," Lois said to herself as she stood beside the van, her arms wrapped around her chest. She watched a flock of geese fly over behind schedule, honking their way south. She scanned the front of the store and could see two of the cashiers, Dori and the new girl, Sydney. They were talking to the janitor, Marvin. She thought about going in. She liked Marvin. He always made her laugh. But she couldn't see Juanita. She squinted her eyes against the glare of the glass and thought she saw the silhouette of her head above the short wall in Aub's office. Her gut tightened. She searched the sky for more geese, but there were none.

Aldora came banging out of the automatic door and raced into the parking lot in front of a car, causing the driver to slam on his brakes and the tires to squeal.

"Aldora! Be careful!" she yelled.

"I thought it was the fifth," Aldora said as she positioned the chair beside the van.

With Aldora secured, Lois drove across the parking lot to the caution light, glancing in the mirror at the front of the store. It was in the shadow of the afternoon sun, making it impossible to see anything through the glass.

"Turn off your chair," she said as she turned onto Livingston Road and headed south. Just outside the city limits, she turned the van west into their gravel driveway and pulled up behind the yellow farmhouse with green shutters and a red metal roof sitting on a small knoll.

Aldora had fallen asleep almost as soon as they left the parking lot, and Lois guided her chair into the house, then into her bedroom before turning the chair off and plugging it into an outlet. She thought of trying to get Aldora into bed, but she knew she couldn't do it without help, so she left her there, her head slumped to one side at an awkward angle. She sleeps like a baby sleeps, she thought.

Lois went back into the living room and sat down at the end of the sofa under a lamp. She picked up a book from the end table, opened it at the bookmark, and read:

> *I have heard what the talkers were talking, the talk*
> *   of the beginning and the end,*
> *But I do not talk of the beginning or the end.*
>
> *There was never any more inception than there is*
> *   now,*
> *Nor any more youth or age than there is now,*
> *And will never be any more perfection than there is*
> *   now,*
> *Nor any more heaven or hell than there is now.*

Urge and urge and urge,
Always the procreant urge of the world.

Out of the dimness opposite equals advance, always
substance and increase, always sex,
Always a knit of identity, always distinction, always a
breed of life.
To elaborate is no avail, learn'd and unlearn'd feel
that it is so.

Sure as the most certain sure, plumb in the uprights,
well entreatied, braced in the beams,
Stout as a horse, affectionate, haughty, electrical,
I and this mystery here we stand.

Clear and sweet is my soul, and clear and sweet is all
that is not my soul.

She put down the book and lay back against the cushions, closing her
eyes. In a moment, she was asleep.

The puppy was yelping, like it was afraid, and she could never bear to
see an animal suffer. She ran out the back door of the house into a cold,
low fog and gathered her robe tightly around her. The path to the barn was
wide and old, but dark and overgrown, and she felt the wet branches of
unkempt privet lash her face and arms as she ran. The puppy began to howl,
a mournful, guttural sound that ran up and down her spine.

When she reached the barn, she ran into the hall and stumbled into
a round bale of hay, which almost knocked her over. She blindly sought
support to keep from falling and felt the large tires of the tractor. She was
gasping for breath. She steadied herself on the wheel. The puppy cried
out from beyond the light of a three-quarter moon that filled the opening
before her. She realized that when she entered the barn, there had been no
moon, but she had no time to think of it. She plunged into the light and
gasped in fear. She was standing near the edge of a large, ragged-edged
erosion ditch that split an old cotton field in full bloom, covering it in black
stalks and white cotton balls bursting from their hulls. The plants tore at
her clothes as she fought her way to the ravine and the puppy, whimpering
now. The poor thing, with bony ribs and the wet eyes of disease, was
clinging to the rim with tiny claws, only its head and chest visible. She

could not see bottom of the ditch until farther on, and knew the puppy would die from the fall. It was so weak and pitiful she wondered if the merciful thing to do would be to let it go. It would be an easy thing to do. But she couldn't, and fought against the rough stems and branches and hulls of the cotton plants to reach it. She must save it. But the plants grew larger until they closed over her head, blocking out the moon, and she cried in anguish to free herself from them.

"Lois! Lois! Help me!"

She bolted awake and ran to the bedroom. Aldora was frantically pushing the buttons on her chair and crying.

"You know it won't work while it's plugged up, Aldora," she said as she pushed the on-off button and unplugged the cord. "Now, see, it works."

"Why do these things keep happening to me!" Aldora wailed as tears rolled down her cheeks.

"Everything is all right now," she said as she touched the old woman's shoulder. Aldora shrugged off her hand. "Would you like something to eat?"

"Is breakfast ready yet?," she sniffled. "I don't want that store-bought bacon."

"It's after 5 p.m., Aldora. Would you like a sandwich to hold you over until supper?"

"Oh."

Lois walked out of the room and through the dining room into the kitchen. Aldora followed.

"I want cookies, but somebody ate them all," she groused, glaring accusingly at Lois.

"Remember, the doctor said you can't have any sweets," Lois said as she searched the refrigerator shelves. "Would you like some tuna fish salad?"

"I want cookies."

"How about some fruit salad. You like that."

Aldora mumbled something unintelligible, but when Lois put a bowl of fruit salad in front of her and handed her a spoon, she ate.

"Have the boys got home yet?" Aldora said between bites.

"Which boys, Aldora?"

"The boys! The boys! They said they were going fishing with Boone."

"Where?"

"I don't know. I never liked fishing. My uncle took me up once and I got really scared out in the woods at night. I haven't been fishing since. So, are they back yet?"

"No. Not yet. Maybe they'll be here soon."

"I hope so."

"Turn off your chair."

While Aldora finished eating, Lois took out a bag of potatoes and began peeling them.

"I used to be a good cook," Aldora said.

"Want to help?"

Lois handed her one of her duller knives and a potato.

"I used to be a good cook, but it hurts my back too much to stand at the stove now," Aldora said as she meticulously peeled the potato. "When I was still a girl, I helped my mama cook Thanksgiving dinner. We fixed fourteen chickens one year. I wrung their necks. None of my brothers would do it, but I did it, or chopped their heads off with a hatchet. I used to fix all kinds of cakes and pies, and sweet potato souffle and Waldorf salad. Are we going to have a lot of pies for Thanksgiving?"

"Some," Lois said.

"I hope we have sweet potato. It's my favorite. My father's favorite joke was about sweet potato pie. A man goes into a restaurant and eats dinner. When he is finished, the waitress comes to the table and asks if he wants pie. The man says yes. The . . . How does it go? Oh. The waitress asks him, 'What kind?' He says, 'There ain't no pie but tater pie.' Daddy used to laugh and laugh."

Lois chuckled. She put the last potato in the bowl and got up to rinse them in the sink. When she finished, she sat back down and began cutting them up into small chunks. She noticed Aldora was staring at her intently.

"What?"

"I don't know what I would do without you, Lois," Aldora said. Her lips began to tremble. "You are of such great help to me since I got sick."

"Thank you, Aldora," Lois said, her eyes softening.

Lois got up and put the potatoes on to boil, then took a package of chicken breasts from the refrigerator. She turned the oven on to preheat, and turned. Aldora was sleeping. Lois pulled the skin from the meat and put it in a bowl lined with seasoning. After she rolled the chicken breasts in the mixture, she put them in a casserole dish and put them in the oven. She then took lettuce and tomatoes and cucumbers from the refrigerator and prepared a salad.

As she put the salad bowl back in the refrigerator, she looked out the kitchen door window. The green pasture was lined with a ridge of green pines and greener cedars interspersed with browning oaks and sweet gum, and bright red maples. A wide path ran down to the barn, then beyond it across the pasture until it entered the trees. Farther up, she could see it turn up along the ridge. She knew it ended a short distance farther at a old home place that overlooked the valley. She had walked up there every day once with Brownie, their old beagle, now dead. There was a nest of red flying squirrels about half-way up the ridge and Brownie ran along under them as they glided from tree to tree, barking furiously. She wondered if they were still there, or only their tattered nests, like the old chimney was all that remained of the family that once lived at the end of the road. She didn't believe in ghosts, but even so, the place was haunted. She could see the family gathered around the hearth, floating three feet above the ground where the old floor used to be, and could hear in the wind them fighting and crying and laughing and loving. And when she no longer saw them when she reached the top of the ridge, she wondered if it was she who was doing the haunting.

She looked at the clock. It was 6:37. Aub would be home in a few minutes. She opened the door to check on the chicken with a fork, but blood seeped out behind it and she closed the oven. She stirred the boiling potatoes and put the dial on medium low. She fixed a cup of hot tea and sat at the table, sipping it while watching Aldora sleep. She slept so soundly that for a moment Lois wondered if she was dead. She knew she could die at any moment. The doctors had told her it was only a matter of time before her heart gave out. The thought stirred nothing inside her. I am going to die, too, the thought. The air in the room thickened. The refrigerator kicked on. The clock on the wall ticked off a minute. What will I do with all the time? The thought frightened her. I could work at the store. But what about Juanita? She clinched her fists in anger then got up and turned off the potatoes. She took them off the eye and put a cover over the pan.

"Honey, I'm home!" Aub chortled as he stepped in the back door, waking Aldora. He stepped over to kiss Lois. She turned to him with a tight smile.

"Is anything wrong?"

"No."

"Hi, mama," he said as he stepped over to Aldora and kissed her cheek, too.

"Did you have a good day?" he asked, turning to Lois. She shrugged.

"No," Aldora said, scowling. "She forgot to take me to Aunt Charlie's. She said she had some pear preserves to give us. She said she made a hundred pints this year and we could have some if we wanted."

"But mama, what are all these jars on the counter? They look like pear preserves to me."

"I don't know."

"Hmmm, something smells good. Come into the living room, mama, and let Lois finish dinner."

He winked at Lois as he led Aldora out of the kitchen, but his smile could not hide the concern lying just below his skin. Lois slowly finished her tea. The yellow overhead light above the table made the room seem cavernous. The last sip of tea was cold and sickly sweet. She raked her tongue against the roof of her mouth. With a start, she smelled the chicken and opened the oven. She took two pot holders and pulled the dish out quickly and sat it on the stove. In the farther reaches of the overhead light, it looked golden brown and she exhaled.

She dawdled as she finished the mashed potatoes, got the salad from the refrigerator, put the chicken on a serving dish, and put out plates and silverware and glasses until her anger had faded, then called them to supper.

"Pull your chair up to the table, Aldora," she said as she chopped a chicken breast into fine pieces on a plate. "What do you want to drink?"

Aldora poked a fork at the salad.

"I don't like rabbit food," she said.

"You need the fiber. What do you want to drink?"

"It doesn't matter."

"Mama, you can have milk or juice or water. What do you want?"

"Milk I guess."

"Did you fry the potatoes?"

"No, Aldora. You can't have fried food."

"I like home fries. That's the only kind I like."

"Here's your pills. Don't forget to take them."

"I won't."

"We had a good day at the store today," Aub said as he scooped up a spoonful of mashed potatoes. "Better than I expected the week after Halloween. Turn off your chair, mama."

"Did you bring the receipts?"

"No, mama. It's the fourth. I'll bring the receipts home tomorrow."

He winked at Lois and whispered, "Do you think you'll have the time tomorrow to get the totals? If you don't, Jaworski can do it. That's what I hired him for. Then all you will have to do is stuff and mail the envelopes."

"I won't have time," Lois said. "She's got an appointment with the cardiologist in Brownsboro tomorrow at 11."

"Oh, yeah. I forgot. We'll take care of it. I'll just bring her a bundle of the old receipts like I usually do."

"I hear you whispering," Aldora said hotly. "I know what you're doing. You're going to send me to a nursing home. I won't have it. I won't have it!"

"No, mama, we weren't talking about that at all. You know you will always have a home with us, isn't that right Lois?"

Lois nodded her head.

"She wants to put me in a nursing home!" Aldora shrieked, choking on her food. "I won't have it! I won't have it!"

"Now, calm down mama," Aub said sternly. "You're just getting yourself upset over nothing. Take a drink of a milk."

Aub handed it to her and Aldora took a drink, swallowing hard, and gasped.

"It's all right, Aldora. Don't forget your pills."

They finished the meal in silence. Afterwards, Aub took Aldora into the living room to watch television while Lois cleaned up and loaded the dishwasher. She listened to them from the kitchen, not to their words, which she could not make out, but to the sound of them. Periodically, Aub would groan and Aldora would laugh. It was a pretty laugh, almost girlish. As she wiped the table down, she noticed Aldora's pills. When she finished, she took them into the livingroom with a glass of water.

Aldora and Aub were playing checkers. Aldora was winning the game and laughing with each piece she took. Lois stood by silently. Aldora's eyes were sparkling, and years seemed to have sloughed off her face. For a moment, Lois could see her as she once was, so pretty and vibrant. When Aub, with a loud groan, was defeated, Lois handed Aldora the glass.

"Take your pills, Aldora."

Aldora took them one by one as she smiled at her son.

Aub turned on the television then, to a crime show Aldora loved to watch, and sat down in his easy chair with the latest edition of the *Brownsboro Beacon*. Lois sat on the end of the sofa by the lamp and picked up her book.

"Did you hear about Plum Thompson and his wife?" Aub asked as he scanned the front page.

"No," Lois said, not taking her eyes from the book.

"He killed his wife and himself."

"Look out! He's right behind you!" Aldora shouted at the television, shaking her fist.

"Who is he?"

"Plum Thompson. You know, the developer from Oak Log."

"Ohhh. That's terrible. I think I saw his wife once in the store."

"Watch out! Stupid girl! Poor stupid girl."

"She used to come in all the time. She said she liked our meats better than anybody's. She was one of my best customers."

"Uh huh."

"What are you reading?"

"Walt Whitman.

"The poet? Is he any good"

"Fair to middling."

"You're teasing."

"Uh huh."

Aub settled back in his chair. The pages rustled as he read them. Lois read:

> Trippers and askers surround me,
> People I meet, the effect upon me of my early life or
>   the ward and city I live in, or the nation,
> The latest dates, discoveries, inventions, societies,
>   authors old and new,
> My dinner, dress, associates, looks, compliments,
>   dues,
> The real or fancied indifference of some man or
>   woman I love,
> The sickness of one of my folks or of myself, or ill-
>   doing or loss or lack of money, or depressions or
>   exaltations,
> Battles, the horrors of fratricidal war, the fever of
>   doubtful news, the fitful events;
> These come to me days and nights and go from me
>   again,
> But they are not the Me myself.

The phone rang.

"I'll get it," Lois said. She walked to the entertainment center and picked up the receiver. "Yes. Oh, hello. How are you? Oh, we're fine. Yes, she's here. Aldora, it's Paul."

"Paul?"

"Mama, it's Paul. Paul, my brother."

"Hi, Paul. How was the fishing? You didn't go? But you said you were. Uh huh. Uh huh. We went to Aunt Charlie's and got some pear preserves. No. We haven't put up a thing yet. I keep telling Lois we've got to get canning soon or we won't have nothing."

Lois and Aub exchanged a knowing smile.

"No, our garden's all growed up with weeds. I had a garden when Daddy and I lived in Talking Spring before he died. I broke the ground with a hoe. It was the prettiest thing. It didn't have a weed in it. Daddy said, 'Mama, that's a good garden.' This gal from the newspaper came out and took my picture. When they ran it in the paper, it said, 'One old woman with a hoe.' I don't know why they said that. I'm not old. Uh huh. How's your back? It is? OK. 'Bye, Paul. Mama loves you. That was Paul. He said he didn't go fishing. I'm sure he told me he and the boys was going with Boone."

The crime drama ended and Lois said, "It's time for bed, Aldora. I'll go turn back the covers."

Aldora followed her into the bedroom.

"Back up your chair, Aldora, while I fix the bed."

"It won't work."

"Stop! You've got it a wheel tangled in the cord again. There. Now back up."

"When we lived in the house up on the ridge, we had a screened in porch. I used to love sleeping on it in the summer. You could hear the crickets and the bullfrogs so clear up there."

"You never lived there, Aldora. You lived in the old house at Talking Spring until you met Aubrey and y'all moved in here."

"I thought I did. I can see the porch just like it was yesterday."

"There was a big screened porch in the house at Talking Spring."

Aldora began to hum an old gospel song, "Just a Closer Walk With Thee."

"Aub, I need your help!" Lois shouted.

"Coming."

Aub helped her lift Aldora out of her chair and into bed. Lois pulled the covers up over her and Aub bent down to kiss her on the forehead. Aldora continued to hum.

"Goodnight, mama."

Lois patted her hand.

"Goodnight, Aldora."

"Are the boys home yet?"

"No, but they should be home soon."

They smiled as Aldora closed her eyes and her humming resumed, then walked back into the living room.

Lois said, "I'm tired. We had a long day. I think I'll go to bed."

"Me, too. I'm bushed," Aub said. He turned off the television and followed her.

Lois stood by the bed and took off her dress and underwear, then put on a long flannel gown.

"What did the doctor say?" Aub said as he removed his pants and shirt.

"She's lost a little weight but her blood pressure is still high," Lois said as she got into bed. "He gave me a prescription for some hemorrhoid cream, and some pills to help her memory. He said it might take a little time for them to work. He said he was giving her a low dose to start, but will increase it. We go back in a month."

"I'll take them with me tomorrow and get them filled in Hall's Corner," he said as he got into bed. The springs creaked loudly. "I hope we get some good news from the cardiologist tomorrow."

"Don't get your hopes up."

"I know. Her heart is very weak. Wasn't that something tonight how she was when we played checkers? I haven't seen her that happy in a long time."

"She almost looked like I remember her when I first met you."

"It seems like so long ago," he said as he turned his back to her and switched the lamp off.

"Yes," she said.

She turned off her lamp and stared out the window. The faint yellow glow through the curtains told her the moon was rising. She wondered what phase it was in as the veil of sleep descended on her. She could hear Aub softly snoring. She snuggled down into the warmth of the covers and lay the palm of her hand on his wide bare back. She knew what she would dream.

⟋⫿⟍

XIV. The Mystery of God

The Brownsboro Beacon and Carter County News

— Thursday, November 4, 1998.

Developer kills wife, self
Deputies find Plum Thompson, wife
Imogene dead in mansion at Oak Log

By Brad Randall
Editor

Carter County sheriff's deputies made a gruesome discovery late Sunday night when they responded to a 911 call from the mansion home of developer Thaddeus "Plum" Thompson and his wife, Imogene, on Six Mile Road. When police went inside, they found Mrs. Thompson, 54, in the kitchen slumped over a table, dead of a single 22-caliber gunshot to the chest. After searching the house, they found her husband, 62, lying on an upstairs porch with a single 22-caliber gunshot wound to the forehead.

When EMTs arrived, Mr. Thompson, owner of Thompson Development, was still breathing, but was pronounced dead at the hospital, according to Barry Sandeford, county director of emergency services.

"We tried to save him," Sandeford said, "but it was hopeless. He had lost too much blood."

Mrs. Thompson was pronounced dead at the scene. Sheriff Will Billings refused to speculate on whether it was a case of murder-suicide.

"The investigation is still on-going," he said.

Plum Thompson was one of the county's leading businessmen. Thompson Development, established in 1948 by his father Phil, built the courthouse annex in 1957, and is the general contractor on Hall's Creek Village, the new subdivision four miles from Hall's Corner on the Brownsboro Road.

As Thompson Development, he was the county's largest landowner, including extensive acreage in the northern part of the county as well as many lots of prime real estate in Brownsboro including the Cherokee Mall. The couple's home, known as Plum Nearly, is a multi-storied mansion sitting on several hundred acres.

"It's a great loss, not only to the county, but he was a personal friend," said Art Lincoln, chairman of the Carter County Chamber of Commerce. "I never met a finer man in my life."

County Commission Chairman Ronnie Hall said Mr. Thompson will be long remembered.

"He was one of a kind. There'll never be anyone like him again. He was why I got into politics in the first place. If he had not encouraged me to run for county commissioner in 1990, I wouldn't be where I am today."

Zebediah Schultz of Hall's Corner, his adopted son, former business partner, and fellow member of the Carter County Golf Club, expressed disbelief that Thompson had killed his wife and then himself.

"That's not the Plum I knew," he said. "He was a good Christian man. Not a mean bone in his body. We might have had our differences, but that's just the way it is in business."

Mrs. Thompson, the former Ivanell Imogene Butler of Macon, was very active in civic affairs. She was on the board of the Carter County Library, and chaired the "Save the Pemberton" committee, a group dedicated to restoring the old Pemberton Theater in Brownsboro. She was also past-president of the Carter County League of Women Voters and treasurer of the Brownsboro Garden Club.

"It's just terrible," said Mavis Gilbert, president of the library board. "Genie was like a sister to me. I can't understand it. They were always such a happy couple."

The Thompsons were longtime members of the First Baptist Church, where Mr. Thompson served as a deacon and Mrs. Thompson was active in the North American Baptists Missions Society. Both of them taught Sunday school.

"They were fine, upstanding Christians," said Pastor James Oglivie. "They were just quiet, ordinary folks around their friends. Salt of the earth. I still can't believe it. At Sunday morning service, they seemed fine. They were both excited about the new nursery we're building in the annex."

The Rev. Oglivie was the one who contacted local authorities after they failed to show up for evening services and did not answer their phone.

The couple had one daughter, Mary and Milton Dennis, and three grandchildren, Tracy Elliot Dennis, Roger Dewayne Jennings and Michelle Yvonne Jennings, all of Washington, D. C., and an adopted son, Mr. Schultz of Hall's Corner. They were preceded in death by a daughter, Jennifer Ann.

Phillip Thaddeus "Plum" Thompson was born July 12, 1936, and was a lifelong resident of Carter County. He is the son of the late Mr. and Mrs. Phil and Luvenia "Livy" Thompson of Brownsboro. He was a veteran of the Korean Conflict and member of the Brownsboro chapter of the Veterans of Foreign Wars. He was a deacon at the First Baptist Church of Brownsboro and taught Sunday school.

He was preceded in death by four brothers, Robert Ellis, Alexander "Alex" Bryan, George Washington, and Jasper Daniel Thompson, all of Brownsboro, and Franklin Roosevelt Thompson of Anderson, South Carolina, and five sisters, Mrs. Margaret (James) Parnell, and Mrs. Grace (Arthur) Brady of Brownsboro, Mrs. Octavia (Earnest) Carnes of Centerville, Mrs. Eugenia (Jacob) Carnes of Atlanta, and Mrs. Flonnie (Franklin) Brownlow of Chattanooga, Tennessee. He is survived by a brother, William Carter, of Brownsboro, and three sisters, Mrs. Elaine Crandall and Mrs. Bernice Barton, both of Brownsboro, and Ms. Sylvia Thompson of Nashville, Tennessee; cousins, nieces and nephews also survive.

Ivanelle Imogene Butler Thompson was born April 2, 1944 in Norfolk, Virginia. She came to Carter County in 1954 to attend the Chamblee Women's Academy in Hall's Corner. She was a founding member of the Carter County Library board, chaired the "Save the Pemberton" committee, was a member of the Brownsboro Garden Club, and was a past-president of the Carter County League of Women Voters. She was a member of the First Baptist Church of Brownsboro, where she taught Sunday school, and was active in the North American Baptist Mission.

Mrs. Thompson was the daughter of the late Col. Charles Evan Butler and Mrs. Susan (Harold) Barnes, both of Macon. She was preceded in death by two brothers, Shield David and Euclid Thomas Butler, both of Macon, and two sisters, Mrs. Catherine (Caleb) Hall of Macon, and Mrs. Marlene (Joseph) Bunch of the Six Mile community. She is survived by two sisters, Mrs. Jennifer Ann and the late Thomas "Shorty" Peterson of Hall's Corner, and Mrs. Mary Sue (Jim) Adams of Macon; and one brother, Timothy Elwood of Philadelphia, Pennsylvania; cousins, nieces and nephews also survive.

Funeral services will be held Wednesday at 2
p.m. at the First Baptist Church of Brownsboro
with the Rev. James Oglivie presiding. Burial will
be in the Little Prairie Holiness Church Cemetery
in Six Mile.

William Thompson Funeral Home is in charge
of arrangements.

In lieu of flowers, the family requests that
donations be made to the "Save the Pemberton"
fund.

xxxxxxxxxxxxxxxxxxxxxxxx

Light is streaking across the sky like in some old war movie. My head
hurts. There she is. She's trying to get away from me, but I'll catch her. She
is running around the kitchen table in the old house giggling, but I cut her
off. We run in to each other. "Excuse me, Elizabeth," I say, "I didn't know
you cared."

"Plum, I need you."

"I'm coming, Genie."

She's fixing pear preserves again. That woman's got a thing about
canning. She insists we have a garden every year, even though she could buy
whatever she wants store made. She's like mama that way. Mama died right
before I got home from Korea. I didn't even get to go to the funeral, because
I was on a ship in the Pacific. I enlisted in '53. I lied about my age, just so
I could fight the Commies. But by the time I got to Korea, it was about all
over. Didn't even get in combat. But seeing the bodies was enough; those
poor boys, kids really. I never want to see anything like that again. I came
home with one of them, Jimmy Cox, from down in Fort Yeager. He was
killed by a mine more than a year after the fighting stopped. Had a wife and
three kids.

"Plum, I need you."

"I'm coming, Genie."

She was so pretty, you know, back then. Not the first time, though. She
was just a gawky kid, kinda ugly. She came over from Macon with her sister
Jennifer Ann to visit their sister Marlene. I guess she was about eight. I
was working on shares that summer for Marlene's husband Joe, helping
him with his cotton, 'cause daddy insisted that I know what hard work is.
I learned, too. Joe was about the hardest-working man I ever knew, and he
expected anyone who worked with him to keep up. She was always under
my feet, pestering me about this or that. I'd get so mad I swear I could have
wrung her scrawny neck, but I didn't. Joe would've killed me if Marlene

didn't get to me first. She gave me my nickname, you know, first time she saw me. She said, "Why you're plum handsome." I ain't let her forget it since.

Am I moving? It feels like I'm moving?

I'm a gonna have a little talk with Jesus,

I'm a gonna tell him all about my troubles.

Hmmm hmmm hmmm hmmm hmmm hmmm hmmm.

He will answer by and by.

I never was much for religion, but my Genie insisted I go to church and teach Sunday school. Wouldn't let me get a word in edgeways about it. Finally, I said, OK, if you are so goldarn set — she wouldn't let me cuss, either, at least around her — goldarn set on going to church, we'll go to daddy's. She about had apoplexy 'cause her daddy was a Methodist and her mother was a Holiness. He he. She fussed about everything, at least until we got Jimmy Oglivie for a preacher. I think he's more'n a little full of himself, but she likes him cause he looks like Clark Gable. She fussed about the pews being too hard, but daddy replaced them, then she fussed about the hymnals being old and worn out. I replaced them. When me and daddy kicked everybody's butt until they built the first annex, she hushed then. She knew when she was whupped.

"Plum, I need you."

"I'm coming, Genie."

I will say this for her. When she sets her mind to something, there's no shaking it loose. When Taylor and Margie Schultz died in that horrible car wreck, it wouldn't do but that we adopted their boy. His brother was already up and out of the house, you know, but he wasn't making enough money to make a home for the boy. He was an ornery little cuss; still is. But I don't hold nothing against him for his ways. Never did. You know, he's the one who insisted I write him out of my will. I don't think he ever felt like he was a part of the family.

People might think just because daddy had a lot of money that we had it easy from the start, but they'd be wrong. Daddy didn't give us nothing. I mean, nothing. I went to work on the framing crew to start. Didn't get paid any more than an any other apprentice. It was five years before I made foreman. I might be a foreman still if daddy hadn't died. He was out looking over a job site on Sunday after church when he saw one of the walls was crooked. Daddy had an eye for that stuff. He could see a crooked board a mile away. So he took off his Sunday shirt, and took a hammer and a crowbar out of the trunk of that old Cadillac he used to drive. It's the one out in the shed now. He took down the whole wall out in the hot sun — it was July — and him nearly 80. He about got it all back up, too, straight as an arrow. When he didn't come home for supper, mama called me, since I was the only one of my brothers still working for him. Daddy was a hard SOB to work for and he had run all of them off by then. He never ran me off, thought. I wouldn't let him. Some people said he shouldn't have been working on the Sabbath, that it was God's way of punishing him, but I couldn't ever believe that God was that mean and spiteful. I didn't cry at the funeral. None of us boys did.

There's the bus. Old Tom Gravely is still driving it. Come on, Jenny Ann. She's like a butterfly, that girl, always flitting about here and there. I don't blame Tom that he didn't see her. She was halfway across the road when she remembered she had left some silly thing on the seat. I think it was a box of scarves she got at school. It was the last school day before Christmas and some boy who got her name bought them for her. Even now all I can remember is seeing the tire run over her and Genie screaming in the car. I can't remember nothing else. Not even the funeral.

Is it getting dark? It looks like it's coming up a cloud. I hope we can get all the houses done before the winter really sets in. They're nice houses, too, for the money, and well made. I don't care what Art Lincoln says about us building too many "starter homes" and depressing property values and all that. Oh, people have told me plenty about it. But Art and that pack of his, some of them my own damn tenants at the mall, can just go to hell. Who do they think built that place?

"Plum, I need you."

"I'm coming, Genie."

You know what I always liked best about her. She's like a plow mule. You just put her in the traces and she goes. She don't ever complain about working. That's what I used to tell her we were, just a couple of plow mules. I meant it as a compliment, but she got all puffed up about it first time I said it. But I really think is was all for show, you know. I loved her and she knew it. Many's the time we would lie together in bed after . . . well, you know, and I would just stare at her with her face all flushed and she would look at me so shy. She knew. I know she did.

"Plum, I need you."

"I'm coming, Genie."

Now where is she?

xxxxxxxxxxxxxxxxxxxxxxxx

The Brownsboro Beacon
and Carter County News
– Thursday, November 12, 1998.

Sermon delivered at
Thompson funeral

By Brad Randall
Editor

Since we reported last week on the tragic deaths of Plum and Genie Thompson, several of our readers have contacted us about printing the sermon the Rev. James Oglivie delivered at their funeral last Thursday at the First Baptist Church. They have told us it helped them try to come to terms with such an unexpected loss. Therefore, in lieu of our usual editorial, we are reprinting the reverend's sermon in the hope that others may gain some comfort form it.

Text of the sermon given by the Rev. James Oglivie at the funeral of Mr. and Mrs. Philip "Plum" Thompson, November 4, 1998, at the First Baptist Church of Brownsboro.

'Think now, who that was innocent ever perished? Or where were the upright cut off? As I have seen, those who plow iniquity and sow trouble reap the same.' Job, Chapter 4, verse 7-8.

Death comes to each of us unbidden in the blink of an eye. The Bible says it is like a thief in the night. We might be cooking supper, or washing our car, or watching television with our family. We might be thinking about cleaning out the garage, or what we're going to spend our next paycheck on, or how we're going to handle some conflict with a co-worker. We might have just had a fight with a loved one, the bitter words still on our tongue, or we might be hugging a grandchild and about to tell them how much we love them. We might be doing nothing at all, just resting in a rocking chair on the porch watching the lightning bugs come out at night. But I say to you that in the blink of an eye, we will all come fact to face with eternity!

Now, this thief has come to Plum and Genie Thompson and stolen them away from us. And it is left to us to try to make sense of why they had to go now, and in such a tragic manner. My heart goes out to their brothers and sisters, and their son and daughter, and the many friends, business associates, nieces and nephews and cousins who are with us today. I count myself among you. We are with you in this terrible hour of grief. We are all asking 'Why?' Why now? Why this way?'

But as Job said to his wife, Chapter 2, verse 10: 'Shall we indeed accept good from God, and shall we not accept adversity?' It's easy to believe in God when we are enjoying His blessings. It can be so easy, we don't think we need to read our Bibles every night. It can be so easy, we don't think we need to go to church except on Christmas and Easter. It can be so easy, we can even forget that it is He from whom all our blessings flow. It is He who is the light! It is He who is the word! It is He and only He who can wash our sins away.

But like Job's wife, when troubles come upon us, we immediately begin to doubt. At the first sign, we cry,'Why is God doing this to me? Why is he making me suffer so?' Like Job's wife, we say, maybe we ought to just curse God and die. Just get it over with! Just give up!

'I am blameless. . . . .' Job says, chapter 9, verses 21-24. 'It is all one; therefore I say, he destroys both the blameless and the wicked. When disaster brings sudden death, he mocks at the calamity of the innocent. . . . If it is not he, who then is it?' Ah, it is a mystery beyond all human understanding, 'For God speaks in one way, and in two, though man does not perceive it.' Chapter 33, verse14.

God has spoken to us today in one way and in two. Plum and Genie are gone. This kind, sweet couple are no more on this earth and we don't know why. Now, some of us might be sitting in judgement on Plum, but the Bible says, 'Judge not lest ye be judged." We do not know just what happened last Sunday afternoon that led to this horrible tragedy. Satan would have us presume guilt and lay blame, but I tell you it is a snare to trap the wicked! I knew Plum Thompson a long time. We all did. He was as fine a Christian as I ever met. So was Genie. It makes no more sense to me than it does to all of you. It makes no sense, but who can presume to know God's will in everything?

We can never know why! Only God knows why! So I do not come to you today like Eliphaz the Temanite, or Bildad the Shuhite, or Zophar the Naamathite, with 'proverbs of ashes' and 'defenses of clay.' None of us can be righteous before God.

As Job says, chapter 1, verses 21: 'The Lord gave, and the Lord has taken away; Blessed be the name of the Lord.'

Blessed be the name of the Lord in all things. In all things. He tests us with fire. He afflicts us with boils. He overthrows all our hopes. 'He destroys both the blameless and the wicked.' Why? There is no human why. There is only God's why and His grace. By His grace we are saved from hell and eternal torment! By His afflictions we are shown the path of righteousness! By His terrible trials we are shown the way to heaven!

As we are gathered here today to say goodbye to Plum and Genie, let us remember all the goodness we saw in their hearts. Let us remember their kind and gentle ways. Let us remember their generosity. Let us remember how they helped so many of us. And let us not presume to ask why they are gone. 'Get behind me Satan,' Jesus said. Get behind us Satan, for we are the Children of God!

Let us pray. Our Father who is in heaven, hallowed be your name. Your kingdom come. Your will be done on earth as in heaven. Give us today our daily bread. Forgive us our sins, as we forgive those who sin against us. Save us from this time of trial and deliver us from evil. For the kingdom, the power, and the glory are yours, now and for ever.

Amen.

xxxxxxxxxxxxxxxxxxxxxxxxxx

"He shot her once in the chest," said Barry Sandeford to the four men sitting around the front table at the Cozy Café in Hall's Corner. He was a tall man who wore a dark blue uniform. His shirt's buttons were stretched tight, revealing larger and larger slivers of his tee shirt as they descended to form a blue and white cat's eye over his belt buckle. The group, all old men, met each morning during the week to drink coffee, eat Linelle DuBose's ham, sausage, and tenderloin biscuits—she was the best cook in twenty-five miles, and some said the best in the county— talk politics and chew over the latest news. Barry wasn't a member, since he was the head of the county's emergency services and lived in Brownsboro, but he "just happened to be in Hall's Corner this morning and thought he'd drop in for some of Linelle's cooking."

"The paper said he shot her with a .22 revolver," said Abe Carter, an old white-haired man dressed in overalls who lived out at the Six Mile crossroads on Brownsboro Road. He spoke from behind a plastic menu, the only one left on the table. On the front of it was a turquoise drawing of a smiling waitress pouring a steaming cup of coffee. Across the top, in gold letters, were the words, "The Cozy Café. On the corner in the Corner," and at the bottom, "Who wants pie?"

"It's a wonder he killed her," said Julius Pinkus III, a portly man who owned the antiques store next door, as he fingered the lapel of his dark brown, ill-fitting suit. "A little pistol like that ain't good for nothing but scaring somebody with."

"Still, if he shot her in the chest . . . ?" said Jim Cochran, a lanky, skinny man in a flannel shirt and jeans who was a semi-retired farmer that lived near Macedonia Church.

"Yeah, you would think so," said Barry. "The coroner said she had powder burns on her dress. He must have snuck up on her. There's no way to tell if the first shot killed her right away. Either way, I never saw so much blood in my life."

"I heard his business was going under. You know his supervisor Walt Carter took the payroll and ran off to who knows where," said Josh Pennick, a square-faced man of average height and build wearing a pair of khaki pants and a blue chambray button-down shirt. He was the newest and youngest member of the group at 62.

Everybody but Abe laughed. He just glared over his menu.

"Oh," Josh sputtered. "Was he a relative?"

"He's my son, you fish-eyed fool."

"Oh, Abe, settle down," Linelle said as she refilled their coffee cups. "You cussed that boy for a week when you found out what he had done. If I remember right, you said you were going to strangle his fool neck."

"If you ever find him!" Milton hooted.

When the laughter died down, Barry said, "No, I don't think that's it. Jared Adams at the bank told me they had more money that God."

"Now Abe, are you going to order or are you just going to read the menu?"

Abe flushed and said, "I think I'll have . . . ah . . . I guess . . . ."

"Country ham and biscuit it is," Linelle said as she yanked the menu from his hand and walked away.

"Don't mess with her, Abe. That's what you always order. She's liable to spit on that biscuit just to spite you," said Milton.

"Would she?" Josh asked with a grimace.

"No telling what that Linelle's going to do," Milton said, trying to keep a straight face.

"Do you think she might have been running around on him?" said Jim, daring Milton to make a joke about his troubles. He did not suffer lightly any mention of his daughter Mandy, who everybody knew had gotten caught with another man just a couple of weeks ago and her husband had thrown her out of the house.

"Genie Thompson? Nah. When would she have had the time?" Barry said. "When she wasn't heading up some civic improvement, she was working right along side her husband. I don't think I ever saw her out by herself."

"But she was a widow woman, wasn't she, when he married her?" Josh said. "The paper said Zebediah Schultz was their adopted son."

"Nah. Zebediah's parents were killed in a car wreck and Genie insisted that they adopt him," said Jim.

"I heard that the two of them never did get along that well," said Abe.

"Oh, you can't pay an attention to Hilda Biddle's gossip."

"Speaking of widows. Remember Mama Wallace after old Tom died?" said Abe Carter. "I went over to see her a month later, to pay my respects, and I swear she acted like she wanted me to stay a while, if you know what I mean."

"Remember Abby Carnes?" Milton said. Everybody groaned.

"That woman was colder than a Canada trout," said Josh.

"Was he on drugs?" said Abe.

"Nah. The state crime lab said neither one of them had anything in their systems. I never knew either of them to even take a drink at all, in public at least."

"Maybe they were what they call 'closet alcoholics,'" offered Josh.

"Drinking in a closet? What the hell fun is there in that?" Milton laughed.

"But I will tell you one thing, and don't let this out," said Barry, his voice so low the old men had to crane their heads toward him just to hear. "The coroner said that she had semen in her. Said it couldn't have been more than a couple hours old."

"I guess there's no telling," said Jim.

"Did any of you hear about Wal-Mart coming?" Josh asked.

"Yeah. This is on the Q T, but Art Lincoln says they're looking at some land on 146," said Barry.

xxxxxxxxxxxxxxxxxxxxxxx

"Are we going to talk about fall pruning at all?" said Darby Howard, president of the Brownsboro Garden Club, and widow of Thad Howard, a local realtor. She was a matronly gray-haired woman wearing a floral print dress. The club was meeting in her house, a big white rambling antebellum festooned with gingerbread a couple of blocks from downtown Brownsboro.

"I don't think I can," said Mavis Gilbert, a thin, gaunt woman wearing a black pantsuit. She was the wife of Moss Gilbert, who owned a clothing store in Brownsboro, and Genie's closest friend.

"I wish we would," said Jennifer Ann Peterson, widow of Thomas "Shorty" Peterson, a Brownsboro druggist, and Genie's sister. She was a tall and thin blue-haired woman with broad shoulders, and was wearing a bright yellow and white polka dot dress with a solid yellow jacket, and a wide white straw hat with a yellow ribbon.

"We have to elect a new treasurer at least," said Darby.

Mavis broke down in tears.

"Now, now, Mavis," Darby said, patting her hand.

"Oh, go ahead and cry, Mave. Cry it all out," said Elizabeth Hall, the youngest of the group. Her tailored dark green suit and permed auburn hair made her look even younger. She was the wife of the county commission chairman.

"God moves in mysterious ways," said Adelaide Cochran, a stocky woman wearing a simple green smock with narrow white vertical stripes over a pair of matching green stretch pants. She was the wife of a local farmer and smiled at Beth Oglivie, wife of the pastor of the First Baptist Church.

"Men, however, are more predictable," said Mary Beth, ignoring Adelaide. Mavis sobbed.

"Mary Beth!" Elizabeth cried as she held Mavis against her ample bosom.

"Well, it had to be something," Mary Beth said. "They had plenty of money, and I don't think Genie would have been cheating on him."

"Never can tell by appearances," Jennifer Ann said.

"Hush, Jennifer Ann," said Elizabeth, without taking her eyes off Beth. "Y'all don't seriously think that Plum . . . ?"

"Oh, god! And she found out . . . ?" Mavis squalled.

"No, Mavis, no. They're just speculating, that's all, and they ought to stop it," Elizabeth said, glaring.

"Worse things have happened," Mary Beth said, glaring back. They all knew she and the pastor were having trouble.

"But they seemed to be so happy," said Adelaide.

"Pah!" Jennifer Ann said. "My sister had a mean temper and you all know it. She and Plum got into some real rows. And she held a grudge, too."

All the ladies knew that Jennifer Ann and Genie had once been rivals for the affections of "Plum," and had a big fight years ago when Genie won him. Publicly, it played out as a dispute over a flock of dominique chickens that Jennifer Ann said one of Plum's dogs was harassing. The incident was known in the unofficial history of Carter County as "The Dominecker War." Publicly and privately, the sisters reconciled, for family's sake, but some thought a small kernel of bitterness remained in both of them.

"Don't speak poorly of the dead," said Adelaide in a hushed tone.

"None of us is perfect," said Marsha Gail Lincoln, wife of the president of the Brownsboro Chamber of Commerce as she smoothed the waist of her blue business suit. "Genie, God love her, had her faults. Remember the mud pie?"

Ragged, uneven laughter rose among the ladies, except Mavis.

"Won the blue ribbon at the county fair and everything!" cackled Lu Adams as she slapped the table. She was a pallid, squinty-faced woman with black frizzy hair streaked with gray, which matched her suit, and the wife of the president of the Citizens Bank of Brownsboro.

"Then she had to give it back because somebody found the exact same recipe in a magazine," laughed Mary Beth.

"I wonder who snitched on her?" said Elizabeth, casting an eye toward Jennifer Ann.

"Well, it wasn't me," huffed Jennifer Ann, who had found something fascinating about the centerpiece of fading Indian paintbrush nested in stalks of golden sagebrush.

"She . . . she didn't . . . steal it," muttered Mavis. "She told me it was just a coincidence. I believed her, too."

"Well, she did win that contest about every year," said Lu.

"It was a good pie," said Adelaide.

"Yes, dear," said Jennifer Ann. "Well, in the end, she might have felt it was a blessing she died the way she did."

"How can you say that Jennifer Ann Peterson!" Mavis cried.

"Jennifer Ann, you're going too far," scolded Elizabeth.

"Why, Jennifer Ann?" asked Mary Beth.

"Well, you know our mama died when Genie and I were pretty young, in our twenties. I was the only one still at home, but Genie moved in with me to help take care of her."

"Yes," said Mary Beth.

"She had cancer of the stomach or intestines or something."

"Could it have been ovarian?" asked Dell Phillips, wife of a local doctor and a nurse herself. She was very tall and lean, with high cheekbones framed by long brown hair still curling after she had released it from its customary bun. In her starched white uniform, she could have been a model.

"I don't think so," said Jennifer Ann, "but I can't remember for sure. All I know is that she was seven-months pregnant when she died and the baby died with her."

Collectively, the other women gasped.

"How sad," said Adelaide, frowning. "I know when my mama died, I never thought I was going to stop crying."

"Your mama's not dead, dear," said Jennifer Ann gently.

"She isn't?"

"Anyway, all our brothers and sisters had married, except for Timothy and me, and he had already moved to Philadelphia. They had their own lives to live, so Genie and I took care of her most of the time. Mama suffered a long time. I think she already had it when she got pregnant. She had been complaining of stomach pains, but mama was a hypo . . . hypo . . ."

"Hypochondriac?" said Dell.

"Hypochondriac. She was always complaining about one ailment or another. If she ever read or heard of a disease, she soon got it. It was a joke in the family that the only thing she had never had was cancer of the heart. She found out she had the cancer when she went to the doctor to find out for sure if she was pregnant."

"How horrible," gasped Mavis. "She never told me."

"It was not something Genie wanted to remember. For nearly the whole seven months, mama was in bed and had to be cared for hand and foot. She got so weak, she could barely stand, and us girls had to do everything from feeding her to bathing her to emptying her bedpan. Daddy tried to help, but I don't think he could bear seeing her like she was."

"She must have been in a lot of pain," said Dell.

"A lot."

"Because the doctor couldn't give her morphine because of the baby."

"Yes. The last couple of months, she barely slept. And she would have these terrible spasms. I can still remember her screaming and holding our hands so tight they bruised. I tried to block it all out. I just went somewhere else in my mind, sort of. I don't know why I'm able to do that. It's just the way I've always been. But Genie couldn't. It was like she felt every bit of mama's pain."

"Oh, poor Genie," groaned Mavis.

"Mama died in December. The 11th. It was really cold outside. I had come down with a cold and didn't want to risk giving it to her, so Genie took care of her for three straight days. I hated it, because I could tell taking care of mama by herself was wearing her out, but I didn't know what else to do. If I hadn't been sick, I would have been with mama when she died. She was very religious, you know. A strict Holiness. I could hear her praying day and night while I lay in my bed with a fever."

"That must have been hard on you," said Elizabeth, with tears in her eyes.

"Not as hard as it was on Genie, right there in the room with her all the time. It was 11:14 p.m. on the dot when I heard Genie screaming. I got up out of bed and ran into the room. Mama was gone, and Genie was holding this poor little dead baby in her hands, squalling her eyes out. The sheet was soaked with blood. I remember it now just like it was yesterday."

"Oh, god!" cried Mavis.

"It was the most horrible thing I've ever seen," said Jennifer Ann. "Genie didn't speak for months after that. She just walked around like she was alive and dead at the same time. Plum got so worried he thought about sending her to Milledgeville, but I begged him not to, and eventually she snapped out of it. But she wasn't the same ever again. Oh, she bore it well, as we all know, but I knew she was . . . traumatized by it?"

"Traumatized," said Dell.

Her word spread out in the silence like the ripples on a pond until it faintly echoed off the dark wainscoting, the green and purple grapevines on the wallpaper. and coppery red pressed tin ceiling, and made its way back to the women.

"Is there a history of cancer in your family?" whispered Dell.

"On both sides."

"Genie . . . Genie told me once she was not afraid of death," sobbed Mavis. "She said she was only afraid of dying."

"Oh, my," said Dell.

xxxxxxxxxxxxxxxxxxxxxxxxxx

"Did you hear that Old Man Thompson killed his wife and then himself?" Bean, a tall skinny boy of sixteen with dark frizzy hair, asked as he climbed the steps up the large multi-level deck that reached up and over a trailer on C Street in the EZ Mobile Home Park. "Mama Wallace said she read it in the paper."

"Yeah, I did, Bean. She was my great aunt, on my father's side," Jake Peterson said. He was sitting in an aluminum lounge chair woven with green and white bands of polyethylene fiber, drinking a cup of hot tea and smoking a cigar. He gestured to Bean to take a seat in an identical chair beside him.

"Oh, I'm sorry."

"I didn't really know her, or the Thompsons for that matter. He came out the construction site more than a few times, but he never talked to anybody but Walt. I don't even think he knew who I was. But I knew their daughter, though, Jenny Ann. I went to school with her."

"Yeah?"

"Well, sort of. Back in the '70s all the kids rode the same bus. They weren't separated by age like they are today. She was in the eighth grade I think when I was in the first. She died, though. Got run over by the school bus. That's something I don't want to ever see again."

"Oh, man!"

"You know Zebediah Schultz is their adopted son."

"Really. Ekee's daddy? Is he going to inherit all that property? He'll be a millionaire."

"No. Zeb had a falling out with the old man years ago and was written out of the will. I guess their daughter Mary will get it all. She lives up in Washington, D. C., I think."

"Hmmm. It sure is nice up here, Mr. Peterson. You can see all the way to Hall's Corner."

"Thanks, Bean. I like it, too," Jake said as he exhaled.

They watched the gray tendrils weave their way into the shadows of the brisk night air.

/|\

XV. A Requited Love

From his very first day at work for his uncle Zeb in 1965 as maintenance man and general gofer, Ezekiel "Ekee" Schultz was told to be sure to introduce himself to all the residents of the EZ Mobile Home Park in Hall's Corner. It took him a whole weekend, partly because the park was so big and partly because he was so unsure of himself that introducing himself to strangers always unnerved him a little. So introducing himself to a lot of strangers all at one time made him stutter and talk to himself, and he dawdled.

It was a relief when no one was home. He felt like he had escaped jail. But when Zeb asked him if he had missed anyone, Ekee couldn't lie to his uncle's stern bony face and piercing blue eyes, and was ordered to go back to those trailers time and again until someone was home. Over the next eighteen years, Ekee had to introduce himself to all new residents and the task never got easier, but it didn't occur too often, usually no more than three or four a month, and he managed it, although not without great personal struggle.

The task took on exponential dimensions in 1983 when Zeb integrated the park by renting a trailer to a black woman, Polly Ann Jones. The lot was in the back corner of the park, on D Street, and immediately three nearby residents moved out. Zeb seemed undisturbed, and soon replaced them with more black families until that area of the park became known as the "black section."

Ekee had the natural racial prejudice that many others had in that part of the state, born as much from a native fear of the strange and unusual as it was from the South's legacy of slavery. Blacks numbered fewer than five hundred in all of Carter County, since the plantation system very rarely took hold in the narrow valleys and sharp ridges of Northwest Georgia. The majority of them lived on the east side of the county, within a few miles of Brownsboro, the county seat, or in Carter, a small settlement a dozen miles south on the Atlanta Road. In the whole west side of the county there were only a handful, so few that when Carter County High was integrated in 1971, the school population of Brownsboro High did not increase much despite the enrollment of over two hundred black children, mainly because of the formation of Carter Christian Academy, to which many white students fled. But even so, there was only minimal racial tension because among the number of black males transferring from Central, the black school, was a running back who ran a 4.39 in the forty-yard dash; a six-five wide receiver who also played center on the basketball team, and two tackles over 250 pounds. And at Carter County High, they numbered fewer than forty in a school population of over five hundred.

Ekee had graduated from Carter County High in 1966 and his entire experience with black people consisted of hunting rabbits on Thanksgiving in 1964 with Fifteen's beagles. Fifteen was a tall and seemingly ageless black man who swapped the use of his pack of beagles in the morning by Ekee and his daddy in the sagebrush fields behind their house at the foot of Sulagade Mountain for the opportunity to hunt those fields in the afternoon. His daddy had sent Ekee over to Fifteen's house, a weathered old relic of a farm house now little more than a shack farther up Switchback Road, to ask him about using his dogs.

Ekee remembered knocking on the door, which was answered by a "blue black" young woman several years older than he. She was wearing a homemade pastel blue shift so thin and worn it fit her curves like a second skin. His groin tightened when he saw her nipples rise beneath the fabric. She was so sensual and pretty and strange and wild-eyed that Ekee stammered out his request.

When she went back into the house, Ekee looked through the screen as if he was peering into another universe, one of clean-swept graying pine floors, cardboard nailed to the walls, a straight ladder-back chair with a new oak-split bottom by the hearth, and a high-backed sofa whose muted pattern blended into the shadows of a kerosene lamp on top of a large radio covered in dark, splitting veneer with a golden dial. The air came through the screen warm and heavy with the smell of collards cooking.

"Why is he called Fifteen?" he asked his daddy later. His daddy laughed.

"He says it's his shoe size. He has a brother named Sixteen, too."

Ekee never quite knew whether to believe him, but he did know that that day, he and his daddy shot five rabbits in the morning and Fifteen shot seven by himself that afternoon.

And that night, the "blue black" girl took up permanent residence in his fantasies. All that he had been told and heard about the animal nature of blacks was affirmed by the way the girl's nipples had gotten hard. From then on, he spent many nights visiting the shack and finding her alone and overcome with desire for him.

xxxxxxxxxxxxxxxxxxxxxxxxx

"Have you seen Polly Ann yet, boy?" Zeb asked him two days after she moved in.

Ekee shook his head.

"Then do it. I don't want her calling me about some strange man messing around her trailer. And don't forget, you've got to fix that hot water heater in 32A today. They've been calling all morning."

Still, it was late in the afternoon, after he fixed the water heater, when he knocked on her door.

Later Ekee couldn't describe in any real detail what happened, except for vivid flashes of memory. Polly Ann opened the door wearing a silky dress that reached down to her ankles with buttons from the neck to the hem. She was a little tall, with almond skin. Enough of the top buttons were open to reveal the narrow valley between her large breasts, which seemed to continually oscillate, and enough of the bottom ones open to give him a glimpse of the soft fold of her thigh above her knee. Her almond face, with its high round cheeks, small wide nose, and glinting black eyes, seemed to shimmer in a warm mist of lilac and chocolate that rushed out the door to envelope him.

"Come on in, young man. I've got a fresh chocolate pie," she said and extended her hand to him. Ekee gulped and took it. It was the first time he had ever touched a black person in his life. Her pink palm was soft and warm.

He remembered eating a piece of pie and looking around the room. Everything seemed to shine. Polly Ann was sitting by him on the couch, asking about who he was and what were his plans. Later, he could only conclude she was casting some kind of spell on him because he couldn't remember any more. He was trembling, shaken, and weak as a baby by the time she handed him another piece of pie to take with him and closed the door. Once outside, he gasped for breath, and wondered where he had gotten the pie.

That night, when he lay in bed, Ekee could see only see her pendulous breasts. Her dress had gapped open when she sat down and they looked like soft, brown cushions. He could hear her voice, low and melodious, somewhere far away. Mindlessly, he reached out to touch them and she clasped his hand, pressing it to her flesh, and laughed.

Polly Ann was calling him "sweet boy" as she wallowed beneath him, her hands on his buttocks holding him tightly. Her beasts and thighs enveloped him like the welcome warmth of a featherbed on a cold night. He was shivering and burrowed deeper into her soft flesh as her words seemed to hold his raw desire in suspension until at long last they released him to cry out in amazement and wonder.

Ekee walked around in a fog all that evening and the next day, his mind addlepated as he sought to grasp the fleeting images and hold them. Zeb said he was acting "tetched." And Ekee had been tetched. To Ekee, who had only gotten to third base and that only once in his thirty-three years, Polly Ann was a goddess whose very presence had blinded him and burned his skin. Yet she was a forbidden goddess, and had set off a war within him that constricted his chest until he could not breathe. It was this agony that drove him to knock on her door again two days later.

"Oh, poor darling," Polly Ann said when she opened the door and saw his careworn face.

"I want you," he grunted.

"Sweet boy," she said softly, "I'm just a figment of your imagination. Now go on."

As his mind slowly emerged from the fog, Ekee was mortified, not only that his lust and desperation had finally driven him to confess his desire for a black woman, but that she had sent him away, as if out of pity. A kernel of bitterness deep in his soul hardened. Its seeds had long flourished in him in the fertile soil of ignorance and violence cultivated in many children by long red rows left by a father's belt or a mother's switch.

"If I ever get to be manager of this park, I'll throw her out on her big black ass," he vowed, but that path was a winding one with unexpected twists and turns.

Over the years, he seldom saw her, and then only at a distance, but when he did, he cursed both her and himself. Yet at night, she had supplanted the blue black girl and she spent many hours submitting to his desires, always wantonly, sometimes by force.

Ekee assumed the position of manager of the EZ in the summer of 1998, and like a former lieutenant puffed up by shiny new captain's bars, he used every opportunity to assert his new authority. But he ran into a roadblock immediately. His first act was to serve an eviction notice on Polly Ann. He felt supremely confident in throwing her out. In the last six months, Zeb seemed to have lost interest in the park all together, anyway.

But Ekee chose the wrong hill to die on. His complaints to his uncle Zeb about her, fabrications of her whorishness he felt sure his uncle would surely believe because she was black, surprisingly fell on deaf ears.

"She stays and that's that," Zeb told him dismissively.

"But Uncle Zeb, she's got strange men coming and going in the middle of the night," he lied.

"I said she stays," Zeb said with finality, staring hard at his nephew. Ekee's frustration only grew when Zeb insisted that Polly Ann and Mama Wallace, an old woman whose brother-in-law was once state representative, alone among the tenants, would keep paying her monthly lot rent directly to him. Mama Wallace he could understand, but was the old man getting some from Polly Ann, he wondered? He couldn't imagine it. Polly Ann almost never left her trailer, and he never saw Zeb's Cadillac parked in her space or anywhere near it.

"But, Uncle Zeb . . . "

"Listen to me, boy," Zeb snarled, his face hard, and his brown eyes tightening into small black circles as he pulled Ekee to him by his shirt. His breath smelled of peppermint. "Leave that woman alone, or I'll kick your ass so hard your teeth will rattle. I told you once, and I won't tell you again, leave her to me."

He released Ekee then, pushing him back with his fist, and Ekee knew better than to say anything more. He was convinced now that Zeb must be getting some on the side from her, although he couldn't for the life of him figure out how.

It was only a few months later that he came face-to-face with her again. He was sitting in the Cozy Café, Hall's Corner's finest and only local eatery, and was surprised when Polly Ann brought his food to him. When he glared at her, she smiled and said, "Hello, Ekee. I'm helping out Linelle now, during the rush because of the funeral," and walked away, her "big, fat ass" waving at him. Ekee groaned.

He had a vague realization that she was referring to the funerals of Plum Thompson, a local developer and the county's richest man, and his wife. He had killed his wife and himself on Sunday and was being buried that day. But the thought faded quickly in his anger at Polly Ann. How dare she act so friendly, like nothing had ever happened between them? Ekee looked down at his plate of beef tips and gravy over rice and toyed with it until he saw Linelle walk to the front to serve Dave Stone, a Yankee who had moved his travel trailer into the park last month, and Doris Pilgrim, the Church of God woman who lived with her daughter Elsie in 49C. Even that strange pairing could not distract him, and he waved to get Linelle's attention.

"Yes, Ekee," the tall red-headed woman said as she stood beside his table with her hands on her hips. She looked like a mountain woman guarding a still and keeping a look-out for revenuers.

Ekee swallowed hard, and, nodding toward the back of the room, said, "Did she fix this?"

"You mean, Polly Ann?"

"Yes," he whispered, almost hissing.

Linelle's face hardened. Ekee blanched.

"So what if she did?"

"Because I ain't gonna eat it if she did," Ekee said, his voice low and rasping.

"You're a real piece of work, you know that, Ekee Shultz," Linelle said as she turned and walked away.

Ekee cursed himself, and cursed Linelle, Polly Ann, his uncle Zeb, and everyone within five miles of Hall's Corner. It might as well have been Hell's Corner for all he knew. In the meantime, however, the soft, warm aroma of the beef tips and gravy unconsciously prompted his hand to scoop up a big spoonful and put it in his mouth.

"What! White people have always eat black folks' cookin'. Hell, some of them even sucked at a black teat!"

The beef and rice turned to clay in Ekee's mouth as the words exploded from the back of the dining room. He quickly turned his face to the window. Outside, two cars were stopped at the caution light in the north lane of Livingston Road where it intersected Brownsboro Road and Switchback Road, even though there were no cars in the other directions. He saw a hubcap rolling down the road beside them and the door of the first car open. A man leaned out and caught the hubcap, then threw it in the back seat. Ekee felt his cheeks warm and his ears began to itch.

He didn't know how long he sat there, his mouth full of clay, but at some point he must have swallowed. And time had passed, because when he finally looked around, the place was empty and Linelle was sweeping up and preparing to close. He did not see Polly Ann anywhere.

With a grunt, he got up and walked to the register. He knew Linelle saw him, but she turned and walked back into the kitchen. In a few seconds, Polly Ann emerged and walked to the register.

When he glanced up at her to hand her his ticket, she was smiling. Their hands touched, and he dropped his head.

"That will be $4.32," she said.

He fished out a five and dropped it on the counter, then left without waiting for his change.

The next day, Ekee's feelings of humiliation and anger kept growing. He cursed his missing bookkeeper, who had taken off on the first for god knows where and left him to figure out the register by himself. He was rudely abrupt in his dealings with any tenants who had the misfortune to cross his path, which almost all of them had to in order to pay their lot rent or trailer rent, which was due in the first five days of each month.

That night, he watched television, but his mind was too distracted to pay it any attention, and he woke up each morning in a funk from tossing and turning all night.

As he labored over the books the next day, it was one of the two names nowhere in it that kept floating in front of his eyes. All day long he seethed. What in the hell makes that old nigger woman so special, he thought? She wouldn't let me fuck her, for godsakes. She actually called me "boy."

Dark, malefic clouds began to form in Ekee's mind like thunderheads that afternoon. He locked the office up early and drove across the highway to J's Grocery. The first cold front of the Georgia winter was coming in. Like the weather, the heater was only blowing chilly air, so he left the motor running.

Without a word to Teg, the owner, who eyed him curiously, Ekee bought a 12-pack of Stroh's and got back in his car. He shivered and cursed his car's heater, as if it were a willful, spoiled child only put on this earth to thwart his ambitions, then slammed the shifter into drive and backed rapidly back across the road, strewing gravel as he slammed on the brakes in front of his trailer. Once inside, he turned up the heat in grim defiance of his usual frugality. Cost? he muttered. The hell with it. His whole life felt like nothing but costs.

As he emptied the 12-pack beer by beer, he fumed over all the wrongs people had done to him. He remembered the time his daddy beat him until he thought he was going to die because some girl at school had stolen his math book, even though he tried to explain that the girl who took it had failed a couple of grades and was bigger than him and meaner than a cross-eyed snake. And he remembered the time his boyhood friend Danny has set him up with a sure thing, but forgot to tell him her daddy was an ornery cuss who didn't like boys coming around sniffing at his daughter like hounds on the scent and had a shotgun. And he remembered walking up to Polly Ann's door and feeling so wicked good, only to be shooed away like a bothersome child. And now all these humiliations had been compounded on Halloween when Adam Pinson's little boy had cold-cocked him with a golf club when he tried to scare him out of a sewer pipe for good in his gorilla suit. These, and many other wrongs, real and imagined, he fingered like a string of pearls which were, in his alcoholic haze, identical. As the sun went down along with his eighth beer, he could stand it no more, and stormed out into the twilight in the direction of D Street.

The chill air cut through his coat to leave open wounds, cleaving his skin and fat and muscle down to the bone. By the time he got to 78D, his face was chapped and he could no longer tell if his body was quaking from rage or chill.

"Oh, Ekee, you've been hurt," Polly Ann said, but he pushed her back into the room and closed the door.

"Shut up," he growled, waving off the warm scents of rose and cinnamon that embraced him, and the room with it polish and sheen that seemed to blind him, and the calm concern on her shimmering round face that enveloped him.

"What is really bothering you, Ekee?" she said, her voice as soothing as that of a whippoorwill on a hot summer night.

"I said shut the hell up, goddamn it!" he yelled and pushed her again, until she sat down on the sofa. He put his hand on his belt buckle to undo his pants, but his hands were numb and his body was weaving. "Goddamn it!"

"When I was a little girl, I snuck into the kitchen and stole butter from the ice box that my mother had made. I hid it in my dress, because I knew if my mama caught me she would give me a switching," Polly Ann said softly.

"Huh?" Ekee said, his voice slurred.

"I sat down behind the barn and ate it. It was a craving and I ate until I got sick and threw up. Lord, by that time my whole face was greasy. My dress too. Thinking back on it now, my mama had to know I stole her butter."

Ekee looked confused. She took his hand and pulled him down beside her on the couch.

"I bet my mama was looking out the back door and laughing the whole time. She knew it was just mischief, and I was a mischievous child I'll tell you that. And I learned my lesson. Life has a way of coming back on you, but it's just God's way of giving us an education. He don't mean anything personal by it. Oh, I didn't eat cow butter for the longest time, but my mama used to make these big old biscuits, cat heads she called them. I swear, cat head biscuits with a big slice of fresh cow butter between them are one of God's gifts to mankind. Mama or daddy didn't have to call us to get out of bed every morning; mama let the smell of her biscuits do it for her. Hmmm, I can still smell them if I close my eyes and think on it. You ever have cat head biscuits, Ekee?"

"My . . . my mama used to make them, before she died," Ekee whispered.

"I'm so sorry," Polly Ann said as touched his arm. "Was she a good cook? My mama sure was."

"I was eight," Ekee said softly. "She was standing in the kitchen at the stove, and I came into the house to ask her something. When she turned around, she opened her mouth to answer me but nothing came out. This stunned look came over her face, then she just smiled at me and fell over dead right there in the floor."

"I bet you miss her every day," Polly Ann said as she pulled him to her, leaning his body into hers until his head rested in the crook of her arm, his cheek atop her breast. Ekee began to sob, his tears wetting her dress. She softly stroked his hair. "Yes, I bet you do."

xxxxxxxxxxxxxxxxxxxxxxxx

Two months later, Zeb Schultz had an attack of severe stomach pains and was rushed to the Brownsboro Medical Center. The family was called to the hospital because Zeb's mysterious ailment seemed severe enough to kill him. His heartbeat was irregular, and had even stopped for over a minute, so they put him in the ICU.

The family members were few in number since Ekee's father was the only living sibling in his generation. Zeb's father and mother died in a car accident many years ago. When Ekee got to the waiting room in the ICU, only his father, Caleb, was there. Although Zeb was the adopted son of the late Plum and Genie Thompson, his falling out with Plum had divided the family, most of them siding with Plum. So only Plum's brother, Carter, and Genie's sister Jennifer Ann, were sitting with his parents.

"How is he?" he whispered to his father.

"Don't know. They can't figure out what he's got, but it's causing him a lot of pain."

Ekee sat in the waiting room as the seconds stretched into minutes and the minutes into hours until Carter, who was old and feeble, said his goodbyes with assurances he would return in the morning. When the doctor came in and said that Zeb's pain was now under control and the crisis had passed, Ekee said he would stay so his father could go home and rest.

"Your uncle is a tough old bird," Jennifer Ann said when only she and Ekee remained in the waiting room. She was a tall and thin, blue-haired woman wearing a brown knee-high cowgirl dress with white thigh-high cowboy boots and a large cowboy hat. "He saved my life once."

"He did?"

"When I was, oh, about twenty-five, I was over at Plum and Genie's new house, the first one they built below Six Mile, not the big one. They had just put in a well pump, but they had not built a cover over it yet. It had rained that morning, so everything was wet. I had an argument with Genie and went outside. We were always arguing about something or another. We were too close, I guess."

"I am sorry to hear of her passing, and her husband's, too," Ekee said.

"It was a great loss to many."

Beneath her large white cowboy hat, Ekee could see a tear on her cheek. He handed her his handkerchief.

"Thank you," she said, sniffling. "I was so mad I could chew nails, as they say, so I wasn't thinking straight. That's the only reason I can think of for standing on the concrete base of that pump. I believe I wanted to see father down the valley. It sits on a flat by the creek, you know. But when I lost my balance and put my hand on the pump to brace myself, I felt like I was hit by lightning."

"It was 220 volts," Ekee said.

"I guess. But whatever it was, it wouldn't turn me lose. Every muscle in me was jerking and twitching. It was an awful pain. I screamed and screamed. Zeb was there that day. It was before he and Plum had their falling out. He came running out of the house and just ran into me like one of those football players. Knocked me twenty feet past the pump into the mud. I was barely breathing. They thought I might die, and I did."

"You did?" Ekee said in wonder.

"At the hospital. They said I had no heartbeat when they got me there, and the doctor was about to pronounce me dead when my heart started beating again. It was a near-death experience, like they talk about on television. I could see myself lying on the gurney like I was floating in the air. I saw all my dead relatives. I even went through the tunnel into the light, just like they say. When I woke up, I was changed."

"Changed?"

"Yes. I started wearing big hats, for one thing. And, I don't buy any green bananas."

Ekee couldn't read her face well enough to know if she was teasing him or not, but the story didn't make him feel like laughing anyway.

"Ezekiel Shultz," the nurse said as she came into the waiting room. "Your uncle wants to see you."

Ekee went into the ICU and stood by Zeb's bedside. His uncle looked like a scientific experiment with all the tubes and sensors attached to him.

"Ekee, come here. I've got something to tell you," Zeb said hoarsely as he pointed to a spare, thin-cushioned chair by the bed.

"Some years ago now, an old friend of my adopted grandfather, Phil Thompson, asked him for a favor before he died. My grandfather promised him he would respect his wishes. He was a man of honor, Grandpa Phil was. The friend did die soon enough. but then Grandpa Phil died, too, right after. It's the strangest thing. Grandpa Phil knew it. He was just going to the hospital for gallbladder surgery, but the week before, he started giving things away. He gave me his pocket knife. I've still got it. They botched the surgery, you know. His gallbladder had abscessed, and they didn't get all of it out. He died the next day of blood poisoning.

"I wanted to sue the hospital, but Plum and Genie refused. Grandpa Phil had just given them most of the money they needed to build this ICU unit, although they never put his name on it because he insisted they not do it. He was like a daddy to me, and I was so mad with grief, I wanted to kill those doctors. When Plum and Genie refused to sue them, I moved out. We didn't speak for five years. But before he died, Grandpa Phil made me promise to honor his promise to his friend, and I told him I would.

"Now, I don't imagine I am going to die tonight. Or tomorrow, even if the doctor thinks it is my gallbladder. But I was scared there for a while, and I wondered what would happen if I did not have time to tell you. So, I'm telling you. I promised that I would provide Polly Ann Jones and Mama Wallace and her boy a place to live, scot free, rent and utilities, for as long as they live. And I want you to honor that promise."

"But why, Uncle Zeb?"

"As far as you're concerned, there is no 'why,' boy. There's just do."

He watched his uncle labor to breathe. He seemed smaller somehow, as if he had shrunk. He wondered if he had seen the tunnel and the light, but was afraid to ask.

"I understand."

Ekee's brow was creased with worry, and the old man's eyes softened for a moment.

"Ekee, I'm sorry," he said softly.

"For what, Uncle Zeb?"

"For anything I ever did to hurt you. I grew up hard, and it made me a hard man," Zeb said.

Ekee's eyes filled with tears and he patted Zeb's hand as he slowly closed his eyes.

Zeb Schultz had gallbladder surgery the next day, and survived, but in the process of removing it, the doctors discovered he had stomach and intestinal cancer. The doctors took out part of his stomach and intestines, and gave him six months to live. But in six months, he was back tending his orchards and working his garden. He lived another ten years, and even then, some said he died only because he quit eating and starved.

XVI. The Funeral

Under the unseasonably warm but clear November sky, the line of cars stretched for nearly a mile behind the two new brown Cadillac hearses. Three black limousines, two Cadillacs and a Lincoln followed it, and they in turn were followed by an array of Cadillacs, Lincolns and Chryslers, all black or white or silver or dark green. A large black dually quad-cab was next, then four-door sedan after four-door sedan, silver or white or teal or red, then a brown Hummer. Behind it came a gaggle of four-door sedans, two-door sedans, minivans, compacts, sub-compacts, and pickup trucks, both new and old, like the banded colors of a snake trying to keep up as the long line stretched and contracted. There was not enough room at the Little Prairie Holiness Church Cemetery for all the cars, so they lined the Six Mile-Oak Log Road for hundreds of yards in both directions.

Jake Peterson had to park his old Chevy pickup a quarter-mile away and joined the throng of people dressed in black walking up the road.

"Daddy!" squealed a little girl. Jake whirled around.

"Dede!" he laughed. The girl, a brunette pixie about seven-years-old, jumped up into his arms. He staggered.

"Whoa," he laughed. "You're getting to be a big girl."

She beamed at him. Over her shoulder, he could see the couple following her. He was a tall man, with hair as dark as the child's, and he had a handsome, if angular, face. He was wearing a dark blue sport coat and a pair of khakis.

"Luther," he nodded.

Luther nodded back.

"Sandy."

The woman was wearing a dark blue dress that covered her knees, and a gray jacket. She was tall, too, and slim, with long, curly brown hair. Anxiety creased her oval face, darkening her eyes.

"Hi, Jake."

He put the girl down and shook her hand. The four of them walked on slowly, not looking at each other.

"Jake . . ." Sandy said haltingly.

He looked at her, but said nothing.

"Jake, I'm sorry about DFACs. I just got mad when I didn't get your checks on time. I told them I didn't want to go through with it later, but they said I would have to re-do all the paperwork again if I dropped it."

"You know I'm not making as much at my new job at the Lumber Barn," he said as he picked the girl up and put her on his hip.

"I know. Like I said, I'm sorry. It's just that I got laid off when they closed the towel plant, and Deanna needed shoes and a coat for school."

"It's no problem," he said.

"Things have been pretty tight for us." She was holding Luther's hand.

"Like I said, no problem. So, how you been, Punkin?" He nuzzled her neck.

"Daddy, don't call me that!" she giggled.

The three walked on in silence while the girl chattered on about being in the second grade at a new school, her teachers, and her friends. When they reached the hill onto which the crowd converged, she whooped. Several people turned to look. The girl blushed.

"Mama, it's Cindy. She's my best friend," she said as she squirmed off his hip.

"Go on," Sandy said, "but be quiet."

"Yes, mama. 'Bye Luther. 'Bye daddy," the little girl whispered hoarsely, then ran off toward a black girl sitting with her family at the back of the rows of folding chairs surrounding the open burial plot under a large tent that said "Thompson Funeral Home." Sandy glanced at him, her lips pursed in a tight smile, but Jake was looking past her at Deanna. She and Luther followed, leaving Jake alone standing well back of the audience.

He sighed deeply. The sun-drenched air was clear and clean. The deep azure sky stretched over the small knoll like a dome, broken by few clouds. The muted chirps of birds radiated out from the trees lining the pasture by the cemetery. A blue jay groused in the field, overgrown with grass and bitterweed and musk thistle. A cricket chirped from an old, gnarled cedar tree nearby. He tried to count the intervals between its chirps, but stopped when he realized that he could no longer remember how to use it to calculate the temperature. Sobs from the front line of chairs drifted over the crowd.

"Hi, Jake."

He turned to see Brad, Grace, Adam, and Rachel, all former classmates at Carter County High, Class of 1986, walking toward him.

"Hi, guys," he said, keeping his voice low, out of earshot of the crowd. "Long time, no see. How's the paper business, Brad?"

"We're doing all right. Next time you're in Brownsboro, stop in. I'll show you the new color unit we just bought. I'll even take you to lunch, my treat."

"Tempting. Maybe I can come over on my lunch break."

"Hell, you can't get from C Street to A Street."

"Hey, big guy," he laughed softly as he shook Adam's hand. "I see you're off your crutches, but you're still dragging that same old ball and chain."

Rachel blushed.

"*So, Gracie, did your nurse drop you when you were a child?*"

"See!" Grace said, poking Brad in the ribs. "Even he does a better George Burns than you do. *No, we were poor. Mama had to do it.*"

"So, what's up with you guys?"

"Ah, it's such a beautiful day we couldn't stay inside," said Adam.

"So, we decided what the heck, let's go to a funeral," said Grace.

"I had to be here anyway," Brad said. "Did you see the story in the paper?"

"Yeah," Jake said. "It was really a shock."

"Who would have thought Plum Thompson, of all people, would do a thing like that, killing his wife and then himself," said Adam.

"The sheriff didn't say it was a murder-suicide," said Brad.

"How could it have been anything else?" said Rachel.

"Hush, Rache," Adam whispered. "He was Grace's great uncle."

"No, shit! I mean, no kidding," Brad said.

"Sorry, Grace. I didn't mean anything."

"She was my great aunt," Jake said.

"Then this is old home week," Brad said.

"Shut up, you jerk." Grace hissed as she hit him on the arm.

"Ow!"

"I didn't really know her. I saw him a lot more often than I saw her, but only on the construction site. I don't think either of them knew me from Adam's house cat."

"I don't have a cat," Adam smiled.

"I didn't know him either, or her," said Grace, pensively.

"I wonder what would make a man do such a thing?" asked Rachel.

He questioned was left unanswered as the minister began to speak. His deep monotone only formed a bass line to the birds' melody and the cricket's percussion.

"I can't hear him," Rachel whispered from the other side of Adam.

"Does it matter?" Grace whispered back across the broad expanse of his chest. When she turned to the other two men, Jake was smiling at her. She stepped around Brad to stand beside him.

"What are you grinning about?" she whispered. She had to stand on her tiptoes to reach his ear.

"Oh, nothing," he said.

In that moment, she looked so beautiful, up on her toes, all skinny legs and boy hips and breasts flattened by her tight shirt, with her small, smiling face framed by her close-cropped brown hair, that if he had a rock, he would hit her with it.

The grave side sermon ended and the mourners filed past the family, shaking their hands and giving condolences.

"Who was the skinny guy who was taking it so hard?" Rachel asked as they walked back to their cars.

"That was her brother, Tim. He lives in Philadelphia. He's never married," said Brad.

"He looked kind of gay," Adam said.

"Is he, Grace?"

"Shut up, Brad."

"Let's all go over to Linelle's for coffee," Brad said.

"Who wants pie?" Grace said cheerily. Adam hooted, then quickly hushed himself, but Rachel only blushed. Jake looked at them in curiosity.

"It's a long story, champ," Grace said, taking his arm. "I'll tell you on the way."

Jake took the long way back to Hall's Corners. He turned north up the Six Mile-Oak Log Road, then west on the Macedonia Church Road. As they passed through a vast green rolling pasture, they rode over an old iron bridge across Oak Log Creek. The old oak boards clattered loudly beneath the wheels of the truck. Across the pasture, they could see a line of hardwood, mostly bare but with a lot of oaks still clinging to their dull orange leaves. Through the trees, they could see the ridge line and above it, blue sky.

"When I was in New Mexico, this is what I missed most," she said. "Don't get me wrong. It is so beautiful there. Every night is a light show. Once I rode from Ruidoso to El Paso and saw the sun sparkle off the frozen waterfalls on the Organ Mountains as it set. And once we rode into the White Sands Desert in the summer. It was like 104. But we turned the air conditioning up and pretended it was snow."

"Green and water," he said.

"What?"

"That's what you missed. Green and water."

"How did you know?"

"I hitchhiked to California, remember? It was right after high school."

"You and Sandy?"

"Are you kidding? She didn't like it, but I had itchy feet. I just had to see San Francisco and the Pacific once in my life."

"I didn't know that. You should have stopped in Alamogordo. I was in the Air Force then."

"I should have. But I got this ride with a guy just east of Amarillo who was going to San Jose. We drove straight through. My sister lives there."

"In San Jose?"

"Yeah, well she did. But by the time I got there, she had moved to L. A. A little town called Belle that sort of got swallowed up by the city."

"You should have called first."

"I wanted to surprise her. So, how about you, Sarge? What was it like defending America's freedom?"

Grace laughed.

"Boring, mostly. A lot of spit and polish and all that bullshit. I liked Germany, though. At least until this snot-nosed Airman First tried to rape me. I reported him, but all I did was create a big hassle because it was my word against his. In the end, I was the one who got transferred. After that, I just wanted to get out."

"Sounds like a lot of crap."

"Let's talk about something else."

"OK, what's the deal with 'Who wants pie?'"

"I should have kept my mouth shut."

Jake glanced at her as they crossed a low hill between a weathered two-story farm house on pillars, most of its white paint flaked off, and an equally weathered red barn with a side-shed whose outer wall was tilting over. A green '69 Plymouth four-door sedan sat beside the house, and as they passed, two hounds walked toward the road, barking.

"All right. You know about Sophie's revenge," Grace said.

"I was there."

Grace blushed. The event would long remain a highlight in the unofficial history of Carter County. Carl Thornborough's wife, Sophie, a girl of seventeen, had caught him running around with Rachel a couple of months back, and exposed the whole affair publicly at a dinner for about fifty people held behind Linelle's Cozy Café in Hall's Corner just for the occasion. But what made the event legendary was that Sophie announced that she had taken her revenge by making love to Carl's daddy, Rachel's daddy, Adam, and Grace, Carl's cousin. After the dinner, she left him and moved to New Orleans.

"Did she really screw all those guys?" Jake said, his voice rising slightly.

"I don't know," Grace said. She turned her face to the window.

"And you?"

"I ain't saying." Around her reddened cheek he could see her smile.

"Don't be coy with me, Grace," he teased.

"Do you want to know about 'Who wants pie?' or not?" She was giggling. "Good. Well, after the dinner, Brad and I tried to cheer Adam and Rachel up. They looked like two whipped dogs. I don't think they've really gotten over it all yet, but anyway, Brad invited us out to his place on the Old Brownsboro Road. You know, the house he inherited from his aunt that he was restoring when he found out that it was originally an old cabin."

"I read his column about it."

"It's a great place, way back off the road in some trees. So, we got them out there and got them drunk and stoned, then we all got naked, and one thing led to another."

"You mean, all four of you? Gracie, you are a one bad girl."

"Do you really think so," she said, cocking her head to one side and fluttering her eyelashes. "Or are you just jealous 'cause you weren't there?"

Jake turned to watch the road. She could see his Adam's apple bob as he swallowed.

"You know me, Grace," he said, turning back to face her. "I'm a one-woman man."

"I know," she said, her green eyes leaping from his face to slide across the horizon. "You can imagine what kind of shape we were in the next day. We slept until past noon, but even then I still had a buzz when I woke up. We were all as hungry as hibernating bears, so we went to Linelle's. It was a slow day and we had the place to ourselves. She wouldn't take our order, but just shushed us and went into the kitchen. We were too zombified to object. I think she's some kind of witch because she fixed us this incredible linguini in white sauce with homemade Italian bread, buttered with real cow butter. It was perfect. Just perfect. By the time we got through eating, we could hardly speak. So, when she came to the table with these big cups of hot coffee and asked us, 'Who wants pie?' we all lost it. I told her, 'I think we've had enough.' "

Jake chuckled. "Well, here we are, right in the Middle."

He pulled off the road and parked the truck at a slant to a row of old buildings so that it faced the pasture and woods that reached to the horizon beyond the town. The Middle consisted of five abandoned buildings, four connected by a common covered walk. They faced a large tin cotton warehouse across the road guarded by two ancient tractors hiding in a stand of dead poke salad, one with metal wheels, both rusted like the Tin Man. Their back was to Talking Spring Creek and their battlement was an abandoned railroad track whose rails and ties had been replaced with fescue. It was a giant green berm that stretched out of sight in either direction, breached only by a dirt drive crossing over it in front of the warehouse.

Signs on the four buildings said they were the remnants of A. J. Culberson's General Store, Peterson's Feed and Seed, G. W. Hill & Co. and the Wayside Café. The names of Culberson's and Peterson's were in faded paint on large glass windows through which could be seen dusty shapes piled against the walls. G. W. Hill & Co. was set in marble across the top of a two-story brick facade. Only the red and white Wayside Café sign with Coca-Cola logos flanking the words showed any sign of recent life, and streaks of rust ran from each of the four bolts holding it to the building.

"The Middle of nowhere," Grace said.

"Nooo. This place used to be called Spring City a long time ago. When they organized Carter County in 1850, it was the county seat for a while because G. W. Hill's granddaddy built a big mill on the creek to make cloth. It's long gone now, but my granddaddy said it used to be near that clump of trees over there behind the warehouse. There was a bank vault in the back of the G. W. Hill & Co. building there, and Culberson's still has a section just inside—see the banisters?—that was a U. S. Post Office."

"So how do you know all this?"

"I guess I got it from my granddaddy, Jasper. My great-granddaddy owned that store, and granddaddy grew up around here. He was named after J. W. Culberson who owned this store. I got my name from him through my grandfather."

"Oh, yeah. I remember from graduation. Jasper Wilcox Peterson," Grace said, imitating a PA system. "I don't which got the bigger laugh, Jasper or Wilcox."

"Now you know why I chose to be called Jake. Anyway, there was a problem with the name Spring City. Some place in Northeast Georgia had the same name and their post office was older, so they had to change it.

They decided on Hillsborough, or rather G. W. Hill decided, my grandpa said. But after the mill burned down in 1949, and then G. W. died, the place kind of died with him, and the post office closed. That's pretty rare, you know, for a post office to close. Hell, Oak Log's got a post office. Finally, by the late 1950s, the Hills, the Culbersons, and the Petersons were long gone, and only the Wayside Cafe was left, then it closed when the railroad abandoned the track. Only it was known as the Spring City Café first. The Taylor Atkins' family owned it in the beginning and the Atkins never got along with the Hills even though they were neighbors for over a hundred years. See those two old houses back up against the ridge? So the Atkins kept the name just to spite G. W. Somebody rented the place in the '60s for a while and tried to make a go of it as the Wayside Cafe, but they closed after only a couple of years."

"So, how did it get the name Middle?" asked Grace as she rolled down the truck window to get a better look.

"The story is that back in the '30s someone asked Taylor Atkins—he was the third, or maybe fourth. I don't know which— why he didn't just close up the café and leave. 'Why should I want to be anywhere else?' he said. 'I live right here in the middle of the world.' The name just stuck."

"Right here in the middle of the world," Grace said as she slid her butt forward and lay back against the truck seat. She looked at the landscape through heavily lidded eyes, and soon her chest rose and fell in a slow, steady rhythm.

"Yeah," said Jake. He rolled down his window and rested his elbow on the frame while he looked at the line of distant woods dividing the green rolling pastures from the blue and white dome above.

A mild November breeze scurried through the truck windows smelling of green grass and old, musty hay.

Where does the road end? Jake wondered. I know that if we go up here about a quarter-mile and take a left, then go a few hundred yards, we're in Talking Spring. And if I turn right there, the Talking Spring Road goes to Hall's Corner. And if I get on Livingston Road there and go north, eventually I would get to Tennessee, then West Virginia, Ohio, Canada. But where then? If I just kept driving, would I end up at some fishing resort on a cold, clear lake full of big lake trout, or would a pig trail road go on from there to some settlement of just a few families out in the wilderness like Middle once was? And from there, maybe a trail twists and turns even further, maybe even to the Arctic Ocean and some tiny Inuit fishing village somewhere. It's a long way to somewhere from the middle of the world.

He cranked the truck reluctantly, then drove the short distance to the cut-off leading to Talking Springs Road. As they drove over the old railroad crossing and pulled to a stop, they saw a woman a little way down the road, looking at a stream that ran from a culvert. She turned to them and they waved. She waved back, then turned back to watching the stream.

"Who is that?" Jake said as they turned toward Hall's Corner.

"I think that's Lois, Aub Folsom's wife," Grace said.

"I don't know her. But it's going to get a little too cool to be out walking in short sleeves," he said.

"She probably is just getting away from her mother-in-law. I don't know how she stands taking care of her day after day."

"Then she's nothing like your mama?"

Grace balled up her fist, but Jake wagged his finger at her.

"Uh uh."

"Darn," she said as she slumped back against the seat.

Jake watched the woman's back in his rearview mirror until a bend in the road put her out of sight.

By the time they got to the Cozy Café, the place was nearly empty of customers. As they walked in, they heard a woman's loud voice coming from the "house table" in the back of the dining room.

"What! White people have always eat black folks' cookin'. Hell, some of them even sucked at a black teat!"

Grace cackled as Jake led her to a booth near the front, smiling. The irate woman looked like Polly Ann Jones from the back. She was sitting at the house table with Linelle. She was an older black woman of expanding girth who had once looked like a fashion model. Two young men in worn jeans and faded flannel shirts sitting on stools at the counter turned to look. Their faces were hard, but they said nothing and turned back to their meals. A somewhat dowdy and plain woman two booths down whispered something to her companion and got up and left.

"Hi, Doris," Grace said as she passed, but the woman didn't seem to hear her. Her companion slowly got up and walked to the cash register at the end of the counter. Linelle left the table at the back to meet him there.

"Hey, Yankee," Jake said.

"Hey, redneck," Dave Stone said as he paid his ticket. He had a Boston accent and was a ruggedly handsome, broad-shouldered man with graying temples and just the beginnings of a paunch. He walked over to them.

"Did you get all the insulation in under your trailer?" Jake said as they shook hands.

"Almost. If it's clear tomorrow, I'll be able to finish."

"Well, let me know if you need any help. Oh, Grace, this is Dave Stone. Dave, Grace Brady. Dave just moved into the park a few weeks ago. He's got this big travel trailer, one with two slide-outs. It's nicer inside than most of the trailers in the EZ. He's traveling the country."

Gracie looked at him with open curiosity.

"I'm retired Navy," Dave said.

"Must be nice to live wherever you want and if you get tired of it, just pick up and leave," said Grace.

"I guess so, if you can afford the gas," he laughed.

"So, how did you wind up in Hall's Corner?"

"Oh, it's not obvious? Linelle's cooking," he teased as the proprietor joined them. Linelle smiled. "Well, I've got to go. My date is waiting."

"Now that's a match," Grace said, shaking her head in wonder after he went out the door. "Plain old Doris hooking up with some Yankee traveler."

"It is a wonder," grinned Jake.

"Brad said to tell you they had to leave," Linelle said. "He had to get back to the paper, and Adam and Rachel had to go home to meet the school bus, which should be by here any minute. If you are really hungry, you're out of luck. After the funeral, there was a big crowd came in. I don't even have scraps to feed Maurice."

Maurice was her pot-bellied pig.

"Oh, crap!" Grace suddenly exclaimed. "I forgot I've got to meet the plumber. Right now, too. I'm renovating Miss Clarie's, the old clothing store down the block. It's going to be a boutique, mostly tourist stuff, but I'm going to have a lot of local art, too. Linelle, did you get those cloth samples yet?"

"No, but I should have them by tomorrow."

"There's no rush. Bye, Jake. Thanks for the ride."

Grace leaned over to squeeze his hand, then flew out the door like a dove out of a cage.

"Talk about wonders. Stay sit, Jake, and I'll make a fresh pot of coffee."

"Ah, don't go to all that trouble, Linelle," he said absently, without turning around until Grace had passed out of view.

"Would you care for a piece of pie, then, to take with you? I've got some apple and some coconut creme left."

"Yeah, I'll take a piece."

"Which kind?"

"Surprise me."

Jake sat back in the booth as Linelle stepped behind the counter. It was only then that he saw Ezekiel "Ekee" Schultz, the manager of the EZ, sitting at a table in the front window alone. He sat with his back partially turned to Jake, staring out the front window. The fat little man's flushed cheeks were bulging as if he had a mouth full of food he had forgotten to chew. Deciding to leave well enough alone, Jake paid Linelle and left.

xxxxxxxxxxxxxxxxxxxxxxx

Jake walked up the steps of the large tri-level deck that dwarfed his trailer with a slice of mystery in a white paper bag in one hand and a glass of milk in the other. The unseasonably warmth of the day was already giving way to the long shadows of winter's cool evening. He put the bag and milk down on a small metal table made of curled black wrought iron legs holding up a plywood top painted blue and cracked, and dusted the oak leaves out of a green and white plastic and aluminum lounge chair before sitting down.

He took a big drink of the cold milk and was about to open the bag when Ekee, the park manager, drove up. He lowered the power window.

"Looks like it will be a cool night," Jake hollered down.

"Yeah," said Ekee, his voice flat. "Ah, Jake, about this deck . . ."

"I told you, Ekee, it was some computer glitch over at the Lumber Barn. I didn't order all this stuff, but when you threatened to throw me out of the park, I had no choice but to go ahead and build it. I tried to explain it to them, but they still said they have no record of it. But I figure one day someone will show up and make me tear it all down."

Ekee waved off his complaint.

"About that, Jake. I've changed my mind. It's become some kind of landmark. I was over in Brownsboro today and I heard someone giving directions. They said, 'If you get to the Big Deck, you've gone too far.' I think it might be good for business."

"Then I'm glad," Jake said, laughing, but Ekee had already put the car in gear and driven off.

He sat back in the chair and inhaled as he looked into the oak tree towering over him. He knew that if he could see it from the top, its limbs would look like a whirly-gig. He exhaled. Farther down, just below the fringe of the dull orange canopy, he could just see the roofs and back of the facades of the buildings of Hall's Corner. He thought of Grace there, in the white-painted brick one almost in the middle, and wondered what she was doing.

Without looking, he found the bag and opened it, then took a big bite. It was coconut.

XVII. The Women's Circle

"Grace, you feel like a block of ice!" Jake laughed as he snuggled against her. They were lying naked on an air mattress inside two full-size sleeping bags zipped together on the top level of a deck that rose by and above Jake's trailer in the EZ Mobile Home Park. The temperature was just below freezing and the sky was very clear.

"Not everywhere," she purred. "Not here."

He groaned.

"Or here."

Jake rolled over on top of her as she giggled.

"Now you've made me lose count. Where was I? Oh, yes, one hundred billion . . . ahhh . . . and one, one hundred billion and oooo . . ."

Jake pulled the sleeping bags back over their heads and it was close to midnight before they re-emerged. They lay back against the pillows and breathed deeply of the crisp night air.

"Are you ready now to abandon your pagan ways?" he asked softly as he turned to face her.

"No," she said as she turned to face him, smiling. "But please keep trying."

He kissed her, but their kiss was interrupted by someone calling her name from the ground below.

"Yes!" she said.

"Grace, the circle needs you."

"I'll be down in a second."

Jake's lips pursed in an exaggerated pout. She kissed his nose and whispered, "I'll be back."

"What is it?" she asked Linelle Dubose, owner and operator of the Cozy Café, a short walk away in Hall's Corner when she got to the bottom of the stairs.

"Polly Ann says it is time," the tall red-headed woman answered.

The two walked in silence around the corner of Jake's trailer and onto D Street, passing in and out of the circles of security lights until they reached the black section at the end. They went into the trailer at 78D. As Grace pulled the door closed, two shots rang out close by. She screamed.

"What was that?" Linelle gasped.

"I've been afraid of this," said Polly Ann, a short, stout black woman who lived in the trailer. "I've been listening to them yell at each other all evening."

"Who?" Grace asked, but the question was not immediately answered. A police siren suddenly grew louder and louder until a bright blue light, like a frantic lighthouse, throbbed through the kitchen windows.

As Grace clung to Linelle, Polly Ann went to the door and looked out.

"Please stay inside, ma'am," someone yelled from beyond the light.

Polly Ann closed the door.

Someone yelled, "He's got a gun!"

In rapid succession, five gunshots crackled outside on the street, then everything was silent but for a child crying.

The women waited without talking until three more police cars and an ambulance arrived and left. Through the kitchen windows they could see that a crowd had gathered in front of the trailer across from them, some of whom remained long after the ambulance left and the blue lights finally stopped flashing but for one. The front door at 68D was open and light streamed from it onto the front steps and the thick grass encasing them.

There was a knock on the door at 78D.

"Police officer! Open up!"

Polly Ann opened the door.

"Ma'am, there's been a serious domestic dispute across the street and I would like to ask you a few questions," said the young officer very seriously.

"Jimmy Daniel, is that you?" Linelle asked as she stepped beside Polly Ann.

"Hi, Miss Linelle," the officer said. "Grace. Now ma'am . . ."

"Jimmy, we didn't see or hear anything except some gunshots and a bunch of shouting," Linelle said.

"Well, even so . . ."

"That drunk Gabe Lanier shot his wife, didn't he?" interrupted Polly Ann. "Is she dead?"

"No, ma'am. She's badly hurt, but the paramedics think she'll live. Now if I could just . . ."

"Excuse me," said Jennifer Ann Peterson as she barged past the officer into the room, then turned to face him. She was no less tall nor intimidating than Linelle, and Jimmy gulped.

"Come on in, Doris," Jennifer Ann said over his shoulder.

"I just want to ask a few questions."

"Jennifer Ann!" Linelle cried disapprovingly.

"Where is their little boy?" asked Polly Ann.

"She wanted to come," Jennifer Ann said with a wave of her hand as she sat down on the couch.

"He's been taken to a foster home for the night."

"But Doris?"

"He was pretty shook up."

"Jennifer Ann, you didn't tell me Grace would be here," groused Doris, a plain middle-aged woman with long brown hair pulled back in a bun.

"Oh, poor child."

"You're the one who said you wanted to come."

"Now, ma'am, what did you hear prior to 11:45 p.m.?"

"Is Gabe dead?"

"But you didn't tell me Grace would be here."

"Yes, ma'am. Now, what . . .?"

"What have you got against me, Doris?"

"Were you the one who killed him?"

All four women faced Jimmy Daniel, whose face was alternately yellow with his eyes in the shadow of his hat and blue with one cheek in shadow. A hound bayed in the west. Sounds like it is one of Zeb Shultz's, Jimmy thought. He swallowed.

"No, ma'am. A GBI agent did. He had no choice."

"Poor boy," said Polly Ann.

"You're a harlot, that's why."

"Jimmy, why don't you go on home now," Linelle said as she stepped out onto the small porch of the trailer and took his arm.

"Me? What about you and Dave Stone, and you still married."

"Doris! Grace! Hush!" said Jennifer Ann.

"Are y'all having some kind of New Year's party?" Jimmy asked, craning his neck to look back toward the door as Linelle led him down to his car.

"No. It's just a little women's circle we've got going. It's like the quilting club your mama used to belong to."

"But it's after mid- . . ."

Linelle closed his car door and went back into the trailer. Mama Wallace, an elderly gray-haired woman from the other end of C Street, tapped on his window and waved, then followed Linelle.

Now alone for the first time since he saw the shots fired that killed Gabe Lanier, a deep chill settled in Jimmy's bones. He began to shiver and turned the temperature and fan on high. He turned off the blue light and looked out of the passenger side window at the trailer on lot 78D. The porch light went out, then the kitchen lights. He would come back tomorrow. Right now, he just wanted to go home.

"One of y'all check on that boy tomorrow," said Polly Ann as Mama Wallace entered the trailer.

"I will," Mama Wallace said.

"Let's form the circle," said Linelle as she pulled two chairs from the kitchen into the living room. Grace lit three candles and placed them on the coffee table and four of the women sat down facing them.

"Sit down, Doris," Polly Ann kindly said.

"You *are* witches!"

"No, Doris, just women. Now sit down," said Jennifer Ann.

The stares of the four women pulled her down into the seat.

"What are you going to do?" she said, trembling.

"We're going to talk, Doris," said Jennifer Ann.

"I called this circle because it is time to tell Bean Wallace the truth," said Polly Ann.

"Wait. Doris, do you swear on your immortal soul that nothing you hear in this room will ever leave it?" Jennifer Ann said lowly.

Doris looked from face to face flickering in the candlelight and felt that their eyes pierced her with visions of hell fire.

"Well, do you?" Mama Wallace said.

"Y . . . yes."

"Where is Bean?" said Grace.

"He'll be coming along directly," said Mama Wallace.

"What is this all about?" said Doris.

"All in due time, Doris," said Linelle. "Now let us join hands and close our eyes."

"Oh, Lord, forgive me."

"We have gathered together to form this sacred circle to help Polly Ann and Bean Wallace through a great trial," said Linelle softly. "We do not sit in judgement; we dwell in a circle of love and acceptance. Let us each look deep into our hearts for snares and tangles that might keep us from this holy purpose, and rid ourselves of them. Let us separate our lives from their fate so that we might be of true service to them, like circles of women have done from time immemorial. This is our power and our burden. Let us bear them up in joy and kindness, and embrace them in the warmth of our hearts."

"Yes." said Grace and Mama Wallace and Polly Ann.

"Amen," said Doris. There were tears in her eyes.

There was a knock on the door.

"Mama Wallace?"

"Come in, Bean."

The tall, skinny boy with wild frizzy hair stepped into the room a pace and stopped, staring from face to glowing face.

"It's OK, Bean," said Mama Wallace as she fetched him into the circle. Each of the women reached out to touch him briefly as he sat down, then included him in the circle of hands.

"Wha . . . what's gggoing on?"

"Bean, you know my friend Polly Ann. She has a story to tell you."

Bean looked into the black woman's round face and drowned in the deep pools of her large, shimmering eyes. She spoke, and her words were like the elusive songs of bobwhites heard at a distance.

"When I was young, almost as young as you, I fell in love with a wonderful man. He was a powerful man, not in physical strength or stature, for he was unexceptional in both, but in intelligence and charisma. He wasn't handsome either, not handsome at all, but to me he was beautiful. He had a powerful voice and when he spoke, others listened, but not just because of it, but because when he spoke, he had something important to say. He was not a man of mindless principles, and he was certainly no saint, but he was a man of great heart. As you might expect, such a man was admired by both men and women, and power and influence came easily to him like it was his birthright.

"He loved me, too. There are no words for a love like ours, and even with a voice that could stir the heart and inspire the soul, he could not find any. But we didn't need words, or any of the trappings of love you see on television and in the movies. He never bought me flowers or candy or any of that, or even provide me with a home, and I never cooked or kept house for him. I am a terrible cook. But none of that mattered because we were friends first, then lovers. He asked nothing more of me than that I be what I am, and I asked nothing more than that of him. Remember this, Bean. If you can ever find someone who can love you like that, do not let her get away, for it is a rare thing.

"Now you might ask, where is this man that I love? Why am I not with him? He died fifteen years ago at the age of 72. But even when he was alive, I could not live with him because he was white. Because of his status in Carter County, we could not even live in the same place. So, for all the twenty-five years we shared, he lived here and I lived in Atlanta. I graduated from Spelman College and taught school in Fulton County. I had my own apartment and my own friends. I had my own life and he had his. It was the way it had to be, you see, because he was a man of great moral convictions and believed that he could help people. So the only way he could serve the people, and love me at the same time, was to live two separate lives."

"Who was he?" Bean asked.

"He was Uncle Dave Wallace, the state representative for Carter County for over thirty years until he retired in 1980."

Doris gasped.

"We never intended to have any children, but despite taking precautions, we had two. The first was Levon. He was a beautiful boy with the shiniest ebony face you ever saw. My Levon was always a proud boy, and grew into a proud black man. When I went into labor with him, Uncle Dave had Mama Wallace come to live with me and help raise him. She loved him just like she was his own mama, and Davey always gave me money to help raise him. But those were troubling times. Black people had struggled so long and suffered so much at the hands of white people in America that Levon could not help but be resentful. I even had my own resentments. Almost all of us did. I guess that's why I made such a mistake. I was afraid that if Levon knew who his daddy was, he might hate him and me too. So, when Davey came to visit, Mama Wallace would always take him somewhere. He never saw Davey at all after he was old enough to remember. But Davey loved that boy. He didn't want to hide from him. It was all my doing. But when he was eighteen, Levon fell in love with this pretty poor girl named Tamara from Cabbagetown and said they were getting married. Although I was greatly afraid to tell him, I couldn't keep it a secret any longer because they wanted to have children."

Polly Ann began to cry. Hands squeezed hands tightly.

"It was as I feared. When I told him, Davey was with me and tried to explain why things were the way they were, but Levon would have none of it. He stormed out of the house and I didn't hear from him for years. I found out later from Tamara's mama that he married the girl and moved to Detroit. They had three sweet little babies that are now about grown, but he won't let me come and see them. He won't even speak to me, still. My only hope is that after they get out on their own, they might seek me out themselves.

"I grieved for that child so bad I thought about killing myself, and I might have if it had not been for Davey insisting that Mama Wallace stay on with me."

"It took no coaxing," said Mama Wallace. "Polly Ann and I were already best friends."

"Eventually, things went back to normal, as normal as they could, until Davey's health began to fail in 1980 and he had to retire from the legislature. He started feeling bad during the session and went to see the doctor. He had leukemia. His family wanted him to come back home, but he insisted that he needed to be close to his doctor, so he took an apartment right next to mine in North Atlanta. I only had seventeen years in the public schools, but I retired so I could be with him every minute. It was painful watching him die away a little every day, but it was even more painful when he seemed to rally in the last year only to fail rapidly afterwards. I began to have stomach trouble in 1983 and I thought it was because I was so worn down after nearly three years of nursing him. But when I went to the doctor, he told me I was pregnant again. I couldn't believe it. I was forty-two years old.

"However I might not want to add to his concerns, I knew I couldn't keep it from Davey. But he just smiled, like I knew he would, and said, 'It will be all right, Polly.' He was staring death in the face and he was comforting me! I just cried and cried."

Polly Ann blew her nose and sniffled.

"My Davey died in June. It was a warm, rainy day. I was holding him in my arms and he was trying to get his breath. 'I will see you soon,' he said, and passed. My baby was born two months later. Everything came out when the family read the will. Davey had left equal parts of his estate to his son, Dave Jr., from his marriage to Janet Whitton—they divorced right after I met Davey—and to me and my son. It wasn't much, but with my part there's enough to pay for college. Dave, Jr., took it real hard, and he won't have anything to do with me. He didn't even want me moving back to Carter County. He's got his father's name, and he wasn't shy about using it to win election to his father's old seat. I even hear he might run for governor. But he's not the man his father was. But I think my son will be."

Polly Ann smiled at Bean.

"Welcome," said Grace.

Bean felt the floor begin to shift like sand. For a moment he feared it would simply fall away and he would drop into an endless void. His parents were dead. They had died when he was real young. His mother

was Mama Wallace's daughter, and she and her late husband Elton had
adopted him and taken him to raise. She had shown him their picture.
Mama Wallace was poor after Elton died when he was almost too little to
remember, living on a small pension and Social Security. He was a gawky
sixteen-year-old white boy with frizzy black hair from a trailer park in
North Georgia who sometimes fancied himself to be a poet when he wasn't
fancying himself to be nothing, or doomed to misery because in the last few
months, he had loved a grown crazy woman, and lost something he never
had. But he knew, as he watched it all fall slowly into the void beneath his
feet, that the story was true. It was too elegant not to be.

"Mama?" he said as the circle of women closed in to embrace him.

xxxxxxxxxxxxxxxxxxxxxxxx

Grace quickly stripped and stood in the cool air looking out over the EZ
Mobile Home Park. In the distance, she could see the caution light at Hall's
Corner and she took a deep breath to feel the air sear her lungs. Her small
nipples hardened and goose bumps pebbled her skin.

"You are turning into an icicle," Jake laughed as he leaned on his elbow
and threw the sleeping bag back to his waist.

Grace scurried under the covers and pressed every inch of her body that
she could against his. He yelped.

"Happy New Year," she said.

XVIII. A Brief History of Hall's Corner, Georgia

Written by Julius Pinkus, Jr.
On the occasion of the Nation's Bicentennial, 1775-1976.
© 1976, 1998.

Hall's Corner, Georgia, population 1,167, was incorporated on July 4, 1855, five years after Carter County was created. The town is named for Jasper Higgins Hall, the land surveyor who drew up the initial plots for the town and was its first mayor. The original city council included D. R. Peterson, O. R. "Ort" Davis, H. M. Marion, and F. T. Dubois. The earliest settlers also included the Wallace, Smith, England, Carnes, and Humphries families.

Hall's Corner was an early trading post in the Cherokee Nation known as Sulagade and lay on an ancient trade route from New Echota, the last Cherokee capitol, to the Creek Territory at its juncture with an Indian trail over nearby Sulagade Mountain. Sulagade in Cherokee is variously interpreted as "strong mountain" or "mountain of the buzzards."

Hall's Corner is located in the Amama Valley, or "valley of the springs," and is known for its large natural spring that serves as the headwaters of Talking Spring Creek. It lies in the extreme northwest corner of Carter County at the junction of the Brownsboro Road and Livingston Road. Three miles to the west is Sulagade Mountain and a mile to the east is Little Texas Ridge. Two miles to the north, Sulagade Mountain and Little Texas Ridge converge to form the narrow pass known as Trimble's Pinch, and to the south the valley extends to the Piedmont.

Hall's Corner in the War of Northern Aggression

Hall's Corner's large tanyard, owned by the Wallace family, provided much-needed cowhides for the Confederate Army. G. W. Hill's textile mill on Talking Spring Creek four miles to the southeast was a source of cloth for soldiers' uniforms.

The town was also the site of one battle, a skirmish at Trimble's Pinch during Sherman's March to the Sea. The Hall's Corner Home Guard, under the command of Col. Christmas Nowlin, ambushed a small Union scouting party there on May 28, 1864, routing them. The Yankees fled south, only to encounter cannon fire at Talking Spring (modern Hillsborough), four and a-half miles away, before straggling back to Sherman's Army with light casualties. Col. Nowlin was killed in the initial battle and is buried in the First Baptist Church cemetery. An unknown Union soldier who died in the skirmish is buried on the lawn of the old Chamblee School for Women, now the Pennick Funeral Home.

Hall's Corner in Its Heyday

Hall's Corner thrived in the latter half of the 19th century, primarily due to cotton. The Keown and Folsom Railway Company completed spur lines from Keown's Junction and Talking Spring to the Chattanooga, Rome and Southern Railway in 1870, which naturally made the town a prosperous hub for commerce. The tanyard closed after the war, but was soon replaced with other industries, including a second textile mill, the Primrose Textile Co., a furniture company, and a large cotton gin that served most of the Amama Valley. By 1890, Hall's Corner boasted a population of 3,206 whites and about 300 Negroes, and had a hotel (the Lacey Hotel), five churches, three banks, two general stores, two newspapers, a women's clothing store, a dance school, a drug store, a farm supply company, and four livery stables. The Chamblee School for Women, established in 1888 on First Street, has long been considered one of the premiere schools for young women in this section, a reputation it continued to enjoy into modern times under the leadership of Headmaster Dr. Julius Pinkus, Jr.

The financial turmoil of the 1890s made the prosperity of Hall's Corner short-lived, and by 1895, the K&W Railway Company was near bankrupt. The company leased the spur lines to the Chattanooga, Rome, and Southern Railway, which was acquired by the Central Rail Road and Banking Company of Georgia in 1901.

Hall's Corner in Modern Times

Hall's Corner recovered and enjoyed modest prosperity up until the First World War, when cotton farming began to decline after the drought of 1917. Cotton fields were replaced with pastures for beef and dairy cattle, which remains the primary agricultural industry today. The local economy went into stagnation after the drought, and the Great Depression proved devastating to the town, as it did to many other small towns in America. Two of the banks closed, as did many of the industrial enterprises, including the Primrose Textile Co., and several commercial businesses. The town's decline was interrupted by a brief revival during World War II, but suffered a further blow when the G. W. Hill Textile Co. burned in 1949 and was not rebuilt, leading the Central of Georgia Railway Co. to abandon the spur line to Hillsborough.

By 1950, the town's population had declined to less than 2,000. The Lacey Hotel closed in 1951 when it was seriously damaged by a tornado, which also destroyed the Admore Cotton Ginning Co., later rebuilt, but closed permanently in 1957. In 1952, Hall's Corner High School was consolidated with Carter County High. The building is now the home of Hall's Corner Elementary School. In 1955, a five-alarm fire destroyed the Smith Feed & Seed Co. and threatened to burn down the entire downtown area, but quick efforts by the Hall's Corner Volunteer Fire Department saved it. By 1958, the trains no longer stopped at Hall's Corner on their way to the terminus at Keown's Junction, and in 1975, the railroad announced that it was closing the spur line altogether.

The town's two newspapers, the Hall's Corner Clarion and the Sulagade Sentinel, in competition since 1879, merged in 1951, and the combined newspaper, the Hall's Corner Clarion-Sentinel, survived for another fourteen years before it ceased publication in 1965.

By 1960, the town's industrial activity consisted of the Wallace Furniture Company, which produced cabinets, and the Palmer Pecan Company, whose large pecan orchard begins inside the city limits and extends several hundred acres to the south even today, plus numerous small dairies. Commercial businesses included the People's Savings Bank, Hall's Corner Drugs, Miss Clarie's Hi Fashion, the Norris General Store, Admore's Used Cars, the Baker School of Dance, the Curl Up and Dye Beauty Shop, and two gas stations. Churches included the First Baptist Church of Hall's Corner, Mt. Carmel Methodist Church, Trimble's Pinch Pentecostal Church, and the Hall's Corner Church of God. Local Negroes attend the Mt. Jubilee AME Church.

As of this writing, the Palmer Pecan Company has closed, but Hall's Corner is in revival. It is now the home of Ostow Mills, a shirt manufacturer, which built a plant on Livingston Road just south of town in 1962. Several commercial enterprises have sprung up as a result, including Taylor's NAPA Auto Parts Co., Norris Feed & Seed, Hall & Wallace Real Estate, Pinkus Furniture and Antiques, the Cozy Café, the Law Offices of Baker, Jackson & Smith, and the E. Z. Mobile Home Park. Plans are also underway to establish a new local newspaper, but they are only in the planning stages.

The current mayor is Julius Pinkus, Jr., the second consecutive member of the Pinkus family to serve in that position. Councilmen include Abraham Norris, Jr., Samuel Wilson, Odell Admore, and J. D. Smith. The City Judge is Victor Simms, who has served the town in that capacity since 1952, and the Police Chief is Harold Dunning. In 1972, the city established the position of City Manager, a post currently held by Thomas Elleby. The Chief of the Hall's Corner Volunteer Fire Department is Darby Elliot, Jr., and the City Attorney is J. D. Smith.

State Representative "Uncle" Dave Wallace, who has served in the legislature since 1952, also resides in Hall's Corner.

Other notable people from Hall's Corner include concert pianist Bartholomew Simpson, professional middleweight boxer Paddy "Big Irish" O'Neal, and Sammy Johnson, who played in the Negro league.

Hall's Corner was the first town in Carter County to establish a "leash law" for dogs, in 1959.

With good governance, the future of Hall's Corner looks to be a bright and prosperous one.

A Short Amendment (1998)

In the last 22 years, Hall's Corner has gone through several major changes. Dr. Julius Pinkus, Jr., died in 1977 and the Chamblee School for Women closed permanently upon his death. State Rep. Uncle Dave Wallace died in 1983, which was a great loss to the entire county. And in 1986, twins Abraham and Albert Norris, two of the most prominent commercial entrepreneurs in the town's history, were killed in an automobile accident at the ages of 91.

In 1986, Ostow Mills was sold to an international corporation which immediately shut down the plant and moved production to Mexico, with a loss to the local economy of nearly 300 jobs. The Hall's Corner Business Association bought the building in 1987 and has been actively seeking new tenants.

As the 20th century comes to an end, Hall's Corner remains a vital community with excellent prospects for growth. Several small industries, including a lamp fob plant and a manufacturer of specialty auto racing parts, have located here, and efforts are underway to develop a resort at Talking Spring, which should increase tourism. The town's continued spirit of cooperation and determination to succeed will bode well as it adapts to the changing needs of the new century.

(Julius Pinkus, III. 1998)

www.ingramcontent.com/pod-product-compliance
Lightning Source LLC
Chambersburg PA
CBHW071834020726
47502CB00004B/1355